THE Mutilators

THE Mutilators

A Novel

Robert L. Foster

SANTA FE

Sunstone books may be purchased for educational, business, or sales promotional use.
For information please write: Special Markets Department, Sunstone Press,
P.O. Box 2321, Santa Fe, New Mexico 87504-2321.

Cover art by Riley Milion
Book and Cover design › Vicki Ahl
Body typeface › Perpetua
Printed on acid-free paper
⊗
eBook 978-1-61139-282-1

Library of Congress Cataloging-in-Publication Data

Foster, Robert L. (Robert Lee), 1933-
 The Mutilators : a novel / by Robert L. Foster.
   pages cm
 ISBN 978-0-86534-994-0 (softcover : alk. paper)
 1. Mutilation--Fiction. 2. Ranch life--Utah--Fiction. 3. Mystery fiction. I. Title.
 PS3606.O766M88 2014
 813'.6--dc23
                        2014016478

WWW.SUNSTONEPRESS.COM
SUNSTONE PRESS / POST OFFICE BOX 2321 / SANTA FE, NM 87504-2321 /USA
(505) 988-4418 / ORDERS ONLY (800) 243-5644 / FAX (505) 988-1025

The author gratefully acknowledges the editorial expertise of Darrel L. Foster who edited much of this novel.

Preface

IDAHO'S ANIMAL KILLINGS ENDED IN 1976. Ranching and farming folks in Idaho talked about the animal mutilations for many months and speculated on who or what the mutilators were. Sometimes details were exaggerated which increased the speculations. In restaurants where ranchers gathered for morning coffee, many of whom had lost valuable animals, talked about the unusual flashing blue lights hovering over their pastures the night their animals were killed. Some said they saw "cigar shaped" UFOs, others said they saw round shaped UFOs. The general consensus, however, was that the mutilators were aliens.

In my interview notes with Randy Johnson, before I wrote this story, he emphatically told me there was not the slightest doubt in his mind that the mutilators were aliens. Idaho law enforcement officials I interviewed told me predators were the culprits—but off the record, several believed aliens committed the animal butchery.

Amid the speculation, an interesting article appeared in several western newspapers. "FBI Joins Investigation of Animal Mutilations Linked to UFOs." It stated that at least 8000 cattle and horses have been butchered with surgical precision over an estimated 1.28-square- mile-area stretching from Tennessee to Oregon since the mutilations began around 1970. Those 1.28-million-square-miles are more than a third of the total land area of the continental United States.

An engineering physicist at Sandia Laboratories in New Mexico, which handles secret government projects, revealed that Native Americans are so terrified by animal mutilations on Indian Reservations, they bury the carcasses immediately and are reluctant to discuss what happened. Even their dogs refuse to go near the carcasses.

In many cases the attacks have coincided with UFO sightings. Baffled investigators say the strange pattern of the mutilations includes these startling facts:

No tire marks, footprints or other signs of human activity are found near the mutilated carcasses.

Only the blood and certain parts of the animals—usually the reproductive organs—are removed.

Trace elements found on and in some carcasses are the same as those collected after a UFO sighting in New Mexico.

Buzzards and coyotes refuse to eat the mutilated horses and cattle.

A notable psychologist and UFO researcher in Boulder, Colorado, stated: "What few clues we have concerning those responsible for the mutilations suggest that we are dealing with well-equipped, highly capable airborne entities... We are forced, I feel, to the hypothesis that unidentified aircraft are the means—UFOs."

✝

Scattered reports of animal mutilations continue to surface from time to time in various western newspapers. For example, on August 31, 1996, Utah's *Deseret News* carried a story attributed to the *Associated Press*, titled: "What—or who—keeps killing Idaho's Cattle?"

Again, on July 28-29, 1999, the *Deseret News* delved into the mutilations with a story titled: "Answers actively sought in bizarre cattle mutilations—Patterns are being found—but not explanations."

So the mystery remains. Who or what are the mutilators?

Prologue

Late Summer, 1975

NOTHING FROM RANDY JOHNSON'S PAST prepared him for what he was about to face.

Imagine the ground rising up over the scrub oak covered hills south of Randy Johnson's Idaho ranch, then rolling north through the velvety green pasture, continuing past his uniquely styled western log home, skirting around the old wooden barn and outbuildings. Further north the land gently sloped down to the rim of the rugged half-mile deep Snake River Gorge, twisting and turning its way through the breathtaking broken landscape like a huge dark serpent.

Randy and his nearest neighbors, ranchers and farmers, often watched with wide-eyed curiosity as shiny saucer-shaped objects, with strange strobing blue lights, rose from or descended into the crest of the deep gorge, as though on some secret mission.

Randy, six foot two, was a rangy brown haired man who ranched with his family in Central Idaho along the Snake River. This evening like every other evening, Randy was feeding the livestock, several head of red and white Herefords and twenty five riding horses. Though the horse herd was small Randy always referred to his place as a horse ranch.

He fed the animals thick stemmed green alfalfa. The Herefords trotted toward Randy. Several stretched out their necks to moo. The horses stayed bunched together at the far end of the pasture, milling about, waiting for Randy to feed them.

Randy's high spirited yellow lab, Buster, was continually underfoot, very skittish and nervous, and followed Randy's every movement, almost tripping him twice.

"Crazy damn dog! What the hell's the matter with you?" Randy growled. "Get outta' here!" he shouted, pointing toward the house. But something wasn't right! It was too quiet so Buster stood his ground, and wasn't about to budge.

As twilight slowly settled over Twin Falls Valley Randy finished up by pitching some hay over the pasture fence to the hungry horses then walked toward the house, Buster tight on his heels, The sky was clear and a full moon leisurely peaked over the mountains in the east.

Suddenly Buster stopped dead in his tracks and stared skyward, growling deep in his throat, crowding in close to Randy who tipped his cowboy hat back and craned his neck. He couldn't see anything to be alarmed about, though he could hear a powerful, low-throbbing rumble overhead. Then he saw several pulsating blue lights suddenly flash on out of nowhere, as if someone had thrown a switch and the light beams slowly moved along the ground toward the far end of the pasture where the horses whinnied and milled frantically, some running away from the lights. The encroaching darkness made it difficult to see exactly where the lights were coming from. *Perhaps the audible reverberations could be low rumbling thunder echoing in from the distant mountains* he told himself. *Probably some freaky weather phenomenon.* Though he'd seen flashing blue lights before in the Snake River Gorge, he'd never seen them come this close to his ranch.

"As I neared the house I couldn't figure out what was wrong with Buster, slinking and skulking along like a whipped, maltreated dog, whining mournfully, frightened half to death—from what I had no idea." The big lab's peculiar behavior puzzled Randy because Buster was a strapping aggressive ranch dog that had tangled with coyotes, cougars, even sour-tempered badgers, and so far he'd never lost a rumble.

"Maybe Buster was trying to alert me to some kind of danger emanating from the flashing blue lights," Randy said. "I really didn't pay much attention to the dog because I was watching several of my horses running to the far side of the pasture to escape the lights.

"I was a little worried by this unusually weird situation, but what the hell? Nothing I could do about it and so far no harm had been done."

His worry stemmed from recent television breaking news flashes which repeatedly spewed out gory details about dead cattle which had been strangely mutilated, or butchered, many of them right here in Twin Falls County.

To date the mutilators had not been identified and the puzzling unsolved mystery was the talk of the county—even the whole state of Idaho—as veterinary surgeons who performed autopsies on the mutilated animals reported the surgery and resections used to extract the butchered cattles' eyes, ears, lips, intestines and sexual organs were performed with skill levels completely unknown by our current veterinary science,

Idaho lawmen, without exception, agreed the mutilations were indeed gruesome, but in every investigation they attributed the killings to predatory animals.

Quit your worrying, Randy told himself, as he sat on the back porch and pulled off his work boots. *Whoever is killing and mutilating cattle won't bother me. This is a horse ranch!*

Five hours later the mutilators struck Randy Johnson's ranch!

1

RANDY JOHNSON'S RANCH IS NESTLED IN A remote corner of Twin Falls County's Magic Valley in south central Idaho. In 1975, brutal domestic animal killings, accompanied by bizarre mutilations, kept Randy and his neighbors on edge as they wondered whose ranch the mutilators would strike next.

The summer sun over Idaho's Twin Falls Valley was hot. Bill Martin had no idea this sweaty day would be any different from yesterday, last week or last year. As long as Union Pacific's heavy freight trains came rolling along the tracks, through the valley, he and his six-man section crew had a steady job maintaining the rails.

They were tough hard working men who admired and respected Bill. They knew he had been a first sergeant with the U.S. Army Rangers in Vietnam, though he never spoke about that time in his life ten years ago; nor did his cousin Randy Johnson, his lieutenant and platoon leader, who owned the ranch land on both sides of the tracks where UP's section crew was now working.

Bill shielded his eyes from the glare of the mid-afternoon sun glinting off the shiny steel railroad tracks stretching ahead as far as the eye could see. The next freight train wasn't due for another three hours, plenty of time for his crew to finish replacing two cracked steel fish plates with new ones and tighten the bolts, securing each plate to the ties.

He watched Emilio Sanchez, on his knees, twist the big wrench with all his strength and tighten the last bolt.

"Need some help?" Bill offered.

The short stout man with a dark hard face that was creased and leathery looked up. "No, Senor Bill. I've got it." He stood slowly, twisting and stretching to ease his aching back, then pulled a red bandana from his back pocket and wiped his sweaty brow.

With a grin, Bill said, "I think we're all a little too old for all this hard work, amigo."

"I agree, Senor Bill," Emilio nodded, twisting his head from side to side trying to work the kinks out of his neck. "I think some day I take all my money and go back to Mexico, maybe buy a little ranch and let my sons work it while I supervise."

"Sounds like a plan," Bill said. "Maybe I'll go with you. It would beat hell out of working our guts out along these rails every day."

Emilio smiled at that, and waved his hand around. "Isn't this land part of your Cousin Randy's ranch?"

"It is—everything on both sides of the track for the next mile."

"I thought so," Emilio said slowly. "Back down the track a ways," he pointed, "I saw one of his horses sleeping on a hillside."

Bill rubbed his jaw and nodded. "Hmm. That's odd. Randy always keeps his horses in that big pasture next to the house. Maybe this one jumped the fence and came looking for a little adventure. Where did you see it?"

"About two blocks back, halfway up that big hill with the rocky outcrop. It's hard to see the horse. It blends into the brush." Again Emilio pointed.

"Keep an eye on things, Emilio. I'll wander back and have a look see."

"Okay Senor Bill."

Bill walked back along the tracks, his eyes searching the surrounding hills. As he neared the hill Emilio mentioned, he suddenly felt a tingling sense of foreboding—similar to that time in 'Nam when he and Randy led a patrol straight into a cleverly laid Viet Cong ambush. *Strange!* He hadn't had a single thought about that for a long time. He held a hand above his eyes to block the sun, squinted, and saw the horse's hind quarters, midway up the brush covered hillside. He could tell just from the way it was positioned it wasn't sleeping. Horses sleep horizontal, not vertical. This horse had dropped dead where it stood!

Bill puffed hard as he climbed over the fence and struggled his way up the hill's steep slope, grabbing brush, pulling himself up foot by foot to the rocky ledge, just below the summit. There he got his first close up look at Randy's horse, Miss BJ! He knew the sturdy little mare. He'd ridden her several times when he and Randy saddled up each fall and headed for the high country to hunt for trophy bucks.

The fourteen-year-old registered thoroughbred mare, worth a thousand dollars, was lying on her side, her head uphill. But what in God's name had happened to her? Her stomach was sliced open from chest to anus and everything normally found in a body cavity was gone.

The look of incredulity that crossed Bill's face was immediately replaced by anger. *Who would do something like this?* Bill bent down for a closer look, stepping slowly and cautiously toward the horse's head.

"Jesus H. Christ!" he gasped aloud, and jumped back. Dumbfounded, he stared into Miss BJ's face, grinning at him. Her lips had been neatly sliced off, fully displaying her teeth in a hideous grin. Her eyeballs were gone and one ear had been sliced off. Bill had no way to know how long she'd been dead.

His savage Vietnam War experience kicked in, keeping him from complete panic, but not fear. He knew what he needed to do. *Check for clues. Find out who did this. When? Why? Look for blood. Look for tracks. Look for missing body parts. No human would take guts, lips, eyeballs, ears. Was it hunters killing for fun? Maybe. Predators? Hell no. No predator could do this! They have teeth that rip and tear flesh. These mutilations were accomplished with extremely sharp or advanced instruments, the incisions accomplished with a surgeon's skill.*

The extent of the horrible mutilations puzzled and frightened Bill. Carefully and methodically he examined the loose soil on which the horse was positioned, looking for traces of blood. There was none anywhere on the ground nor on the horse itself, almost as if it had been siphoned off before the horse died.

Bending low he scanned the ground in all directions looking for footprints. There were none, except Bill's—no predator tracks, no human tracks and most puzzling of all, no tracks of the horse itself.

Bill tipped his hat back and wiped his sweating brow. He speculated that with this late summer heat the horse should have started to bloat. Bill had seen enough death in forests and jungles in his time to know how quickly decay sets in. There is always bloating, a rancid stench and flies buzzing around, attracted by that sweet rotten smell at the beginning stages of putrefaction. Insects and carrion clean up everything but the bones. The bones begin to decompose and feed the ever evolving landscape.

And that was a paradox. Miss BJ's carcass was in perfect condition except for the weird mutilations covering her remains—no stench, no decay, no insects. There was nothing for Bill to do now except quickly get to a phone, call Randy and let him know what he'd discovered.

Bill walked briskly north along the tracks back to his section crew. Emilio stared searchingly at Bill's troubled face. Bill motioned Emilio over, out of ear shot of the men.

"What's wrong, Senor Bill?" Emilio asked with concern. "You look like you see a ghost."

"I don't have time to talk right now, amigo. Can you take over for me? It's kind of an emergency."

"Yes sir, Senor," Emilio said respectfully. "Did you find Senor Randy's horse?"

"It wasn't sleeping, my friend. It was dead. I'm glad you noticed it and brought it to my attention."

"So now you go to tell Senor Randy his horse is dead?"

"Yes. He needs to know. I should be back by quitting time, but if not, let the men go and we'll finish up tomorrow."

Bill eased into the driver's seat of the UP pickup and turned over the engine. He hit the accelerator and slewed down the dirt road alongside the track, spraying mud patterns of dirt and rocks.

He screeched to a stop in front of his house, jumped out and rushed in through the unlocked front door. The house was empty. His wife was at work and the kids were in school. He grabbed the phone and dialed Randy's number, absently wondering if he should call the county sheriff first. But it was Randy's horse and Randy's business; and he knew Randy didn't want strangers poking around his property. He valued his privacy. *No,* Bill thought. *I'll take Randy out to see his horse and let him decide how he wants to handle it.*

Randy's phone rang several times. Impatient, Bill was about to hang up and drive over to Randy's ranch.

""Hello," came Tessie's voice, Randy's wife of twenty five years.

"Tess, is Randy there?"

"He's out by the barn working on the tractor. He can't get it started. Can he call you back?"

"I really need to talk to him right now. I'll wait while you get him."

Usually Bill was easy going, and Tessie was a little concerned with the urgency in his voice. She stepped out on the porch and shouted, "Randy! Telephone for you."

Randy looked up from the tractor engine and tipped his battered cowboy hat back. "Who is it?" he called, wiping his greasy hands on a dirty towel.

"It's Bill," Tessie shouted back. "He says it's very important."

"Oh all right, I'm coming."

Randy picked up the phone and heard Bill's voice. "I found Miss BJ over by the tracks on that scrub hill where the tracks turn south."

"Okay, Bill. Thanks for letting me know. As soon as I get this damned tractor running I'll saddle one of my horses and ride over there and bring her home."

"No, Randy, you don't understand," Bill said. "Miss BJ is dead. I found her about an hour ago at the south end of your ranch."

"Dead?" Randy gasped. "Good God, Bill, what happened to her—was she shot, bloated, run over by one of your trains, what?"

Bill cleared his throat, finding it difficult to speak. "I don't think it's something we should discuss on the phone." He tried to make his voice sound casual.

"All right," Randy said, "If I come over to your house can you take me to her? I can be there in thirty minutes, as soon as I wash this grease off my hands."

"You bet! I'll be waiting."

Tessie was standing in the kitchen doorway listening. "What's happened? Bill sounded pretty serious."

Randy's face tightened with displeasure. "Bill found Miss BJ dead, over on the south side of the ranch."

Tessie stared at Randy in astonishment. "Oh, Randy," she said, "How did it happen? I loved that horse. We raised her from a colt…"

"I don't know." Randy's voice was flat and sharp. "Bill said he didn't want to discuss it on the phone. I'm going over to Bill's, and he will take me to the spot where he found her."

"Do you think she wandered onto the tracks and got hit by a train?"

"I have no idea," Randy answered. "I think Bill would have told me if that were the case. No, Tess, from the sound of Bill's voice I think there's more to it than that."

✝

Tessie walked with Randy out on the front porch and watched him walk to his pickup parked in the drive. He paused for a moment and glanced across the horse pasture, staring at the log fence. His horses contentedly chewed the last of the alfalfa he'd scattered along the fence early that morning. How had Miss BJ managed to break out of the pasture? The gate was securely closed—and no horse had ever made it over or around that fence. How was it he hadn't noticed Miss BJ was gone? *Damn*, he thought, *I should pay more attention.*

"Something wrong, Honey?" Tessie called out

"No, Dear," he replied. "I was just trying to figure out how Miss BJ got loose."

✝

Randy looked worried as Bill sped along the highway toward the side road along the railroad tracks. Bill, not much of a talker, hadn't said much, beyond a quick howdy, and "jump in, Randy, and I'll take you out there."

"C'mon Bill, give," Randy prodded. "What the hell happened to my horse?"

Bill's words sent a chill down Randy's spine. "Miss BJ was butchered, I mean completely gutted!"

Their eyes locked for only a moment, but in that moment Randy knew something was terribly wrong. "Gutted?" he growled in disbelief. "Are you sure? Who the hell would gut and butcher a horse?"

"I have no idea," Bill answered. "The whole damn deal is mighty strange though. There are no tracks or footprints around the horse, not of man, beast, ATV, truck or anything else—not even the tracks of Miss BJ herself."

"Then how did she get up there on that hill?" Randy asked.

Bill shook his head. "Damned if I know. Maybe you can figure it out when we get there." He pulled the pickup truck alongside the section crew gathering up their tools, finished for the day.

Emilio walked over to the truck and talked to Bill through the open window. "Senor Bill, we finish with the fish plates. We go now. We do the others tomorrow."

"All right," Bill said. "I'll see you in the morning."

Emilio glanced past Bill to Randy on the passenger side. "Ah, Senor Randy, I am very sorry to hear about your horse."

Randy nodded. "Did you see or hear anything unusual yesterday?"

"No, Senor. Nothing out of the ordinary. When the trains come by we hear nothing but their whistles and the usual clickity clak rumble they make."

"Thanks, Emilio," Randy said, and waved as Emilio walked off and joined the others.

Randy turned to Bill. "Where is she?"

"C'mon. I'll take you up to her."

They walked down the railroad tracks, climbed over the barbed wire fence and made their way up the steep hillside.

"She's just a bit further up," Bill said, breathing hard, as he scrambled over loose rock. When he stopped to catch his breath Randy moved around him and kept climbing until he reached the rocky outcrop—and saw Miss BJ. She appeared to be sleeping, but when Randy stepped up close, he tasted bile forming in his throat.

He quickly and nervously glanced over his shoulder as Bill scrambled up behind him, then returned his attention to the horse. He couldn't take his eyes off her. He just stood there motionless, paralyzed by the unfamiliar feeling of menace, wondering if he should go home and get his gun or make a run for it. *But run from what or who?*

Bill read Randy's face in an instant—it was the very same expression the first sergeant saw on Randy's face when the young lieutenant cautiously led his platoon into a remote Vietnamese village where bodies lay scattered about in various attitudes of death. Every man, woman and child had been brutally massacred. Their killers even used machine guns to kill the dogs, chickens and two old water buffalos.

"Well?" Bill said, "What..."

Randy threw up a hand to silence Bill, and he walked around Miss BJ, closely examining her mutilated body. "Jesus!" Randy exhaled. "I've never in my life seen anything like this. What kind of sick, crazy person would do this to a horse?"

Bill's heart was hammering in his rib cage and his tone was uneven when he said, "I haven't got a clue, Randy, but before you get all pissed off, and want to kill somebody, let's think this through for a minute. Nothing like this has ever happened before, I mean mutilating horses, at least not around these parts. Then something or someone starts killing animals all over this part of the state, mostly cattle. Over a hundred of them have been gutted and mutilated in the same manner you see here with Miss BJ."

"Yeah, I know all about that, and I've figured out what I'm going to do," Randy said forcefully. "So there's nothing to think about. I'm going to find the asshole who did this and..."

"Oh no, I don't think so," Bill interrupted, cutting Randy off. "Something needs to be done, but you're not the one to do it."

"And just who is going to do it for me, Sergeant? Will you tell me that?" Randy always called Bill Sergeant when he raised strong objections to any argument at hand.

"The sheriff and his deputies."

"Oh c'mon, Bill, get real!" Randy said forcefully. "They're as worthless as tits on a big ol' boar hog."

"Maybe so," Bill replied, "but they're all you've got. They're investigating all the cattle mutilations and they probably have some leads you don't even know about. You've gotta' give 'em a chance."

"And if I don't?"

"Then it's back to square one, right where you are now."

Randy knew there was sound and convincing logic in Bill's thinking—there really wasn't much in the way of other choices. He knew he couldn't find the culprits himself when he didn't have a clue as to who or what they were.

"All right, then," Randy conceded grudgingly. "But right now let's look around and see if we can find any clues ourselves as to what happened to Miss BJ."

They examined the ground within a ten foot radius, and found no footprints or tracks, just as Bill had said. Yet their cowboy boots made noticeable impressions in the soft soil as they searched about.

"Hey Randy," Bill called out excitedly, "Take a look at this!"

Randy walked over and stared at a large patch of skin and hair from Miss BJ's flank, clinging to the rocky outcropping. Randy rubbed his hand over the patch of hair, looked around, then glanced up.

"What are you thinking?" Bill asked.

"If I didn't know better I'd say the horse was suspended from something in the air, lowered and its flank scraped against the rocks as she came down."

"A helicopter, maybe?" Bill asked.

"No. There aren't any choppers around here."

"What then?"

Randy shook his head. "I just don't know."

On the ground approximately twelve feet out from the horse Randy and Bill discovered a peculiar oblong shaped indentation in the ground, measuring twenty four inches long, eight inches wide and eight inches deep. Following in a circular direction away from the horse they found an identical indentation exactly seven feet from the first one. Continuing on, they located a third indentation, completing a circle twenty five feet in diameter. The position of the three identical indentations in relation to the dead horse indicated the horse could have been lowered to its exact position by an object resting above the ground on tripod legs or struts.

Randy thought through some silent calculations, second nature to him because of his long time experience as a helicopter pilot. "Bill," he said, "Based on the density of this soil, the circumference and diameter and depth of these indentations; whatever produced them must have weighed close to seventy five tons."

"What are you saying? A UFO maybe?" Bill leaned back against a rock, took a pack of cigarettes from his shirt pocket, pulled one out, placed it in his mouth, and struck a match. "So what do we do?" Bill asked, drawing smoke into his lungs. "You want to leave Miss BJ here for the predators and forget the whole thing?"

From the expression on Randy's face Bill saw he'd said the wrong thing.

"No, I can't just forget about it. The risk is too high. I've got other horses and cattle to worry about." A truculent note had crept into his voice. "I don't think we're dealing with humankind here, Bill."

Bill's eyes widened and he took a long drag on his cigarette. "What then?"

"If you want my honest opinion, based on what I've read recently and what we've seen here today, I think we need to at least consider that all these mutilations have something to do with an unidentified force or even UFOs or whatever operates them. If anyone of this earth is involved they are some sick sonsabitches to do something this weird." Randy wondered in speculative silence if someone could actually be this deranged and demented and what the purpose of such acts could be.

Bill stared at Randy for a long silent moment, and his eyes quickly narrowed. "You better be damn careful before you go sayin' something like that to the authorities. They'll think you're slipped a cog and are ready for the nut house."

"I know," Randy nodded, concurring quietly, mulling over the implications. "But whoever is mutilating the stock in this area have us all between a rock and a hard place. If I keep silent, they'll likely go on killing; if I report it to the police, they may think I've lost my mind, or at least accuse me of having delusions. You know how that goes!"

"Yeah. I do," Bill answered. "They've throwed me in jail a time or two— but not because of some butchered animal. They told me I was drunk, got in fights, raised hell."

Randy smiled. "Did you?"

"Hell, I really don't remember." Then Bill stared at Randy, and it passed through his mind that they were like brothers, and if Bill expressed his inner feelings at the moment, it would go no further. He looked at the ground for a moment, and asked in a very quiet tone, "Randy, did you feel anything different when you first saw Miss BJ?"

Randy wrinkled his brow, his eyes wide. "Different? Like what?"

Bill stared at him in silence, wondering how to say it. "An eerie feeling. Kind of like foreboding. Like maybe we shouldn't be here. Like we're messing in someone else's business. I don't know. I had the strangest feeling come over me as soon as I climbed over the fence down there by the tracks, like a warning, don't go any further. Look at Miss BJ there. There's no flies, no bugs, no predators have been at her, no birds. You have to admit it's mighty damn weird. Or am I imagining things?"

With a grimness on his face, Randy shook his head. "No, Bill, you're not imagining things. I had those same feelings the minute we started to climb up here. It's hard to put into words. Almost like an unspoken warning. But how can that be?"

The two men stood silent for a moment. "Well, it's too late now," Randy said. "We've been here and we've seen what they did to Miss BJ. The ball's in their court now. We'll have to see how the game plays out."

Bill chuckled. "This is more than a game, Randy!"

"I know!"

They took a final look at Miss BJ, then started to walk away. A cool evening breeze blew across the hillside, and a pair of magpies circled on an air current, then dipped down intending to feast on Miss BJ's carcass. Five feet above the horse the magpies squawked raucously, their wings flapping furiously to stop their descent—seemingly before they flew into a dangerous, invisible barrier.

The moment passed without a word, until Bill asked, "did you see that?"

Randy nodded his head slowly. "Yeah. I saw it." He looked as frightened as he felt.

"Pretty damned weird, huh?" Bill said, and took the last drag on his smoke, then dropped it on the ground and stepped on it.

"It is," Randy agreed. "But that little episode just made up my mind for me. I'll call Sheriff Dan Jeffords first thing in the morning. I've got a hunch we're dealing with something that's way out of our league."

✝

Later that evening Randy was beat when he walked into the house and sat down at the kitchen table. Tessie poured him a cup of coffee. "Well," she asked anxiously, "Did you see our horse?"

"I did," Randy said and described in gruesome detail the strange mutilations he saw on Miss BJ's butchered carcass.

Tessie didn't speak or interrupt until he finished. Then, eyes wide, she stared at him and asked, "And you have no idea who or what killed her?"

"None at all," he replied, avoiding his UFO theory, so as not to unduly frighten her. "I do know it wasn't coyotes or cougars, and she wasn't shot. But I'm not so concerned about how she died. I'm more interested in finding out why she was mutilated and what it could mean for our other livestock. We've got a ranch to run here."

"Are you going to call Sheriff Jeffords as Bill suggested?"

"I don't want to," Randy said and drank down the last of his coffee. "But I don't think we have a choice. I'll call him tomorrow. Maybe he can figure out what's going on."

Tessie smiled gently. "Good. That's the smart thing to do." She leaned over and gave him a kiss on the cheek. "Let's turn in, Honey, sounds like we've a big day ahead of us tomorrow."

2

THE NEXT MORNING RANDY CALLED Sheriff Dan Jeffords on the phone to report Miss BJ's mysterious killing and mutilation and explained in accurate detail exactly what he'd discovered at the site, leaving nothing out.

There was astonishment mixed with disbelief in Jeffords' voice when he said, "You're telling me someone gutted one of your horses?" What do you mean gutted?" Jeffords asked. "Are you sure?"

"Yes, Dan, I'm sure! As I told you, she was sliced open from one end to the other and all her internal organs are gone. Whoever did it also cut off her lips, an ear and took her eyeballs."

A pause followed, then Jeffords' voice came again. "Any chance coyotes got to her?"

Randy's hiss-snapping reply startled Jeffords. "Hell no! I know the difference between a coyote bite and a knife cut. BJ was one of my best horses. Someone butchered her and I want you or one of your deputies to get out here and take a look at her and find her killer."

Jeffords ignored the abrupt demand and tried to keep his voice pleasant. "It'll be at least four of five days, Randy. That's the best I can do. I'm completely swamped. Nearly every rancher in the county is losing livestock to predators. Me and my deputies are stretched to the breaking point."

"Four or five days?" Randy repeated his words. "What am I supposed to do in the meantime?" What if…"

"Look, Randy," Jeffords interrupted bluntly, "You'll have to do like everyone else. Keep your eyes open and guard your animals. I wish there was more we could do, but you'll have to wait until we figure out what the hell is going on. I've tried to get some help from the state police but they've got their hands full. In fact every law enforcement officer in the state is busy investigating livestock killings. Right now that's their number one priority."

Jeffords' words evoked anger and frustration in Randy but there was really nothing he could do but wait his turn. "Well, make it as soon as you can," Randy said disgustedly, and hung up the phone.

He sat back in his chair pondering, *what now?* He knew Dan was a man of his word. They'd been life-long friends, gone to school together, been on the high school football team and socialized from time to time.

"Well? What did Dan have to say?" Tessie asked as she sat four places at the breakfast table. The pleasant odor of frying bacon and baking biscuits filled the kitchen. She was a slender, lively woman with a fair complexion even the harsh Idaho weather never seemed to affect and a mass of light brown hair, neatly combed straight down to her shoulders. Two or three times a week she would whisk together her special very delicious biscuits, which Randy loved and would eat to the last little crumb. She'd tell folks she learned biscuit making from her mother, who always said, 'a rancher must have a hearty breakfast.'"

Randy looked up at her and shook his head. "Dan said he's swamped and can't get anyone to out here for four or five days."

"What are we supposed to do in the meantime?" she asked.

Randy shrugged. "Hope and pray none of our other animals end up like Miss BJ. That's all we can do for now."

"That's not very reassuring, is it?" she smiled.

"No it isn't"

He changed the subject. "Are the kids up yet?"

"Yes. They'll be here in a minute. Joe is going to drop Jennie off at school this morning. She's got a homework project due today, and it's too big for her to take on the school bus. She'll ride the bus home. Joe has football practice after school, then he'll drive from there to his job."

Randy smiled. "I worry about our boy driving that beat up old pickup truck to his job in Twin Falls. It doesn't have too many miles left in it. The tires are bald and the engine is only hitting on about three cylinders. I've been thinking about asking Joe to quit working at the drive-in and help me with the evening chores. I could pay him more than he's making at that fast food joint."

Tessie nodded as she brought the coffee pot from the stove and poured Randy a cup. "I know you could," she said, "But he has friends at work and has fun working with them. It's his last year in school. Let him enjoy his friends. This old ranch will always be here."

He grinned. "Yeah, maybe so—and I've always got you here to help me, right?" He patted her teasingly on the behind.

Seventeen-year-old Joe, half asleep stumbled into the kitchen, followed by ten-year-old Jennie, skipping happily and jumping into her chair at the table.

"Good morning, Jennie, my lil' darlin'," Randy chuckled. "You look ready to take on the world, but take a look at your miserable looking excuse of a brother. He looks like something the cat dragged in." Randy turned to Joe. "Did you work another late shift at the drive-in? I didn't hear you come in last night."

"Yeah," Joe answered, rubbing sleep from his eyes. "I didn't get off until one a.m. And I've got another late shift tonight." He shook his head. "I'm glad tomorrow is Saturday. I'll have the whole weekend off. In the morning some of us guys are going to have a football practice at school."

Randy nodded. "Better dig in, before I eat your share of these scrumptious biscuits. There's magic in your mother's cooking. Eat enough of her biscuits and you'll be a tougher man than your father."

"Oh Randy!" Tessie shook her head and walked over to her son. "Did you hear what your father said, Joe?" Tessie tousled Joe's mussed up hair. "I think he's trying to butter me up so I'll help him get the rickety ol' tractor fixed, or something worse. Go ahead and eat. Then you can drop Jennie off at her school and get your sleepy butt to class."

"Okay, Mom."

Joe turned to Randy, and with a sheepish tone asked, "Hey, Dad, did you call the sheriff about Miss BJ?"

Randy nodded. "I did, but it didn't do much good. He said he'll send someone over here in a few days."

Joe stared curiously at his father. "What if more of our animals get killed before he gets here?" It came out in with a bit more bewilderment than he intended to convey.

"Oh I don't think that will happen," Randy replied casually, trying to put a note of reassurance in his answer. "Whoever killed Miss BJ is probably long gone by now." However Randy was much more apprehensive about the whole episode than he wanted to be.

✝

After another late summer typical ranching day on their Idaho spread, Randy and Tessie bid goodnight to Jennie, with their ritual evening hugs and prayers and retired to their bedroom.

"No need waiting up for Joe," Tessie said. "He won't be home until two a.m."

"Good!" Randy grinned. "That means no interruptions for what I have in mind."

He gazed in adoration as Tessie slipped into a sheer nightgown, then teasingly continued with her nightly routine of brushing her hair and her teeth, washing her face and finally climbing into the simple but beautifully adorned double bed. She pulled the home spun blanket up to her shoulder as she rolled to her side; and with a lascivious glint in her bewitching hazel eyes watched Randy continue his slow, awkward undress. He removed his boots, then his Levi's and shirt, and stood there grinning, in his boxer shorts. As he climbed into bed she felt the mattress yield beneath his weight. He took her in his arms and kissed her. His hand began their familiar journey over her divine lithe figure, and her entire being relaxed as a soft petal.

A couple of hours later Tessie sat up suddenly, listening in the dark to Buster. He generally slept outside on the back porch in the summer and fall and never caused a problem. Now he was whining and frantically scratching at the back door. She'd never heard him whine like that before. She slipped quietly out of bed and tip-toed through the dark house to the back door. Buster came slinking in, whimpering, his tail clamped between his hind legs.

"Buster," she whispered, "What's wrong? You all right?" she patted his head. The dog licked her hand and retreated across the kitchen, sliding his huge bulk under the kitchen table.

Tessie looked out the back door into pitch black darkness. There was no moon. At what seemed precise intervals, flashing blue lights crackled at the south end of the pasture, almost like a flickering neon sign. Something out there had scared Buster half to death. Tessie listened and thought she heard some kind of low throbbing or deep humming reverberations, definitely too low-pitched to be a helicopter, but it didn't sound like a jet engine either.

Something strange and eerie was going on out there in the pasture. Tessie hurried back to the bedroom and shook Randy. "Wake up Honey, we've got trouble!"

"What?" he mumbled groggily, cleared his throat and jerked up in bed.

"Get up, Randy, get up right now!" Tessie's voice came out in a thin, frightened whisper.

"Those miserable blue lights are flashing above the pasture again and they've spooked the horses; they're scattering like bats out of hell in every direction."

Randy tried to shake the cobwebs from his brain. He closed his eyes momentarily, then shaking his head back and forth jerked them wide. He'd almost drifted back to sleep, then he rolled over, opened the night stand drawer, searching for his Colt .45 semi-automatic pistol. It wasn't there.

"Where in the hell is my pistol?" he asked angrily.

"I took the clip out and put it and the gun in the bottom dresser drawer so Joe or Jennie wouldn't fool around with it."

"Damn it, Tess, I wish you wouldn't do that," Randy said in a tense, cranky voice, "I've taught them to both better than to mess with my guns. I need to be able to get to them quickly to protect our family."

Tess apologized softly, "I'm sorry, Randy."

"Never mind, Honey," Randy said as he retrieved his .45 from the dresser drawer. Methodically he popped the clip into the handle and racked the action, then slowly let the hammer down.

Startled, Tess asked, "What are you going to do?" as she stared at big .45, watching his hand curl sensuously around the decorative pearl pistol grip and caress the cold steel trigger with his finger. "If someone or something is messing with our horses they're going to get the hell scared out of them or worse," Randy said with a menacing scowl.

She stiffened. "Oh Randy, please be careful before you shoot someone. Calm down darlin', please."

"You just stay right in behind me and let me handle whoever or whatever is out there. It'll be up to them whether they get shot or not. C'mon. Let's find out who's screwing around with our horses."

He crept through the darkened house, and stepped out on to the back porch. There were no lights over the pasture, no movement, no sound. His eyes swept and scanned across the darkened pasture and he didn't see anything unusual—however his curiosity was highly piqued, given the events of the last few days, having found Miss BJ butchered, seen Buster holed up under the table and the fear in Tess' face, all contributing to his uneasiness. He looked back over his shoulder at Tessie.

"It looks like whoever was out there is gone. It's too dark to see the horses. I'll check on them in the morning. We might as well go back to bed." He lowered his pistol and reached out his left hand, tenderly took her hand in his and led her back to the bedroom trying to calm his hidden, nagging fears.

She was trembling as Randy set his pistol on the nightstand, within easy reach. The worry deep in her voice, she asked, "What's happening, Randy? It's like waking up from a nightmare. Our horse killed, mysterious blue lights..."

Softly Randy completed the thought for her. "And you're scared. Me too," he confessed. "I've never been really scared of anything—but this...I don't know. How can I fight something this elusive? I feel so inept and helpless. I don't know what to do." He paused. "I'm thinking I'll just have to let the law deal with it."

Tessie walked to the bed and sat on the edge of it, her hands pressing her nightgown between her knees. "That's seems to be about all we can do right now. Let's pray that they can figure out what's going on around here."

Randy nodded. "Well, I think we've had about enough excitement for one evening. Are you all right?"

"Fine," she answered, though her voice didn't sound overly convincing.

"Okay. Let's get some shut eye. Oh, I forgot to ask, did you hear Joe come in?"

"No. He won't be here for at least another hour."

Tessie tossed and turned fitfully and couldn't sleep for worrying. Her recent dreams and secret jitters kept her nerves on edge. What troubled her more than she cared to admit, even to her husband, was the thought that whoever or whatever was mutilating animals might soon try to do the same to humans right here in Idaho.

✝

The sun was barely peaking above the east mountains as Randy stood at the pasture gate counting his horses, standing huddled tightly together, not stirring in this cold gray of early morning. It was difficult to count them because of long shadows across the expanse of rocky, scrub-oak covered hills and the green pasture where his horses generally flourished and dwelled in relative calm.

Shock and terror chased each other across Randy's face when his slow methodical count came up one short.

Daylight grew steadily. Randy leaned forward, squinting his eyes for a better view to determine which horse was missing. One of his favorite mares, Little Girl, was heavy with foal, which always made it quite easy to identify her in the herd—but she wasn't there!

My God! How can that be? Both gates are closed and locked. The fence is secure all the way around. How did she get out?

Randy's mind raced, wondering what to do—how can I find her? Where should I look? He was taut as a watch spring, ready to snap. The horses stirred and whinnied when they noticed him standing there, and Randy listened to the light thud of their hooves on the hard ground as they walked toward him, Big Caballo the tall palomino stallion out front. The friendly horse stuck his head out over the fence and softly nuzzled Randy's outstretched hand. Randy gently patted the side of Caballo's head. "What happened here last night Big Fella? Where's Little Girl?" he asked, wishing the horse could talk.

Confused and worried, Randy sauntered slowly to the house and through the back door and went inside.

Tessie appeared at the kitchen door and began to say something, glanced at his troubled face and asked with concern, "What's wrong, Honey?"

"One of our horses is missing."

"What?" her mouth dropped open. "Which one?"

"My Little Girl."

"Oh no, not her," Tessie gasped. "Her colt is due any day now."

"I know," Randy said sympathetically, searching his mind for answers.

"Is Joe awake? Maybe he knows something or saw something when he came home last night."

"No. I'm letting him sleep in this morning."

"Why don't you wake him while I wash up?"

"All right, Hon," Tessie said as she turned on her heel and walked down the hallway, knocked on Joe's bedroom door and called softly. "Joe, wake up. Your father wants to talk to you."

Joe's sleep-reddened eyes slowly began to open. Tiredly he brought himself up on one elbow and hollered out irritably, "Get the hell out and leave me alone for once!"

His angry words and tone surprised and frightened Tessie. She stepped back and slowly closed the door.

Randy, wiping his hands on a towel, jerked his head around. "What the sam hill did he say?" He threw the towel down and stomped down the hallway where he ran into a very irritated yet concerned Tessie. She raised her hands, dumbfounded, her eyes were wide, and they glanced at each other. "All I did was ask him to get up," Tessie said, with exasperation.

Randy grabbed the doorknob and threw his son's door open. "What did you just say to your mother?"

"It's okay, Randy," Tessie said meekly. "Go easy. He's just tired."

Like lightning, he turned on her thundering, "it's not okay. He's never talked to you like that before and he's not going to start now, damn it!"

Randy's eyes blazed with controlled rage and anger as he stared at Joe lying in his bed. "Get yourself up! Right now! This damn minute! We have some talking to do."

"Get out, Dad! You and Mom leave me alone!" Joe shouted.

Randy's lower jaw worked from side to side, before he said, with a balance of calm and temper, "Don't you ever use that tone of voice with me, or your mother for that matter, and don't ever tell me to get out of my own house. You get your ass out of that bed and get dressed, and I mean right now! Then meet me in my den in fifteen minutes."

"And if I don't?" Joe muttered.

"You don't even want to go there!" And with that Randy turned and abruptly, marched out of the room and down the hallway.

✝

Fifteen minutes later, Randy's anger had simmered down somewhat and Joe stood before him near the threshold of the den.

"Come in, Joe. Have a seat." Randy motioned him to a chair in front of his desk.

"Now son, what do you have to say for yourself?"

"I'm sorry I yelled at you and Mom," he responded timidly.

Randy looked into Joe's blue eyes and saw an honesty that convinced him to forego any further chastisement of the lad. "Next time you get feeling so damn grumpy, take a second to think about what's going to come out of your pie hole before you speak and save us all a heap of trouble. Promise?"

"Yeah, Dad, I promise." Joe answered truthfully. "Okay if I go now? I've got football practice."

"In a few minutes," Randy said with concerned deliberation. "Close the door, will you? This will only take a minute. I want to ask you about last night."

Color instantly drained from Joe's face, and he was visibly shaken. "Can't we talk about it later Dad—please?"

Disturbed by Joe's frightened demeanor, Randy asked softly, "what's wrong, Joe? Did anything out of the ordinary happen last night?"

Joe felt awkward and was slow to answer. "No," he bluffed. "I just went to work and came home as usual."

"That's not what I meant, son. Did you see anything unusual around the south pasture when you drove in last night?"

Joe slumped down in his chair, not meeting his father's eyes, and didn't answer.

"Well?" Randy pressed, cocking an eyebrow.

"I don't want to talk about it!" Joe replied, a bit more forcefully than he intended.

"Why not?" Randy pressed further, and with a more intense gaze into Joe's deceitful eyes, which told Randy he was probing into an area Joe wanted to completely avoid.

"I just don't, okay?" Joe argued.

"No, it's not okay. If you saw something I need to know, you've got to tell me."

"Why?"

"Our mare Little Girl is missing."

"Oh Jesus H. Christ!" Joe gasped and grimaced as his face filled with terror.

"Did you see who took her?" Randy asked, calmer now.

Joe nodded affirmatively.

"Well, who was it?"

"*They...*" Joe stuttered, and couldn't force the words out.

"They? Who, Joe? I need to know, son."

Joe stared at his father as his first tears in years trickled slowly down his face. "I can't tell you," he blurted out. "*They'll* hurt you and Mom," he said with an uncontrollable sob.

"Oh no they won't!" Randy said forcefully. "C'mon, tell me. No one is going to hurt me, and I can guarantee they won't hurt your mother or you or Jennie! I need to know who *they* are."

Joe took a deep breath. "I just can't, Dad. *They* made me promise not to tell anyone."

The immediate paleness of his face and the quivering of his lip foretold the absolute and terrifying fear he felt about telling his father of his horribly frightening experience last night while he was driving home along that lonely stretch of dirt road and stopped to see why their horses were running helter skelter in every direction.

3

"ALL RIGHT, YOUNG MAN, HAVE IT YOUR WAY," Randy's tone was calm and even. "You're old enough to make your own decisions. Go to your football practice, but keep this in mind, while you're out on the field running the ball, I'm planning to find out what happened to Little Girl with or without your help. This ranch will be yours one of these days. I'll let you decide whether you want to help me preserve it for your future. When you're ready to tell me what you saw last night maybe we can figure out what this mutilation business is all about right here on our own ranch. In the meantime we've got to find Little Girl. Will you help me look for her first thing Sunday morning? We'll saddle two of our best horses and head out at sun up and scour every inch of the ranch until we find her. What do you say?"

"Sure, Dad," Joe replied, with less trepidation than he was actually feeling, tempted to spill what happened to him last night, every vivid crazy detail of which he could recall with uncanny clarity. Those eerie details played over and over in his mind's eye, like a horror movie he couldn't turn off. So he just sat there, his hands clasped firmly in his lap. He felt like the sap had drained right out of him. Though lingering, nagging fear for his parent's safety was uppermost in his mind, deep down in his heart and soul, he knew he'd have to shoulder the responsibility of telling his father who abducted Little Girl and how, at least from what he knew. But for now, all he could do was get away to the football field and try to decide what he should do.

✝

The dusty, dented black and white sheriff's patrol car pulled to a stop off the dirt road near Randy's ranch and uniformed Deputy Jake Henline surveyed the tranquil peaceful scene before him. The log ranch homestead was an imposing two-storied building, surrounded by a wrap-around porch, with rocking chairs, tables and a barbeque grill. But what was more imposing still, were the outbuildings, the barn, stables, a big tack room, a granary store and a couple of sheds. Jake fondly recalled the time he worked for Randy around the ranch when he returned from Vietnam five years ago, shattered in body and mind. His body healed but his mind remained plagued by recurring nightmares of his marine buddies being gruesomely killed, while others were wounded, mangled and maimed during vicious gun battles and hand to hand combat. Finding and securing a ranch hand job at Randy Johnson's place provided the mental escape he needed from his upside-down world of war, and its corresponding continual confusion, and compassionately eased him into a slow return to a world of peace time reality. As a working cowboy, alone in Idaho's high country, riding herd on wild range cattle, he'd been reborn in mind and spirit—finally reclaiming the civilian values he grew up learning and living, but got misplaced long ago in Southeast Asia's killing fields. And when he was whole again, Randy put in a good word for him with

Dan Jeffords. That recommendation, coupled with Jake's military experience, landed him a deputy sheriff's job.

Jake pulled into Randy's drive way and unwound his six foot four frame from the driver's seat and stepped out.

Jennie was romping around on front lawn with Buster, throwing a Frisbee for the old dog, "Hi, Mr. Henline," she shouted as the old dog came running up to her with the Frisbee in his mouth.

"Hi Jennie. Is Joe here?"

"No, he's over at the high school practicing football."

"Is your Daddy here?"

'He's in the house. C'mon in, Mr. Henline. I'll get him."

Jake followed the pretty young girl through the door into the front room. Randy came from the kitchen and quickly thrust his hand out and grabbed Jake's big beefy hand in a hearty handshake. "This is a pleasant surprise, Jake. Long time no see. Have a seat." He motioned Jake to an overstuff rocking chair. "What brings you out this way? "

"Two reasons, Randy. Sheriff Jeffords assigned me to nightly patrol duty in this part of the valley. There's something very strange going on, and we've got to come up with some answers—and fast."

"Are you referring to animal mutilations?" Randy asked.

"Yes, and we're especially interested in Miss BJ's strange killing and mutilation. She's the only horse so far that's been killed and mutilated. The Sheriff has assigned me and another deputy to investigate that next week, with your permission, of course. We apologize for not coming sooner, but we're working sixty hours a week, mostly night patrols, when farm animals are being slaughtered. After our investigation we'll write up a detailed description of the mutilations inflicted on your horse and also any pertinent evidence on the site where Bill Martin found her and pass it along to the attorney general's command post and to the FBI in Boise."

That took Randy by surprise! "The feds are now involved?"

"They are. The FBI office in Boise is becoming very interested in these animal killings."

"Why?" Randy asked.

"I don't know, unless they feel local police can't handle the problem. Everything with the feds is hush hush. They're hard people to work with."

Randy nodded. "And what's that about a command post?"

"The command post was authorized and set up in Boise by Idaho's Attorney General to coordinate the numerous reports of animal mutilations pouring in from all over the state."

"How does it work?" Randy asked.

"I've not been involved with it personally, but from what we in the sheriff's office have been told, the state police put a huge map of Idaho on the wall and hired retired police officers to answer phone calls reporting animal mutilations. A yellow thumb tack is stuck into the map at those locations. Wherever the pins cluster, that's where the mutilations are occurring. One of those pins represents your ranch."

Randy's eyes were hard on Jake now, when he asked tentatively, "How many other pins are stuck into the map?"

"Way over a hundred, the way I hear it."

Randy chewed on that silently for a few moments. "The feds? A command post? My God, Jake this sounds serious."

"More than serious! Goddamn scary."

Randy nodded thorough agreement! "Jake, you mentioned two reasons for your visit today. We've taken care of one of them. What's the other one?"

"I wanted to talk to Joe. but Jennie told me he's over at the high school."

Randy's head jerked up and he stared at Jake hard before asking, "Why? Is Joe in some sort of trouble?"

"Oh no, no," Jake replied with a grin. "I just came by to see how he's feeling this morning after he tangled with me last night."

Randy was clearly puzzled. "How he's feeling? He tangled with you? Did you have a fight? What are you talking about?"

"*What?* You mean he hasn't told you?"

"Told me *what?*"

"About what happened between the two of us at one-thirty this morning."

Tessie stepped into the front room, her car keys still in her hand. "Hi Honey, I got the shopping done. Oh, Hi Jake," she called out enthusiastically. "I saw your patrol car parked out front. Did you come to arrest one of us?" She gave him a playful smile.

"No, not today." Jake returned the grin and started to get up.

"Oh, sit down, Jake, for heaven's sake," she said."You don't have to bow and scrape to me. You're one of the family, just like one of my kids. Can I get you a cup of coffee?"

"I'd love one, Tess! I sure could use a pick me up this morning—it was a long night and I'm dragging around half asleep."

Tessie walked back to the kitchen. When she was gone, Jake leaned forward and said, in a low voice, "Damn, Randy, I'm really sorry to spring this surprise on you. I assumed Joe would have at least told you. I need to talk to you in private. Okay?"

Randy nodded, as Tessie walked in with a steaming mug of hot coffee and handed it to Jake.

"Tess," Randy said, "Jake has some confidential business he needs to discuss with me. Would you mind leaving us alone for a few minutes?"

"Confidential business?" Tess' eyes widened. "What's it about?"

Randy chuckled. "If you knew that, it wouldn't be confidential, now, would it?"

"Oh"—her head wagged just the slightest, "All right," she pouted. "I never get to hear any of the good stuff! Damn men!" She shook her head and made for the kitchen.

Randy craned his neck to make sure she was out of ear shot. "Okay, Jake, what's this all about? Joe told me some crazy stuff about someone or something who told him not to tell, but I have no idea what he was talking about. Whatever it was happened last night, but Joe clammed up and as of now is very reluctant to say anything more about it. If I had any inkling you were involved I would have pressed him much harder. So anyway tell me what happened between the two of you at that ungodly hour of the morning."

Jake took a long sip of coffee. "I'm sorry Joe hasn't told you. I would have preferred you hearing it from him, but here's the way it went down. I was patrolling out this way last night, driving slowly, hoping I might catch some crazy sonsabitch in the act of killing farm animals. It was moonless and cloudy and pitch black. Just after I passed Henry Jamison's place, I thought I saw some kind of blue light pulsating over your south pasture. As I got closer I put my headlights on high beam, but still couldn't see a damn thing but road—until I saw the reflectors on the back of Joe's old pickup parked off on the right side of the road about a quarter of a mile from your pasture. I couldn't see anyone in the truck. I thought maybe Joe had run out of gas and walked on home. I stopped to check it out. As I shined my flashlight in the driver's window, and saw Joe hunkered down on the seat. I thought maybe he was asleep. I shined the light on him and he gave out the most blood-curdling scream. Seriously, it scared the livin' piss right out of me and I darn near had a heart attack! I've never ever heard anyone scream and carry on like that."

"What the hell made him scream like that?" Randy asked puzzled, coming right to the edge of his seat.

"That's what I wanted to know, so I asked him, are you all right, Joe? I'll never forget the look on that boy's face, there in my flashlight beam—like he was scared half to death, and at his wits end. His face was chalk white and his eyes bulged out like he'd seen something too evil to comprehend. He was shaking in every fiber of his being. I jerked the driver's door open and asked him to step out of the truck.

He screamed at me two or three times, 'don't hurt me, don't hurt me,' and backed away. I ordered him to stop screaming and stand still. Joe, I said, it's me, Jake Henline, I'm not going to hurt you. What's the matter with you? Why are you acting like this?"

"Then what?" Randy asked with intense interest. This just did not sound like Joe at all.

"He screamed, 'Get away from me,' then doubled up his fist and took a wild crazy swing at me. I ducked and grabbed his arm. He struggled desperately to get away and screamed at the top of his lungs, 'let me go!'"

"I'm sorry to tell you this, Randy, but I slapped him hard across the face. I really felt I had no choice. He was fighting, screaming, acting like a crazy man. That blow seemed to bring him around and he stopped fighting me. His wild bulging eyes slowly came back into focus. 'Jake? Is that you, Jake?' he asked. "Yeah, Joe, it's me, Jake Henline. I asked him. What's wrong, Joe? What are you doing out here?

He was kind of incoherent, talking fast, and I couldn't make head or tales out of what he was saying. Something about he had to work late, got sick and was sorry he'd taken a swing at me."

"That's all he told you?" Randy asked, perplexed.

"Not a thing more was offered. I wasn't sure what to do next. By then Joe had regained his senses and seemed fairly normal and a whole lot more rational. I asked if he wanted me to drive him home in my patrol car, but he flat out turned me down. He seemed in a hurry and jumped in his pickup, started it up and took off. I followed a ways behind him to make sure he made it home safely. When he pulled into your driveway, I headed on home."

Randy's face reflected his total bewilderment, and he asked Jake, "What the hell would have caused Joe to act like that? Had he been drinking or anything like that?"

"No.," Jake replied. "I've handled dozens of DUI's and would have smelled liquor as soon as I opened the truck door."

Randy nodded, "What then? Did you see anything unusual in the horse pasture or on any other part of the ranch?"

"Nothing out of the ordinary at all. Why? Is there something other than Miss BJ's slaying going on around your ranch I ought to know about?"

"Well, yes. I suppose there is. Last evening our mare Little Girl came up missing, and Jake, I don't mind telling you I'm worried and scared as hell— and I just don't know what to do. I've got other horses and lots of cattle to think about—what if they start killing and mutilating them?"

Jake stared at Randy and his voice almost a croak. "Are you sure Little Girl didn't just slip through the fence and is somewhere on the ranch?"

Randy's face took on a sober expression, "Yeah, I'm damn sure she didn't get out of the pasture on her own. She's a great horse. It's not like her to wander off. We just inspected all the fences and gates this summer. You know my maintenance routine around here! I have a sickening hunch she's probably laying on some hillside, right here on this ranch, butchered and mutilated just like Miss BJ was."

"God, let's hope not. Have you reported her disappearance to the sheriff?" Jake asked.

"Not yet," Randy replied. "Joe and I are going to saddle up and ride around the ranch and try to find her—or what's left of her."

"Perhaps that's best under the circumstances," Jake agreed. "If and when you find her that would be the time to talk to Dan. Right now he's up to his eyeballs trying to field incoming phone calls. The phone lines are jammed with people calling in with the wildest tales you can imagine about their animals being slaughtered. Most of the ranchers around these parts are in a total panic mode, demanding action from the sheriff's office."

"So what are you guys doing?" Randy asked.

With a sardonic grin, Jake came back with, "What the hell can we do, Randy? Not one person has seen a damn thing that gives us even the slightest clue as to who or what is killing livestock. But," Jake smiled broadly, "I've got a hunch our very first clue might come from your Joe. I definitely believe he saw or heard something out there last night that could just open the door for us."

Randy's head jerked upwards. "You really think so?" he asked skeptically.
"I sure do."

"Have you said anything to the sheriff about that—I mean your confrontation with Joe last night? "

"No. Dan's got enough on his mind right now. And what could I tell him? I don't really know what happened out there last night. I take it you want me to keep quiet about that?"

"I'd appreciate that, Jake, I really would, until we can learn a bit more about what might be going on and have at least some specifics. I'd also like to give Joe some more time to calm down and perhaps come clean with me or his mother about what happened to him last night."

"I understand," Jake responded. He put his empty cup on the coffee table and stood, ready to leave. "Anything else?"

"I think we've covered it," Randy said. They shook hands amiably.

Jake's hand was on the doorknob. He stopped and turned slowly, his brows knotted slightly. "Randy, do you think what happened to Joe last night has anything to do with Little Girl being AWOL?"

Randy answered tentatively, his voice grim and quiet, "Yes. Yes I do. And I've got a gut feeling that when Joe and I saddle up two of our best horses and head out at sun up tomorrow to look for her Joe may open up and tell me what the hell happened."

"I wish I could tag along and hear what he has to say, but I've got three investigations scheduled and more piling up after that Will you please let me know as soon as you find Little Girl, and better yet, let me know if Joe tells you something that may provide any vital clues we need to determine whoever or whatever is killing livestock in our area?"

Randy nodded. "You can count on that, my friend!"

4

THE FIRST SHADOW STREAKS OF DAWN
found Randy and Joe out in the horse pasture trying to rope a couple of saddle
horses to ride in their search for Little Girl. The horses were nervous and
skittish, evidently caused by of some kind mysterious episode in or near the
pasture Friday night.

"Slow. Easy, now," Randy's voice said softly in the semi-darkness, as he
held both arms out and hazed a big appaloosa mare against the fence. "Now
Joe! Throw your rope on her, before she takes off running again."

Randy's voice reached Joe's ears dimly, as though in a strong cross
wind. Everything was a little hazy in Joe's consciousness this morning; all
he wanted in the world was sleep. He hadn't slept well—too many things
rumbling around in his mind—things he didn't understand—things that had
never happened before on a peaceful Idaho ranch.

"Damn it, Joe, wake up!" Randy shouted. "Throw your rope around her
neck before she stomps me into the ground!" The sharp command snapped
Joe fully awake, and he shook his head back and forth, stretching his neck.

"Sorry Dad," Joe said as he quickly slipped the noose over the appaloosa's
well muscled neck.

"Take her to the barn and saddle'r up," Randy said. "I'll be along in a
minute, as soon as I catch the palomino." Randy hazed the big stallion into a
corner, threw his rope over the horse's head and tightened it around his neck.
Randy led the tall stallion from the pasture and stopped to close the gate. He
stared at his other horses nervously milling about. Except for Miss BJ and
Little Girl, they were all there, and he couldn't for the life of him figure out
how they'd escaped.

He closed and locked the gate and glanced over at the flag pole in front
of the house where the American flag rippled in the early morning breeze. In
a moment of reflection Randy realized how fortunate he was to live in a free
country, to be blessed with a beautiful wife and kids and to own a working
ranch nestled in the most beautiful mountain country the man upstairs ever
created. Then his eyes fixed on the far horizon, silhouetting the mountains,
north across the winding Snake River.

Randy Johnson had never wanted to be anything but a rancher. A cattle rancher and maybe raise a few horses. He was pushing fifty, and life couldn't be better. He was realizing the reward for the long years of hard work developing the ranch into a modern business enterprise. As a young man he'd learned cattle ranching and frontier-style living from his father and grandfather. It was tough, gut-busting work, six days a week, fifty one weeks a year, except for the annual vacation he and Tessie took to Mazatlan, at which time he paid his cousin Bill Martin to look in on his stock. Maybe this year his son Joe would do it. The boy was seventeen and already turning out to be an outstanding ranch hand.

If that damned war hadn't come along—oh well, that was water under the bridge. *War is hell*! He smiled. *Boy, a truer statement was never made*. Two years lost in the hot humid deadly jungles of Southeast Asia. He wouldn't take a million dollars for the experience, but he wouldn't give a plug nickel to do it over again! If he hadn't signed up for ROTC at the University of Idaho to help pay for tuition and books—oh well, it beat hell out of working in a gas station or a fast food joint. During his sophomore year he married Tessie, the love of his life, whom he'd known since kindergarten and dated from the time their parents allowed them to date.

Scratching out some semblance of life, they lived together in a tiny rented one-bedroom basement apartment in Moscow, Idaho. Tessie worked long hours waiting tables at the La Frontera Mexican Restaurant. And he couldn't remember a single complaint she'd ever made. When Randy graduated and pinned on his new shiny gold second lieutenant's bars, Tessie packed their suitcases and they hopped in the old pickup and headed for a new adventure at Fort Rucker, Alabama, where Randy underwent rigorous helicopter pilot training. After he'd served his time in the army, he joined the Idaho National Guard, unaware that the following month his unit would be called to active duty in Vietnam. He and his cousin Bill Martin shipped out together, fought side any side, and luckily or by the grace of god, both returned to Idaho; and, over time, pushed horrible memories of that bloody killing time to the back of their minds and moved on with the life of their boyhood dreams of ranching and working in Idaho's Snake River Valley.

"Hey, Dad," Joe yelled, "Mom's got breakfast ready."

"Tell her I'll be there as soon as I saddle my horse."

✝

Tessie set cups and plates before Randy and Joe. Sausage, eggs and biscuits, then poured some steaming hot black ranch coffee. Randy didn't talk much in the mornings until he'd had his first cup.

Tessie's intuition told her that Joe would tell Randy sometime today what he saw out there near the pasture the night Little Girl went missing. She wanted to say something, do something that would make everything all right for Joe. But what could she say? She could only bite her tongue and swallow back the empathy she felt at the moment.

Randy lovingly patted her arm. "More coffee please," he said with a wink.

As she poured coffee she said, "I made some sandwiches and a thermos of coffee and packed them in your saddle bags."

"Thanks Honey," Randy said.

She smiled and gave a little nod. "I also stuck your loaded forty-five in the saddle bags, just to be on the safe side."

"I appreciate it." Randy grinned, wondering how she could read him like a book. He chalked it up to that uncanny sixth sense of hers.

"Are you taking Buster with you?" she asked. "He seems pretty anxious to get going."

"We sure are," Randy said, and drank the last of his coffee. "We need him. If Little Girl's somewhere on the ranch he'll help us find her."

✝

The day would be comfortable Randy thought as he rode along following a well-worn cattle trail south towards the spot where Bill had found Miss BJ's remains. If Little Girl was out here, she'd probably be somewhere in that area. Except for the slight breeze things looked gentle. The cattle sauntered along lazily, grazing contentedly. Winter would be along soon. The smell of it was in the air, like the smell of a thing out of sight, yet there it was. Joe traipsed along behind his dad on his appaloosa, and Buster, head down, nose to the ground, ran ahead, weaving enthusiastically through the sagebrush, trying to pick up a scent.

Randy and Joe rode along quietly; and the only sounds under the bright fall sky were the horses loping movements and the saddles squeaking. It was a predominantly silent ride the first hour or so. Joe didn't speak unless spoken to, still seemingly distant, with a great deal on his mind.

Standing in the stirrups Randy turned and said, "Let's head for those cottonwoods, and take five, all right?" Joe kicked his horse up alongside his dad and together they trotted toward the trees.

They dismounted and tied their reins to a low hanging branch on an old knotty cottonwood tree. Joe relaxed and slid his six foot frame down, against a tree, and let his legs sprawl out in front of him.

Randy grabbed a canteen hanging from his saddle, took a drink, and handed it to Joe. Panting, Buster streaked into the trees and plopped himself down beside Joe, resting his head on his outstretched front paws.

Randy said quietly, "Are you ready to tell me what happened Friday night. I really need to know,"

Joe hesitated. "I guess so, but I'm not sure you'll believe me. That's why I've been holding back. I doubt anyone will believe my crazy story."

"I'll believe you, Son," Randy said softly. "You've never lied to me before, and I'd trust you with my life. Just take it slow and from the beginning. It was just a normal night at the drive in, right?"

"Yeah, Dad. The boss asked me to stay late and help clean up. I finished up about one a.m. then headed home."

"On your drive home did you see anything unusual?"

"Not until I was about a quarter of a mile from our pasture."

"What did you see?"

"I'm really not sure, Dad." Joe's face contorted as his mind pulled up memories best left tucked away. "Everything is still all jumbled up in my mind. I really didn't see anything solid—or tangible. It was like a wild crazy dream or hallucinations or..." He hesitated. "But I did see something, if that makes any sense."

Randy nodded affirmatively. "Well? Tell me what you think you saw."

"I saw flashing blue lights like strobe lights over the pasture. Our horses were running amuck, like maybe a mean hungry cougar was chasing them, and was about ready to attack."

"What did you do?"

"I threw on the brakes and stopped to see what was causing the ruckus or what was chasing them."

"Did you see anything that looked suspicious?" Randy asked, his interest intense.

"Not exactly. Not a person, if that's what you mean. I was scared and I don't know why, except the pasture was unexpectedly lit up very bright for a few moments, almost as intense as at noon time. Just after I pulled off to the side of the road I saw a bright clear beam of light, like a spot or searchlight, beaming down from somewhere or something in the sky. The light was moving over the pasture. It seemed as if each horse was being individually scrutinized, sort of like someone was trying to locate one in particular. It seemed an agonizingly long time, except I now know it was more instantaneous."

Joe saw his father's face had a tight look about it. "Why are you looking at me like that?"

"Like what?"

"Well," Joe pursed his lips, "like you don't believe me. See, I told you you wouldn't believe me."

"Relax, son, relax." Randy waved a hand. "I'm with ya. Go ahead. I'm listening. It was a clear light, not blue, right?"

"Yeah, a regular light, you know, like the spotlight we plug into the cigarette lighter when we hunt jackrabbits at night."

"What were the horses doing?"

"Running like hell, scattered, snorting, whinnying, kicking and flailing about with their hind legs."

"Could you see where the light was coming from?"

"As near as I could tell in the dark, it was some kind of a polished shiny metallic circular object about five-hundred feet above the pasture, with flashing or pulsating blue lights and some kind of throbbing motor noise."

"Then what?"

"The bright light finally stopped scanning the herd and came to rest solidly on Little Girl. She skidded to a stop and froze, just like a statue."

"What happened then?"

"Now Dad, this is the part that's really hard to believe. She was slowly being hoisted off the ground in the light beam."

If Randy doubted what he was hearing he didn't show it. "Go on," he urged.

"The moment her feet left the ground she began screaming and kicking, fighting to break free. Her screams sent chills up my back. It's still creeping me out. I never heard such a sound in all my life."

"What caused her to do that?" Randy asked, his face masked with concern.

"I don't know unless it was pain, pure fright or sheer terror. When she was about fifty feet above the pasture the bright beam snapped off. I couldn't see Little Girl any more, but I could still hear her screaming. Next, the blue lights flickered off—and everything went back to darkness. Within a few seconds that bright beam of light flashed on again from the contraption in the night sky and started moving eerily and slowly in my direction, like it was trying to find me. You know, like one of those big searchlights we've seen in the movies, used to spot airplanes."

"And you think they were actually searching for you?" Randy asked, with a look of deep concern and a tad of speculative doubt.

Joe nodded. "Yeah. I know they were," he answered firmly, with a look on his face seeming to indicate he couldn't really convey memories of that terrible night with mere words. "God, Dad, I was so scared I was almost petrified. I thought the light might pick me up like it did Little Girl." Joe took in a deep breath and continued. "I heard a thumping noise, and my heart was beating so hard and so loud I felt as though there was a kettle drum in my chest. Then the light flooded over my pick up and me. I hid my face in my hands to ward off the brilliant light. It was so bright it hurt my eyes and impaired my vision. I felt encased in a warmth like the sun and it wouldn't go away. I put my face down on the seat, but it didn't seem to help much. The light was still engulfing me. That's when I heard the words, 'do not be afraid.'"

"Who was speaking?" Randy asked, astounded at this revelation. "You said you didn't see anyone."

"I didn't. The voice seemed to come from the light. It seemed to…" Joe searched for words, "like penetrate my mind, talking to my mind, not my ears. There were no spoken words, like now when you and me are talking to each other. I can't remember exactly, but they said something like, 'don't be afraid,' and 'do not tell what you saw here.' You must not tell.'"

"What did the voice sound like?" Randy asked. "Was it accented English or what?"

Joe chewed on his bottom lip for a moment. "I don't quite know how to describe it, Dad. Kind of like the voice was coming from the end of a long tunnel, like maybe the voice of a translator, like a computer robot speaks. You know how they talk, SLOW AND DEEP." Joe deepened his voice. "Like DO—NOT—BE—AFRAID. WE—WILL—NOT—HURT—YOU. The voice said something about people being hurt. Like a warning. DO—NOT—TELL—OR—PEOPLE—WILL—BE—HURT. LEAVE NOW."

Randy leaned back, pondering Joe's astonishing story. To say he was amazed would be an understatement. Joe watched Randy place his hand tightly around his chin. Then in a voice, with a slight tone of doubt, Randy asked, "How many were there?"

"I don't know."

"More than one?"

"I think so. The voice said WE a couple of times."

"Did you speak to them?

Joe nodded. "I said out loud, I won't tell."

"Did you say anything else?"

"Yeah. I asked, who are you? What do you want? As soon as I said that the light immediately snapped off."

"Did you high tail it out of there as soon as the light snapped off?"

"No, Dad. It was like I was paralyzed or drugged. I can't explain it any better than that. I think I stayed there for quite a spell. When I started to regain my senses, the pasture was dark. The abnormal lights were gone. I felt so mixed up I didn't know what to do."

"Then what happened?"

"Someone shined a bright light in my face. It scared me so bad I started hyperventilating. I figured they'd come back to kill me, and I had to fight back."

"That must have been Jake Henline using his flashlight, right?"

"Yeah, but I didn't realize it was him. He ordered me to get out of the truck."

Randy grinned. "Jake told me you actually took a wild crazy swing at him! That was a dumb thing to do. Hell boy, he's big enough to wrestle alligators with one hand and whip your ass with the other one."

Clearly embarrassed, Joe said, "I know! And you're right Dad. It was a dumb thing to do. But my whole body was trembling all over. Jake is so big and tall. Standing there in the dark, by the door of my truck, my first thought was that he was some kind of beast or monster, so the second I stepped out of the truck, I tried as hard as I could to deck him."

"In that situation I believe I'd have done the same thing," Randy said. "But getting back to the horses, do you think whomever or whatever talked to you from the beam of light took Little Girl?"

"Yes sir!" Joe was quick to answer, without a trace of doubt. "The last time I saw her they were hoisting her up out of the pasture. She was screaming like a lost soul from the pits of hell. Then the lights went out."

Randy hunched forward, and asked, "Did they seem interested in any of the other horses?"

"Nope. Only Little Girl. That light beam followed her all over the pasture, like they had pre-selected her."

"Any idea why?"

"Well," Joe replied slowly, "I kind of figured Little Girl was the only horse that was going to have a colt. Other than that, she wasn't any different from the other horses."

Randy stared at Joe in silence before he said, "The colt, eh? Damn, that makes sense. But what would they want with an unborn colt?" Randy shook his head. "Son, this situation gets more bizarre by the minute. Thank you for opening up and sharing your experience with me. I can only imagine how terrified you must have been, being out there all alone with no one to help you. Let's hope nothing like this ever happens again!"

Joe drew in a long breath and asked, "Do you believe me Dad?"

Randy nodded, with a slight smile, "Of course I do, son. No one could make up a tale like you've just told me." He paused for a moment. "For the time being I think it would be best if you keep all of this to yourself. Don't tell anyone else until we have more information."

"Jeez Dad, don't worry about that," Joe said with a sigh of relief. "I don't plan to ever tell anyone about this. I'm having a hard enough time believing it myself."

ϯ

"Mount up, Joe," Randy said, "Let's ride." They rode south at a canter, side by side, their horses' steel-shod hoofs drumming along the ridgeline above the Union Pacific railroad tracks. When they came to where the tracks made a looping south curve, Randy reined to a stop and held up a hand. Joe pulled his horse to a stop.

"Over there," Randy pointed, "Just below the top of that hill is where Bill found Miss BJ. So I figure if Little Girl is still on the ranch she'll be somewhere around here."

Joe's eyes widened. "Think we can find her? There's a lot of range land out here."

"Let's split up and start by searching each gully. Take Buster with you. Maybe he'll pick up a scent. Keep me in sight, and holler if you see or find anything."

"All right." Joe snapped his fingers. "C'mon, Buster, let's go." Joe put spurs to his horse. The old dog ran ahead, glanced back and adjusted his speed to the horse so as not to get too far ahead—until a long-eared jackrabbit unexpectedly jumped out from under some rocks and zigzagged flat out through the sagebrush. Old Buster shifted into high gear, in an all out run, trying to catch the rabbit.

Joe slowed his horse to a saunter along the ridgeline, his eyes searching and examining every gully and arroyo. He reined the appaloosa to a stop at the top edge of a deep brushy canyon and leaned forward over the saddle trying to see to the bottom. Halfway down, on a flat outcropping, in a tangle of tall weeds, he noticed a circular space that had been crushed down flat against the ground.

Buster lost his race with the rabbit and came running back, wagging his tail, panting, his tongue hanging out the side of his mouth.

Suddenly, Joe's horse reared up on its hind legs, whinnying shrilly. The sudden bucking maneuver took Joe by surprise; but being an expert horseman, his feet were planted firmly in the stirrups. When the horse's front hoofs jolted back to solid ground, they barely missed Buster as he scurried out of the way. Joe leaned over and studied the ground to find the rattlesnake that caused the horse to rear, figuring that's the only thing which would make the big appaloosa mare buck like that. However there was no snake.

When the dust cleared, Buster raised his head high in the air and caught a whiff of something in the gulley he clearly didn't like. He lifted his lip and bared his teeth and growled way back in his throat letting Joe know something was amiss. Then he lowered his snout closer to the ground and sniffed his way slowly to the brim of the top edge of the ravine, where he set himself in a defensive stand. His tail shot out and his hair stood on end. He growled fiercely.

"What is it, boy?" Joe called. "Is there something down there?"

Buster didn't respond and maintained his protective stance, continuing his low growl.

Two blocks south Randy unsheathed his binoculars and played them across the gullies ahead, trying to recognize anything at all out of the ordinary. He heard Joe's loud whistle, looked back and saw Joe purposely waving his Stetson hat in the air. Randy turned his horse and came galloping up.

"Have you found something?" Randy quizzed.

"Buster's picked up a scent of some kind down in that gulley. Look at him." Buster was still growling. "He's letting us know something's down there."

"It's too steep for the horses to clamber down there," Randy said. "Let's leave them here and work our way down to that weedy outcrop and check it out, maybe find out what set Buster off like that."

Joe nodded affirmatively and dismounted. Randy reached back into his saddle bag, latched on to his Colt 45, and stuck it in the waistband of his Levis, then dismounted.

"Expecting trouble?" Joe grinned sheepishly.

"Nothing me and the ol' peacemaker here can't handle," Randy said lightly. "Let's go." He started down the hill.

Joe clucked his tongue and shouted, "C'mon, Buster." The old dog ignored the command. Joe shouted, "Get yourself down here!" Buster approached reluctantly, slinking toward Joe, his tail between his legs. "That's weird, Dad. That's the first time Buster's ever refused my command." As he said that, Buster turned tail and skedaddled up the hillside to the horses tethered on the promontory.

Randy and Joe slid and shuffled their way down into the rugged loosely rock-lined ravine. When Randy stepped onto the outcropping, he brushed aside the weeds and foliage to create a small clearing where he could get a better look at the eerie sight unfolding a few feet in front of him. As he did, he stopped abruptly and dug his long heeled cowboy boots into the rocky dirt. Stunned and terror struck, he stared at one of the most disturbing sights he'd ever laid eyes on. He threw up a hand. "Whoa, Joe! Stay right there. Don't come any closer."

The absurd, hair-raising grin on Little Girl's face and her empty eye sockets glaring up at Randy froze him dead in his tracks. Partially hidden within some weeds a few feet away was the mutilated carcass of their once beautiful and gentle mare. Her rigor mortis affected body lay horizontally across the weeds, her feet toward the bottom of the ravine.

"What is it, Dad? Did you find something?"

"Yeah. It's the remains of Little Girl," Randy replied with some trepidation.

For a split second Randy felt the horse was still alive, laughing at his frightened face. Bending closer, Randy could see Little Girl's upper and lower lips had been surgically removed, exposing her teeth in a hideous smile, exactly the same as on Miss BJ.

Little Girl's tongue had been removed, and the empty eye sockets had sharp, clean cuts around the outside as though the same type of large auger or scooping device used on Miss BJ had been used on Little Girl to remove her eyeballs and lift them intact from the sockets. Her ears had been cleanly and neatly sliced off. All the incisions on the horses head had been made with extremely sharp instruments, by someone or something who knew how to use them.

Chomping at the bit to see what was going on, Joe stood on his tiptoes trying to get a better look. "Dad, is it okay if I come down now? I've seen dead animals before."

"Not like this you haven't. You might need a barf bag. Oh never mind. C'mon down. But be very careful. This is a crime scene so let's try not to destroy any valuable evidence."

Joe scrambled down and his first glimpse of Little Girl caused him momentary nausea. He sucked air through his teeth and struggled for a moment to keep it under control, dry heaving a couple of times. His face wrinkled with disgust. "How could someone kill and butcher a horse on a small outcropping like this?"

"I don't think it was done here," Randy replied.

"Where then?"

"We'll talk about that later, okay? Right now let's see if we can figure out what happened to Little Girl."

They knelt down and studied a neat, clean 20-inch surgical incision beginning at the mare's chest, curving downward to her vagina, between her legs. Through this opening Little Girl's unborn colt had been pulled from her womb. The mare's sexual organs had been cut out.

"Where's her blood, Dad?" Joe asked.

"I don't have a clue," Randy answered. "There isn't any blood on the ground, on the horse or anywhere else."

"But how can that be?" Joe asked with a baffled look. "There should be blood everywhere, or at least some traces of it."

"I know," Randy answered. "Hey, c'mere and take a look at this." Randy pointed to a seven inch wide band of raised flesh that circled the horse's neck.

"What would cause that?" Joe asked.

"You told me Little Girl was lifted up out of the pasture. Maybe this raised flesh was caused by some kind of lifting device attached around her neck."

Joe's eyes went wide. "Yeah, maybe she was hoisted out of the pasture, into that silver disk thing where she was killed and cut up. The parts they wanted they kept, and dumped her carcass here."

Randy nodded. "That's a very good possibility. Let's see if we can find any missing body parts or any other clues. You look over there." Randy pointed. "I'll see if there are any indentations in the ground like I found close to Miss BJ."

Joe searched carefully in the tall grass and weeds but found nothing. Randy bent down and found three pod marks where the weeds had been crushed into the rocky soil. He measured them with his hands.

He heard a foot crunch on gravelly rock, and a tentative clearing of a throat. He whirled, and pulled his 45. Joe was standing there.

"Next time you come up behind a man," Randy growled, "announce yourself. I almost blew your head off!"

Joe's face was turned toward him. Under his hat brim his face was troubled. His voice was slightly choked. "I'm sorry, Dad."

"Me too," Randy said. "This damn mess has my brain so muddled…" He lost his train of thought. "Look here." He smoothed out the weeds. See this pod mark? There are two more just like it. There and there."

"Something on tripod legs maybe?" Joe said. "Like you found by Miss BJ."

Randy nodded. "Exactly the same."

"Could it have been a helicopter?"

"No. A chopper couldn't land here. I'd say it was a UFO."

"Jeez, Dad, are you sure?"

"No, I'm not sure," Randy shook his head in frustration. "What I don't about this sort of thing could fill and encyclopedia."

Joe started to ask another question. "What are we…"

But Randy wasn't listening. He felt the anger rising in him, the coming explosion. Heat rushed to his face and flushed it to an angry shade of red. "Damn them, damn them all to hell!" he growled as he locked his fist on the grip of the 45 in his waistband.

Joe's last words were drowned in the rolling rapid fire thunder of Randy's army 45. He was shooting indifferently into the earth ten yards from his feet, plowing up dirt. The sharp blasts echoed across the arroyo.

"*What are you doing, Dad?*" Joe asked.

"I don't know," Randy answered sheepishly, "but it sure makes me feel a whole hell of a lot better."

Joe grinned broadly. "Jeez, Dad. And I thought I was losing it!"

5

THE DAY AFTER DISCOVERING LITTLE GIRL dead and mutilated, Randy reported his find to Sheriff Dan Jeffords, the head law enforcement official in the area. After two long apprehensive weeks Deputy Sheriffs Jake Henline and Jim Munford were finally dispatched to the Johnson ranch. After some preliminary discussion surrounding the events leading up to the discovery of the horses Randy escorted them to each of the remote hillsides to study and photograph the carcasses of Miss BJ and Little Girl. Oddly, both carcasses were still in a near perfect state of preservation. Two evenings after the officers' investigation, on his way to another mutilation that had been reported at a nearby ranch, Jake Henline caught up with Randy pitching some hay from his pickup over the fence to his horses. Without much fanfare, he handed Randy a file folder containing a three-page typewritten copy of his investigative report, titled CRIME REPORT. TWIN FALLS SHERIFF, TWIN FALLS COUNTY, IDAHO. Jake was obviously not in a particularly friendly or talkative mood which struck Randy as somewhat peculiar. They'd always had a genial relationship and today shouldn't have been any different. The deputy certainly didn't seem to want to discuss the report at all. He left in somewhat of a hurry without much more than a courteous nod of his head.

Randy, also a bit preoccupied, threw the folder on the seat of the pickup and continued with his evening chores. It was past sundown when he sat down back at home on the porch and removed his boots. As he walked stocking-footed into the darkened kitchen he noticed Tessie watching one of her favorite television programs in the front room. Not wanting to disturb her or get involved in the program, and being very anxious and curious about the report, he stepped into his den and quietly closed the door. He sat at his desk and began reviewing Henline's report. He quickly became perturbed and aggravated with what he was reading, shaking his head in total disbelief! Everything in the report was totally misleading, from beginning to end, at least it was from Randy's point of view.

Randy was very tired and discouraged. He took the folder and walked to the front room, dropped it on the coffee table and slumped back in his overstuff chair. Tessie, sensing Randy's displeasure with something and a need to talk, turned off the TV.

"You look exhausted, Honey," she said with concern.

Randy ran his fingers through his graying black hair. "Oh, it's nothing to worry about. I just finished reading Jake Henline's investigative report, and it kind of left me wondering what the hell is going on." He gestured at the file folder.

"Anything interesting?" she asked, as she walked over and placed a comforting hand on his forehead checking to see if he had a fever, then sliding it tenderly over his cheek trying to sooth the upset or exhaustion she sensed in Randy's mood.

"Poor baby," she said gawking at him. "You've got the quivers and you're sweating."

"I'm fine, Tess. Will you quit fussing over me, please? I'm just a little irritated and confused tonight, that's all."

"You sit still, and I'll make you a cup of hot tea."

He was in no mood to be mothered. "Forget about bringing me tea right now." He said it a bit more callously than he intended.

His sharp retort brought a curious stare from Tessie. "What's in Jake's report that's got you so fired up?" She retrieved the folder and handed it to him.

"Let me read some of it to you." He opened the folder and quickly scanned down to the section marked: (Reconstruct crime—Describe physical evidence, location found. Summarize other details relating to the crime.) "Here it is, Tess, right here. Listen to this: *Our investigation during daylight hours lead these officers to believe that the missing body parts were eaten or destroyed by predators, flies, maggots or whatever other item of nature that assists in decomposition of dead carcasses, rather than some pervert cutting the area away.*

"Predators, Randy?" Tessie asked with anxiety and concern. "That can't be true, can it? You and Joe told me the mutilations were done with sharp instruments, and that when the deputies inspected the carcasses they could plainly see the mutilations."

"That's what's confusing me, Tess. They did see the mutilations, up close and personal! The way they looked at each other during their investigation made me think they were scared half to death—and that they were in tune with how I felt about the situation. The whole damn report is full of these kinds of fabricated notions that nothing was amiss or unnatural about how our horses were mutilated. I can't believe Jake would do such a thing. I had more trust and faith in him than that." Randy paused and shook his head. "He was acting very strange today as well. When he dropped off this folder he hardly said a word and left like he was racing to a fire. He sure didn't want to stay and discuss his report with me, that's for damn sure!" Randy said, with a perplexed shift of the eyebrow. "Listen to this," Randy continued. "The next paragraph of the report really galls me: *The animals are truthfully too far decomposed to be able to make a positive determination. The animals were too far gone to be able to detect any wound marks.*

"But you and Joe told me..."

"I know what we told you," Randy interrupted. "But it's the deputies' conclusions that really baffle and piss me off. I won't read the whole paragraph. It's too long, almost like they made it up as they went along. *The missing parts could easily have been removed by a human.* "What the hell for?" Randy asked condescendingly and continued. "*However, a varmint or bird could have gotten them. It is possible that someone actually ran the animals down with a large truck bumper to cause the animals to be in the shape they are in. There really is quite a bit of doubt in these officers' minds that the death and condition of these animals is connected with other incidents reported in other areas that may involve a deviate drug cult or whatever.*"

"Why would Jake write something like that?" Tessie said with distaste. "Do you plan to confront him about it?"

"You're damn right! Face to face!" Randy replied forcefully. "As soon as I can track him down I'll ask him why he lied when he wrote predators were the culprits when the evidence right there in front of him indicated otherwise."

Randy chewed his lower lip for a moment, deep in thought. "Hell, two days ago, out there on the hillside when Jake and Jim were studying Miss BJ's mutilations, I pointed out to them specific evidence indicating the possibility of other worldly involvement, like laser surgery, missing body parts, no blood, several pod marks and the fact predatory animals wouldn't touch the carcasses because of some type of force field around them."

"Meaning UFOs?" Tess asked curiously.

"Exactly," Randy said. "But Jake just threw it back in my face as if warning me, 'that's pure speculation. You'd better keep your hunches about what happened to your horses and UFOs to yourself. Understand?' When I asked him why, he told me point blank, 'there are enough screwballs spreading rumors about UFOs and mysterious mutilations without any more stories getting started.' Then he softened a bit said, 'as a friend, I owe you a lot, Randy. I'm just warning you for your own good, your theory is going to get you in big trouble.'"

"What are you going to do?" Tessie asked.

"What can I do? All we have in the way of law enforcement around these parts is the Sheriff's office. I've got a hunch, from reading Jake's report, Dan Jeffords has told his deputies that there's only one answer to what or who is killing and mutilating animals—predators—regardless of what the actual facts are. That leads me to believe Jake is just following orders to cover his own ass and explains why he didn't want to discuss this report with me this afternoon."

"But why would Sheriff Jeffords do that?" Tessie asked. "Do you think he's behind or involved in some kind of cover up? If he sticks to the predator theory the mutilators will never be identified much less caught and stopped."

"I don't know, Tess," Randy said, locking questioning and curious eyes with her, "unless..."

"Unless what?" she puzzled.

"Unless the sheriff is getting his orders from higher up!"

"Hm. That's an intriguing thought," Tessie mused. "Well," Tessie yawned, "there's nothing more we can do about it tonight. I'm going to bed. Are you coming?"

"In a few minutes," Randy replied. "I want to catch the late news on TV and see if more animals have been mutilated."

"All right, Hon." She bent down and kissed his cheek. "Goodnight."

†

Seated on the edge of his overstuff chair, Randy turned on the television, flicking through the channels until he found the local news. Afraid he would fall asleep, he went to the kitchen and he made a cup of instant coffee in the microwave, then rushed back to the living room, anxious to find out if there was any new information about state-wide animal mutilations and if anyone had any theories about who the mutilators might be.

After listening to the report of a woman murdered in Nampa, a poacher shooting a fish and game officer and a motorcyclist crashing through a plate glass window, a beautiful brunette reporter smiled into the camera as the words *Breaking News* flashed across the bottom of the screen. The smiling brunette read a report: "We have just learned that near St. Anthony, in Fremont County, over 100 ranchers have been participating in a nightly, county-wide surveillance of the area, patrolling all roads, in an effort to apprehend what they suspect to be devil worshippers butchering their valuable livestock.

Nearly every rancher and farmer in the county is keeping loaded guns at the ready in their vehicles and homes. Many of them suggested to our St. Anthony reporter, Tim Webb, if anyone suspicious is spotted crouched over any of their animals they will shoot first and ask questions later."

The brunette gave a bright toothy smile, and said, "after the break we'll pass along further developments from other parts of our viewing area and some new information just in from the state attorney general's office." After what seemed interminable advertisements, the news resumed.

The brunette said, "Animal mutilations are occurring all over the area and have reached epidemic proportions. Frustration is being expressed by Idaho law enforcement officers throughout the state, who to date, have not apprehended even one suspect. One worried Sheriff told us, speaking about ranchers in his county, 'the damn fools are going to end up killing each other.'" The anchor woman continued in a subdued sober voice. "Vigilante groups are forming around the state and any stranger is suspect. Road blocks, manned by ranchers, farmers and other concerned citizens are making back country travel in Idaho a bit of an adventure, not to mention somewhat dangerous at the moment.

Over in Blaine County, Sheriff Orville Dubbe and his deputies have their hands full investigating the numerous animal mutilations that have been reported, trying to placate angry ranchers who are losing valuable cattle to." The brunette held her hands up like cat claws and hissed, "*Those fiends from hell*, as one distraught pistol-packing rancher referred to them."

After another commercial break the smiling brunette came back on. "Sorry folks, but there are so many reports of animal mutilations coming in we're devoting the rest of tonight's newscast to covering as many of them as we can. Idaho's Attorney General, Sam Kennerton told us, 'We have a unique and unusual situation that calls for some immediate attention.' We tried to get the attorney general to come on the air for an interview but he declined our invitation. He did, however, tell us he's appointed David Randall as chief investigator as well as Larry Spangler, Allan Moen and Neal Harmon, all members of his Boise staff, to gather information on the reported mutilations of domestic livestock here in Idaho. They will compile information, facts and data to determine if there is any overall pattern that would be helpful in apprehending the perpetrators of these crimes."

The brunette switched to her co-anchor, standing on location in the rain, in front of the capitol building. "Charles, you asked AG Kennerton if he could provide more specific details about his newly appointed investigative team. How did he respond?"

Charles Coverly, displaying a doleful look, holding an umbrella in one hand and a microphone in the other, began speaking into the microphone. "Mr. Kennerton said, 'I don't want to characterize using my staff as an investigation per se. That said, I have asked them to look into this serious and ongoing matter. Larry Spangler will cover eastern and southern Idaho; Neal Harmon will scour the middle part of the state, while Allan Moen will work issues in the north and west. David Randall will head up this team. These gentlemen are experts in my office and we hope they will be able to assist the local effort by concentrating on the bigger picture and supplying crucial links and similarities that might lead to slowing or cessation of these animal killings throughout our great state.'"

Neal Harmon? An investigator? Randy's head jerked up, saying to no one in particular, *Good God, I know Neal, if he's the same Neal who was with me in ROTC!* With that, he accidentally splashed boiling coffee onto his Levis, scalding his inner thigh and missing his groin by only a few inches. By the time he recovered from his spill and turned his attention back to the television the weather report was on and the banner at the bottomed of the screen was gone.

"What's going on, dear?" Tessie appeared in the front room hallway in her pajamas. "I fell asleep then I heard you talking and banging around out here. Are you all right?"

"Yeah, Hon," he said with a slight grimace on his face from the pain of the burn. "I just got a little excited with some of the breaking news on TV tonight and spilled boiling hot coffee in my lap."

"You're sure you're okay?" she asked sleepily as she noticed Randy's pained look.

"I'm fine, just a little scald from my coffee. Quit your worrying about your clumsy old man here!"

"If you say so! What was the breaking news about?" Tessie asked.

"The state's attorney general has appointed some investigators to look into the animal mutilations hitting every part of the state, and wants them to try and identify the mutilators and come up with some answers."

"How will that help us?" Tessie asked sleepily.

Randy shook his head. "I don't know exactly, but I believe I know one of the investigators personally. Do you remember Neal Harmon from my college days? A big, broad-shouldered red head. We went through ROTC together. He used to come into the La Frontera Restaurant there in Moscow where you worked. He loved Jorge's tortillas and refried beans."

"Do I remember him?" Tessie grinned. "That man could eat more Mexican food than any customer I ever waited on! He told me once he had a hollow leg and was still growing!"

"That's the man!" Randy said. "I don't know if the Neal Harmon they mentioned on TV is the same man, but I'm sure as hell going to make a phone call to Boise in the morning and find out! The last time I heard anything about Neal he was in military intelligence stationed in Germany keeping tabs on the Russians. If this newly assigned investigator is the same Neal we know, he might want to come take a look at a couple of mutilated horses and hear some of the details surrounding their deaths and mutilations."

6

NEAL HARMON SLIPPED INTO HIS OFFICE
early to avoid phone calls, hoping to get caught up on some paper work before
heading south to Twin Falls County to begin his investigation. He sat at his
desk leafing through some newspaper clippings attached to a memo from
his boss, Chief Investigator David Randall, which read, *Review these mutilation
reports then let's talk before you leave town.* Neal glanced at clipping after clipping
detailing cattle mutilation reports received by law enforcement officers from
all over the western United States. They were basically the same, only the
names and locales were different, such as, *On Monday morning rancher J.D.
Higgins of Albion, Idaho, found two of his prize angus bulls dead and mutilated beyond
human understanding...the animals' body parts had been taken...law enforcement
officials are totally baffled...*

That last part, though absolutely true, riled Neal, as if it were
an accusation. No one had the first damn clue as to the identity of the
mutilators—yet law enforcement was supposed to come up with some quick
answers. But that wasn't about to happen! It was a time of watchful waiting
for Neal and the other investigators, hoping that someone, anyone, civilian or
law enforcement, might come up with a much needed clue that might help
David Randall's investigators identify the mutilators.

Neal's phone rang. *Already? Shit!* He grabbed the phone and uttered a
gruff hello! The caller identified himself as Randy Johnson and Neal's surprise
was completely genuine. "Randy Johnson? That crazy nut case who tried to fly
a helicopter through the airport hanger in Spokane?" Neal heard a chuckle.

"Yeah, Buddy, that's me!"

"It's good to hear your voice again, my friend. What can I do for you?"

"When I heard your name on the news last night I thought you might be
the man who could figure out who killed a couple of my horses. I have a ranch
east of Twin Falls and those sons a bitches everyone is calling the mutilators,
whoever they are, killed and mutilated a couple of my best horses." Randy
explained the unusual circumstances involved in the death of his horses. He
also briefly explained his son Joe's bizarre encounter the night his horses were
taken.

"How long ago were your horses killed?" Neal asked with subdued
enthusiasm.

"A few weeks ago."

"Did you notify the local police?" Neal asked.

"I notified the sheriff and he sent two deputies to investigate."

"Can you tell me their names?"

"Deputy Jake Henline and Deputy Jim Munford."

"Would you have any objections if I contact them and make some inquiries about their investigation?"

"None at all."

"Good," Neal said. "If your horses were killed a few weeks ago wouldn't their carcasses be too putrefied to provide me any clues as to who killed them?"

It was a moment before Randy answered. "Well, you could take a look at what's left of them, and also check out some strange markings on my cattle. There are some very weird things happening down here, Neal. You'll find this as good a place as any to start your official investigation."

Neal thought that over for a moment. "It certainly will. I'll clear it with my boss. And call you back. How about Thursday? Would Thursday work for you?"

"It would."

"All right. I'll have the state police fly me down to Twin Falls in their Cessna Wednesday afternoon. I can get a car there and drive over to your ranch on Thursday morning."

"Need directions?" Randy asked.

"I'll get them when I call you back."

✝

Neal had just said goodbye to Randy when the phone rang again. It was David Randall.

"C'mon over to my office and let's talk. I need your help. Mutilation reports are coming in faster than I can handle them. The attorney general's going to be a basket case if we don't come up with something to get the public and the news media off his back."

"I'm on my way," Neal said as he hung up the phone.

David Randall, shaking his head in frustration, looked up as the door to his office opened and Neal walked in.

"Close the door," Randall said, sounding almost relieved.

Though Neal was a subordinate, he was one of Randall's closest friends. Tall, red headed and broad-shouldered, in his late forties, Neal was a confident successful lawyer, respected by his boss, subordinates and peers alike. A married family man, he lived in Cameo, a short ways north of Boise.

"Do you have anything new to report?" Randall asked hopefully.

"Well, for what it's worth, "I just received a phone call from a ranch owner friend of mine, Randy Johnson. He has a big ranch down in Magic Valley. Two of his prize animals were recently killed and horribly mutilated. While I'm down there I'd like to stop at Randy's ranch and find out what's going on."

Randall scowled. "What makes his slaughtered animals any different from all the other animals that have been killed all over the state?"

"Randy's mutilated animals just happened to be horses."

Randall swallowed hard. "Horses? Sweet Jesus! Now they're starting on horses?"

Neal nodded. "Evidently." He described the horses' mutilations to Randall just as Randy had explained them to him on the phone. He also mentioned Joe Johnson's strange encounter the night the horses were killed.

"Did this Randy Johnson express any ideas about what or who killed his horses?" Randall asked.

Neal nodded, and was silent for a moment, trying to find a way to avoid explaining Randy's UFO theory.

"Well?"

"Randy believes they were killed by someone or something in a UFO."

Randall's heartbeat went wild. "Oh my God! UFOs again? Do you believe him?"

"I can't answer that until I get down there and look around. Randy's a damn good man and I trust him. I detect from your question that UFOs are at the top of the suspect list!"

"They sure as hell are!" Randall said.

"So what's the problem?" Neal asked. "If we have evidence UFOs play into these mutilations, why not explore the possibilities?"

Randall took a deep breath. "We've been instructed to downplay anything that tries to connect UFOs to the mutilations. Right now UFO is a dirty word!"

"Says who?" Neal asked as he studied Randall's worried face.

"Let's talk about that, Neal—and it's to go no further than this room, understand?"

"I'm listening." Neal slid to the edge of his chair.

Randall was stressed and confused by the numerous mutilation reports flooding in to the attorney general's command post just down the hall—his confusion caused by the many differing theories being bandied about by "experts" as to the mutilators' identities. He wanted to explain them to Neal so he would understand exactly what the state of Idaho was up against.

"Neal, Sam Kennerton and I have been sifting and sorting mutilation data gathered from all over the United States to see if there are any similarities with those occurring here in Idaho, or if anyone has tried to identify the mutilators. It's amazing the different ideas that have been expressed in that regard. Some appear logical and reasonable, others stretch the imagination. I'm not sure if I'll be telling you something you already know, but bear with me, and I'll explain what we've come up with."

Neal made a dismissive gesture, waving a hand. "Lay it on me."

"Under some hysteria, farmers back east believe vampires may be involved."

Neal laughed aloud. "Vampires? Oh, c'mon, David!"

"You think that's crazy? Listen up. It gets better. Let me read it to you." Neal watched Randall take a sheet from a file folder on his desk. He held it a moment, then said, "this came out an Indiana paper where the vampire theory was first mentioned.

A farmer reported that overnight, several of his chickens and pigs died quite suddenly. Each pig's forehead had a small wound resembling a rat bite. When the farmer cut the pig's throat it did not bleed. There was not a drop of blood in its entire body..."

"Good God, David!" Neal interrupted. "you're not buying into a..."

Randall shook his head. "Hell no. The Indiana animals weren't mutilated—but if you think that theory is weird you'll love this one. Hairy creatures!"

Neal chuckled involuntarily. "Big tall ones? Ugly? One of your relatives?"

"C'mon, Neal, goddamn it! This is serious!" Randall said, annoyed by Neal's skepticism. But he tried to be patient. "In a remote Montana area where mutilations occurred Monday, a sheriff received reports of large, hairy creatures wandering about! And I'll be a sonofabitch, the very next day we received a "Big Foot" report from just up the road north of us in a remote area south of Rimrock Lake, Yakima County, Washington. Three teenagers observed for several minutes a strange, black hairy creature between eight and nine feet tall, with human like features…"

"Hold up a minute, David," Neal cut in, with a slight grin. "Let me run down to the storeroom and get a shovel. It's getting deep in here!"

"Hey, wait up! It's going to get deeper! I'm just getting started! Right now the main animal mutilation theory law enforcement officials cling to, whenever they are questioned publicly, lays the blame for domestic animal deaths on predatory animals. Of course the fallacy with that is it doesn't explain the bizarre mutilations accompanying the killings. Predators don't mutilate with surgical instruments. They tear the flesh with their teeth."

Neal, who suddenly seemed more interested, stared at Randall for a second and leaned forward in his seat. "Why do you suppose law enforcement is so all fired determined to claim predators are the only killers? Randy Johnson told me he believes that someone or something with surgical skill had sliced his horses open and taken all their internal body parts and even some external body parts, like ears, lips and such. Predators don't do that!"

"We know that. That's why your friend Randy's theory has some merit which could break this case wide open. You might also want to look in on another strange case down that way. Just a few days ago, down in Elmore County, in the little town of Hemmett, which is almost on Mtn. Home Air Force Base's run way, a local farmer, Chad Oliver, who lives about three blocks out of town, found one of his heifers lying dead. The cause of death couldn't be determined. There wasn't a mark of any kind on the animal. Over the following eight days, however, the heifer was mutilated on at least three separate occasions. Now tell me that ain't weird!"

"How could something like that happen?" Neal asked, as his mind whirled with thoughts of how someone could mutilate a dead animal three times, within city limits, and no one saw or heard anything unusual.

Randall shook his head. "Damned if I know. That's why we've appointed you and your coworkers to fan out through Idaho and do some investigating— find out who the mutilators are. You'll be interested to know that in that Hemmett case Veterinarian Dr. Jonathan Thorner and civil defense worker Lyman Stoeffer, with his Geiger counter, performed a hands-on analysis of Mr. Oliver's dead heifer while the local sheriff searched the area for clues as to the mutilators' identity. Stoeffer couldn't get any radiation readings on his

Geiger counter. But this might interest you! Dr. Thorner wrote in his report: *A perfect surgical procedure was used in removing various body parts. With my years of veterinary surgery experience I could in no way duplicate the type of surgery I found on the dead heifer. I took detailed color photographs of the incisions during the autopsy on the animal. I cut flesh samples and sent them, along with the photos, to the Idaho Livestock Disease Control Laboratory in Boise. The chief of pathology there ran several tests on the samples.*

"So what did the chief pathologist find?" Neal asked with evident interest.

"I called and asked him," Randall said. "He told me he was not at liberty to release his findings, unless I produced a court order."

"Did you do that?" Neal asked.

"Good hell no! We've got enough problems without going that route."

"Looks like you're between a rock and a hard place, David, if everything has to be kept hush hush."

"That's right, and that's what makes it so damned frustrating!" Randall replied. "You can imagine what would happen if we started speculating about UFOs, vampires, Big Foot and other wild theories. We'd look foolish, and worse than that, we'd cause a public panic."

Neal nodded agreement. "Just out of curiosity, what are some of those other wild theories? Any chance we can latch on to any of them to calm and soothe ranchers' fears?"

Randall shifted uncomfortably in his chair. "No!" he replied emphatically. "And when you hear them, you'll understand why. One of those theories, which has insurance companies very upset, pissed off might be a more descriptive word, and worried, are allegations that some ranchers are killing their own cattle to collect an insurance settlement."

Neal looked Randall right in the eye. "No rancher would do that!"

"Do you want to bet?" Randall came right back. "Five Idaho ranchers have already filed claims for their dead and mutilated animals—and that has thrown the insurance companies into a complete quandary. If a range cow dies, it usually dies of natural causes, and an insurance claim is in order. But what if an animal is murdered and cut up? That's not dying of natural causes, so no claims are being paid or will be paid, until the mess is straightened out. Get the picture?"

"Uh huh," Neal responded. "And it's not pretty."

Randall slid his chair back, leaned over, his shoulders slouching with weariness, and sank his large clasped hands between his spread knees. With his gaze directed at the floor, he breathed in heavily and released a deep tortured sigh. "You have no idea, Neal, what we're dealing with. The wild theories just keep coming. Vandals! Some of the mutilated animals had been shot and crudely mutilated. Rustlers! Brands Inspector Jim Majors over in Montana said rustlers could be mistaken for mutilators. They might be frightened off from a kill, leaving the half butchered carcass in the field. He thinks that's happening quite often. Then to top it off there are the satanic cultists."

"Satanic cultists?" Neal stared wide-eyed at Randall. "In Idaho?"

Randall nodded. "Believe it or not this is one of the leading theories the press just absolutely loves! Blood sacrifices and sexual excesses both seem to hold a morbid fascination for people around the world. When the predator theory doesn't satisfy ranchers and farmers, law enforcement and the media have found a perfect scapegoat—satanic cultists. Nearly everyone believes these cults exist. It's a logical explanation and acceptable to a few owners of mutilated livestock."

"That's a load of crap, David," Neal said. "There's no such thing as satanic cultists—well, at least not here in Idaho."

Randall shook his head. "Don't be so sure! Advocates of the cult theory, on the surface, seem to have a fair argument. The indisputable facts are that cattle are being killed by some mysterious means, then they're mutilated by sharp instruments, and in most instances blood has been drained or is missing. Maybe you missed the latest UPI news report from Denver. A couple of weeks back they said that Michael Warner, a former member of a California satanic cult says that more than 170 suspected cases of cattle mutilation in Colorado are probably the work of devil worshipers. Warner said, 'I don't think the mutilations are accidental or being done by other animals.' This Warner was a member of a satanic cult from age twelve to twenty. He said they sacrificed dogs during ceremonies and mixed the animal's blood with wine for communion. It was one hell of a report—and Colorado has had animal mutilations in nineteen counties so far this year, exactly like those occurring here in Idaho. Mutilations are so bad down in Utah they're offering a hefty reward to anyone who can positively identify the mutilators."

"Any devil worshipping escapades so far here in Idaho?" Neal asked curiously.

Randall chuckled. "Why hell yes." He grabbed a written report from his desk and held it up. "This just came from District Forest Ranger Danny Jacobsen, east of us at the Ketchum Ranger Station. He spotted two men walking down Cove Creek Canyon, wearing long black robes and cone shaped hats, and he felt they might connected with cattle mutilations in that area. We're receiving reports from Fremont County of cultist activity which the sheriff is calling Satanism. We don't know how much of that is rumor or how much is factual."

Neal shook his head. "That's too far fetched, David, to even be considered."

"You think so? Well let me run a few other theories by you—how about some of these possibilities—the blood and plasma taken from the animals are being used by terrorists for spreading disease through the food or livestock chain. Or maybe the military is secretly doing some blood experimentation in case of mass loss of human blood from a nuclear or biological attack."

"Are you talking about black helicopters sneaking in, flying over Idaho ranches?" Neal asked sarcastically.

"Why not? Randall said.

Neal smiled. "I think what you're telling me is something I already know—we don't have one damn clue as to who is killing our Idaho livestock."

"You got that right, my friend. So get yourself down to Twin Falls find out what happened to Randy Johnson's horses. I'll let the attorney general know that I assigned you to investigate that situation and you'll keep me posted on developments. Any questions?"

"No sir."

"Time is of the essence," Randall said. "We've got to come up with some answers."

"I know."

✝

Neal called Randy and briefed him on David Randall's approval for him to meet with Randy and investigate exactly what happened to his horses. "My boss wants some quick results, so I hope we can come up with something to keep him happy."

Randy sounded pleased. "It'll be good to see you again, Neal. Be here at six-thirty Thursday morning. Tess will have breakfast ready."

"I'll be there!"

After Neal hung up he sat there for a few minutes. *Twin Falls. It was a place to start. It was a beginning. Maybe he'd find that elusive clue that would help identify the mutilators!*

7

IT WAS A COLD, SUNNY DAY, ONE OF THOSE late fall days when clarity of the air makes the sun much brighter than usual. Even so Randy Johnson's morning was plagued by a tractor that wouldn't start, a cow that seemed to be bloated and two of his horses were fighting in the corral. Some days he wondered if he was getting too old for ranching life. Everywhere he looked he saw things that needed fixing, painting or to be torn down and replaced. It didn't improve his disposition when Tessie called to him from the back door.

"Ben Summers is on the phone."

"Damn," Randy muttered. "Tell him I'll call him back."

"He says it's really important."

"Oh, all right," Randy growled, realizing he had no choice but to talk to the old man, who relied on Randy for just about everything. Eighty-five-year old Ben Summers was Randy's closest neighbor, three and a half miles southeast, along the county dirt road.

When Randy got to the living room Tessie handed him the phone.

"Hi Ben. What's going on?"

"I'm damn worried, Randy. Somethin' weird is going on over here."

Ben's tone concerned Randy. He'd never heard the old man sound so worried.

"Like what?"

"Last night I seen them flashing blue lights moving all over my sheep pasture like they was looking for something. Sort of like what you and Tess saw the night them butcherin' bastards killed your horses."

That grabbed Randy's immediate attention! "Are your sheep okay?"

"Well none of 'em is dead if that's what you mean. But they've gone kind of crazy, like they've been eating loco weed—runnin' ever which a way, skittish, like something's after them. Even my dog Aussie is nervous as hell."

"Anything else?" Randy asked.

"Yeah. My big ram, Old Billy attacked me! He's a feisty bugger, but he's never done that before."

"Attacked you?" Randy asked as if he couldn't believe it.

"He did. While I was out checking the herd this morning the next thing I knowed I was flat on my back with all the wind knocked plumb out of me. I was starin' at Billy's huge curved horns pushing against my chest like he meant to drive me right into the ground. I wound up my fist and hit him up side the head as hard as I could, but it hurt my hand more'n I hurt him. Old Billy's never acted like that before. If it hadn't been for Aussie grabbin' Billy's hind leg and dragging him off a me Billy would a killed me!"

"Someone up above must have been looking out for you!" Randy said. "Then what happened?"

"Well, after Billy shook Aussie off, he ran away hell bent for election and I haven't seen him since."

"Do you have any idea why he attacked you?"

"I'm sure it had something to do with them flashing blue lights."

"Are you going to go out and look for him?"

"I am. As soon I get my old mare saddled. Billy can't be too far away."

The phone went dead for a moment. "Ben, are you still there?"

"Yeah, I'm here, Randy. "I hate to ask, but I was wondering if you could you come over..."

"I'm sorry," Randy interrupted. "I'm up to my eyeballs in work today, and first thing in the morning a state investigator from Boise will be here to take a look at my two dead horses. Maybe he and I could ride over after he's completed his inspection. Would that work for you?"

"Well," Ben sounded disappointed, "if that's the best you can do, I'll see you tomorrow."

"You be careful out there looking for Billy," Randy cautioned. "Call me when you find him."

"I will."

When Randy hung up Tessie asked, "What did Ben want?"

"It looks like whoever killed our horses might be after his sheep. He wanted me to come over, but I just can't run over there every time he calls. I wish I could talk Ben into selling that damn weedy patch of ground he calls a ranch and move into town. I mentioned it to him once and he almost tore my head off—the stubborn old fart! But damn it, he shouldn't be living out there all by himself!"

Randy met Tess' eyes and they were brimming with concern for Ben and he wanted to say something, do something to allay her fears. "Don't worry, Honey. Ben can take care of himself. He's a tough old bird."

✝

Eighty-five-year old Ben Summers raised sheep, about a hundred at a time, give or take a few. Rhode Island chickens scratched and pecked in the dry, grassless cement-hard soil in front of Ben's dilapidated unpainted single story ranch house. Two small white goats wandered around a nearby pasture looking for any weeds or cheat grass the sheep may have missed.

Aussie, a twelve-year-old black, brown and white Australian shepherd, with light blue eyes usually napped on front the porch but still kept an eye on Ben's sheep. Five years ago last Christmas Aussie, wet, shivering and hungry, showed up at Ben's front door. Where the starving dog came from the old man never found out—but the two quickly bonded. Evidently Aussie had received some professional training somewhere in his travels because he was a superb watch dog and protected his master and his sheep. He got to know the neighbors, and became especially fond of Randy Johnson. Whenever he'd come to visit Ben, Aussie would bark and run to the front room window, put his forefeet on the windowsill, his tail wagging and bark again. Like all dogs' tails, Aussie's was a semaphore of his feelings: his fear, his welcome and his smile.

Except for Aussie, Ben was now a loner. Bessie, his wife of sixty-two years, passed away ten years ago and was buried on a small hill south of the barn. Never a day passed that Ben didn't stop what he was doing and gaze at Bessie's grave for a few moments, and wait for the myriad of pleasant memories that always came flooding in. He still missed her terribly. Together they'd homesteaded the ranch and in so doing inherited the hard life that went with their choice. They shared life together without a cross word ever passing between them. Since Bessie's passing Ben's life had settled into a dreary ritual, but the old man had everything he needed and he was content.

Once he thought about selling out and moving further into the back country to escape civilization, but no such place existed any more—and he was too old anyway. But glory days of his youth filtered in from time to time as he reminisced about his cowboying adventures in the high country, herding cattle in the summer, and pushing them to lower ground in the fall. But as the years rolled by Ben decided raising sheep was much easier than fighting those wild stubborn range steers

Nothing seemed to matter much any more. He'd been born at the end of the nineteenth century, and often wondered if he even belonged in the twentieth century with its noisy freeways, jet planes cruising at 30,000 feet over his ranch—people rushing every which way, never finding what they were seeking.

One thing Ben truly cherished was his lifelong friendship with Randy Johnson and his family. Randy was more than just a good friend, he was like the son Ben and Bessie never had. Randy stopped by often to check on the old man—and bring him his favorite meal of tasty spare ribs and vegetables specially prepared by Tessie. After Ben had devoured the spare ribs, Randy would slip him a pint of Jim Beam sipping whiskey. It had become a regular ritual.

Not long ago Randy drove up in his pickup and unloaded a TV set. He told Ben it was a used set he haggled for at a garage sale. He installed it in Ben's front room and showed the old man how to change the channels and control the volume. But Ben could tell the TV was brand new and he was too choked up to say much of anything except, "Thank you, Randy." A few weeks later Randy had the telephone company install a phone in Ben's front room so Randy could call him to make sure the old man was all right and ask if he needed any help.

Once in a while, on long summer nights, when Randy was caught up on his own chores, he'd ride one of his horses over to Ben's place and they'd sit together on the front porch, chairs leaned back against the house, and sip whiskey—and Ben would reminisce fondly about the old days when Idaho's mining and logging camps were full of rowdy, smoky piano-tinkling saloons where cattle and sheep men drank and argued—and once in a while enjoyed knock-down drag-out fist fights amongst themselves or with the loud mouthed loggers or miners—which sometimes turned into wild west shoot outs. Randy enjoyed his old friend's stories and often said, "Let's drink to the good old days!" That always brought a smile to Ben's weathered old wrinkle-lined face, and he'd always say, "I never drink unless I'm alone or with someone!" They'd both chuckle.

Ben was getting a little forgetful and often told Randy the same stories over and over. He loved his sheep, several of which he'd given pet names—but of the entire flock he was proudest of Old Billy, his huge curved-horn breeding ram.

"He's a Lincolnshire, Randy. They're the best sheep in the world."

"Says who?" Randy came right back, grinning and baiting Ben. "I have it on good authority that Merinos are by far the world's best breed of sheep!"

"Hell's bells, Randy, who told you a damn lie like that?" Ben took a big swig of whiskey. "Why them Merinos don't hold a candle to a Lincoln. They come right from the old country. Some feller over in England crossed a Leicester with some of them coarse native sheep called Lincolnshires. That's how we got Lincolns. That was back around George Washington's time. Here in the states a lot of folks don't like Lincolns, but they provide the best meat and fleece in the country. There just ain't no question about that. Us folks here in Idaho and over in Oregon love 'em. Why, you take my ram, Old Billy. He weighs two hundred fifty pounds if he weighs an ounce. Sheep don't get much bigger'n that!"

Randy had heard about the origins of Lincolns more times than he cared to remember; so he slowly sipped his whiskey in relaxed silence and nodded affirmatively when Ben glanced over to make sure he was listening.

A few weeks back, after Ben and Randy had had a couple of belts of whiskey, Randy finally told Ben about finding his two prize horses butchered, then described the horrible mutilations and the subsequent police investigation, the old man just stared skeptically at Randy for a few seconds.

"Son of a bitch, Randy" Ben cursed under his breath. "Who'd go and do something like that to them beautiful animals?"

Randy didn't want to unnerve or alarm the old man with his UFO theories, so he merely said, "damned if I know, Ben. My horses aren't the only animals that have been killed. Animal killings and mutilations are happening all over the west."

"Yeah, I seen that on television. Ain't the police got any ideas at all about who's killing all them animals?"

"Not so far," Randy said, and added a warning. "I want you to be mighty damn careful, Ben, living out here alone. Watch your back. No one knows what we're dealing with—but whoever or whatever is messing around killing animals could be mighty dangerous."

"Don't worry about me, Randy. I've got my old thirty-thirty handy." That battered old lever-action rifle hung over Ben's fireplace. It wasn't used much anymore, since the land had become civilized, at least to Ben's way of thinking. He figured if he fired off a shot the police would probably come racing down the dirt road, kicking up dust, lights flashing and sirens blasting and throw him in jail. This damn civilization crowded a man. But Old Ben had forced himself to accept and live with it.

"The first asshole I find messing around with my sheep will get a thirty-thirty slug right between the eyes!"

Randy had no doubts the feisty old cowboy would do exactly what he said he would, and that worried Randy. Neighbors stopped by Old Ben's from time to time, but he didn't see so well any more—and he might just accidentally shoot one of them by mistake!

✝

Disappointed with Randy's refusal to help him find Old Billy Ben mulled over his next move. He'd have to be careful! There was something out there on his ranch, some kind of unseen power, and for the first time in his life he was truly frightened. He didn't want to go looking for Billy alone. Oh sure, he'd faced wild animals, other men, fought in WW1 where it was kill or be killed. But this? This was different. He was up against something he couldn't see, hear or smell. He walked into the kitchen, reached up on the shelf and grabbed the bottle of Jim Beam whiskey and poured himself a stiff shot, and coughed slightly as he gulped it down. He shut his eyes for a second. *Hell, whatever was out there waiting for him was just a scare tactic. Nothing to be afraid of.* The whiskey helped dissipate the gnawing fear in his stomach. He opened his eyes, reached up and took a box of 30-30 cartridges from the cupboard. took out six cartridges, walked to the fireplace, reached up and lovingly lifted his old rifle down, loaded it then headed for the corral.

Ben saddled his aging mare, shoved the rifle in the saddle scabbard, mounted and let the horse pick her along the well-worn sheep path south of the house. Aussie galloped off ahead, his hindquarters flouncing, scattering the ewes peacefully munching what grass they could find. Old Ben's gray eyes swept the tangle of tall sagebrush, trying to spot Old Billy. It was like hunting for a needle in a haystack. If the curved-horn ram was lying down resting somewhere he'd be hard to see, and unlike Aussie, he wouldn't respond to his master's voice.

The afternoon sun broke through some billowing dark clouds hovering over the eastern mountains and the warm wind kicking up dust would soon turn cold.

Ben pulled on the reins, stopped the old mare, took off his Levi jacket and hung it over the saddle horn. Sweat trickled down Ben's forehead, cutting a furrow through the dust on his unshaven face. He wiped his sweaty palms dry on his pants leg, touched his heels to the mare's flanks and let the tired old horse find her way through the nearly saddle-high scrub brush.

Ben stood up in the stirrups and looked around. Aussie trotted about fifty yards ahead. Suddenly the dog stopped abruptly and planted all four feet in the dirt. His ears pricked up like a bat's. The hair stood up on the scruff of his neck.

Aussie's nose told him what his eyes were telling him. He bared his teeth silently and waited for Ben to come up.

"What is it, Aussie? What do you see?"

Aussie instantly turned around, whining, and faced Ben for a moment. Then he tucked his tail between his legs and took off at a dead run back toward the house.

Ben kicked the mare's flank and forced her slowly forward. That's when he saw Old Billy sprawled out on his back, all four feet in the air. *Oh my God!* Ben was stunned. He just sat there in the saddle unsure what to do.

He was conscious that something else was wrong, something that was more disturbing than the dead ram. More eerie.

The silence.

The absolute weird silence.

Nothing. No birds, No insects. No breeze now to shake sounds out of the sagebrush. A zero, as if everything in the place was dead. As if everything had been stilled, silenced by an ungodly, destructive hand. He rubbed his forehead. Sweat. Cold sweat.

Slowly he dismounted and walked cautiously toward the dead ram. *What the holy hell happened here?* Bile bubbled up in his throat and he spit and coughed it back.

The wool covering the huge ram's abdominal region was stretched back, exposing his gaping empty body cavity. The intestines and other internal organs were gone, as was the ram's sexual organs, including his large scrotum.

Confused, frightened and bubbling with anger, the white-haired old man clenched his fists, and began a systematic assessment, trying to figure out what may have happened here just hours ago. Only one other time in his entire life had he seen an animal torn to pieces—when he was eighteen and found a range steer dead and mostly torn to pieces, and fresh grizzly bear footprints around the mangled animal. From the wall of dark pine trees just yards away, Ben heard a loud deep growl that made his hair stand on end. He'd evidently frightened the bear away from its kill—but he was still close by! Ben had been smart enough to jump on his horse and race away.

But old Billy hadn't been killed by a grizzly. There was no question about that! There wasn't a drop of blood on, in or around the carcass. The ram had died where it lay. There were no human footprints, nor clues of any kind, at least none that Ben could identify. He scratched his unshaven jaw and just stood there and staring. *What the hell should I do?* He pushed his dirty old straw cowboy hat back, then removed it and mopped the sweat band. *Randy! I've got to call Randy Johnson! Billy's been butchered just like Randy's two horses. Randy will know what to do!*

Ben mounted, slapped the old mare's flanks with the reins, and raced her back to the house. He jumped off as soon as the horse stopped in front of the house, ran in and grabbed the phone. He was out of breath and shaking when he dialed Randy's phone number.

Randy answered the phone and heard someone gasping for breath. "Hello...Randy..."

"Ben is that you?" Randy asked.

"Yeah...I found Old Billy, he's dead...they killed him."

"Whoa, Ben, slow down. I can't understand you. What about Billy?"

Ben started again, slower this time. "He's dead, Randy, killed and butchered just like your horses. I don't know what to do. Could you get over here right now?" I need you to help me figure things out."

"It would be better for you to call the sheriff's office. Have them come out and take a look. As I told you before, there's just no way I can get over there right now—maybe tomorrow."

Ben's response was immediate. "I don't want no damn law pokin' around my property, Randy. I don't trust any of 'em, not one little bit."

Randy chuckled. "Afraid they'll put you in jail?"

Ben's voice softened. "Already been there and done that. Don't want no more! Can't you get over here any quicker?"

"No, Ben. Like I told you the investigator from Boise and I will come over tomorrow. Old Billy's not going anyplace."

"Is that investigator a damned cop?"

"No, Ben. He's a lawyer, a friend of mine by the name of Neal Harmon."

"A shyster lawyer? They're worse than cops!"

"Maybe you're right, Ben. But I've made arrangements for Neal to take a look at my butchered horses. The sheriff's office hasn't come up with any answers. Maybe Neal can. Then we'll ride over to your place and let him take a look at Old Billy—so don't mess up the crime scene. Okay? Leave everything just as you found it. Then we can talk and decide what to do. Will that work for you?"

"I guess it'll have to!" Ben growled. "I'll be waitin'!"

Fall 1975

EARLY THURSDAY MORNING IT WAS CHILLY, and the sun was just peeking over the eastern horizon when Randy and Joe Johnson walked out of the house to feed the livestock and do their other chores. Buster trailed along behind.

Cows trotted in from all over the pasture as Randy and Joe walked toward the bales of hay they'd stacked near the fence the night before. The cows patiently watched Randy break the bales then stretched their necks to moo as Randy and Joe tossed alfalfa over the fence. Then they crowded in, contentedly munching the fresh hay. Five of the Herefords' necks and shoulders were blackened in spots almost as if they were wearing harnesses. They weren't exactly burn marks. They looked more like they'd been made by some type of extremely tight restraining or lifting device. Randy had no idea how they got there. All he knew was that the morning after Joe's experience with the mutilators, the same night Miss BJ and Little Girl disappeared from the horse corral, his cows had those strange markings around their necks and shoulders, some still bleeding slightly.

Joe stared at the marked Herefords. "Dad, how do think those scars got on our cows?"

Randy shook his head. "Darned if I know." Randy tipped his hat back and watched his Herefords eating the alfalfa. "You'd know more about that than I would. The cows got those markings the same night Miss BJ and Little Girl were killed."

Joe nodded. "Yeah, I know." He cleared his throat and pulled on his ear lobe.

"What?" Randy asked.

"They must have been lifted off the ground and the harness rubbed their skin raw."

Randy stared at the Herefords. "But why? That's puzzled me ever since I first discovered those strange markings."

Joe said, "maybe to see if the cows could be lifted? They weigh over four hundred pounds."

"Lifted where?" Randy asked. "You told me a light beam came down on the pasture that night, chasing the animals around. Did you see any harnesses or ropes coming down?"

Joe shook his head, shielding his eyes from the bright morning sun. He was thinking of something the disturbed him. "No. But you know what, Dad? Maybe whoever put the cows in harnesses to lift them up wanted to take a closer look at them."

"You mean examine them?"

"Yeah."

Randy was silent for a moment, then nodded. "That's certainly a possibility. But why?" He looked down at his watch. "Well, we'd better get cracking and get the horses fed. Neal Harmon is due any time now."

✝

Back at the house Tessie bustled about the kitchen preparing breakfast. Her keen sixth sense or woman's intuition had been nagging her ever since Randy had found Miss BJ and Little Girl dead and mutilated. Today she knew there was a chance to have a meaningful conversation with someone in the know like Neal Harmon. Maybe, if he was lucky, he might come up with some answers for the weird things happening here at the ranch. The strange lights and creepy noises still happening from time to time had her more frightened than she let on to Randy.

She kept an eye open through kitchen window, and promptly at 6:30 a.m. she watched a new Ford LTD pull into the driveway.

Neal climbed out of the car and stood there for a few moments gazing across Randy's sprawling ranch land, admiring the painted barn, the silo and corrals. He was especially impressed with the well-built, fenced-in horse corral, enclosing several sleek well fed horses, their heads down contentedly munching the hay Joe had just thrown over the fence. Randy and Joe waved and Neal waved back. *That must be the corral from which Randy's two horses escaped or were taken.*

Neal walked to the front door and rang the doorbell and Tessie opened the door. "Neal Harmon!" She squealed excitedly, "Is it really you?"

"In the flesh!" he grinned, quickly noting that Tessie had the unlined, sweet, assured face of someone whose life had been lucky, ordered and close to the earth.

She giggled. "You handsome devil, you haven't changed a bit! Well, don't just stand there. Get in here and give me a hug!" She pulled him inside. They embraced and when they parted Neal said, "Damn, Tess, you're still just as beautiful as I remember you."

"Well, thank you! That's nice to hear—especially since I'm getting a few gray hairs! We've got a lot of catching up to do." She took him by the hand and ushered him into the living room. "Randy and Joe are finishing up their morning chores. They'll be in shortly. Are ready for breakfast?"

Neal nodded and smiled. "I've been anticipating one of your fantastic meals ever since I talked to Randy on the phone!"

"Well, make yourself at home. We'll eat as soon as Randy and Joe come in. I'll check and see how my biscuits are doing."

As she walked to the kitchen Tessie looked through the screen door and saw Randy and Joe walking together toward the house, Buster at their heels. He was a young yellow lab in the prime of his strength. And since his frightening experience the night of the flashing blue lights, he was like a brusque watchman as he often roamed from the house to the barn, then to the corral and out buildings, checking scents, but always staying close to Randy to warn him if he picked up that strange unknown odor that had once made him cower under the kitchen table, trembling in terror.

Neal jumped to his feet when Randy and Joe walked into the front room. The two old friends embraced.

"Howdy, Neal," Randy said enthusiastically. "It's been a long time. But damn, my friend, I wish it could have been under more favorable circumstances."

Though it had been several years since they'd seen each other Neal could see that Randy had changed very little. The same intelligent eyes, strong jaw, the same energetic cheerfulness, combined with Idaho hospitality. The warmth of Randy's embrace and his greeting touched Neal and put him immediately at ease. Randy introduced Joe to Neal and they shook hands.

"I hear you're one heck of a football player," Neal said.

Joe grinned. "I play on my high school football team."

"Ever make a touchdown?" Neal asked with a smile.

"Now and then," Joe said modestly.

"Breakfast is ready!" Tessie called out.

Five places were set at the table, and Neal, Randy, Joe and Jenny came in and sat down. Tessie poured coffee.

The aroma of bacon wafted through the house, the Idaho spuds had been fried with onions and green peppers. Tessie took egg orders from those seated at the table—some over hard, some over easy. Tessie always had farm fresh eggs on hand, many with double yolks from some of her treasured laying hens.

Her skills as ranch chef that had been handed down to her over the last generation or two were the way to any man's heart. Her cooking was highly regarded in the valley and she was very proud of her breakfast and lunch skills right down to the best damn cup of coffee in the county.

Among the specialties for this special breakfast were freshly baked, flaky ranch biscuits and homemade fruit preserves to spread on them.

Tessie's eyes sparkled as Neal and Randy ate and talked about the ranch, which had captured Neal's complete attention and approval.

"We've done all right," Randy said modestly. "When I got back from Vietnam my Dad was suffering from cancer, and near the end he deeded the ranch to me. It was mostly cattle then. I thought we might make a little extra money if we raised and sold a few horses. I've had a fondness for fast horses since my grandfather introduced them to me in my early teens. He loved following how his line did at the track, though he wasn't much of a gambler himself. I kind of followed in his foot tracks and got interested in racing horses. So, on a whim, when I had a few extra dollars burning a hole in my pocket, I bought a couple of thoroughbreds I fell in love with. They both won us a little money at the race track."

"Those were the two horses you found butchered and mutilated?"

Randy nodded. "Yeah, and someday I'll find out who killed them and they'll be mighty damn sorry!"

Neal sat back in his chair and sipped the last of his coffee. A faint appreciative expression softened the lean ridges of his face. "Damn, Randy, you've got a lovely spread here. It's so peaceful—almost makes me wish I'd taken up ranching. You and Tess have made it a real show place," Neal smiled. He reached out and pushed his cup across the table toward Tessie.

"I could use another cup of that delicious coffee—but I can't handle another bite of those wonderful biscuits. I'm so full I'm ready to pop!"

Tessie poured more coffee into his cup. The talk ran on among old friends around a familiar table. It was as though there hadn't been a long, fifteen-year separation in their friendship. Finally the conversation moved to a discussion of their military service during the Vietnam War.

Tessie noted some discomforting remorse and regret in Randy's tone when he tried to brush past some experiences he had always felt were best left buried in some dark place in the back of his mind. Randy had always been mild and courteous surrounding his soldiering days, but gave no real details of his out and out heroism during some of the heaviest battles of the war; and Neal was diplomatic enough not to delve further into any specifics.

Tessie quickly jumped in. "The army awarded Randy the silver star for his gallant actions, which he really deserved. That worried me because that meant he'd been in lots of front line action. The happiest day of my life was when I received a telegram he was finally coming home for good! I traveled to San Francisco, and when he got off the plane I greeted him with the tightest hug and biggest kiss he's ever had! What a grand feeling coursed through my body! He was alive, physically okay—and I secretly thanked God I finally had him back again! We spent a delayed honeymoon there in San Francisco! What a wonderful week that was!" She smiled at Randy. "You probably don't even remember, do you?"

"Like hell!" Randy grinned. "A man never forgets something like that!"

Neal smiled. "I'm glad it turned out so well! San Francisco is an exciting place in more ways than one!"

"So, Neal, what happened to you after you graduated from college?" Tessie asked.

Neal described some of his military experiences, when and where he'd served, touching briefly on each. After military service he'd gone back to college and got his law degree. He was now married, had two children and felt lucky to have landed a good job in the Idaho attorney general's office. "So I could live and raise my family in Idaho, where I was born and bred," he concluded.

Never in Neal's wildest imagination would he have pictured himself involved in anything as weird and bizarre as animal mutilation investigations. Homicide and forensics, maybe—perhaps robbery, rape and general mayhem. But dead animals? It was still difficult to believe he was here in rural Idaho investigating animal killings—one hell of a long way down the scale from army intelligence, spy networks, military and political intrigue or even regular mundane courtroom drama. He had really been enticed to the position in the hopes of being able to prosecute criminals, an opportunity he'd been promised if he decided to stay in the AG's office.

"More coffee, Neal?" Tessie asked.

"No thanks. I'm good, any more and I'll get the shakes; but damn, that's good coffee, Tess."

Randy pushed back from the table and started to rise.

Tessie said, "Take Neal in the front room, dear, so you can talk. The kids and I will clean up the kitchen. Jenny has to catch the school bus in a few minutes."

Randy grinned. "The boss has spoken, Neal! Follow me!"

When they were comfortably seated in the front room, Randy said, "Well my friend, are you're ready to get to work and earn your pay?"

"I am."

"Where do you want to start?" Randy asked.

Neal scratched his ear. "I'm not sure. I mentioned my agenda to you on the phone. But I've never been involved in investigating anything that remotely resembles animal killings and mutilations, so I'm flying by the seat of my pants, so to speak."

"Aren't we all?" Randy grinned again.

Neal nodded. "On the phone you mentioned that Deputy Jake Henline and another deputy, Jim Munford, were the investigating officers. I decided to call Deputy Henline and ask him a few questions about his investigation here on your ranch."

Randy looked at him curiously. "What did Jake tell you?"

"It seemed a little odd to me how the investigation was handled. The sheriff's office was so busy they couldn't dispatch any deputies to your ranch for a couple of weeks. Henline told me that delay hindered the investigation because the horses had been dead too long for him to really make any kind of assessment as to the cause of death."

"Is that all he told you?" Randy asked, rather nervously.

"He told me he wrote up an investigative report for the sheriff, and gave you a copy. Is that correct?"

"It is. Let me get it for you." Randy turned and called to Tessie out in the kitchen. "Hon, will you grab Jake's report from my desk in the den and bring it here?"

Randy and Neal chatted a few moments; until Tessie sailed into the living room with a file folder and handed it to Randy. He handed it to Neal who held it for a moment before opening it.

"Oh," Neal said, "Before I forget, Deputy Henline also provided explicit details of his encounter with your son Joe the night your horses were killed."

Randy's jaw hardened of its own accord. "Damn that Jake anyway! He promised he'd keep his mouth shut about that! I hope to hell he hasn't blabbed it to those nosy news reporters hovering around the county like flies around a dead animal!"

Sympathy began to creep into Neal's eyes. "I'm sorry, Randy. That's probably my fault. I ordered Deputy Henline to provide every detail of what went down that night. I'm hoping to develop some leads that might help me succeed in identifying the mutilators. That's what my boss ordered me to do, so I have no choice but to investigate every possible lead. But this I promise you, I'll keep your son's experience absolutely confidential."

Randy shrugged, knowing there was nothing now he could do to suppress Joe's story. It would become a part of Neal's official investigation. "Just out of curiosity," Randy asked, "what did Jake tell you about Joe?"

"He said he discovered the boy sitting in an old pick up parked off the shoulder of the dirt road leading to your house. The boy was frightened half to death. Henline's first impression was that Joe had probably experienced some type of seizure which caused a slight convulsion, causing him to see and hear things that weren't really there, at least none that Henline could see or hear. He said Joe was totally incoherent."

Faint disgust lit up Randy's eyes." He actually told you that?" Randy was thunderstruck.

"Yes. Why? Do you disagree?"

"Your damn right! You haven't heard Joe's side of the story yet."

"I plan to," Neal said, "Just as we discussed on the phone. I want to hear from Joe's own lips exactly what happened out on that lonely road that night."

"I figured you would," Randy agreed, "So I kept Joe home from school today, which is also a football practice day." Randy grinned. "He wasn't too happy about it. He hates to miss even one practice. He's going to try out for a spot on a college football team next spring when he graduates. Shall I call him in?"

Neal shook his head. "Before you do that, let me take a quick look at this police report and see what Deputy Henline wrote."

Randy handed him the folder. "Okay."

Neal opened it and focused on the first sheet, speed reading, doing his best to stash away in his memory the most crucial details. When he flipped to the last page, he looked up, no comprehension on his face. "What you told me on the phone about your horses and what Deputy Henline wrote in this report don't jibe! It's like comparing oranges and apples." He looked at Randy like he was expecting a response.

Randy's head jerked back. "What the hell are you talking about? My horses were butchered and mutilated. That's all there was to it. Case closed!"

Neal shook his head and held up the report. "Have you read what's in this?"

Randy rubbed his chin, somewhat embarrassed. "Not really. I've been so damn busy...Jake gave me that copy and told me to hang onto it. He's a personal friend so I trusted him." Randy paused, a look of concern on his face. "What do you mean it's like comparing apples and oranges?"

"Well, Randy, I'll try to explain it diplomatically so you don't think I'm taking sides. You explained your theory to me about UFOs, a strange unknown type of surgery, body parts missing, no blood, and etcetera. Henline's report clearly states that your horses were probably killed and disemboweled by predatory animals."

"That sneaky son of a bitch!" Randy snorted. "He never said anything to me about that!"

Neal's eyebrows raised. "Are you calling Deputy Henline a liar?"

Randy quickly backed off. "Well, not exactly a liar, but I sure as hell disagree with his conclusions that my horses were killed by predatory animals. There are no predatory animals in these parts that can kill a full grown horse!"

"You have a point. I'm not sure I agree with Deputy Henline either," Neal concluded. "What kind of a fellow is this Henline? You mentioned he used to work for you before he joined the sheriff's department—so you know him pretty well?"

"That's right. He's almost like a member of my family—honest and reliable."

"Then what makes you think he'd falsify a police report—if that's what he did?"

Randy dropped his gaze and mulled the question over. "I don't have a clue—unless Sheriff Jeffords instructed him to."

Neal jerked back and stared at Randy for a moment. "That's a pretty serious allegation against a three-term, well respected sheriff. "

"I'm prepared to back it up—if I have to," Randy said.

"It's a little too early for that," Neal replied. "We've still got a long ways to go before we actually figure out what the hell is going on. I'm planning to meet with Deputy Henline while I'm down here so let's hold off on this for a while, okay?"

Randy nodded.

Neal closed the folder and set it on the coffee table.

"If it's okay with you I'd now like to talk to your son in private. After that, if you don't mind, let's ride out and take a look at your dead horses. I'll change into some levis and put on my cowboy boots. I want to see the site, look at the carcasses, and get the lay of the land. Maybe we can come up with something."

"I sure as hell hope so!" Randy smiled, pleased that finally someone was going to at least try to get at the truth. "I'll send Joe in. While you're talking to him, I'll saddle a couple of horses."

†

Joe had bristled like a porcupine two days ago when Randy told him a special state investigator was coming from Boise and wanted to interview him about his unusual experience on that spooky night last spring when he had a run in with the mutilators.

"Do I have to meet with him?" Joe groused.

"Yes." Randy said emphatically, and stared at Joe's stricken face.

"I want to forget all about it, Dad. Why do I have to repeat it again?"

"Mr. Harmon has his reasons, Joe. He needs to hear your story."

"Aw, Dad, I don't want to." Joe said. "It makes me feel so stupid to tell anyone what happened to me. I'm not sure I even believe it any more, it's so far out! How do you and Mom feel about me? Are you ashamed of me?"

"Oh no, son! Don't ever think that, not even for a minute!" Randy quickly countered. "Your Mom and I are so proud of you. Just throw your shoulders back, walk in and tell Mr. Harmon what happened to you. Whatever he asks, be honest. He's a good friend and whatever you tell him will go no further."

"Oh, all right! If I have to," Joe said acidly.

Joe's thoughts of being treated like a criminal or a lunatic in his own home left him disturbed and angry. Every night since that terrifying incident when Little Girl and Miss BJ had been abducted and slaughtered, he'd been unwittingly haunted by bits and pieces of what really happened, which he'd forcibly forgotten—but the details were slowly filtering back to his consciousness. Even the long hot showers he was taking at night couldn't dispel his apprehension as he tried to sleep. He tossed and turned most nights, hoping the nightmares would go away. Then he'd wake up totally exhausted—often too tired to attend football practice—and if he wasn't in top physical condition no college would even consider letting him try out for their football team.

Neal Harmon ushered Joe to a chair in Randy's den and closed the door then he pulled a chair up close to the nervous young man, who was dressed in jeans, plaid shirt and varsity jacket hoping he could still get to school after this interview.

Neal stared at Joe's frightened face, then smiled. "Relax, Joe. Lighten up! I know I'm an outsider, but, hey Buddy, I'm not a cop! I'm your Mom and Dad's friend. We've known each other for years—and I want to be your friend too. How about it?" Neal stretched out his hand. The gesture melted the ice block in Joe's throat.

Joe grabbed the hand. "All right, Mr. Harmon."

"Good. I really need you to help me figure out who is killing cattle and horses here in Idaho. You could hold the key to solving the whole situation."

That brought a slight smile to Joe's face. "What makes me so important?"

"You're the only one in Idaho who's actually had an encounter with the people mutilating our livestock."

"They're not people, Mr. Harmon!"

"What?" Are you sure?" Neal thought for half a second, until he realized what that implied. He sat straighter in his chair and leaned forward.

Joe's eyes widened at Neal's intensity. "Yeah, I'm sure."

"Why do you think that?" Neal asked.

"If they were people, I would have seen them."

"Your dad told me they talked to you. How did they do that if you didn't see them?"

Joe nodded, as if expecting the question. "Through mental telepathy."

Neal held up a hand. "You just lost me, Joe. Maybe we'd better start at the beginning." Neal pulled a notebook and pen from his jacket pocket. "I'm going to make a few notes as we go along. "Tell me what happened, starting with when you got off work and walk me through the whole situation."

Joe nodded then explained his lonely drive home from Twin Falls.

"Did you feel there was anything wrong when you left work?" Neal asked. His words puzzled Joe.

"Well I always got a creepy feeling driving home alone in the middle of the night on that dark deserted dirt road. The only light out here in the sticks where we live is the moon and twinkling stars. If the moon is behind the clouds, the shadows can be pretty eerie. That particular night when I got close to home I saw a spotlight chasing our horses around the pasture. I nearly freaked out."

"A spotlight was chasing them?" Neal interrupted, almost with disbelief. "What did you think was happening?"

A bewildered nod from Joe answered him. "I've thought a lot about that, Mr. Harmon. At the time, I didn't have a clue as to what was going on. But thinking back, now with a clearer head, I know there was some kind of object in the sky hovering over the pasture."

"You actually saw it?"

Joe nodded. "Yes, but I didn't pay a whole lot of attention to it. My main concern was that damn light sliding along the pasture coming straight at me! I didn't know what to do. I didn't know if the light was dangerous. A few days later it dawned on me that that spotlight was coming down from something in the sky."

Neal opened his mouth, but he read fear in the boy's eyes—fear that Neal and everyone else would think him crazy, or at least imagining things. Neal remained silent.

Joe assembled his thoughts. "Mr. Harmon, there's something I must tell you. Something I've never told anyone. Perhaps now is the best time. I've got to tell someone. I'm pretty sure what I saw was an alien space ship!"

Neal leaned forward in his chair, his eyes wide. "Describe it!"

"It was a huge, triangular shaped object, I mean really huge, like the size of a football field. It made a faint whining sound. At the same time some lights underneath began to glow. There was a white light which I could see at each of its three corners. A red light strobed from the middle of its belly. The spotlight seemed to be beaming down from somewhere in the middle of that belly, near the red strobe light."

"Why haven't you mentioned this to anyone else?" Neal asked.

"I don't really know. It's sort of like my memory was blocked for a time. And when I finally realized what I'd seen, I was afraid to say anything because people would think I'm crazy." Joe paused. "You don't think I'm crazy, do you?"

Neal smiled. "Certainly not, Joe." Neal had his notebook in one hand and his pen in the other, jotting notes.

"What really intrigues me is that you actually saw a UFO up close. Perhaps its occupants may be killing our animals. I am puzzled by one thing however. What happened when Deputy Henline came along? Why didn't he see the UFO?"

"It took off before Jake got there."

"How? Straight ahead? Straight up?"

"It moved straight east like a hockey puck gliding over ice, very smooth and unwavering. And it moved faster than I can even describe."

"You're sure it wasn't a helicopter of any kind?"

"I'm positive. I know helicopters, their size, and their sounds. My dad's a helicopter pilot and I've been flying with him."

A real UFO? Neal's mind spun on the possibilities; the main one the potential of developing a plausible UFO theory to explain numerous animal mutilations. But who would believe him?

"Is that all, Mr. Harmon?" Joe asked, breaking Neal's train of thought.

"Oh, I'm sorry, Joe. Just one thing more. You mentioned someone or something spoke to you—using mental telepathy. Tell me a about that."

Joe explained the deep monotone computer-like voice instructing him not to be afraid and warning him not to tell what he had seen.

"Were you afraid they might hurt or kill you?" Neal asked.

"Not really," Joe answered honestly. "I got the feeling they didn't want to do that. The scariest part was knowing that someone or something could control my mind and thought processes. I couldn't move or think, or I would have started my truck and got the hell out of there."

"Me too!" Neal grinned, then asked," Has anyone you know seen any triangular shapes in the sky, unexplained shadows, heard voices or other unusual sounds out in this area? Maybe at school, in town or from neighbors?"

Joe shook his head. "No sir. None that I know of."

"All right, Joe. I think that's all I need right now. Thank you for sharing your experience with me."

Joe stared at Neal for a moment, choked for words. The set of his mouth got slightly anxious. "Do you believe me, Mr. Harmon?"

Neal nodded. "Yes, Joe. I do believe you—and thank you being honest with me." It was a simple statement, but Neal knew it would bring relief to Joe's mind to know that someone, especially a professional investigator, believed he was telling the truth.

Relief flooded Joe's anxious, worried face. "Thank you, Mr. Harmon!" he exclaimed sincerely. "You have no idea what this means to me."

"I can guess," Neal said. "I remember when I was a young man how hard it was to convince most grownups I was telling the truth about anything we were talking about." Neal leaned forward and looked into Joe's alert blue eyes, which were far more tranquil than he'd seen them this morning. "Joe, if it becomes necessary, would you be willing to tell your story just as you told it to me this morning to a panel of my investigator friends up in Boise?

"Um, ah, I don't know…would you be there with me?" Joe stuttered hesitantly.

"Of course I would. We'd also want at least one of your parents there, for moral support and because you're a minor. Okay?'

"Okay," Joe smiled. "Is it okay if I go to school now?"

Neal nodded and threw out a hand. "Get! And thanks, Joe."

Neal walked into the kitchen and found Randy and Tessie sitting the table drinking coffee and talking.

"You finished with Joe?" Randy asked.

"I am."

"Everything okay?"

Randy nodded. "He told me everything that happened to him and he seemed relieved and happy to get it off his chest. That boy went through one hell of an ordeal! You're lucky he came through it as well as he did."

Randy smiled. "You'll get no argument from us about that. As a family we've all been lucky, very lucky. We're still alive and well." He turned to Tessie. "Pour Neal a cup of coffee."

"I thought we were going to ride out and take a look at your dead horses," Neal said as he sat down at the kitchen table and Tessie poured him a cup.

"We are," Neal said, "and after we do that we'll ride over by Ben Summers' place and take a look at his dead ram."

"Who is Ben Summers?" Neal asked.

"He's a neighbor, a rancher who raises sheep, a real old Idaho original. There's only one Ben! He called me and said he found his prize ram dead and mutilated. He wants me to come take a look before he calls the sheriff. It'll give you a chance to get a close up look at a fresh mutilator kill!"

"Great!" Neal said, "that's even better than I would have hoped. Maybe that might furnish some of the clues I'm looking for."

Tessie tapped her fingers on the table. "Well, Randy, are you going to ask him?"

"Ask me what?" Neal said.

Randy smiled. "Now that the kids are in school and we have some privacy, Tess and I would like know if you have any ideas about who could be killing and mutilating livestock here in Idaho. Are you permitted to share any information with us?"

9

"WHAT WOULD YOU LIKE TO KNOW?" NEAL asked.

"Has the attorney general's office come up with any substantive clues, ideas or leads so far in their investigation?"

Neal sipped his coffee in silence for a moment. "Not really. We've been shooting in the dark trying to come up with something, anything that might help us identify the mutilators. We had high hopes for what we thought might be a solution, but it didn't pan out."

"Tell us about it," Randy said.

"Several reports from ranchers here in Idaho and other western states indicated that some of the butchered animals were radioactive, so the attorney general and the rest of us put our heads together to determine where the radiation could have come from. The answer jumped right out at us—Idaho's Engineering Laboratory at Arco! Those scientists are experimenting with nuclear energy."

"And nuclear energy generates radioactivity, right?" Randy said.

"It does."

"Did you go to Arco to check it out?" Randy asked with heightened interest.

"I did, but they were pretty tight-lipped about specific projects they're working on because they are highly classified. The only information available was basically a history of their operations. On my authorized tour of the facilities the guide told me the first peacetime use of nuclear power occurred when the U.S. government switched on their Experimental Breed Reactor #1, called EBR, #1, right near Arco, on December twentieth, nineteen fifty-one. That was fourteen years ago, and it gave Arco the distinction of becoming the first city in the world to be fully lit by atomic power. More importantly, it paved the way for commercial use of nuclear power."

"That's very interesting, Neal," Randy said, "but what does that have to do with radiation on mutilated animals?"

"I'm getting to that," Neal said. "The guide took me through the building where plutonium two thirty-nine was once produced and used to develop nuclear weapons. He showed me where it's now stored."

"Isn't two thirty-nine a deadly radioactive metal?" Randy asked.

"That's putting it mildly!" Neal said. "I was gaping at it through thirty four layers of oil-separated glass which protected me from its lethal rays! The damn stuff has a shelf life of at least a thousand years. Whoever handles it has to be mighty damn careful. The slightest exposure causes radiation poisoning. A tiny piece of two thirty-nine gives off so much energy it can warm your hands. A fractionally larger piece gives of sufficient heat to boil water in seconds."

"Really?" Randy said, his concern notching up. "Have there ever been any serious problems at the plant with plutonium-two thirty-nine?"

Neal nodded. "In nineteen fifty-five the Arco reactor suffered a partial meltdown, another world first. They kept that from the public as much as possible."

Tessie jumped in. "Neal, I still don't understand the connection you are trying to make between the nuclear plant at Arco and the butchered livestock here in Idaho."

Silence greeted her query for a moment.

"Well, Tess, we thought maybe those scientists at Arco might want to determine how animal flesh responds to intense doses of radiation, how flesh can be preserved, or…"

Randy threw up a hand. "Whoa, hold on, Neal!" Randy interrupted. "That theory has a lot of holes—the first being, how the hell would they get animal parts from all over Idaho to the plant?"

"Ever heard of black helicopters?" Neal asked.

Randy and Tessie laughed out loud. Randy put one hand to his ear and his other hand in front of his mouth like he was speaking into a microphone. "Earth to Neal! You've been watching too many sci-fi movies. Black helicopters are used in fictional stories to throw suspicion on the government agencies involved in unexplained wild conspiracy theories, kidnapping, murders and the like."

Neal pounced back enthusiastically. "That's a bit melodramatic, but we had to take a look at Arco, even though nothing conclusive came of it. However, as a follow up, when I finish my investigation here, I'm heading over to Mountain Home Air Force Base to find out if they're using any helicopters—or if they've picked up any UFO blips on their radar in the past few weeks."

"Mountain Home Air Force Base?" Randy snorted. "Good damn luck with that! They're mighty tight lipped about giving out information. A newspaper reporter found that out the hard way a couple of months back when he tried to get some info. They all but kicked his ass off the base!"

Neal grinned. "Well, the Idaho attorney general pulls a little more water than a newspaper reporter. The AG lined up an appointment for me to meet with the Air Force information officer—maybe he can point us in the right direction. If UFOs are flying around this area surely Mtn. Home's radar would have picked them up."

Randy stared at Neal for a second. The comment made sense. But Neal hadn't seen Randy's butchered horses yet! That's how this all started and maybe there were some answers out there—that's why Neal was here! A strange emotion filled him suddenly. The mutilators wouldn't be identified by the government! It was up to the ranchers. It was a deadly serious situation and a new sense of reality took over—and Randy knew they had to get moving.

"Well, my friend," Randy said, "we won't find any answers sitting here. Let's saddle up and ride out and look at some butchered horses the mutilators left in their wake."

Randy halted his horse atop a rolling ridge east of the ranch, above the Union Pacific railroad tracks. Further down, in a deep gully, the afternoon sun glinted off the peaceful thread of a creek winding through the valley's bottom.

Neal, following behind on a muscled tan buckskin, could smell the aroma of sage and cedars carried along by the breeze as his gaze moved over the vast Idaho landscape.

When he pulled alongside Randy, Randy pointed. "Miss BJ is down there, Neal. Walk down and take a look."

"Aren't you coming with me?" Neal asked.

"No," Randy said. "I want you to form your own opinion. I'll hold your horse, and wait here."

Neal dismounted and stepped away from the horses, scouring patches of dirt lying between the rocks. There were no footprints or pod marks; the steady wind across the top of the ridge had swept them away.

Neal looked back the way they had come, and shivered involuntarily.

This place had secrets, dangerous secrets. There was no way anyone had walked here to kill the horse and there were no horseshoe prints. The mysterious killers had left no signs of their passing. You've been in some weird places in your time, he told himself. But this takes the blue ribbon for sure. What he was about to see would reinforce that thought!

Neal picked his way down the steep trail, his high heeled cowboy boots digging into the shale, and got his first whiff of the noxious stench coming from the dead horse lying on its side a few feet ahead. He could hear buzzing deer flies fighting for their place on the rotting carcass. Reluctantly he forced himself forward. Suddenly he gasped as he spotted Miss BJ's swollen, decomposing body putrefying in the afternoon sun.

Neal gazed in mingled disgust and outrage. *Why in God's name would someone kill a thoroughbred race horse?* The horse's ears and lips were missing, and the gaping, maggot-infested body cavity was empty, which could easily be the results of scavenging coyotes.

Neal carefully inspected the dusty ground twenty feet in every direction around the carcass and found none of the pod marks Randy had described. There was no way Neal could tell what killed the horse, much less determine whether it had been mutilated with a superior type of surgery. With no better evidence, he had to assume the animal died of natural causes on a lonely Idaho hillside, and had become a welcome meal for scavenging birds and predators.

He pulled a small notebook from his pocket, took a seat on a rock some distance from the carcass' odor and jotted a note. *Randy Johnson's horse Miss BJ appears to have died from natural causes. There is nothing to indicate otherwise. The body was too far decomposed to determine if any unusual type of surgery had been used. The missing body parts were probably eaten by predatory animals or birds. The blood may have been absorbed by the soil.*

Neal clambered his way up to the top of the hill, where he stopped to catch his breath. Randy was sitting in the saddle, with one leg wrapped around the saddle horn.

"Well? What do you think?" Randy asked.

Neal stared up at him. "When was the last time you looked at the carcass?"

Randy's brow wrinkled. "A few days after the deputies made their investigation. My son Joe was eager to check the site with a geiger counter to see if we could detect any radiation. When he asked his science teacher, Mr. Meaders, if he could borrow his geiger counter, Meaders not only let us borrow it, he came along with us to help out."

"What happened?" Neal asked.

"The beeper went off and the damn needle went clear past the high mark!"

"What was Meader's reaction to that?"

"He got pretty damned excited," Randy said. "He told me there seemed to be some kind of radiation shield surrounding both horses."

"Radiation shield? What made him think that?"

"The readings on the geiger counter. He said it was like an invisible tent covering the horses."

"Did you believe him?"

Randy thought for a moment and hesitated. "Yes I did. Before the deputies made their investigation, I witnessed my dog Buster back away from the carcass, frightened half to death, when his nose evidently touched some kind of invisible protecting barrier."

"Protecting the carcass from what?" Neal asked.

Randy shook his head. "Damned if I know."

"Oh c'mon, Randy," Neal said, "you must have some idea."

Randy wasn't sure how to put his belief into words. He fidgeted with unaccustomed nervousness. "I figure the barrier was put around the horses to keep predators away."

"Why?" Neal asked.

"In case the killers want to come back and retrieve more parts from their bodies."

There was a moment of silence, before Neal said, "That's pretty far out, Randy…"

"You asked me. I told you," Randy interrupted rather sharply. "Now that you've seen Miss BJ, what do you think killed her?"

"I'd like to see the other horse before I answer that," Neal answered quietly, as he climbed into the saddle.

Randy frowned, pulled his hat down and shouted, "All right. Follow me!" He wheeled and spurred his horse into a gallop, Neal following close behind. They rode single file down and over a couple of smaller hills, crossing and recrossing the meandering creek flowing along the bottom. Randy twisted in his saddle to see how Neal was doing. No problem. He was a very competent horseman as he moved up and down with ease in the saddle.

They came up out of a depression in the ground and Neal saw another draw about a quarter of a mile distant. Randy turned and spoke over his shoulder.

"Little Girl is in that draw up ahead."

✝

Neal tried to look casual as he dismounted at the top of the draw. Randy quickly dismounted, and patiently stood there holding the horses' reins while he watched Neal carefully pick his way down the draw through the rocks and brush.

Neal found Little Girl in exactly the same condition as Miss BJ—a bloated, maggot-infested carcass—no pod marks, no blood, nor footprints of any kind. He hunkered down on his heels not ten feet from Little Girl and jotted some notes, trying to remember if he'd overlooked anything. When he climbed up the hillside he stared at Randy. He kept his feelings strictly to himself. His voice was level, under total control.

"That's a hell of a mess down there, Randy." Neal rubbed his dry lips with the back of his hand.

Randy nodded, hunched his shoulders a little and his eyes widened. "Well? You've studied both horses. Have you drawn any conclusions as to what killed them?"

Neal nodded. "Uh huh. And I won't sugar coat any of it for you. I'm afraid I have to agree with the deputy sheriffs' investigative report."

That blunt answer totally stunned Randy. He shot Neal an angry look. "How can you say that? My God, didn't you see the laser surgery? The mutilations and the pod marks?"

Neal appeared embarrassed as he shook his head. "I studied the ground and the carcasses very thoroughly, my friend. I'm sorry, but I found none of those things."

Randy looked dejected and disappointed. "Then you don't believe me?"

There was an awkward silence for a few moments, before Neal replied cautiously, "I think you believe what you told me. But I need evidence and it's not here. Do you have any photos or anything concrete?"

"Only what you've seen," Randy answered.

"Then I am sorry. Circumstantial evidence won't work for me. The only conclusion I can draw, based on what I've seen out here today, is that your horses died of natural causes. I know that's not what you wanted to hear, and I'm sorry, but that's what goes into my report."

Randy stared at Neal for a moment. His face, Neal thought, had never looked so drawn, so exhausted.

Randy's voice fell and he raised his hands in a helpless gesture. "I guess you have to do what you have to do." *But something sure as hell ain't right! Maybe the killers removed the force field from around the horses so predators could get at them and destroy vital evidence.*

Discouraged, at a loss for words, all Randy said was, "Aw, hell, Neal, let's ride on over to Ben Summers' place so you can take a close up look at his slaughtered ram. At least it's a fresh kill. Maybe you'll see something there a little more supportive of my theory about the mutilators' identity."

He clicked his tongue and urged his horse forward at a gallop, Neal again following closely behind.

✝

In the distance Randy heard a dog barking hysterically. He slowed his big stallion to a lope as he got closer to Ben Summer's dilapidated old ranch house, and motioned Neal to ride up alongside.

"Anything wrong?" Neal asked.

Randy nodded and shrugged. "Something's not right," he said, tight-reining his horse to a stop.

"Like what?" Neal asked.

"I'm not sure," Randy scowled. "Hear that barking? That's Aussie, Ben's sheep dog. I've never ever heard him bark like that. In fact, I've never heard him bark at all."

Neal grinned. "Isn't that what dogs do, bark?"

"Not Ben's dog."

Aussie got uneasy whenever strangers came to the ranch, and if they got too near without a proper introduction, he'd show his teeth. No one could work him except Ben and Randy.

Randy stared across the yard then turned to Neal. "This time of day Ben usually sits out on his front porch with a cup coffee and a smoke, then dozes off, and lets Aussie keep an eye on things."

"He sounds like a smart man!" Neal said good naturedly.

"He is that!" Randy agreed, as his brow wrinkled, a bit puzzled. Normally Ben had coffee brewing when he knew company was coming.

"I told Ben we'd be here this afternoon; I gave him a heads up yesterday so he'd be here to meet us. The old boy sounded so damn worried and frightened when I talked to him on the phone I thought he might have a heart attack."

"Maybe he went to town," Neal offered.

Randy shook his head. "I don't think so. He doesn't own a car or truck. Tess and I usually pick up a few groceries for him when we go shopping."

Randy raised a hand. "C'mon. Let's look in the house." Randy nudged his horse forward. Neal followed him in silence. They pulled up at the house and dismounted. Randy opened his saddle bag, cautiously grabbed his 45 and stuck it in the waist band of his Levis.

Neal groaned as his feet touched the ground. He pressed his hands in the small of his back and straightened. "Oh my God. I'm butt sprung! My back and legs are killing me. It's been a long time since I've ridden a horse." He glanced at Randy's 45. "Expecting trouble?"

"I hope not," Randy said as he stepped up onto the porch and raised his hand to knock on the door. At that instant Aussie came racing from somewhere out back, and planted his feet in attack mode in front of Randy, growling ferociously, challenging him to enter the house.

Randy took a deliberate step forward and called out in a soft voice, "Hey, Aussie, you old mutt, you know me. What's the problem? Get over here and let me give you a hug!"

Aussie's eyes narrowed, and his tail wagged, but still he was very wary. But why? Randy knelt and ran his hand through Aussie's lustrous long gray-black fur. The dog shivered and rubbed against Randy's hand.

Randy again stepped to the front door, pounded vigorously several times and shouted, "Ben, hey Ben, you old rascal! It's me, Randy. Open up!"

"I don't think he's home," Neal said.

"Let's find out." Randy turned the doorknob, the door opened and they cautiously walked into the unpainted old house, closely followed by Aussie sniffing here and there.

An odor like old gym socks and unwashed dishes drifted out. Neal clamped his teeth over the urge to gag and tried to smile.

Randy grinned. "Ben wasn't the world's best housekeeper. "Ben!" Randy shouted again. "Are you in here?"

No answer.

The front room and kitchen lights were burning brightly. A chill ran over Randy! Frugal ol' Ben would never leave lights on during the afternoon.

The front room wallpaper was a bit dirty, though definitely selected by a woman who liked roses with raised petals; the furniture was old and well worn, but otherwise the room appeared normal for an old Idaho ranch house. *Strange,* Randy thought, as he glanced at the empty gun rack nailed over the fireplace where Ben kept his battered old model 1893 Winchester 30-30. The old man took it down only once in a while to shoot pesky coyotes menacing his sheep—or to run snoopy visitors off his property.

Randy turned from the front room and walked into the kitchen. The linoleum was coming up in small curls along the edges. Randy peered at a half empty box of Remington 30-30 shells on the kitchen table. *What was Ben doing with his 30-30? There's no sign of a struggle.* A large, dented blue graniteware coffee pot sat on the wood and coal stove. Randy put his hand on the coffee pot, then felt the stove.

"Cold," he said. "Where the hell is he?" Randy growled and exhaled slowly, a tight knot of muscle was now squeezing at his chest, he stepped across the hallway to the bedroom and glanced inside. The bed was made up and hadn't been slept in.

"Has the old fellow had trouble with anyone?" Neal asked. "Maybe someone looking for a little payback?"

"None that I know of. Ben didn't have an enemy in the world."

Aussie brushed nervously against Randy's leg. He reached down and patted the dog's head and scratched behind his ears. "Where's Ben?"

Neal grinned. "Does Aussie understand English?"

"Yeah! Australian English!"

Aussie's ears perked up as if he understood. He stared up at Randy with his moonstone blue eyes for a moment, then barked and scrambled for the open doorway.

"C'mon, Neal. Let's follow him."

Aussie barked happily and loped along a well-worn sheep through the tall sagebrush. Randy spurred his horse to a gallop, square on the dog's heels. Neal followed Randy. Three blocks from the old farm house, near Ben's dilapidated, falling down barn, the sage brush opened onto a wide sheep pasture where several Lincolnshire sheep milled nervously about.

Aussie stopped dead in his tracks, bared his fangs and began growling fiercely.

Randy's stallion almost ran over the dog as Randy jerked back on the reins and stopped just in time.

"What's going on?" Neal called out.

Randy turned in the saddle. "I'm not sure. But look over there." Randy pointed off to the left where Ben Summer's saddled old mare stood patiently waiting for her master. "That's Ben's horse. I don't like the looks of this, Neal," Randy said and dismounted.

He walked up to Aussie. "What's wrong Boy? He asked. "Where's Ben?"

Aussie took off and Randy and Neal followed on foot. Aussie disappeared through an opening in the brush and began barking.

Randy walked up and suddenly stopped short. He drew in his breath involuntarily, which brought his heart into his mouth and he gasped with revulsion.

Old Ben was stretched out on the cold ground on his back, eyes open, staring skyward, his old lever action 30-30 clutched in his dead hands, across his chest. Five empty shell casings were scattered on the ground near his body. Randy just stood there and stared at his old friend's bristly face, which held a horrified look as if he'd encountered something that defied logic.

For a time Randy couldn't say anything. He just stared at the body. Then he was shaken back into awareness of the present situation when Neal asked, "Is that Ben Summers?" His stomach tightened as he stepped closer to the body.

Randy nodded. "It was." It was obvious to both of them that Ben was dead, but Randy knelt down and placed a finger on the old man's carotid artery and checked for a pulse. His eyes met Neal's, and he shook his head, grimacing.

"Look at his face, Neal," Randy pointed. "It's twisted and contorted like he was frightened to death. Have you ever seen anything like that?"

Neal shook his head." No, I never have. Do you think maybe he was shooting to protect himself from something or someone who was after him?"

"I think that's a damn good possibility," Randy said.

"So what do we do now?" Randy asked. "Should we take his body back to the house?"

"No," Neal replied. "Let's not disturb a possible crime scene. When we get back to Ben's house you can call the sheriff and ask him to send a deputy and the medical examiner out here. We'll let them determine what happened."

"Sounds like a plan," Randy agreed. "But let's at least cover him up."

Randy walked over to his horse, untied his rolled up rain poncho from behind the saddle, walked back and carefully spread it over Ben's body. He hated to leave his old friend lying there in the sagebrush, but there was nothing more he could do for him at the moment.

Neal stood there staring down at the covered body. "Had you known Mr. Summers very long?" he asked quietly.

"All my life," Randy said wistfully. "I'm going to miss the old codger a lot. He was a soldier like us in his younger days. He fought in WW One. Once in a while he'd open up and tell me about being a sergeant at the battle of Chateau Thierry—and how he fought under General Black Jack Pershing. Told me how they took the Germans by surprise without even a preparatory artillery bombardment. Then he'd ask me how it was in Vietnam." Randy paused for a moment before he continued, a bit of emotion in his voice. "He took me fishing, taught me to use guns. We had some wonderful times hunting. He could really spin some yarns about old time gunfighters and outlaws."

Neal nodded. "They don't make 'em like that any more, my friend. I wish I could have known him." Neal licked his dry lips and took a deep breath. "What now?"

Randy rubbed his chin. "Before we call the police let's find Ben's mutilated ram so you can examine it. He told me he'd never seen butchery like that!"

"Do you know where it is?"

"Uh huh," Randy said, and pointed. "Down this trail a mile or so."

Neal lit a cigarette. Nervously, Randy thought.

"Something on your mind?" Randy asked.

Neal nodded. "I know this is going to sound insane, but these animal mutilations occurring all over the state scare the living daylights out of me. They make me feel like I'm a little kid. It's all in my imagination of course." Neal took a long drag on his cigarette, his hand shaking slightly. "There's something around here that's not of this earth. I sensed it when I talked to your son Joe, again when I looked at your butchered horses and even right now—and it's scaring the hell out of me!" Neal took another drag on his cigarette. Suddenly his eyes went wide and he coughed as his breath caught in his throat.

"Oh my God, Randy, look!" Neal pointed to Aussie backing slowly toward them, growling deep in his throat, his hair standing on end.

Randy was silent. His hand went to the butt of the 45 in his waistband! He hadn't realized it until this very second, but he shared the misgivings Neal had articulated so perfectly—and like Neal, Randy was scared. Damn scared! So was Aussie!

10

RANDY WAS SUDDENLY AWARE OF A POWER so inexpressible, so cosmic, it was as if the real world had disintegrated and he and Neal were in a strange uncharted world and at the mercy of something evil and destructive. He pulled the 45 from his waistband, cocked it and pointed it toward the empty space above Ben's poncho-covered body.

"C'mon, Neal," he said quietly, and gestured for him to move back to the horses. "There's something here we don't want to screw around with."

"Just a minute, Randy," Neal said, reaching inside his jacket for the notebook. "I want to write something..."

Suddenly the wiry hair on Aussies back bristled and he crouched into attack mode. His lips drew back over his yellow teeth, and from deep within his throat came a snarling growl.

"Damn it, Neal, move your ass! And move it now! I'll cover us. C'mon!"

They backed away from Ben's body until they bumped into their horses.

"What the hell was that all about?" Neal asked.

"I really don't know," Randy answered truthfully, "But I think we've been warned to get away from this place. Aussie either smells or senses something we can't see." Then with a wry smile he asked, "are you sure you want to find Old Ben's dead ram?"

Neal nodded. "Hell yes! We can't quit now! We're in too deep." He put his foot in the stirrup and climbed onto the saddle. "Let's go!"

"All right, my friend, it's your funeral," Randy said and threw a leg over his stallion. "Follow me." He touched his heels to the horse's flank and took off at a gallop. Neal and Aussie followed closely behind.

The almost imperceptible sheep trail wound through a tangle of arroyos and shadowy ravines. Uneasy, Randy occasionally glanced back the way they'd come. He also kept a careful lookout ahead, though he saw nothing to be alarmed about. Yet he shivered involuntarily as a foreboding feeling crept down his spine, like it had many times in the dense jungles of Vietnam, when he was so close to invisible enemies he could smell them, yet there was no way of knowing how many there were or where they were concealed.

"Hey, Randy," Neal shouted, "It's going to be dark soon. How much further?"

"Hang on. We're almost there," Randy said, nosing his horse along the old ram's tracks which curled behind the knee of a steep hill which threw a shadow across them. Randy slowed his stallion to a walk and leaned down to inspect the ground, following the shallow indentations left by the ram's feet.

Finally Randy held up a hand and reined his horse to a stop. "I think this is pretty close to the spot where Ben found Old Billy's carcass. I'll take a look just to make sure." He grunted and eased himself out of the saddle and had a long look around. Then he stared up at Neal. "You may as well step down and hold the horses. Be ready to move and move fast if I give you the signal."

Neal dismounted and Randy handed him his horse's reins, then walked slowly to a wide clearing in the sagebrush fifty yards ahead, still unable to shake a nagging sense they were still not alone. They were being watched, their progress carefully monitored. But by whom? He was convinced that whoever or whatever it was, it wasn't human, not out here. He wasn't sure why he was thinking that; but it had a lot to do with his son Joe's encounter with the mutilators and the mysterious deaths of his horses—and maybe because of Old Ben's strange death back there closer to the house. But no matter how he rolled it around in his mind or picked it apart, he couldn't conceive of any way that the watchers or mutilators could be human. One thing he did know for damn sure—they were close by. Mighty close! He felt it and knew it, just as sure as he knew the sun would come up in the morning.

Aussie raced ahead through the sagebrush toward the clearing and quickly located the dead ram's carcass. His muzzle slammed into a solid invisible force field covering the Ram's body like a tent. Startled, Aussie let out a high-pitched blood-curdling yelp, and tumbled sideways. Quickly regaining his balance, he shook himself, and gingerly extended one front paw out to try and determine exactly where the invisible object was. Before that paw touched anything, he heard a loud shout:

"Aussie! Stop!" Randy shouted. "Come here!"

Stop! How the dog hated that command! The ram he was supposed to protect was dead and Aussie was ready to fight whoever killed it! But he'd been trained to obey. Slinking apprehensively, five feet from the carcass, he cautiously circled the ram once more, then dashed to Randy's side, drawn as surely as if by a wire.

"Good dog!" Randy patted Aussie's head.

"What's going on?" Neal hollered. "Did you find something?"

"Yes. Leave the horses there and come over here and take a look. This will interest you."

"Be right there." Neal took his camera from the saddlebag anxious to get some pictures and walked toward Randy. He stopped for a moment and cocked his head as he heard a strange vibrating sound. He looked around in every direction, then back over his shoulder as if he expected to see someone following him—but no one was there.

He sidled up alongside Randy, and gawked at the butchered ram as shock and disgust engulfed his features. "Who in their right mind could do something like this?"

The big ram was stretched out on its side. Only empty holes remained in the skull where his solid, curved horns used to be. His eye sockets were empty; the eyeballs had been removed, along with its ears. A precise surgical incision split the ram wide open, from throat to anus and all its internal organs were gone, as well as its sexual organs.

Neal cautiously stepped closer, examining the ground. With astonishment, he gasped, "Randy, look here!" He pointed to the dry ground. "There's no blood anywhere, not even on or in the carcass. How can an animal be butchered like this and there's no blood spatter? It doesn't make any sense."

"Maybe it's not supposed to. I'll be damned if can come up with any answers. This is almost identical to the way I found my butchered horses. Not a drop of blood anywhere."

Randy stepped in close to the carcass. Evidently the invisible shield didn't deter humans. He stood there studying the razor-straight stomach incision.

Squinting, Neal bent down and walked slowly around the carcass, examining it in minute detail. Even in this gruesome state the old ram seemed almost alive, as if it was only sleeping. Just to make sure, Neal forced himself to put his hand down and touch the ram's nose.

He jerked back. "Jesus, Randy," "Old Billy's nose is still warm. I've got to get a picture of this. He uncased his camera and worked with the settings. When he looked up his eyes went wide as he stared past Randy out across the endless sea of tall gray sagebrush, where a breeze created patterns along the tops, bending them toward the two men, followed by a rolling white mist which immediately settled over them—not a cold mist but something almost like a cloud. It happened so fast there was no time to retreat.

"I think we're going to be killed, Randy," Neal said softly, "unless you've got something figured out."

Randy, barely hearing him, said nothing: something else was on his mind.

"Go away you crazy evil bastards!" he shouted, grabbed his pistol and fired in the direction from which the mist came.

For a split second nothing happened. Then came a faint whirring noise and the sound of something swooshing through the air. Randy was hit with an unseen force stronger than anything he'd ever experienced and his pistol flew from his hand as he hit the ground like a pole-axed cow.

Aussie barked only once before he was instantly frozen to immobility.

Randy was down and out. Aussie was a canine statue. All hell was breaking loose and it all happened before Neal could do anything about it. His heart ran wildly. What should I do" He bent down. "Randy?" *Oh my God, he's dead.*

No Neal, he is not dead. He threatened us. No one must ever do that.

Neal trembled, stood up and glanced around, but he couldn't see anyone—then it dawned on him a voice was talking to him through some kind telepathy, which immediately formed questions in his mind: *Who are you? Why are you here? What do you want?*

Have no fear. We will not harm you. Leave this place and take your friend and your animals with you. Do not come back again.

Neal heard the stilted English words, echoing as if coming from far off through a long tunnel, though with perfect diction as though the man was speaking vocally.

"Who are you?" Neal asked again, this time verbally.

There was no answer. "Are you still here?" Neal asked.

Silence.

Neal looked around, speechlessly. The mutilators were gone. He stared down at Randy.

Aussie started barking loudly.

"Randy! Randy!" Neal shouted. "Are you all right?"

Dazed, still flat of his back on the ground, Randy looked up and regarded Neal through dazed murky eyes, which slowly cleared as they came into focus, and he was fully conscious again. He slowly raised his hand. "Help me up."

Neal reached down and pulled Randy to his feet.

"What's going on, Neal?" He asked. "Who hit me? It's like I'm waking up from a bad dream!"

"More like a nightmare," Neal said. "I think we just had a run in with the mutilators and they weren't finished with whatever they were doing to Ben's ram. We stumbled in at the wrong time!"

"I think you're right," Randy said, "At least that sounds logical." He leaned forward and gingerly felt his ribs with both hands.

"Anything broken?" Neal asked.

"Not broken, but mighty damned sore. I've never been hit that hard before, not even when I was playing football!"

"Do you think you can you ride?" Neal asked.

Randy nodded and grinned, "As long as the horse doesn't trot."

"Okay," Neal said and mounted his horse. "Let's ride back to old man's house and phone the sheriff."

Randy and Neal had a hundred questions to ask each other, but they didn't ask a single one. Nothing made the least bit of sense. They knew they'd ridden into a mysterious situation beyond their control! but at the moment it didn't seem to matter.

They kicked their horses to a gallop as the sun dropped behind the western mountains, creating a brilliant reddish orange sunset. Aussie followed them, at an even-paced, steady run.

When they came to the spot where they'd left Old Ben and his mare Randy drew rein near the mare. When Neal pulled up alongside he asked, "Shall we load the old man onto his horse and take him back to the house."

Randy shook his head. "No. The sheriff will want to take a look at Ben just as we found him. This area may be a crime scene, so let's not mess it up."

Neal didn't like the idea. "What about predators? We can't just leave him…"

Randy smiled. "I don't think he's going anywhere and Aussie will take care of any stray coyotes." Randy grabbed the old mare's reins and led her toward the house, Neal trailing along behind.

11

THEY REINED UP IN FRONT OF BEN'S darkened ranch house, dismounted and tied the three horses to the fence. Randy walked into the house and flipped on the lights then turned to Neal. "I don't know about you my friend, but it's been one hell of a day. I could use a drink, how about you?"

"I'll vote for that," Neal grinned. He was so tired he slumped gratefully into a kitchen chair and exhaled loudly. "You're right, you know. It's been a hell of a day! I feel like I've been run over by a freight train!"

Randy opened the kitchen cupboard, reached up to the top shelf and grabbed a fifth of whiskey. "Ben always kept some Jim Beam handy in case the weather suddenly turned freezing or blazing hot." He sat two water glasses on the table and poured three fingers of whiskey into each, and pushed one across the table to Neal.

Neal took a long pull on his whiskey, then shook his head. "What the hell happened out there today, Randy? I'm still trying to figure it out and I can't come up with any logical answers."

"I believe we just had our first close encounter with aliens!"

"You mean aliens from another world?" Neal asked with surprise.

"Do you have any doubts?"

"Well," Neal said cautiously, "I know what I saw and what I heard. But aliens? That makes no sense at all. Why would aliens be killing domestic farm animals?"

"If we knew the answer to that you wouldn't be here. There's some hefty reward money waiting for the lucky person who can come up with some clues that will help identify the mutilators."

Neal's eyebrows rose in question. "Are you going to tell the sheriff what happened out there today?"

Randy nodded. "Part of it—that we found Ben dead and his prize ram butchered."

Neal shook his head. "I don't think that's going to work. There's quite a bit more to add to this story that needs telling—if you want to try and convince the sheriff that aliens may be involved."

Randy nodded. "I'm aware of that. But why not let the sheriff investigate and form his own conclusions?"

"You make a good point," Neal said firmly. "What kind of man is your sheriff? Do you know him personally?"

Randy nodded. "He's a long time friend. We get together once in a while for a drink, and we've shared some great hunting adventures here in Idaho. He's ex-marine and tough nails."

"Is he any good?" Neal asked. "I mean is he a good cop?"

"He gets re-elected every time he runs. I've helped with some of his campaigns."

"That's not what I meant," Neal said. "Do you think he's up to handling a case that may involve UFOs and aliens? If he even hints at anything extraterrestrial to state or federal authorities it'll put him in a hell of an awkward situation. Maybe we should save him the embarrassment and call in the state police—let them handle this investigation."

"Oh hell no!" Randy quickly interjected. "Not a good idea!"

"Do you mind telling me why?"

"This is Jeffords' county and he runs it like it's his personal fiefdom. But no one minds. He makes folks around here feel safe and secure. Going over his head to the state police would be a mistake. You'd find he's not the forgiving kind."

"Well, since you put it that way," Neal said, "We'd be better work with him."

Randy chuckled. "Wise choice. Would you like another drink before I call Tessie and let her know we'll spend the night here? Then I'll call Dan Jeffords."

Neal held out his empty glass and Randy poured him another shot of Jim Beam.

†

Tessie sounded relieved when Randy told her they were safe. "I've been so worried. So many crazy things are going on. How is Ben getting along?"

"I'm sorry to have to tell you this, Tess, but Ben is dead. Neal and I found him out in his sheep pasture."

"Oh Randy," the words came out on a thin whisper, "Not old Ben," followed by "What happened to him?"

"We think he may have had a heart attack."

A weird feeling settled in on Tessie. "But he was as strong as a horse the last time I saw him. Are you sure it was a heart attack?"

"We don't know."

"Have you notified Dan Jeffords?" she asked.

"I will, but I wanted to talk to you first."

Her voice was soft when she asked, "Would you like me to drive over in the pickup and get you?"

"Thanks, Honey, But I think it best if we stick around here for the night. Kind of keep an eye on things. I'll ride my horse home tomorrow."

Tessie felt a chill travel down her spine. She didn't like the idea of being home alone at night, but she held her fear in check, knowing Randy was doing the right thing, taking care of Ben's situation. "Then I'll see you tomorrow. You be careful, Randy."

†

"Is Tess okay?" Neal asked.

"She's fine. I'll call the sheriff now and ask him to come over here in the morning."

"Tell him to bring the medical examiner along."

"Why?" Randy asked, and drank down the rest of his whiskey.

"We need to obtain a medical opinion as to Ben's cause of death."

"Good idea," Randy agreed, "and maybe have him take a look at the butchered ram while he's here?"

"You're way ahead of me, Randy! But yeah, it sure won't hurt my investigation to secure a medical opinion about a butchered animal, even though the medical examiner isn't a veterinarian. The results of such an examination would at least give me something credible to take to my boss back in Boise."

"Sounds good!" Randy said. Then he dialed the sheriff's office.

"Sheriff's office," said a woman's voice. "How may I direct your call?"

"Hi Beth. This is Randy Johnson. I need to speak to the sheriff."

"I'm sorry Randy, he left for home about an hour ago. May I take a message?"

"Keeping pretty late hours, is he?"

"You got that right!" Beth answered. "He's practically worked the clock around the last two weeks. Calls reporting animal mutilations are coming in almost hourly."

"I hate to bother him at home, but this is urgent. Can you put me through?"

"Hang on, Randy. I'm ringing him right now." In a moment she said, "Go ahead, Randy. He's on the phone."

"Hi Dan. This is Randy Johnson. I apologize for calling you at home, but I'm calling you from Ben Summers' place."

"Ben's place?" Jeffords asked sharply. "This time of night? What the hell are you doing out there? Is something wrong?"

"We found Ben dead out in his sheep pasture."

"Dead? What happened?" A slight pause. "You said we. You got someone out there with you?"

"Yeah. Neal Harmon from the attorney general's office up in Boise. He came down to take a look at my dead horses."

"Damn it would be nice if those sonsabitches up in Boise would let me know when they're sending someone into my jurisdiction!" Jeffords growled.

Randy let it pass and provided Jeffords additional information. "Don't sweat it, Dan. Neal's all right. He's an old friend of mine. He could be very helpful to you in this mutilation mystery if you'd give him a chance and not get your balls in such a big uproar! We're staying out here at Ben's place tonight. Can you get out here in the morning and take a look, and bring Dr. Jim Austin with you?"

"Why?" Jeffords asked.

"Because of the condition of Ben's body when we found him."

"What are the circumstances? Was he murdered?"

"I don't know, but I don't think so." Randy explained how they found Ben lying dead with his rifle across his chest.

"Sounds like it could have been of a heart attack."

"Maybe so, Dan. But there's another complication. We found Ben's prize ram dead. The poor bugger was mutilated beyond recognition."

Jeffords sighed disgustedly, "Oh Jesus H. Christ, another butchered animal? You figure there's any connection between the old man's death and the dead ram?"

"I hate to keep saying I don't know," Randy said. "We left Ben's body where we found it. We checked out the ram, and tried to be very careful so as not to destroy any essential evidence. Everything's pretty much as we found it. That's why we need you to come out here and investigate. Can you make it in the morning?"

"Christ almighty, Randy, I'm swamped," Jeffords growled grudgingly. "I've had ten friggin' calls in the last two days about butchered animals…"

"C'mon Dan," Randy interrupted sharply, "You owe Old Ben at least a few minutes of your time! You knew him as well as I did."

The enormity of the fact that Ben and his ram may have been killed by mysterious means was slowly sinking into Jeffords' confused mind. "Yeah, Randy, you're right. Don't mind me. I'm just in a pissy mood this evening. Too goddamn much work and not enough help. I need about ten more deputies. You interested in a job?"

"Are you kidding?" Randy asked. "I wouldn't think of pinning a damn badge on, not with this indiscriminate butchery of animals taking place all over the state."

"That's what I figured, you chicken shit," Dan chuckled. "I'll be out there in the morning and I'll drag Jim Austin along with me."

"Thanks Dan. We'll be waiting."

Jeffords shook his head and gritted his teeth as he slammed the phone down. *This goddamn job is going to get me committed to the funny farm!* He gathered his thoughts, for few moments, regained his composure then dialed Dr. James Austin, Twin Falls County medical examiner.

✝

Dr. James Austin was fifty five, healthy and fit. As a young man he'd been trained as an army corpsman and went ashore with his regiment when it hit Omaha Beach at Normandy in June, 1944. He'd seen his share of death and suffering and had two purple hearts to show for his own wounds, a gut shot that laid him up for several weeks, and shrapnel form a machine gun round still being carried in his calf, both wounds long since healed. It was while he hovered near death's door after the gut shot, in a woebegone tent hospital, watching dozens of overburdened medical staff workers frantically trying to save lives, succeeding so often with massive battlefield injuries that he decided to become a medical doctor—that is if he lived long enough to get back to Idaho, his boyhood home!

Jim Austin had a real soft spot for rural farmers and ranchers and often received payment for his services in produce or chickens and once in a while a nice cured ham during the holidays. He had a little farm himself, a short ways out of Twin Falls. But much of the ranch work was left to Barbara, his bride of thirty five years. They'd known each other since they were children. Barb had been a pert, lively teen-ager. She bloomed as a woman and often told neighbors doing chores kept her lean and mean! She loved Jim with all her heart and had stuck with him through the tough times of the war, his therapy upon return from the battlefield, and the long torturous struggles of medical school.

A few minutes after Sheriff Jeffords' late evening phone call to Dr. Austin, Barbara came from the bathroom, her face scrubbed and cheeks flushed. "Who was that on the phone, Jim? You look mighty unnerved."

"Sheriff Jeffords wants me to go with him on a call in the morning." He explained that Ben Summers had died and he needed to go take a look at the body and make necessary arrangements.

Barb gave a sigh of relief. "Just a routine examination, then?"

"Perhaps. One of Ben's prize sheep was found butchered near the old man's body.

I got a feeling the sheriff wants me to take a look at the animal."

"Oh Jim," she said with alarm, "Please tell me you're not going to get mixed up in all that craziness again—are you? That's not really your job or concern," she went on abashedly, "you've already looked into several animal killings and you're not a qualified veterinarian."

Jim smiled, and with a wink said, "maybe I should have been. Animals can't talk back and their owners usually pay cash money for services rendered."

"Oh, be serious," she chided not so lightheartedly. "It could be dangerous to go poking around those dead, mutilated animals. I'm not sure what you hope to learn for your troubles and frankly it scares the hell out of me."

"The danger is a slight possibility," he agreed, "But there's something mighty strange going on with these animal mutilations and I want to try and find out what it is."

Barb nodded with a slight grin. "I bet you would—you Sherlock Holmes! That's why you purchased that new geiger counter, right?" She knew Jim was extremely anxious to break in his new toy and perhaps come up with some kind of theory to help solve the lingering dilemma of all these recent animal mutilations.

"Exactly what is this new toy you call a geiger counter? What does it do?" Barb asked curiously.

"Well," Jim explained, "Naturally there's a long technical definition in the operating manual, but to put it in laymen's terms, it's a small hand-held device or machine that can detect whether objects emit nuclear radiation."

"Do those objects include dead animals?" she asked, putting a harsh and prolonged emphasis on the word objects.

"Yes, however if the geiger counter detects any radiation on dead animals that's really all it does. It doesn't tell me where the radiation came from, what kind of radiation it is or how long it's been there."

"Hmm," Barb responded, "When you put it that way, a geiger counter doesn't sound all that damn useful."

"I know." Jim smiled despite himself, really unsure whether a geiger counter would actually make any difference at all in trying to solve mutilation problems. Still he really loved the mystery of learning something new or solving a problem—and this was one situation that really needed some solving.

✝

Jim had trouble falling asleep this evening. Maybe other people didn't, even those who'd had their farm animals butchered by something mysterious. Maybe they'd found some way to shrug in the face of what might be an invisible enemy—but he sure as hell hadn't!

He was a medical doctor and human beings were his patients, whether alive or dead, especially dead now that he was the medical examiner. He'd quickly learned that a couple of days after being appointed to his new and challenging position, when he autopsied his first murder victim.

He still wondered how the hell he'd gotten so deeply involved in animal mutilations. It snuck up on him so innocently. A veterinary surgeon in Burley quietly asked him if he'd mind taking a look at the delicate surgery he'd discovered on a butchered cow. Then another veterinarian in Twin Falls asked a similar favor. As Jim examined the dead animals he was drawn into a situation that aroused his curiosity as never before! He noted that each vet's questions to him were the same.

"What do you think, Dr. Austin? Was this animal butchered by someone with medical skills? I've never seen any surgery like this before."

Jim wasn't sure how to answer. He'd never encountered such an amazingly advanced type of surgery—so perfectly precise in every detail. He knew at first glance it was a type surgery currently unknown to American veterinary or medical science. And strangest of all, without exception, Jim found the same type of surgery every time he was asked to inspect a dead animal—and always there was a corresponding story from the animals' owners, ranchers and farmers, who reported sighting UFOs shortly before finding their animals dead and butchered.

In the back of Jim's mind he was recalling a very strange episode down in Albion last month. He was still pondering that one over and over in his mind!

The small town of Albion, with less than 300 people sits at the edge of the Sawtooth National Forest, just south of Burley. The first sightings of "large strange objects" in the sky were attributed to weather phenomena by local police—or perhaps, they added, some type of balloons loosed from their moorings. Of course moored balloons out in the middle of Idaho's Mini-Cassia area wasn't exactly an everyday occurrence, to say the least. It would be a very unusual area for hot air ballooning enthusiasts.

Around the time all this was happening high school teacher Martin Quinn, and his wife, began seeing strange lights in the sky about 11:30 p.m. They hovered north of the city for about 45 minutes, then moved seemingly instantaneously to hang over the airfield. While there, two smaller objects glided out from the larger one and traveled in opposite directions quickly and silently out of eye sight, but shortly thereafter returned and were engulfed by the larger one.

Perplexed law enforcement officials grudgingly admitted there was some kind of bright light in the northern sky that night, evidently a star. They seemed okay to leave it at that.

Curiously, animal owners stated their cattle acted very peculiar from early that evening through twilight and into night time. Cows bawled and bellowed, and it was difficult to sleep because of the tremendous racket.

Barking, terrified dogs ran into houses and refused to go out again.

Meanwhile in other nearby communities residents saw unusual lights and objects in the sky. The next morning and throughout the day several farmers and ranchers discovered dozens of butchered cattle scattered over many ranches. The entire area was a buzz with talk of flying saucers. Several ranchers were now carrying rifles in their trucks.

Three days later, after Jim visited a patient in Albion, he stopped by the Cowboy Grub Café for a cup of coffee. It was a slow day and the café was empty. Jim chatted with owner, Sarah Rontoski, who told him about a very strange sight she'd seen three nights ago while she was driving home.

"From the corner of my eye I saw a long silvery object in the sky. It didn't appear to be moving, more like it was hovering, like a big bird trying to spot something to eat. I pulled my car over at the top of Connor Creek Pass and watched it. It was sort of cigar shaped, maybe two thousand feet up, off to the northwest toward Howell Canyon. I'd never seen nothing like that before."

Jim casually sipped his coffee and asked, "What were your first thoughts? I mean were you frightened?"

"Yeah, Doc. I was scared half to death. I was up there all alone."

"Did you report it to the police?" Jim asked.

"I didn't want to," she said, "Because they'd think I was a whacko nut case. But when my customers started talking about what they'd seen that night I had a sit down with our local town marshal and told him what I'd seen."

"What did he say?" Jim asked with interest.

"He thought I was hallucinating! He didn't believe me, not one damn word! Me and my neighbors feel like it's a waste of time talking to the police. Hell, they think we're all a bunch of nutty fruitcakes!" She hesitated a moment and lowered her eyes. "Well, they don't come right out and say it to our faces, but it's like they laugh behind our backs. Every one of the townsfolk who've reported such sightings to the police say they got the same treatment I did."

Jim's troubled mind flashed back to that particular incident, in and around Albion, and the follow up speculation reported in local newspapers. The one that really grabbed his attention, and still troubled him, was from the U.S. military: *AF Not Probing UFO Sightings*

Mountain Home Air Force Base has not sent jets to investigate recent UFO sightings in the Magic Valley. The base information officer said, "To the best of my knowledge the base has not sent out chase planes and I don't think we would do that. We are no longer in the business of officially doing it," he added, referring to the defunct Air Force project of observing and analyzing sightings and information (Project Blue Book). "UFO sightings have created a stir in Magic Valley during the last three weeks. Some people relate the UFO sightings to the recent cattle mutilations that have spread statewide. But that is sheer speculation and has no basis in fact."

✝

Outside the Austin home it was pitch black. The autumn sun had been chased away by the cold winds of winter blowing in from the west. Snow wasn't too far off. Jim tried not to think of tomorrow, He slipped quietly out of bed so as not to wake Barb, and paced back and forth in the dimly lit front room.

Within minutes, sleepy-eyed Barbara slipped into the room. "Can't sleep, Honey? You're worrying about tomorrow, right?"

Jim nodded gravely. "I am, though I hate to admit it."

"Are you still theorizing that the mutilations are being committed by extraterrestrial beings?"

"I am. But I know the sheriff isn't. One of his deputies told me that."

"Are you scared?" she asked quietly.

"Yeah, damn scared."

"Well it's a free country, Honey. You don't have to go with the Sheriff in the morning."

"Yeah, I do," he answered forcefully. "I don't know how to explain it to you. It's like some kind of ominous energy force is pulling me out to Ben Summer's ranch to keep me digging into this puzzle. I've just got to go."

"I can't dissuade you?" Barb asked.

Jim shook his head. "No."

"Then you'd better take along some protection!"

That sent a chill down Jim's back! He knew she meant his Browning 45 pistol.

Barb moved close to him, took both his hands in hers. And when she saw the strange look in his eyes, she knew what he had just told her was the truth.

"Please promise me you'll be careful?"

He shrugged and said, "I promise."

Barb smiled. "All right, my love." She took his hand and gave him a peck on the cheek. "We'd better get some rest. Your mind needs to be sharp—you have a very challenging day coming up tomorrow!"

12

IT WAS CHILLY OUT. SHERIFF DAN JEFFORDS stared out his kitchen window. Wind howled and swirled leaves around on the lawn. November nights are generally very cold in Idaho and Jeffords hoped early winter snow would hold off until he could complete his investigation of Ben Summers' death.

The sheriff was unnerved by Randy Johnson's late evening phone call informing him about Ben, and finding the old man's prize ram a little further on, butchered practically beyond all recognition.

Goddamn! Jeffords shook his head at the almost unbelievable mysterious events taking place all over his county—phone calls pouring into his office almost hourly, irate ranchers demanding action to identify the mutilators and stop them, dead animals, and now dead people! And to top it off, some hot shot investigator from the attorney general's office was poking his nose into a situation that technically was none of his damn business. All of this flashed through the sheriff's mind for a couple of minutes as he tried to come to grips with what he could or should do, but the answers just wouldn't come. *What the hell is an old country sheriff supposed to do?*

He walked to the fridge and grabbed a Bud, popped the top and chugged down half a can of cool, refreshing brew. The clock on the kitchen wall read ten. Time to catch the local newscast. He turned the TV on to see a pretty female anchorperson delivering *Breaking News.* "Today more mysterious cattle mutilations were discovered at several remote Idaho ranches—and reports are just coming in that the mutilators have now spread into the neighboring states of Utah, Wyoming and Nevada, where ranchers are reporting dozens of slaughters that had taken place in the last few days. Law enforcement agencies in the intermountain west are reeling from the number of reports flooding in.

We tried to get interviews with federal and state agencies, but so far none of our phone calls have been returned."

Jeffords had heard enough and disgustedly flicked off the TV. *Three of those mutilated cows mentioned were discovered just hours ago right here in Twin Falls County—not ten miles from my house!*

He grabbed the phone and dialed his chief deputy Jake Henline. It rang several times before he heard Jake's voice.

"Sorry to be calling so late, Jake. I hope I didn't wake you. Got a minute? I need to talk to you."

"No problem, Sheriff. What's on your mind?" as if he didn't already have some idea.

Jeffords ran down an abridged version of the situation at Ben Summers' sheep ranch, and added, "I'm heading out there in the morning. I'm taking Doc Austin with me to aid in the investigation by examining old Ben's remains."

"Do you want me to tag along?" Jake probed, feeling he should be more involved in a major investigation.

"No. I need you to keep a lid on things around the office. Right now the whole county is close to a civil meltdown. We've got to get a handle on what the hell is happening around here with all these mutilations. Can you step in and take charge for me tomorrow while I'm out at Ben's place? I've got a gut feeling there may be some positive leads out there to help break this case wide open."

"Sure thing, Sheriff. Don't worry about it," Jake replied, upbeat now about being trusted to manage the sheriff's office for a spell.

"I appreciate that, Jake, but whatever you do, don't disclose any information to anyone about our on-going investigation. Understand?"

"Not even to the feds or the state police?"

"No one! Goddamnit Jake. You got that?"

"Yes sir! Anything else?"

"Yeah. I'll be with Randy tomorrow and I know damn good and well the first thing he's gonna' hook me with is what's the status of our investigation into the death of his horses."

"What'll you tell him?"

"I haven't got the first damn clue," Jeffords answered. "Your report of the incident was a bit too sketchy for me to draw any conclusions. You should have checked it out more thoroughly and provided more details."

"Like what?" Jake interrupted, his voice a bit edgy.

"Well, the surgical cuts for starters…"

"Whoa, Sheriff, you hold on for one damn minute," Jake growled, his voice rising, a bit angry and frustrated. "You specifically told Deputy Munford and me before we left your office that Randy's horses were more than likely killed by predators. I, and Jim too, both assumed that's what you wanted put in our report—so that's what I did!"

"Hold your taters Jake and calm down! I'm not blaming you for anything." Jeffords' voice took on a softer tone. "I guess what I'm trying to find out is exactly what you and Jim really saw when you got a long, hard look at those wasted horses. Could you actually tell if they were killed by predators, like you put in your report?"

The phone went silent for a moment, before Jake answered hesitantly. "Look, Dan, I'm not denying that maybe my report had a little spin on it, but that was to please you. I assumed that's what you wanted. I'm sorry."

"Never mind that now. Just tell me the truth exactly as you really saw it, Jake," Jeffords interrupted. "That's all I want. Were Randy's horses killed and mutilated by predators or not—in your opinion?"

"Well good hell no!" came Jake's swift reply. "You want the truth? Okay, here it is. There are no predators in this area big enough to take down a full grown horse. You know that! I have no idea how Randy's horses were killed, but I'm pretty sure they were butchered by someone or something with a medical person's skill."

Jake's forthright confession shocked Jeffords, who until now, hadn't put much credence in lame brain stories about laser surgery or other nonsensical theories.

"Really?" Jeffords quipped with total surprise. "What about radiation or some kind of force field around the carcasses? I've heard rumors from some of the local yokels that substantial doses of radiation were found around Randy's dead horses."

"They're not rumors, Sheriff. I know that for a fact. I saw and felt it myself. To be honest with you, if you'll pardon my French, it damn near scared the living shit out of Jim and me when we saw Randy's big dog Buster practically croak with a coronary when he got within ten feet of those creepy lookin' bloodless horses. There certainly was some kind of force field around the animals, like protecting them, and not only Randy's, but most of the other mutilations I've investigated around here recently."

"I was afraid of that," Jeffords said forcefully. "I suppose I've had my head in the sand hoping and wanting to believe that predators had to be the answer to the animal killings right here in my jurisdiction. I suppose deep down inside I knew it had to be something else—so I started doing a little research, asking around, making a few phone calls to some professors and scientists and a few others. But instead of coming up with enlightening answers, I'm more confused than ever, and it's driving me crazy—eating away at me day and night."

"Why? What did you find out?" Jake asked with piqued interest.

"Lots of things," Jeffords replied. "Not only do we have an epidemic of animal mutilations here in Idaho, hundreds of cattle across the west have been found mutilated under unusual circumstances, exactly like the ones we've investigated. Sheep, horses and, believe it or not, even humans have also been similarly mutilated. No one knows what kills them, but all their blood has been removed. And like you mentioned with Randy's horses, precise laser cuts have been found on the mutilated animals, and certain organs removed from their bodies, especially their reproductive and rectal organs."

"Did you learn anything worthwhile about radiation?" Jake asked.

"Yeah. Abnormally high radiation levels have been detected wherever mutilated cattle are found and scavengers won't go near much less touch the carcass. There are seldom any footprints leading to or from the livestock."

"Anything else?" Jake asked.

Jeffords paused for a moment. "Well, what I've just told you is enough to keep me awake most nights—but, Jake, the most difficult thing for me to wrap my brain around is that on many of the dead animals there are clamp marks on their legs and necks that seem to indicate they were somehow taken from their normal habitats and mutilated elsewhere and dumped—UFO sightings and/or bright lights in the sky coincide with most of the cattle mutilations."

"So what's your thinking about all of this? Did it make a card-carrying believer out of you?" Jake asked, somewhat jokingly.

Jeffords answered with a question. "You've seen more mutilated animals than I have, what do you believe?"

Jake, taking a more serious turn, replied, "Well, you asked me for the truth. Here it is. Everything you just mentioned Jim and I found when we inspected Randy's horses. I hope we're not in trouble leaving some of that out or our report. We…"

"Hell no!" Jeffords interrupted. "Don't give that a second thought! I appreciate your honesty. Anything else?"

"Yeah. Let me bring you up to speed on Randy's boy Joe. He's still having some mental issues with what the military calls post traumatic stress disorder or PTSD from something he witnessed one midnight on his way home from work. I told you about that, remember?"

"I do. A close encounter I believe you called it—the boy said he saw a space ship. Probably a hallucination. Anyway, how's Joe getting along now?"

There was a short pause before Jake said, "Not good. Randy has scheduled an appointment for Joe with a psychiatrist down in Salt Lake later this month. Hopefully that doctor can provide Joe the help he needs to get back to his old self. It really has him all whacked out. It's sure been one hell of an ordeal for the Johnson family. It's little comfort to them that we don't seem to be much closer to solving this mess for them or anyone else either. The pressure is getting turned up on all law enforcement and none of them wants to be the first one to go on record with UFO theories. The world outside our little intermountain area already thinks we are a bit loco for living out here in the sticks."

Jeffords nodded. "I totally agree that it's been a wrenching ordeal for the Johnsons. I really like Joe. He's a great kid, and a hell of a ball player. I get over once in a while to see some of his football games. Let's hope things work out for him."

"Yeah," Jake replied, "He's almost like one of my own kids. Well, Sheriff, you'd better get some shuteye. Sounds like you have a hell of a big day tomorrow. Are you sure you don't want me to go along and provide a little backup?"

Jeffords chugged down the rest of his beer. "I appreciate the offer, but no, I want you in the office. Don't worry about me. Hell, Jake, I'm as brave as the next man, but I'm no fool. I'll have enough backup for anything out the ordinary that might pop up. Randy's as good as they come with fists or a gun and I understand the investigator from Boise is ex-army and good with a gun."

"I'll take your word for it, Sheriff," Jake said. "You can count on me to take care of things on this end. Who knows? Maybe you'll run something down out there on Ben's ranch to help move things along and clear up this mystery, like you said."

"Maybe so," Jeffords sighed, but his voice didn't sound too positive.

✝

Early the next morning Sheriff Dan Jeffords slowly eased his patrol car into Dr. James Austin's long circular driveway and stopped at the front door of the two-story red brick home. Dr. Austin opened the door and waved. Barbara gave her husband a peck on the cheek and handed him his medical bag and small Geiger counter and he headed for the car.

"Throw your stuff on the back seat, Doc," Jeffords said." Is that a Geiger counter?"

Austin nodded. "Yep. Brand new. I just got it a couple of weeks ago. I thought today might be a good time to try it out."

"Why?" Jeffords asked.

"To see if there are any signs of radiation around Ben Summers' place." Jeffords let it go.

Austin climbed in on the passenger side and Jeffords handed him a paper sack with a bran muffin and coffee.

"Ah, that smells good, Dan. Thanks."

Jeffords smiled. "We don't have much around these parts to brag about but our little bakery makes the best dang muffins in the whole state."

"I won't argue with you on that!" Austin responded and took a bite of muffin which was fresh and tasted as good as its aroma had hinted at.

"What's on the agenda for today?" Austin asked and took a sip of hot coffee.

Jeffords drove down Main Street then pulled out into highway traffic and headed south out of Twin Falls.

"Randy Johnson and Neal Harmon, a state investigator, will meet us at Ben Summers' ranch at eight. As I mentioned last night, they discovered Ben's body in his sheep pasture and further on the mutilated carcass of that big ram which ran loose all over the ranch."

"A state investigator?" Austin asked with a bit surprise. "What is he doing out in these parts?"

"I assume he's investigating the animal mutilations hitting in this part of the state just like we are."

"But that's your job isn't it?" Austin asked.

Jeffords was silent for a moment. "I thought so," Jeffords said.

"Is this guy a police officer or veterinarian?" Austin asked, finishing off the muffin.

"Neither. He's an attorney whose boss evidently thinks he's a cop." Jeffords voice took on an exasperated tone.

"Do you know him?"

"I've never met the man. He's out of the attorney general's office in Boise. Evidently the AG is launching his own investigation. He probably doesn't trust us pecker neck country bumpkin cops to come up with anything new to help him identify the killers."

"Oh, I don't know about that," Austin countered. "The news indicates the AG is getting hammered by the governor and everyone else in Idaho to come up with some answers. I'm guessing the AG will be grateful for any help he can get no matter where it comes from."

Jeffords pondered that for a moment, finding nothing objectionable, and changed the subject. "How about you, Doc? Have you ever studied a mutilated animal close up?"

"Several times."

"Well?"

"Well what?"

"Have you formed any opinions as to who killed them?" Jeffords asked as he turned off the highway onto a gravel road bordered on both sides by walls of thick, tall sagebrush, which soon faded into miles of gorgeous range land, dotted with cattle grazing peacefully.

Doc Austin threw the same question right back at Jeffords. "Have you seen any mutilated animals?"

Jeffords nodded. "One or two. I usually send my deputies to handle the investigations while I field all the incoming phone calls."

"How about Randy Johnson's horses? The way I heard it from the ranchers' co-op in town his horses were mutilated just like all the cattle here in the county. "Did you see those horses?"

Jeffords shook his head. "I didn't have time. Two of my best deputies handled that investigation."

"Did they find any clues or come up with any ideas about who the killers might be?"

Jeffords nodded. "Their official police report indicated predators."

Austin threw up his hands, as if in disgust. "Do you actually believe that? The way I heard it Randy's horses were mysteriously transported out of the pasture near his house, killed and mutilated someplace else then dumped in the hills next to the Union Pacific tracks."

Jeffords swallowed, unsure what to say. "Yeah, I've heard that rumor floating around town. Right now that's all it is, a rumor!" he said defensively. "I'm not buying into any rumor or theory about little green men from Mars—not yet anyway."

"Maybe you should!" Austin said seriously. "Your predator theory isn't getting you anywhere in solving the mystery, is it? Think about what happened with Randy's horses. Pod marks and restraint wounds on both horses, along with radioactivity. No blood on, in, or around the carcasses. All kinds of body parts taken—and Randy and Tessie saw what they thought was a UFO." Austin raised an eyebrow. "What more do you want? How can you just dismiss all of that like it doesn't exist?"

Jeffords gave a curt nod of the head, still skeptical and kept his eyes on the road. "You're an educated man, Doc. You're sitting there telling me you believe aliens are visiting the earth, killing domestic animals?"

"Hell yes! Would you even be investigating the killings if they weren't? Law enforcement officers all over the west are investigating mutilated animals. If the killings were being done by predators local fish and game departments would take care of the problem. They have sharpshooters that take care of rogue predators. You know, they fly around in helicopters and shoot predators." Dr. Austin stared at Jeffords. "No. The mutilators are not predators!"

Jeffords jaw dropped and he took his eyes off the road for a second and glared at Austin in disbelief. "You too? Has the whole freakin' world gone crazy?" His words slipped out with utter contempt. "There's no definite proof aliens are the culprits."

"Yeah, right," Austin replied, "and there's no proof they're not." From the conversation it was obvious to Austin that Jeffords had been thinking about this. Heavily!

Austin smiled. "Do you want to hear my opinion?"

"I suppose you'll tell me whether I want to hear it or not!" Jeffords said.

Austin nodded. "I'm not totally converted to a UFO alien theory—yet. But I'm leaning that way, trying to keep an open mind—perhaps you should too. I believe we have to look at every possible angle if we expect to identify the killers and what's gone on out here." Dr. Austin hesitated to say the rest of it, but continued. "You're locked into a predator theory. But if you'd paid closer attention to the mutilated animals you inspected, I'm sure you'd have concluded predators didn't have a damn thing to do with their mutilations—you're just reluctant to admit it. What the hell are you afraid of, public ridicule?"

The question took Jeffords by surprise and he frantically fished his mind for an answer, and gave in slightly. "Okay, for the sake of argument, let's say the culprits are aliens. What's their motive?"

Dr. Austin smiled triumphantly. "That's what we should be trying to find out, don't you think"

"I don't deal in speculation, only in facts," Jeffords said.

Austin nodded. "I'm absolutely glad you do! If we're lucky today, maybe we'll discover some of those facts."

13

JEFFORDS PULLED UP IN FRONT OF BEN'S house and stopped. Randy and Neal were standing on the wrap around front porch drinking morning coffee. Aussie growled and scrambled toward the patrol car.

"Get!" Randy growled and pointed. Aussie slunk back to the porch.

Dr. Austin grabbed his things and climbed out of the patrol car and waved. "Hi Randy."

Randy waved back. "C'mon over here, Jim, and meet Neal Harmon, down from Boise."

Austin was six feet, solid, with graying hair and a mustache. He wore jeans, denim shirt and scuffed pointy brown boots. He grabbed Neal's hand. "Glad to meet you, Mr. Harmon. Welcome to the Magic Valley."

"Good to be here, Doctor," Neal replied.

Sheriff Jeffords lingered for a few moments in the patrol car, talking on the radio to his dispatcher. When he finished, he put the mike down and climbed out of the car.

Neal studied the Twin Falls County Sheriff who looked like he'd stepped out of a John Ford movie. Tall, slightly gray, well built, tanned. He was dressed western style, but not duded up—twill slacks, hand-tooled leather boots, crisp kaki shirt with snaps instead of buttons, with the large Twin Falls county sheriff insignia near the shoulder part of the left sleeve. On his hip he wore a holstered 357 magnum revolver.

Randy grabbed Jeffords' hand. "Glad you could make it, Dan. Meet Neal Harmon from the attorney general's office.

The two men stared and sized each other up for a moment. Then Jeffords extended his hand, nodded, and said, "pleased to meet you," looking anything but. He shook Neal's hand.

"Sheriff," Neal responded, noting Jeffords' handshake was firm, his gaze direct, almost confrontational. He radiated a tough energy.

"What can I do to help out here?" Neal asked. "I want to help as much as I can."

"I don't know," Jeffords replied candidly. "You won't be part of the official county investigation—I need to maintain my independent stance. The rest of us," he pointed to Randy, Dr. Austin and himself, "live here. So I'm investigating for Twin Falls County. Any questions or comments?"

"Just one," Sheriff," Neal responded pleasantly, "Right now I'm just an observer—and I don't want to get in your way or screw up your investigation."

"I appreciate that Mr. Harmon," Jeffords replied coolly, but with a slight smile.

"Well," Randy grinned, "now all the hand shaking is out of the way follow me and I'll take you over to see Ben."

As Jeffords walked past the house Aussie ran out and greeted him by happily, jumping up, placing his huge front paws against Jeffords' chest.

"How are you, Aussie, you big old lazy loafer?" Jeffords smiled and rubbed the dog's head with both hands. Then he turned to Randy. "What are we going to do with this worthless hound?"

"If no one objects, I figured I'd take him over to my place. He and Buster are good friends. And old Aussie is a good herd dog. "

"Great idea, Randy!" Jeffords said with a sigh of relief. "I figured if you didn't want him, I'd take him. I just want to make sure he has a good home. I don't have the heart to see the old boy go to the humane shelter, not after he's been such a loyal companion to Ben."

Randy nodded. "Yeah. Ben loved that dog!"

The men followed Randy along the hard-packed sheep trail to the pasture. He pushed open the age-weathered wooden gate.

"Ben is right over there, Doc." Randy pointed, about fifty yards ahead.

"I see him." Austin handed Randy his bag. "Hold this for a minute. I want to check my Geiger counter and make sure it's working." He turned it on.

Randy watched a startled, puzzled expression cross Austin's face when his head jerked up and he quickly pulled the Geiger counter in closer to get a better look at the dial. .

"Anything wrong, Doc?" Randy asked.

"No, nothing." But the tone of his voice seemed to belie his words.

"Well, let's move it then, Jim," Sheriff Jeffords said impatiently. "Time's a wasting." He started walking through the open gate.

Austin reached out and grabbed Jeffords elbow. "Why don't you fellows wait here for a minute? Let me check things out first."

"Hell, Jim, we're not scared of a dead body," Jeffords said.

"It's not that, Dan," Austin said. "Just stay here and give me a few minutes," his voice trailed off, as he walked toward slowly Ben's body, sweeping the Geiger counter back and forth across the frozen ground.

"What the hell is he doing?" Jeffords asked.

"He's checking for radiation," Neal said. "It can be very dangerous."

Dr. Austin turned off the Geiger counter, leaned over Ben's body and pulled the poncho off. The old 30-30 rifle was still firmly clutched in old man's gnarled fingers and his glazed eyes stared skyward.

Austin stood there for a moment studying the body's position, then slowly walked around, absorbing details. No footprints of any kind. No surgery. Still fully clothed. Then he turned on the Geiger counter and leaned in to body scan the old man, starting at his head and moving in down toward chest, the Geiger counter about a foot above the body.

Instantly the needle zipped over to high and the buzzer went off with a high-pitched staticky sound.

Startled, Dr. Austin jumped back and shouted, "Goddamn!" His surprise wasn't feigned! "Stay away!" he shouted. "Don't come over here. He's radioactive!"

Dr. Austin stood there for a moment breathing rapidly, trying to collect himself.

Then he walked back to the others standing by the gate.

"Randy, did you or Neal touch Ben's body?"

Randy and Neal stared at each other for a moment, trying to remember.

"No, Doc," Randy answered. "We just covered him with a poncho."

"Ah, that's good, my friends. I doubt you've been affected by the radiation. We can test you later." Austin turned and stared across the pasture at Ben's body.

"My God. What a terrible way for the old man to die," he sighed solemnly. "But if it's any consolation he didn't suffer. He died quickly."

"Of what?" Sheriff Jeffords asked.

"Some kind of radiation poisoning."

"Can you be more specific?" Jeffords leaned forward with intense interest.

"I suspect it was external radiation that first entered Ben's body. How it was administered I have no idea. Just off the top of my head I'd say it was probably some kind of death ray gun."

"Death ray gun?" Jeffords scoffed. "You're kidding right?"

Neal jumped in. "Please, Sheriff, let the man finish."

"Sorry Doc," Jeffords apologized. "Go ahead."

"I base my assumption on the fact that Ben's clothing exhibits external contamination, which my Geiger counter picked up. I can even pick it up at this distance from his body, because once anywhere inside the body radioactive material continues to move to various sites throughout the body, and it continues to emit radiation until it is removed or decays."

"Wouldn't that take quite a bit of time?" Jeffords asked.

Dr. Austin nodded. "It most certainly would, and that's what has me puzzled, Sheriff. I think it's safe to say Ben died almost instantaneously. He died where the radiation was administered, or in laymen's terms, dropped dead on the spot where he's lying."

"How do you know that?" Jeffords asked with increasing interest.

"From the position of Ben's body," Dr. Austin replied. "See the rifle still clutched in his hands, pressed against his chest? If he hadn't died instantly my guess is he would have walked or crawled back to his house and phoned for help, wouldn't you agree?"

"Good point. I think I understand." Jeffords conceded. "But let's backtrack for a moment to your death ray statement. Where the hell would someone obtain a ray gun that kills someone instantaneously with radiation?"

Dr. Austin shook his head. "As far as I know, Sheriff, no such weapon currently exists on this planet."

Sheriff Jeffords voiced a disturbing thought. "I think somebody out there someplace is setting us up. Maybe we're next, and I can tell you that it's making me mighty damn nervous."

"I wouldn't worry about something like that, Sheriff," Dr. Austin said. "I believe whoever or whatever is killing and mutilating animals won't bother humans—unless, of course, they happen to interfere at the wrong time!"

"Do you think maybe that's what happened to Ben?" Jeffords asked.

"I certainly do. He wasn't out in his pasture target shooting. He just happened to be in the wrong place at the wrong time, and probably saw someone or something he wasn't intended to see."

Randy interrupted. "What are you going to do with Ben's body, Jim? He has no next of kin. He made arrangements a year or two ago with Fower's Funeral Home to take care of his funeral and burial when he passed away. Do you want me to call them to come out with their hearse and pick him up?"

Dr. Austin shook his head. "No, Randy, that would be too dangerous. I'll call Dr. Jordan, a renowned radiation expert at the Atomic Energy Commission in Arco, and explain the situation. He'll have to dispatch a special vehicle and personnel with radiation suits. They are trained to deal with dangerous situations like this."

"What will they do with Ben's body?" Randy asked with concern.

"Perform some type of special autopsy, I assume. I really don't know for sure, but I'll do everything I can to find out for you."

Neal stared at Randy. "As Dr. Austin was explaining about high levels of radiation I was thinking about your butchered horses—didn't you tell me no dogs, predators or birds would touch the carcasses. Maybe it was the radiation that kept them away."

Before Randy could answer Dr. Austin said, "I'm sure it was the radiation. It's the same wherever we find these types of mutilated animals—highly elevated levels of radioactivity exist."

"Damn, this is getting messy," Neal said uneasily. I don't know where it's going to lead. Now we're dealing with murderers using radiation guns!"

The men walked back to Ben's house and Dr. Austin called Dr. Jordan at the Atomic Energy Commission in Arco. Evidently it was difficult to get through to Dr. Jordan, because Austin stated his name into the phone, his location and why he was calling. When a connection was finally made, the two doctors talked for ten minutes. When Dr. Austin hung up, he turned to the others. "Well, my friends, there's good news and bad news. Which would you like to hear first?"

"The good news," Sheriff Jeffords said, hoping that it didn't involve more people screwing and meddling around in Twin Falls County police business.

"Dr. Jordan said he'll send his specially equipped truck and two of his best trained people to pick up Ben's body. They'll be here in about five hours."

"So what's the bad news?" the Sheriff asked.

"Dr. Jordan warned all of us to remain silent about this situation with Ben or we could be charged with a federal felony. From here on, Dr. Jordan is in charge. He will perform an autopsy and return the body to me for burial."

"Are you shitting me, Doc?" Jeffords growled. "Good God! I can't believe this is happening. Now the feds are threatening us?"

Dr. Austin nodded. "They are. And if I were you I'd heed Dr. Jordan's warning. You don't want to screw around with that particular agency. People have a habit of disappearing when that happens."

"That's very true!" Neal said forcefully. "I know from personal experience in the army what those people are capable of. They are authorized to use federal police agencies or the military to investigate anyone of whom they become suspicious."

Jeffords just nodded and swore under his breath. Randy grinned and poured whiskey, putting an ample portion in Sheriff Jeffords glass. "You'd better chug a lug it down, Dan, before you bust a blood vessel."

Jeffords hated feeling helpless in front of the others. He swirled some of the whiskey in his mouth before swallowing. The stuff wasn't really so bad! He reached his glass out to Randy, who poured him another shot.

"So what are we going to do, Doc?" Jeffords asked as he took a pack of cigarettes out of his shirt pocket, pulled one out and lit up. His blue-smoke exhale curled up toward the ceiling.

"It's your call," Dr. Austin answered.

"Well, it looks like we're between a rock and a hard place. Old Ben is out of our jurisdiction now. All we can do now is try to figure out what happened to his dead ram." He took a long nerve-calming drag on his cigarette.

Dr. Austin squinted at Jeffords through a haze of cigarette smoke, and asked impatiently, "You're going to continue your investigation?"

"Of course," Jeffords replied. "This is my jurisdiction."

"Then what?" Dr. Austin asked.

Feeling the whiskey's warming effects Jeffords said, "One thing at a time, Doc." He picked a loose piece of tobacco off his lower lip. "Let's get off our lard asses and find out what those mutilatin'sonsabitches did to Ben's old ram, before some other federal bureaucrat sticks his long nose in where it ain't needed! You got your gun?"

Dr. Austin nodded and patted his medical bag. "Right in here."

Randy said, "Dan, you can use my horse, the one Neal's been using. Jim you can use Ben's old mare. Both are saddled."

Dr. Austin's head jerked up. "Aren't you coming with us?"

"No!" came Randy and Neal's emphatic, resounding response.

Dr. Austin stared at them in utter surprise, waiting for some explanation.

"We've already been out there," Randy said. "Tessie is home alone, worried and scared half to death and the chores need doing, I've got to get back."

Neal said, "I'll stick around here with Aussie and wait for the Atomic Energy people who are enroute to pick up Ben's body."

Sheriff Jeffords chuckled and shook his head. "What a couple of candy asses!"

"It takes one to know one!" Randy grinned.

Jeffords chuckled again. "Well, if it's not asking too much, Randy, old buddy, at least tell me where the hell to look for the dead ram."

"It's in the tall sagebrush just below the hill with the twin cedar trees," Randy said.

"Where we saw that big six-point buck a couple of years ago?"

Randy nodded. "That's the place. Anything else I can do for you."

"No." Jeffords replied, as they walked out of the house toward the saddled horses. Jeffords climbed aboard the horse Randy pointed out and adjusted his weight in the saddle. Randy handed him the reins. Dr. Austin climbed aboard Ben's old mare.

With a tight smile Randy stared up at Jeffords. "You be careful out there and take care of Doc.

Jeffords shrugged, just a shade too nonchalantly. "Quit your worryin'

Randy! Hell, there's nothing out there 'cept sagebrush and a dead sheep." He touched heels to the horse's flank and rode off at a gallop. Dr. Austin followed close behind.

"I hope they'll be all right," Neal said, sounding worried.

"Don't sweat it. The sheriff knows his way around," Randy responded. "Maybe we'd better watch out for our own skins. Something is going on around here that's mighty damned creepy." Randy climbed aboard his horse and Neal handed him the reins." Randy said, "if you have any problems with those people from Arco, give me a call."

Neal waved as Randy whirled the horse around and galloped off toward his ranch.

✝

Tessie sensed trouble in the air as soon as Randy walked in the house and she studied his troubled expression.

Randy met his wife's eyes and they were brimming with concern—and he wanted to say something that would put her fears to rest.

"I've got coffee ready," she said.

"Sounds good," Randy said and plopped down in a chair at the kitchen table. Tessie poured coffee then sat down across from him. She leaned forward in her chair. "Well?"

"Well what?"

Tessie was earnest and intent. "I want to know what caused Ben's sudden death. There's something you're not telling me."

Randy hesitated for a long moment. "I can't. It's best that you don't get involved."

Tessie shook her head. "I have a right to know. I'm part of this too."

"Yes you are," Randy agreed, "but things are going on here in the valley that have never happened before."

"What are you trying to say? What happened over at Ben's place?"

Randy held up a hand. "Please Tessie, just drop it. Okay?"

"Damn it, are you trying to make me mad?"

Randy shook his head slowly. "No, Honey. I'm just trying to protect from what's coming."

When she spoke again her voice faltered. "Will you tell me when you can?"

Randy nodded. "Soon, Honey. Things are moving pretty fast."

14

SHERIFF DAN JEFFORDS WAS BEGINNING TO think being out here in the middle of nowhere on horseback was a very bad idea—when he could be back in town working with his deputies to come up with some clues to help solve the mutilation mystery. Besides, it gave him the creeps wasting time out here.

He settled into the saddle with half his weight on the balls of his feet in the stirrups, adjusted the reins in the fingers of his left hand, tucked his hat brim down tight against the breeze, turned up the collar of his jacket and clucked his horse ahead.

The blue Idaho sky was a thousand miles wide and a nippy fall breeze wafted through the sagebrush, filling the air with its pungent aroma.

As Jeffords rode along, deep in thought, the dilemma of animal mutilations and their consequences in Twin Falls County slowly began to sink deep down into his subconscious mind. They were occurring with ever increasing frequency and there was nothing he could do to stop them, yet it was up to him to catch the culprits, though he had not the slightest idea who or where they were.

He reflected on his recent phone conversation with Sheriff Gus Wallace in nearby Blaine County, advertised as the birthplace of the Sun Valley resort in 1936 and at the heart of Idaho's great outdoors, to see if he'd discovered any new leads to help solve the cattle killings in his county.

"Not a one!" Wallace growled. "Me and my deputies are working our asses off, day and night, investigating mutilated animals. In fact I was just heading out to the Wood River area when you called. Five more cattle were butchered there last night."

"Do you think it's predators?" Jeffords asked.

"Off the record?" Wallace asked.

"Yeah."

"Hell no, Dan. I've seen cows killed by cougars, wolves and bears. Well, so have you! It ain't no predators that's killed cows in my jurisdiction. That's the gospel according to Wallace. You got any ideas?"

"Off the record?"

"Yeah," Wallace responded.

"There's a lot of talk floating around Twin Falls about UFOs and aliens beings involved."

Wallace's response surprised Jeffords. "I believe it's more than talk, Dan. But I'm keeping an open mind."

"Have you talked to Sheriff Pritchard over in Camas County?" Jeffords asked. "The Times-News in Boise reported several cows butchered in his area last week."

"Funny you should ask," Wallace replied. "I just talked to him yesterday, but he doesn't know any more about what's going on than we do. He did tell me the Idaho Cattlemen's Association is putting up a thousand dollar reward for anyone with information leading to the arrest and conviction of cattle mutilators. I don't think it will do a bit of good. Cattlemen down in Utah and Colorado and over in Wyoming have offered rewards too, but so far no one has collected."

Yeah, and no one in Idaho will collect it either! Jeffords thought. *Why can't the muckety-mucks from the state or even the feds come up with some answers?*

"Dan!" Dr. Austin hollered for the second time, "which way?"

"Huh?" Jeffords' head jerked and he turned in the saddle. "What? Oh, just follow me."

"Where were you?" Dr. Austin smiled. "You seemed a million miles away."

"Sorry. This mutilation thing has my mind so screwed up it's whirling in a dozen directions. No one anywhere has any ideas…"

"How about aliens from outer space?" Dr. Austin interrupted. "Have you given that idea much thought?"

Jeffords quick response surprised Dr. Austin. "Yeah, Lots of thought."

"Well?"

Jeffords' eyes narrowed and he shook his head. "Naw! It's not possible."

Austin started to say something but Jeffords threw up a hand. "I know! I know! You don't need to say it. It has to be aliens from outer space, that's the only answer, right? Well, I don't buy it, Jim. Do you realize how stupid it would be for me to just sweep everything that's happened into a corner and lay the blame on aliens? That doesn't make any sense. How did they do it? Why did they do it? What the hell do aliens want with a bunch of butchered cows?"

"You do have a point," Dr. Austin conceded. "But if you discount aliens what else do you have?"

"Not a damn thing—and it's driving me nuts!"

Dr. Austin smiled. "Well, Dan my friend, aliens or no aliens this Idaho countryside is a perfect place for the mutilators to ply their trade." With a sweep of his hand he added, "thousands of acres of range land where they can roam undeterred in search of prime beef, or other animals they happen to want or need."

Jeffords only grunted, without responding. He kneed his tough hard mouthed gray gelding forward, setting the pace—walk, trot, canter, then walk again. Jeffords and Austin slid down the steep bank of an arroyo, leaning back in their saddles, then clawed up the hill on the opposite side, working their way up toward the windswept twin cedar trees at the top. Suddenly Jeffords' gray threw his head, fought the bit and reared up as he crested the hill between the cedars. *You squirrelly sonofabitch!* Jeffords swore under his breath, jerked the reins and pulled the horse to a stop, then eased himself out of the saddle. He stood for a moment, holding the horse's reins, as he surveyed the flatland below, until he spotted the dead ram.

"There he is, Jim." Jeffords pointed, "In that thicket of tall brush, right where Randy said it would be. Step down, and let's walk our horses so they don't tromp the ground and destroy any clues or evidence."

They walked and slid down the steep hill, leading their horses by the reins to the bottom where Jeffords tied the gray to tall sagebrush.

Dr. Austin handed his reins to Jeffords. "Tie my horse too, if you don't mind, Sheriff. I want to take a look at what's left of Ben's ram." He walked briskly toward the butchered carcass, then stopped and stood there for a few moments, taking in every detail of the ground, the surrounding brush and grass, then shifted his attention to the ram's awkwardly sprawled position, on its back, feet in the air.

Jeffords tied Austin's horse next to his, then ambled over incuriously for a routine look at another dead animal.

Dr. Austin was down on one knee, his head lowered, intent on his examination of the ram's grinning, lipless mouth.

"Hey Dan, get over here and take a look at this! The ram's lips have been sliced away and his tongue is halfway sliced in two."

"Is he radioactive?" Jeffords asked, as he moved closer.

"I don't know. I haven't geigered him yet."

Suddenly the sun was blocked out by a huge dark gray cloud three hundred feet overhead, slowly floating across the sagebrush-covered land, casting a lengthening shadow over the ground.

Jeffords craned his neck and stared up; and his face drained of color! For a moment panic set in! He'd never seen a cloud that close to the ground—the only cloud in an otherwise perfectly clear twilight sky, where the sun was settling in the west.

Without taking his eyes off the mysterious cloud, Jeffords reached down and tapped Dr. Austin on the back.

"Hold on a minute, Dan, something isn't right with this ram. Its tongue looks weird, like its being surgically worked on even as we speak. Get yourself down here and take a look."

Jeffords tapped Austin again, harder this time. Austin stood up and glared at him. "What?" he growled with irritation.

Jeffords was staring up and didn't answer.

Slowly Austin's gaze shifted up, and he gasped, "Sweet Jesus!"

The cloud slowly eased into position directly overhead. A brilliant light beam instantly shot down and completely enveloped them.

Jeffords stiffened. He didn't cotton to the idea of doing nothing! A knotted muscle rippled in his neck. He swiftly reached down, loosened the strap on his 357 magnum and with a swift fluid movement drew it from the holster.

Dr. Austin threw up a hand. "Don't!" he shouted. But the warning came too late!

Jeffords' 357 was in his hand. The revolver's muzzle lifted and roared as he squeezed off six rounds in rapid succession directly into the cloud.

"Goddamnit Dan, put that gun away or they'll kill us just like they did old Ben."

Jeffords didn't pay any attention. He quickly ejected six empty shell casings, pulled a bullet from his belt and started to reload the empty chambers.

Dr. Austin grabbed Jeffords' gun hand and jerked the 357 away. "Knock it off!" he shouted and stuck the empty revolver back in Jeffords' holster. "I don't think they mean us any harm. If they wanted us dead, you can bet your ass we'd be dead! Hang tough until we find out what's going on. They've got us by the balls, Buddy—we can't fight 'em and we sure as heck can't outrun 'em even on horses! Where the hell did it come from anyway?"

"I don't know," Jeffords replied, with a deep breath from the bottom of his gut. "The damned thing just materialized out that deep arroyo." He pointed.

Dr. Austin knew there was nothing in current American space technology that could duplicate that brilliant light beam, as bright as burning magnesium. The cloud was obviously under some kind of intelligent control.

"Well, no matter. There's nothing we can do now except do what we're told—and if we happen to live through this weird ordeal, we'll know a whole lot more about the mutilators!"

"How do you know it's the mutilators?" Jeffords asked. "You have no way of knowing that."

"Oh no? Well my friend, if you have any doubts I think you are in for a reality check!"

Jeffords' head jerked up and he gazed at Dr. Austin, and in that glance they exchanged there was certainty on one side and fear on the other.

✝

Deputy Sheriff Jake Henline was at his wits end! After a frustrating morning plagued by several emergencies at the sheriff's office, every one concerning butchered livestock, phones ringing, Levi-clad ranchers driving up in battered pickup trucks, stomping in, red faced with their fists a shakin', demanding some kind of police action and protection. Enough! Jake slammed his office door shut and phoned Randy Johnson.

As soon as Randy answered, Jake growled, "Where the hell is the Sheriff? I need him back here in town—now!"

Randy detected total disgruntlement in Jake's voice and said, "Whoa, Jake, stay cool my good man, you're going to blow a gasket. Last time I saw him, he and Dr. Austin galloped south on a couple of Ben's borrowed horses to inspect Ben's butchered ram."

"When was that?" Jake asked.

"About ten o'clock."

"Goddamn it, Randy, it's three o'clock! They should've been done by now, and on their way back. It's a damn circus over here. I need the Sheriff."

"Maybe they are back. You haven't heard from either of them?"

"Not a word. "I've radioed Dan's patrol car several times but got no answer."

"Why don't you call Neal Harmon at Ben's place," Randy suggested, "and ask him where they are. He's keeping an eye on things over there."

"Who is Neal Harmon?"

"He's an investigator from the AG's office in Boise. He's waiting for the Atomic Energy Commission's people coming to pick up Ben's body. Do you have Ben's phone number?"

"Yeah," Jake replied.

"Anything I can do to help?" Randy offered.

Jake sighed. "Right now I don't think there's anything anyone can do. The ranchers are getting so scared and worked up they may start shooting each other. I'll call Mr. Harmon and see if he knows the sheriff's whereabouts. It's urgent that I get in touch with the him."

"Good luck, Jake," Randy said. "If you need me, I'll be here at my ranch."

There was a slight pause before Jake responded. "Randy, would it be too much trouble for you to meet me at Ben's place?"

"When?"

"In a couple of hours—and Randy bring your pistol. We may have to organize a search party. The other deputies are scattered all over the county."

"I understand. I'll meet you at Ben's ranch."

†

Neal Harmon seated at Ben's kitchen table jotted a few notes about his investigations in Twin Falls County, which he planned to review with his boss, David Randall, when he returned to Boise.

When a loud knock came on the front door Neal answered it. The man standing there might as well been a billboard, he was that obvious—tailored dark suit, crispy starched white shirt, conservative tie, lean cheeks, and an almost imperceptible bulge at the waist where Neal could see the butt of a revolver.

"Are you Neal Harmon?"

"I am."

"I'm John Jones, here to pick up the body of one Ben Summers." He flipped open his wallet and flashed his credentials so quickly Neal couldn't make out the department.

John Jones? A phony name! Neal stepped out on the porch and pointed. "He's over there in the pasture. Do you want me to take you to him?"

"That won't be necessary," Jones replied. His voice was a subdued baritone, his straight back and broad shoulders gave him an air of authority. "My two highly trained specialists know what to do."

Neal studied those men standing by the side of the unmarked, windowless navy-gray van, its rear doors open. They were dressed in bulky, dark blue head-to-toe coveralls of some kind, their faces masked, each wearing gloves and heavy boots.

Jones shouted, "He's over there in the pasture, boys. Use the stretcher."

One of the men pulled a stretcher from the truck and they quickly walked to the pasture.

"So, Mr. Jones," Neal asked, "Are you with the Atomic Energy Commission?"

"They shuffle me around to different agencies," Jones answered evasively. "How about you, Mr. Harmon?"

"I'm with the Idaho Attorney General's office in Boise. Do you need me to sign anything official before you take Ben's body away?"

Jones shook his head. "That won't be necessary. It's merely routine."

"Where are you taking Ben?" Neal asked, as he watched Jones' specialists straining to carry Ben's body from the pasture to the truck. They'd concealed the body in some sort of metallic-looking body bag.

Jones didn't answer.

"Are you people planning to perform an autopsy?" Neal probed.

"I'm afraid that's none of your business, Mr. Harmon."

The arrogant bastard! Neal clenched his fists, startled by a rush of anger. *None of my business? The hell it's not!* However he suppressed the anger. "Will you at least call me or the attorney general if you do perform an autopsy—and let us know the results?"

"That's not up to me." Jones responded in a more friendly tone, and with a slight smile. "But I'll see what I can do." With that, he turned on his heel and walked briskly to the truck, which sped off in a cloud of spiraling dust as if there was some great need to be in a hurry.

Chills ran down Jake Henline's neck when Neal Harmon called and advised him that the sheriff had still not returned and some very mysterious people had taken Ben's body away.

"Where did they take him?" Jake asked.

"I'll be damned if I know," Neal answered, But I sure as hell plan to find out when I get back to Boise."

Jake hung up the phone and stroked his chin, pondering what to do next. Something was mighty wrong out at Ben Summers' place if the sheriff wasn't back from his examination of the dead ram! Where the hell was he? Jake knew he had to drive out to Ben's place as fast as he could get there and find out just what the hell was going on.

Though he'd given up smoking, he pulled a cigarette from an open pack in the sheriff's desk drawer and lit up. He puffed on the cigarette like he might never have another one. As he walked out of the office, Dispatcher Beth smiled. "Taken up the weed again?" Jake took a deep lungful of smoke and blew it over her head.

"Yeah."

"What's up, Jake? You look like your grandma just got run over by a train...hold on." She answered an incoming phone call. She looked up. "It's George Atkins. Says one of his cows is missing. Want to talk to him?"

Jake shook his head vigorously and took a long drag on his cigarette.

"He insists," she answered.

"Oh piss on him!"

"You want me to tell him that?" she grinned.

Jake glared at her. "God no!" He was sorry he snapped at Beth, and quickly apologized. "Don't mind me today, Beth. I'm just in a crappy mood! I'm heading out to Ben Summer's place to see if I can find the sheriff."

"Good idea, you're such an ornery old fart today! A little fresh air might put you in a better frame of mind." Beth waved as Jake walked toward the door, and shouted, "Keep in touch."

Jake jumped in his patrol car and gunned it toward the highway, lights flashing, siren wailing. Just three blocks from the sheriff's office a dozen irate ranchers blocked the street. A couple of them carried 30-30 rifles, others carried holstered pistols. They all knew Jake by sight, and Jake would have given anything for a little anonymity right about now!

With a screech of brakes and a long scrape of tires sliding on asphalt, Jake's patrol car skidded to a stop just before slamming into the ranchers. He doused the lights and flipped off the siren, as the inflamed ranchers crowded up to the driver's side, peppering Jake with questions as he stepped out.

Jules Schofield, a tough, grizzled rancher from Hollister, their self-appointed leader, was instantly in Jake's face. "Ten more cattle were killed last night, Jake. Why don't you cops get off your asses and find out what's going on and stop it? Who's doing it? Is it the Russians?"

Before Jake could answer, another shouted, "Why won't my phone work when I see those UFOs zipping around the sky over my ranch? My wife's scared out of her freakin' mind!"

"What causes the power to fluctuate up and down?" someone shouted.

Another hollered, "Where the hell's the Air Force? Why don't them fighter planes from Mountain Home Air Force Base shoot down them sonofabitchin' UFOs?"

"Quiet down! Knock it off! All of you!" Jake shouted, waving his hands. "Tomorrow afternoon we'll have an informational meeting at the high school auditorium. We'll address all of your concerns then."

"Will the Sheriff be there?" someone called out.

Jake didn't answer that. Instead, resolve hardened his tone. "We're not walking away from this, believe me." He held up his hands. "Hey guys, I know you have lots of questions, but don't panic. That's not going to solve anything. Stay calm. Right now Sheriff Jeffords, Dr. Austin and a state investigator are chasing down some promising leads. They'll be back here with some answers before the day is out. We'll sort it all out for our meeting tomorrow! So please, go on home. You're not helping the situation by milling around here in the street. In the meantime, if anything newsworthy breaks, we'll broadcast it over the local radio station."

"Does that mean help is on the way, Jake?" Jules Schofield pressed. "Will we find out who's killing our cattle?"

Jules was a hard sell! Jake nervously eyed the circle of ranchers and forced a smile. "Of course, Jules. Just be patient and give us a little time."

"Let's say we buy this bullshit," Jules growled, "We still want to know who's killing and butchering our cattle!"

Jake rolled his eyes. Oh for God's sake, Jules, give it a rest and get the hell out of my way. I've got work to do."

"Not until we get some straight answers," Jules insisted.

"That's enough, goddamn it!" Jake exploded. "Get the hell out of my way, Jules, or I'll kick your ass up between your shoulder blades—and take these others with you!"

Sullenly Jules backed away from the patrol car, and nodded for the others to do the same.

Jake waved, climbed back in his car and sped off toward Ben Summers' ranch, siren wailing, lights flashing. Half way there, he flinched as a staticky radio call blurted in from Beth. "Jake, Billy Gonzales just called in. One of his large Angus breeding bulls is missing."

"Who took it, mutilators or rustlers?" Jake asked wearily, hoping it was rustlers. He could catch and deal with rustlers!

"Who knows?" Beth replied. "Last night Billy locked the bull in an enclosed, gated pasture so no one could take him. Billy assured me there was no way he could get out."

"Well how the hell did he get out then?" Jake growled, totally frustrated.

"That's what Billy wants you to find out!"

15

DR. JIM AUSTIN HADN'T EXPECTED anything like this! He stiffened and his eyes went wide as he stared up at the huge dark cloud hovering over them, knowing it was more than a mere weather phenomenon. They were encased in a light beam coming directly from an alien spaceship, which emitted a low humming sound.

Bewildered, Sheriff Jeffords stepped to the edge of the light and tried to push a fist through it. It was strong as steel. He rubbed his knuckles and knew they were trapped. "They've got us, Jim," then blurted, "What do we do now?"

Austin held up a hand. "Shh!" There was a movement, a shadow, a breezy swishing sound. There was movement. A shadow came across the ground toward them. Squinting Austin made out the form of a man dressed in black, his right hand held up in a sign of peace. Breathless, Austin and Jeffords just stood there silent. For a moment nothing happened.

Then the alien spoke. "Good afternoon, gentlemen." And he spoke English with a perfect American accent!

He appeared fit for a middle-aged man, straight, muscular, with a distinguished mane of shining white hair which contrasted with his one piece, black spandex-type outfit, from his neck to the tops of his shined black boots.

"I'm sorry if we frightened you, but you interrupted our work." His voice was smooth and calm, inviting trust. Before the stranger could say another word, Jeffords glared angrily at him.

"What are you doing here? This property belongs to Ben Summers. I'm going to have to arrest you for trespassing until we can figure this out."

The man just stood there not moving a muscle. "I don't think that's a good idea, Sheriff."

Jeffords, irritated and confused by the man's non-compliance, lunged, arms outstretched to take him down. He came up empty. There was nothing there! Dumbfounded, Jeffords stared at his empty hands, then swiveled his head around searching for the elusive alien.

"Where'd he go?" Jeffords asked, now totally confused, wondering how in the hell a man just disappears into thin air.

Dr. Austin knew at that moment the stranger wasn't a body of flesh and bones, but some kind of illusion or apparition, a projection in the form of a person, almost like a 3-D movie character—*Maybe a hallucination!*

"Damn it, Dan!" Austin growled, "Settle your ass down! The man wants to communicate with us, so let's find out what this is all about!"

Austin's warning came at Jeffords like noises muffled by a fog. But deep down he knew Jim was right—*and maybe he could get them out of this situation alive.*

Suddenly, out of nowhere the alien reappeared in exactly the same spot as before.

"I'm sorry about that," Dr. Austin apologized. "Sheriff Jeffords is a lawman..."

"It's all right, Doctor," the stranger nodded calmly. "I know about Sheriff Jeffords, and about you too."

How could that be? Austin thought, but he let it go. "May I ask who you are and where you come from?"

"Certainly. My name in your language is probably too difficult for you to pronounce, so please, call me Captain John. It's a common English name I selected at random."

"How is it you speak our language so well?" Dr. Austin asked.

"For several years we've monitored your planet's radio and television transmissions through our unique computerized translation system. From listening and watching we've been able to translate and learn your language and much about your culture, though it is rather barbaric by our standards." He followed up, almost by way of apology, "Barbaric though your language and culture may be, to us your planet appears to be the most beautiful in the heavens—a haven of peace and tranquility. But gentlemen, under that deceiving façade, we know your true condition. Earth people are predisposed to war and killing. We've hoped that would change eventually."

"Does that make us so much different from your people?" Dr. Austin asked curiously.

"Not really," came Captain John's reply. "We've had our share of wars."

"Can you tell us where you come from?"

Captain John nodded. "From a planet very similar to this one on the far side of the Milky Way galaxy."

That statement surprised Dr. Austin. "We're also in that galaxy."

"Yes you are, Doctor," acknowledged Captain John. "We could almost be neighbors, were it not for the extremely vast distance that separates our two planets. Though you earth people can observe the Milky Way with your naked eyes on a clear night, it's not possible for you to see our planet even with your most powerful telescopes."

"Why is that?" Dr. Austin asked.

"There are bright star clusters and hundreds of thousands of massive stars and dust swirls of hot ionized gas, creating an almost impenetrable wall between our two planets. We confine our travels exclusively within the Milky Way which we've been exploring for many years searching for other habitable planets. Though the Milky Way is huge, its nearby neighbor, the one your astronomers call the Andromeda galaxy, is even larger. We don't really know very much about it, though we have skirted its outer edges."

Jeffords stared at the alien; his anger had passed, replaced by doubt, incredulity. He started to say something—and Austin held up a hand and glared at Jeffords with a look that said, *you're not making this easy for me!*

"That's most interesting, Captain," Dr. Austin said. "Can you tell us how long it took you to get here?"

Captain John hesitated. "I could—but you would not understand. Time and distance as earth people measure it means nothing to us. We do not use the same measurement standards that you do. Expressed in your terms the Milky Way itself is a hundred twenty thousand light years across. That being said, can you imagine how difficult it would be for us to navigate our way around this vast universe using your antiquated measurement system?"

"No, Captain. I can't imagine it at all," Dr. Austin answered honestly. "But it does raise a couple of questions in my mind. In this vast universe in which you travel, what type of propulsion system do you use, and how is it possible for you to appear and reappear from one place to another as you have just done?"

"I'm afraid I'm not at liberty to disclose the workings of our propulsion system other than to say we have overcome the force you call gravity, mastered magnetic levitation, and developed it into a power you would find difficult to believe. Concerning appearing and reappearing, we've finally developed dematerialization into an exact science."

Dr. Austin stared at him, puzzled. "I'm not familiar with that term."

"Then let me try to explain it to you. In your terms it means the disappearance of a person, animal or object at one place and reappearance at another place some distance away. We sometimes call it teleportation."

Captain John noted a brief expression of doubt on Dr. Austin's face when he said, "Are you saying you can make yourself and your ship invisible?"

"Yes."

"And you expect us to believe that?"

"Believe what you wish, Doctor!" the Captain snapped, his smile disappearing.

Dr. Austin spread his hands apologetically and said, "I'm sorry," and pursued the matter no further; but a wild thought flashed through his mind—*this dematerialization thing might explain how animals are lifted from the ground, butchered, then returned to the ground and no footprints are ever found around any of the carcasses!*

Dr. Austin shifted his weight, pursed his lips and asked quietly, "Have you come across any inhabited planets in your travels?"

"Oh, my yes!" Captain John answered positively as his smile returned. "Worlds without number!"

Dr. Austin's eyes went wide. "With advanced life forms?"

"Yes, certainly. Like us in many ways. Some further advanced in their technology than we are, others rather quaint—but all are in an evolutionary process as they try to perfect a utopian state."

"How about your planet, Captain?" Dr. Austin asked hoping he was not being too intrusive.

Captain John shook his head sadly. "Ah, my friend, like earth's civilization where war has been prevalent since its beginning; we've also had our conflicts over the centuries. It's rather ironic that after we finally learned to live together in peace and harmony, a huge meteor crashed into our planet. Nearly all living things were destroyed, most of our people, our plants, animals, everything. However, a few of us managed to survive."

Sheriff Jeffords remained silent as the conversation continued, unable to fully comprehend what he was hearing. Like a college freshman trying to absorb the fundamentals of philosophy or physics, he tried to visualize other planets, space travel and aliens now butchering cattle in Twin Falls County! He listened, trying to stave off panic, and learn more about this person claiming to be from another planet. He rubbed his face, strain showing in his eyes, as he stared contemptuously at Captain John, who caught the look.

"Something on your mind, Sheriff? You appear a bit confused—perhaps a little troubled?"

Jeffords forced a smile, took a deep breath, and said, "I'm okay. Just a little bit lost, that's all. If you'll pardon my skepticism, Captain, I'm just not sure I can believe some of the things you are telling us."

"That's quite understandable. I'd probably be skeptical too, were I in your shoes," Captain John responded patiently." I sense you have a question. What is it?"

"It's more of a personal matter—and I don't want to offend you."

"Just go ahead and say what's on your mind."

"Since you've learned our language and seem to understand our culture, you may also know it's my job to be suspicious. So I must ask if you had anything to do with killing Ben Summers!"

Jesus! Can't he get off Ben's case for five minutes? Dr. Austin shook his head in exasperation, cringed and opened his mouth, unsure what to say to hinder Captain John's anger, which he assumed was coming.

Captain John waved him off. "It's all right, Dr. Austin. I'll answer the Sheriff's question. "Yes, I did," he answered candidly. "Is that what you wanted to hear?"

The Captain's admission raised Jeffords' hackles! He stared at him and growled, "You're actually confessing that you're guilty of murder? May I ask why you murdered Ben?"

"Be careful with your allegations, Sheriff," Captain John hissed a warning, in a scathing tone, "especially the crime of murder. You don't have all the facts. You weren't there—and before you say anything further, let me reveal to you my perfectly legal justification for taking Ben Summers life. I'm not confessing to any such thing as murder! I am quite dismayed that you'd jump to such a conclusion, considering that I have presented myself to you in such a manner I had hoped would be something you could grasp and understand."

Captain John's frank answer stunned Jeffords, almost as if he was contradicting himself from one sentence to the next.

"Legal justification?" Jeffords asked. "What the hell are you talking about?"

"You mean to tell me you haven't figured it out yet?" Captain John retorted sharply.

"Figured what out?" Jeffords sneered.

"Ben Summers broke the agreement, though he may not have known anything about it."

Jeffords' head jerked up as if he'd been slapped. With a startled look, he asked, "agreement? What agreement? Old Ben didn't mention anything to me about any agreement. He was just a piss-poor old sheep rancher."

"So he was," Captain John nodded in agreement, then followed with a remark that stunned both Jeffords and Austin. "Are you so naïve as to believe your government doesn't know we are here?"

That statement left Jeffords speechless, so Dr. Austin jumped in. "Are you telling us our government is aware of your presence—they know you are here butchering livestock and killing people?"

Captain John didn't even blink! "Of course they do! They agreed to let us take the animals we need for our purposes. Unfortunately, what was intended by us as a friendly visit quickly mutated into a definitive show down."

To Jeffords this sounded completely preposterous. "Who is this 'they' you refer to? Our government in Washington?"

"Yes."

Jeffords shook his head. "I don't believe you or any of this nonsense!"

"I don't care whether you believe me or not, Sheriff," Captain John snapped, with a cynical, razor-edged voice. "Your government really had no choice. In our verbal agreement we asserted that we would not harm your planet or any of its inhabitants as long as no hostile action was taken against us."

"Harm our planet?" Jeffords squinted. "What the hell are you talking about?"

"We have enough weapons to destroy almost every living thing on your planet in the blink of an eye. But I assure that's not our intent. It was most unfortunate that Ben Summers took hostile action and fired on us. We responded immediately and with force. Your law books call that self defense, do they not?"

Jeffords was at a loss for words.

For some reason, Captain John's confession of an agreement with the U.S. government resonated with Dr. Austin. Yet he wondered if the alien was pulling some kind of ruse? Could his revelation of an agreement be true, or just some wild fabrication to justify his presence in Idaho? Maybe Captain John was lying through his teeth, and maybe the two of them were gullible dimwits to accept Captain John's story at face value.

On the other side, Jeffords didn't seem as interested in the treaty as in solving Ben's murder. He wouldn't let it go. "You killed Ben's prize ram and he had every right to protect what was his".

Captain John's smile suddenly disappeared and his voice turned sharp and angry again. He glared at Jeffords. "That's enough, Sheriff!" Captain John growled. "I have neither the time nor the patience to stand here and quibble with you! If anyone, and I mean people, governments, or anything else interferes with or threatens our mission they will be destroyed. We tried to pave a path through the proper channels to accomplish our mission and I am not going to explain this to every law enforcement officer I happen to encounter. Understand?"

That got Jeffords' attention! *Get a grip* he told himself, and he quickly apologized. "I'm sorry, Captain. I meant no disrespect."

Captain John's pleasant friendly smile returned and he threw up both hands up in appeasement. "Gentlemen, gentlemen, I'm just trying to explain our actions so you'll know we actually come in peace. We assumed your government would agree to let us select a few domestic animals for our purposes in exchange for your peoples' safety. Whether or not your government informed the populace of the agreement is of no concern to us."

"But sir," Sheriff Jeffords lightly protested, "people around here are getting scared. I've never been advised of any such agreement by anyone in our government."

"And you won't be either, Sheriff," Captain John said. "Perhaps your government is worried about the possibility of creating a panic of global proportions if such information leaks out to the public."

Captain John was silent for a moment as the two men stared at him, trying to sort out the information they'd received, wondering if he had anything else to spring on them.

He smiled. "Concerning this agreement we've discussed, I strongly caution both of you to realize the grave danger you will place yourselves in, from your own government, if you so much as mention the agreement or your encounter with me to the press, law enforcement agencies or the military."

Jeffords looked disgusted. "Are you saying our own government would bump us off?"

Captain John smiled, but only briefly, then nodded. "What other choice would they have?"

"Are you serious? Our own government would kill us?" Jeffords asked.

"I don't have to answer that, Sheriff. You know the workings of your own government better than I do. Figure it out for yourself! Anything else?"

"Yes," Dr. Austin said, "and I hope I won't offend you, Captain, but this poor ignorant country doctor has to ask the big question. With all the other planets you've visited why did you single out our earth and travel light years to get here—just to kill and butcher domestic livestock? That's something I absolutely cannot understand!"

Captain John chuckled. "I wondered when you'd get around to inquiring about that!"

16

CAPTAIN JOHN, SPEAKING IN THE FRIENDLY manner of a small-town university professor, said, "Since you are so curious to learn why we are killing and mutilating animals, may I ask if either of you would care to hazard a guess?"

Both men shook their heads negatively.

"I assume you've both observed some of the butchered animals and searched for clues as to what happened to them?"

Both men nodded.

"What type of animals were they?"

Dr. Austin said, "The ones I autopsied were cattle—all healthy well-fed animals."

Captain John fixed Jeffords with his gaze. "And how about you, Sheriff?"

"Same as Jim. Prime beef—however two of my deputies did investigate a couple of dead horses."

"What kind of horses?"

"Pure bred racing horses."

"Did the two of you develop any ideas or theories as to how or why they were selected?"

Dr. Austin scratched his chin. "I assumed that whoever was killing the animals selected only the strongest and healthiest animals they could find?"

"Aaah," Captain John said, rubbing his hands with an exaggerated air. "Brilliant deduction, Doctor!"

Dr. Austin's eyes went wide. "But why would…"

Captain John held up a hand. "Please, let me finish. We need them! You recall I told you about the giant meteor that crashed into our planet? It devastated nearly everything, cities, people, animals and vegetation. Our domestic animals are similar to yours in form, but quite different genetically. Something happened within the herds after the meteor strike and the animals started dying off. After extensive research, our scientists came up with a solution to save what few animals we have and increase the size of our herds. If we can obtain crucial body parts from healthy animals, like we've found here, we can use them to…"

"Are you talking about cloning?" Dr. Austin interrupted, his eyebrows elevated.

Captain John stared at him in surprise. "Do you know something about cloning?"

Dr. Austin nodded. He did indeed! Well, as much as was currently known in scientific circles. He swallowed, silent for a moment, as he let his mind quickly journey, conjuring up images formed from experiences some years ago in medical school at the University of Utah in Salt Lake City where he studied medicine. Dr. Orville Mortimer, head of the university's med school promoted a theory that the individual cell of any organism, plant or animal, might contain a full genetic blueprint for the entire organism. This, he claimed, could be the first step in the cloning process. Doc Mortimer however was very cautious how he worded his lectures, always providing more questions than answers, because several of his colleagues believed cloning to be impossible, and even if it was, they agreed, it would be unethical, perhaps even immoral!

Dr. Austin was intrigued by Mortimer's cloning theories then, and even more so now that cloning was gaining respect in scientific circles around the globe on several fronts, even to believing it might help develop healthier breeds of animal life.

"Cloning? What the hell is cloning?" Jeffords piped up, having no desire to listen to some long-winded diatribe on something he knew nothing about and cared even less.

Dismayed by this temporary annoyance, Jeffords' curt remark brought another disapproving scowl from Captain John. "Cloning is a sophisticated scientific method we've almost perfected which we hope will save our people from starvation and ultimately from extinction! It's the only known option open to us, Sheriff. So let me assure you we're not playing some cops and robbers game, and we're not here on a pleasure cruise. We are soldiers on a mission from our world to bring life resources back to our planet."

Jeffords felt a surge of resentment at the rebuke, but kept his volatile temper under control and his mouth shut. He gave Dr. Austin a funny look, like he was starting to get the picture, but couldn't quite figure all of it out. Yet.

Captain John gave Jeffords a sardonic smile. "I sense your resentment, Sheriff, but we're not the bad guys and certainly don't want to become your enemy! There are other intergalactic travelers in the universe!—rapacious raiders traveling throughout the cosmos. They strike fast, pillage, plunder and kill. They take what they want and move on, leaving death and destruction in their wake. Luckily they've been a little slow in developing their navigational skills; however, if they accidentally discover this beautiful planet of yours, beware! They will strike without warning."

His voice fell. "They raided our planet once but we easily defeated them because of our advanced early detection and weapons systems. So far they've never returned."

"Interesting," Dr. Austin said, "But I think we got off the track, Captain. "You were going to explain your cloning process."

Captain John nodded. "You're right, Doctor..." Suddenly he raised both hands requesting silence. He cocked his head listening to something neither Dr. Austin nor Jeffords could hear. The Captain looked skyward, shook his head and muttered something in a strange unintelligible language neither man could understand.

Dr. Austin's alarm at this strange interruption abated when Captain John said, "Sorry about that, gentlemen. I've received word that we must leave this place very shortly. One of your military installations picked us up on their radar."

"Mountain Home Air Force Base?" Dr. Austin asked.

"No. A place called NORAD, sometimes called Cheyenne Mountain. They're scrambling some fighter jets at Hill Air Force Base to do a fly over."

"Hill is down in northern Utah," Dr. Austin said.

Captain John nodded. "We know where all your military installations are located. Time is critical so let me finish up then we must be on our way. We've overstayed our welcome. Our allotted time from your government ended yesterday. The problem with Ben Summers delayed us."

"Are you afraid of our fighter planes?" Sheriff Jeffords scoffed.

Captain John shook his head. "Not really. But we want to avoid any confrontation with your military that would cause embarrassment or draw media attention to your government's involvement with us."

Captain John turned his attention back to the matter at hand. "Our scientists discovered that the electrochemical pattern of a living organism, whether it be animal or plant, is found in every embodiment of cells. We are now hoping to successfully clone a cow through cell reproduction. Such cloning also calls for the equivalent of a blood supply."

"Ah ha!" exclaimed Dr. Austin."That's the reason no blood has ever been found in the carcasses of mutilated animals."

"Exactly! This procedure, known as reproductive cloning presents some difficulties and challenges for us, even barriers to the clonal development of animals. However our scientists tell us there is no reason an entire clone can't be grown and kept in storage and used as needed. I'm not sure I understand or agree. I am only a soldier, not a scientist, but I think you get the general drift."

My God! Dr. Austin thought. *That's their motive! They're actually selecting and killing animals so they can use their tissue and blood for cloning purposes.* He opened his mouth to speak, but Captain John interrupted.

"Your range cattle have been bred for this rough western land, and are ideally suited for the extremes in temperature, both hot and cold, found on our planet. Mixing your animals with ours, through the cloning process may be the solution to our food shortage."

Jeffords had difficulty understanding any of this. He didn't have the vaguest notion what cloning entailed. Part of his irritation was based on a vague irrational threat he felt to his position as sheriff—the man entrusted to apprehend and arrest cattle rustlers and thieves. But he kept quiet, knowing that if Captain John left with what he came for the threat to his authority would vanish with him.

Captain John, now speaking faster, said, "After we select a suitable animal for cloning, we beam it aboard our ship. It is euthanized and its body parts and blood are surgically removed. We then return the carcass to the same area from which it was taken."

"U-u-u euthanize them?" Jeffords stuttered.

Captain John nodded. "Certainly! It's more humane to kill them before we take their body parts, don't you think? I probably shouldn't have told you any of this. But now you know our purpose for coming here. I firmly believe both of you will be discreet in disseminating this information, if that's what you decide to do. But I caution you to remain silent. Your lives may be in danger if you disclose this information to your government officials. Of course the decision is entirely up to you. It makes no difference to us."

Jeffords protested. "How can we keep this information under wraps? Our people want answers..."

Captain John held up a hand. "Keeping this information under wraps as you call it will prevent wide spread panic among your people—and possible bloodshed if our ships are forced to defend themselves."

Jeffords head jerked up. "How many ships do you have?"

"We have two vessels operating in the Idaho area."

"Why two?" Jeffords asked.

"It's a very long, hazardous journey back to our planet, even with our intricate vehicles. Our council is of the opinion that at least one of our ships will make it home with it precious and hopefully life-sustaining cargo."

Dr. Austin started to say something, but again Captain John held up a hand for silence, cocking his head to one side, listening. "Gentlemen, I'm informed fighter planes have scrambled at Hill Air Force Base and will be here in a few minutes. I must leave you now."

Suddenly the light beam snapped off and Dr. Adams and Sheriff Jeffords found themselves standing in the stark Idaho darkness, near their restless horses still tied to tall sagebrush.

Dr. Austin and Sheriff Jeffords watched in awe as the black cloud above them dissipated and a huge circular spacecraft, now fully lighted, revved its engines with a growl that echoed across the range land, and it lifted slowly, straight up like a helicopter. Then the engines stopped, silent propulsion kicked in and the ship grew smaller as it shot with unimaginable speed into the starlit depths of the night sky.

Off in the distance came the roar of three F-15 fighter jets streaking in at tree top level, their afterburners spitting fire. Hitting Mach 2, each plane armed with Sparrow missiles and look down/shoot down radar that could distinguish low-flying moving targets from ground clutter, were on top of Dr. Austin and Sheriff Jeffords before the sound of their roaring jet engines caught up.

"Go get them sonsabitches!" Jeffords cheered, jumping up and down, wildly waving his hat.

Dr. Austin grinned. "I think they're a little late and a dollar short."

Jeffords put his hat on, adjusted it and walked off, following the beam of his flashlight.

"Where are you going?" Dr. Austin called after him.

"To retrieve my pistol!"

That damn gun again!

Jeffords returned a moment later, shoving his pistol into its holster. "I'll be goddamned, Jim. Those sonsabitches even took Old Ben's dead ram with them!"

"Well, maybe they also want to clone some sheep," Dr. Austin said.

Jeffords brows furrowed with his frustration. "You're not buying into that cloning bullshit, are you?"

"Yeah, Dan, I am. It sounded logical to me. I think Captain John was being honest with us. However, that leaves us in one hell of a tight spot. Now we must decide what to do the information he shared with us."

Sheriff Jeffords swallowed hard. "What do you think will happen if we tell anyone about meeting an alien? Would we be risking our asses—I mean our jobs?"

Dr. Austin looked at him and nodded. "You can count on it, Dan. We'll have to be extremely careful who we tell, if we tell anyone at all. Remember Captain John's warning?"

Jeffords hesitated before answering. "Well, I think we've got to tell somebody," he said somberly. "If you're saying we should remain silent you're asking for big trouble."

"I'm open for suggestions," Austin said.

Jeffords thought for a few moments. "How about telling Neal Harmon what happened to us?"

"Now there's an idea! He's the only person we know who could really do anything about it—and I'm sure he'd handle it discreetly."

Jeffords felt his heart accelerate. "Do you think we should?"

"It's up to you, Dan. You represent the law. I'm just a private citizen. Think it through, and if you feel good about it, let's do it! But for right now let's head back to Ben's place. People are probably already out searching for us."

✝

Neal Harmon paced nervously back and forth between the kitchen and living room in Ben Summers' home. He looked at a picture of Ben's wife hanging on the wall. She was a very pretty young woman when the photo was taken. He wondered what kind of woman she might have been and how she and Ben had lived.

Daylight was fading quickly and Neal was worried. Where the hell were Dr. Austin and Sheriff Jeffords? They'd been gone well over three hours. He couldn't wait any longer to take action. He picked up the phone and called Randy Johnson and expressed his deep concern for the missing men.

"Well," came Randy's deep voice, "I'll come over and we'll saddle some horses and go look for them. Deputy Jake Henline is also headed out that way. He ran into some troublesome ranchers in town or he'd have been there sooner. He's really worried about the sheriff."

"Between the three of us," Neal said, "I think we can find our missing friends. See you shortly."

Relieved that help was on the way Neal sat down, turned the TV on to *Breaking News*. Idaho's Governor Stan Nordgren was starting a press conference in Boise.

"I have a brief statement concerning the rash of animal killings then I'll take a few questions." Looking grim he said, "This week my office has received eighty five phone calls reporting animal mutilations. My experienced investigators are following several promising new leads which will help us identify the mutilators and bring them to justice." He started to say something more, but newsmen and women interrupted, all shouting questions at the same time, clamoring for more detailed information.

The governor held up both hands to simmer the raucous shouting. "One at a time!" When the racket subsided he pointed. "Charlie Murdock. You have a question?"

"Yes sir, Governor. What are the federal authorities doing? Have you been in contact with the FBI or the military?"

"I have."

"Well? What did they have to say?" Murdock pressed.

"They told me they were not involved in the matter since it's a state crisis, but if we need any assistance they would see what they could do."

"In other words," Murdock said, "they're doing nothing?"

"What can they do, Charlie?"

Murdock shook his head disgustedly. "Well, someone ought to do something!"

"Well, Charlie," the governor responded cautiously, "we're open for suggestions."

Governor Nordgren took a few more questions which he diplomatically deflected. Then his aide threw up a hand. "That's all for now. The governor will keep you posted!"

ϯ

Randy Johnson, in a battered cowboy hat, strode out of Ben's barn, leading two horses and tied them next to his horse, hitched to the fence. He glanced at his watch, which he could barely see in the settling darkness.

"Where the hell is Deputy Henline?" Neal called from the porch.

Randy shrugged. "He'll be here, Neal. Some irate pistol-packing ranchers made it a necessary delay if Jake wanted to prevent bloodshed!"

"Well, he'd better get here in the next fifteen minutes or it'll be too damn dark to find anyone. You might as well come in the house. I've got some coffee brewing."

No sooner had Randy poured himself a cup, than the headlights of Jake Henline's patrol car swung across the porch of Ben's house, scissoring through a cloud of dust. Jake slid to a stop behind Sheriff Jeffords' parked police cruiser. He stepped out into the cool evening breeze and looked around. It was already too dark to see the distant mountains. Venus was rising in the east, a sharp fleck against the velvet sky.

Randy, coffee cup in hand, opened the screen door. "That you, Jake?"

"Yeah. Did they get back yet?"

"Not yet," Randy said. "Get in here and grab a cup of coffee then we'll ride out and see if we can find them."

Jake stepped up onto the porch and noticed old Aussie sprawled in a corner sound asleep He hadn't even barked or growled an alarm that someone was coming. It was as if the life had gone out of him. He was probably dreaming of woolies and of thrilling outruns getting away from the big tough old ram that wasn't the least bit intimidated by a mere herd dog, and of Old Ben's hand gestures directing him to chase the sheep into the pens. How terribly he missed Ben, wondering where he was. Wherever he was Aussie wanted to be there with him and feel that gentle wrinkled old hand rub his head. He whimpered, his legs jerking in his troubled sleep.

Neal brought Jake a steaming cup of coffee and handed it him.

"Jake," Randy said, "This is Neal Harmon, from the Attorney General's office in Boise."

"Pleased to meet you, Mr. Harmon."

"It's Neal. Pleased to meet you, Jake."

155

That introduction left Jake a bit uneasy, wondering who was in charge of things, the honchos up in Boise, or the local sheriff.

Randy ushered them both to chairs at the kitchen table.

"Neal," Jake asked, "Did the Doc or the Sheriff say anything to you about how long they'd be gone?"

"No," Neal said.

"Do you have any idea where they could be?" Jake asked.

"Not a clue. You and Randy know this area better than I do. All I know is they went to take a look at Ben's dead ram. Seemed pretty routine to me. Maybe they got lost."

"Not a chance," Randy chimed in. "Dan knows this area like the back on his hand."

"Mighty damn strange," Jake said, rubbing his chin. "Why didn't you go with them, Neal?"

"They wanted me to stay here to turn Ben's body over to the Atomic Energy people coming down from Arco."

"Did you?"

Neal nodded affirmation. "That was a strange outfit! Something fishing going on up there in Arco. I'd pay good money to know what their connection is with these animal mutilations!"

Jake started to say something when Aussie growled and started barking ferociously. Jake sat his coffee down. He didn't say anything, merely indicated with a backward nod of his head that Randy and Neal were to follow him.

✝

Dr. Austin and Sheriff Jeffords urged their horses along the darkened trail leading to Ben Summers' well lighted house. The horses picked their way instinctively and carefully, Dr. Austin leading the way, followed by Sheriff Jeffords.

Dr. Austin clucked his tongue and urged his horse to a faster pace. For a moment he shut his eyes, wondering if he'd really seen and talked to someone named Captain John—and about something the Captain said, which stuck in his mind. *The others—out there beyond the horizon, exploring, looking for a planet like earth, ripe for the picking. If Captain John had found earth, it wouldn't be difficult for others roaming around the universe to do the same.*

Dr. Austin heard Aussie barking in the distance. He turned in the saddle. "C'mon, Dan. We're almost home." He couldn't see Jeffords very well in the dark, but the man hadn't said a word since Captain John zoomed away in his space ship.

"Are you awake back there?" Austin called.

No answer.

The waking nightmare of reality rubbed against Jeffords' brain like coarse grit driving him into a state he'd never before experienced. There was little likelihood he would ever be the same again. He wondered if Jim Austin's thoughts were like his own. His mind drifted. His exhaustion was physical, emotional, mental. It was as if some sort of sorcery was at work, like a spell had been cast over him by an alien who didn't seem to like Jeffords very much!

Deputy Jake Henline, Randy Johnson and Neal Harmon stood on Ben Summer's front porch and watched them ride in.

"Where the hell have you been?" were the first words out of Jake Henline's mouth!

17

DAN JEFFORDS DISMOUNTED AND EX-changed a scowling glance with his deputy. "Don't you speak to me with that tone of voice, goddamnit, Jake! Who the hell do you think you are?"

Jake's jaw was set and he forced himself to keep his tongue in check, took a deep breath and apologized. "I'm sorry Dan. It's just that I've been worried about you. We've got problems in town..."

"Well? I left you in charge. Why the hell didn't you take care of things?"

"Whoa! Take it easy everybody," Neal Harmon said. "We've all had a rough day. C'mon into the house and let's have a cup of coffee and talk and figure out what's going on." Neal ushered the four men to chairs around the kitchen table and poured them each a cup of steaming coffee, then offered up a fifth of Jim Beam and poured a liberal shot of soul-warming whiskey into their coffee.

All eyes, full of anticipation, focused on Dr. James Austin, who seemed rather upbeat, almost jubilant.

"Well, Dr. Austin," Neal said, "You seem none the worse for wear. Do you want to tell us what happened out there today?"

"Just a moment." Dr. Austin leaned over and whispered to Sheriff Jeffords, "Do you want to tell it or shall I?" Jeffords nodded slowly like he didn't care one way or the other. He felt old. Well he was, for a lawman, most of whom retired after twenty years. He was dead tired to the point of exhaustion and had the mother of all headaches. It took him a couple of minutes to figure out what was going down, which thirty years ago he'd have figured out instinctively in a matter of seconds. He was depressed and felt the crawl of uncertainty in his mind about the upcoming revelation to a group of men who hadn't been there to see what he'd seen and hear what he'd heard. He licked his upper lip. "You go ahead and tell it, Jim. Hell, they ain't going to believe a word of it anyway!"

"Are you all right, Sheriff?" Neal asked with concern, noting Jeffords' sullen face appeared changed from just a few short hours ago, and not for the better.

"Yeah, Neal. He's all right," Dr. Austin said. "Just worn thin, that's all,"

"Okay then," Neal said. "Let's move on. Did you find Ben's dead ram?"

"We did, and a lot more. It's so weird I'm still not sure I believe it myself."

"Just spit it out, Doctor," Neal said, "and don't leave out a single detail. I need to know everything that happened."

Dr. Austin, thoughtful for a moment, was seized by the thought he'd somehow been selected by fate to be the first earthling to actually speak to an alien so close he could reach out and touch him. Awed. Overwhelmed. A humbling feeling—but excitement too. He took a long sip of coffee.

"Well?" Neal urged.

"Sheriff Jeffords and I came face to face with the mutilators this afternoon."

"The mutilators?" Neal quickly interrupted. "The honest to god mutilators?"

Randy, Jake and Neal rocked forward in unison, staring with piqued interest.

Dr. Austin nodded, got up and began moving around restlessly, holding his coffee cup in both hands. "A huge spacecraft mysteriously appeared and hovered directly over us as we studied Ben's dead ram. A man came down from the spaceship, seemingly in a strange beam of light and talked to us. He called himself Captain John and told us he was the vessel's commanding officer."

"You're telling us you actually encountered and talked to an alien?" Neal asked incredulously, suddenly feeling a sense of anticipation, a rise in his temperature.

"We certainly did!" Dr. Austin smiled, then paused for a moment. "Well, at least a projection of some kind, an apparition in the form of a man. He was courteous and explained why they killed Ben Summers and also why they are butchering our livestock."

"They what?" Neal asked. "You mean this Captain John gave you such sensitive information about his operations—just like that? Why did he kill Ben Summers? And why are they killing our animals?"

"Captain John said Ben fired his rifle at their spaceship, and they do not tolerate acts of aggression. They kill animals because they need the body parts."

It crossed Neal's mind that Dr. Austin wasn't lying, but perhaps he had been delusional and imagined things that hadn't actually happened. But Jeffords was sitting there at the table and he would have certainly said something if Austin was lying. Neal rubbed his chin, thinking it through.

Dr. Austin noticed Neal's solemn skeptical look. "I sense you don't you believe me, do you?"

"I'm trying really hard to keep an open mind," Neal said. "But it just seems too far fetched to be true—spaceships coming here, aliens killing people and animals?" Neal thumped his fingers on the table. "Go ahead and let's hear the rest of it."

Dr. Austin nodded and recounted precisely what Captain John had described to them about his far off planet and its devastated condition caused by a huge meteor.

When Austin finished Randy Johnson looked tolerantly at him. "Well Jim, what the hell has that got to do with him killing and butchering my horses? I'm not sure I follow you."

"They need the body parts and blood to clone new animals on their planet..."

"They what?" Randy interrupted, his eyes wide. "Again in English. Please!"

Dr. Austin drank down the last of his whiskey-laced coffee. "Well, Randy, to put it in laymen's terms, the aliens believe that using cells from our animals on their devastated herds they can develop a new stronger strain. Some of our scientists call that cloning, some call it gene splicing and others call it genetic engineering."

Randy's head jerked up. Jake Henline and Neal Harmon were stupefied. They all chewed on that for a few moments.

"You mean they're using our butchered animals for cloning? Is that possible?" Jake asked.

"Yeah, Jake, I believe it is possible. Perhaps a few years down the road we may also be able to clone animals right here in the USA."

Jake was puzzled. "But what gives them the right to zoom in here and kill our animals without permission from anyone, especially their owners?"

Dr. Austin knew the question was coming and it provided the opening he needed. "Oh they have all the permission the need!"

Neal Harmon jumped on that! "Did I hear you right? Permission from whom?"

"From the United States government!" Austin said. "The aliens have worked out a secret agreement with the government to take whatever animals the need for their cloning purposes!"

Shock and alarm chased each other across the four startled faces staring at Austin with disbelief.

Sheriff Jeffords sat bolt upright. "Good God, Jim, you're not buying into that cock and bull story that our own government is involved, are you?"

"Yes, Dan! Unlike you I believe everything the alien told us!"

Sheriff Jeffords gritted his teeth angrily, shifted in his chair and growled, "For Christ's sake Jim, get real. I'm warning all of you, you start screwing around with bullshit like this, saying the government is partly responsible for these killings, you'll get us all hung or landed in federal prison!"

Neal threw up a hand. "Hold it, Sheriff. And you Dr. Austin, back up. You just lost me." He stared at Austin, totally staggered at his stunning disclosure. "Run that government cover up accusation by us one more time, just a little slower. You're telling us that our own government has entered into a conspiracy with this Captain John to let him select and butcher our livestock?"

"I am," Dr. Austin said. "I had my doubts at first and didn't believe it, but the more I've thought about it the more I've come to realize that it's entirely possible. It would certainly answer a lot of questions we all have about animal mutilations." Dr. Austin was silent for a moment, sifting ideas. "Perhaps Captain John threatened or intimidated our government into cooperating. Who knows? Anyway, if our government and the aliens are in bed with each other that might explain why the mutilators have never been identified."

Neal fought to keep a look of incredulity from his face, not sure he could believe or accept anything the Doctor was saying.

Dr. Austin noted that strange look and wished there was some way he could imbue Neal and the others with the same kind of enthusiasm he was beginning to feel then maybe they could figure out some way solve this mutilation nightmare and get things back to normal here in Idaho's Magic Valley.

"Think about it, Neal," Dr. Austin continued persuasively. "Hundreds of butchered cattle sprawled out dead on ranches across the entire west—and the only plausible theory advanced by the authorities to date is that predators killed them? Lots of other theories have surfaced and then been discarded—and the blame always comes back to rest on predatory animals? C'mon, does that make any sense? All of us here have seen firsthand the precision surgery that was performed on many of the mutilated animals. We all know this wasn't done by the kind of predators found here in Idaho. The predator theory just doesn't make sense to anyone who has been involved in this investigation. It's only a very convenient explanation that plays well with the public without opening a can of worms."

Before Dr. Austin could respond, Randy Johnson cut in enthusiastically. "By damn, Jim, a government cover up makes more sense to me than any of the nonsense the news media has been trying to shove down our throats! I know for a fact my horses weren't killed by some scrawny coyote."

"And I totally agree with both of you," Jake said. "It has to be a cover up! I investigated several dead animals myself and I hope I never have to see anything like that again. I'm pretty damn sure no predatory animal could have done the kind of butchery I've witnessed. In fact I'd be willing stake my reputation on it."

Neal held up a hand, "All right! Let's move on." He sat there, silent for a few moments, staring at Dr. Austin.

"What are you thinking, Neal?" he asked.

"You've almost convinced me there is a government cover-up—and if that's true I'm really concerned about that other alien ship Captain John told you about.

According to him, both are still hanging around Idaho. How the hell am I going to explain all of this to my boss when I get back to Boise?" He paused for a moment. "Rest assured gentlemen that whatever I decide to tell him your identities will be kept from the public and the press."

Dr. Austin smiled cynically. "I find it's totally ironic that we really have nothing to fear from the aliens, except the loss of a few animals. It's our own government we have to watch out for. If what Captain John told me about a government cover up is true this could get pretty ugly!"

There was silence around the table as it dawned on the men how dangerous Captain John's stunning information could be for all of them—if it leaked out!

Neal nodded. "Ugly is right! Therefore you must not discuss this with anyone. Not a soul. Do you all understand?"

His gaze came to rest on Sheriff Jeffords, who scowled at him. "Is that a problem, Sheriff?" Neal asked.

Jeffords nodded. "Where the hell does that leave me?" Jeffords growled and rubbed a hand abrasively over his face. "This is my jurisdiction and I should have some say in how this situation is handled!"

"It's not your job, Sheriff!" Neal countered. "If our government is involved, and I'm not fully convinced it is, the feds should handle it—professionals, like the FBI."

"Hell no!" Jeffords shook his head and slammed his big fist down on the table. This is my jurisdiction!"

"Not any more its not!" Neal said forcefully. "You let the feds worry about it, unless you want to tangle with them. Do you understand me?"

"Goddamnit Neal, why are you shoving me off into a corner?" Jeffords was a country sheriff. He liked things clear cut, him leading the investigations, and solving the cases—none of this secretive alien conspiracy cloak and dagger stuff. But though he'd never admit it he was smart enough to know that Neal was right. He'd sure as hell come out on the short end if he got in the FBI's way. He finally gave up, exhaled disgustedly and said, "Yeah, Neal. I understand,"

To smooth it over and show the sheriff he was still his friend, Neal said, "Don't worry Sheriff, I'll keep you in the loop so you'll know what's going on."

"How about you, Randy?" Neal asked.

Randy nodded. "No problem. Keep me in the loop too. I've still got horses and cattle to worry about, and I don't want to end up like Ben Summers!"

Neal turned to Jake Henline. "Jake?" Jake nodded. "No problem."

"And you, Doctor?"

"You have my word, Neal."

"Very well," Neal concluded. I think we're finished here. We're all tired and it's been a hell of a day for each one of us."

There was a round of handshakes, then Neal escorted the four men to the front door, where he handed them each a business card with his private Boise telephone number. "If any of you come up with additional information, call me anytime. I mean it. Day or night."

Jake Henline waved and walked to his police cruiser and took off for Twin Falls.

✝

"Wait here, Jim," Jeffords said. "I'll go start my car and warm it up then I'll take you home."

Neal, Randy and Dr. Austin watched him the sheriff walk to his car. Neal took Austin's elbow and they stepped back into the house and he nodded for Randy to follow.

"Something on your mind, Neal?" Austin asked.

Neal nodded. "Tell me, Doctor, is Sheriff Jeffords always so disagreeable—he seems to have a burr under his saddle. What's his problem?"

"I believe I can answer that better than Jim," Randy said. "I've known Dan all my life and I've never seen him like this. I think his experience with the alien was more than he was prepared for, and it got him rattled." He stared at Dr. Austin for a moment. "I wonder, Jim—that beam of light you said was coming from the spaceship—did it completely envelop you and Dan?"

"Yes. Why?"

"Well since his experience with the alien he seems to have had a complete personality change. Yet you seem the same. Can you explain that?"

Dr. Austin was silent for a moment. "I'm not sure. Dan and the alien didn't hit it off very well."

"Meaning?" Randy asked.

"You didn't hear this from me, Randy, but Dan was down right rude to the alien at first, wanting to shoot him and when I stopped him from doing that he wanted to arrest him."

Neal picked up on that. "But Doctor, you got along very well with the alien. Right?"

"I certainly did. I wish I could have spent more time with him."

Neal pondered that. "Randy may be on to something, Doctor. Do you think something in the light beam or the alien himself, or both could have had something to do with the sheriff's weird behavior?"

"How do you mean?" Austin asked.

Neal smiled thinly. "This is kind of far out—but could the alien have cast some kind of spell on him, hypnotized him or something like that?"

Dr. Austin rubbed his chin. "I haven't given it much thought, but I suppose it's a possibility."

Sheriff Jeffords backed his police cruiser to the porch, then opened the driver's door and hollered, "C'mon, Jim. Let's go. I haven't got all night! Neal, you want a ride back to town?"

"No thanks, Sheriff," Neal said. "Randy and I are going to ride the horses back to his place."

Neal and Randy watched Jeffords gun the car down the dirt road to Twin Falls.

Randy flipped off the lights in Ben's house and walked out with Neal to the restless horses tied to the fence.

"Have you come with any ideas about how you're going to tell the honchos up in Boise what happened here today?" Randy asked.

"I've been thinking on it."

"And?"

Neal shook his head. "I'm not sure. I guess I'll have to tell them the truth, but they'll probably think I've lost my mind."

"Well, whatever you do, good luck my friend."

Neal smiled. "I'll need it! Well no matter. When this mess is cleaned up how about getting together for some fly fishing up in the high country?"

Neal climbed aboard his horse.

"Sounds good," Randy said. He put his foot in the stirrup and swung himself into the saddle. "Ready?"

"Lead the way, Randy. I'd get us lost before we're out of sight of the house!"

"Okay," Randy said, "follow me." He lifted the reins, touched heels to the horse's flanks and galloped off toward his ranch, Neal close behind.

✝

The rest of his week in Twin Falls Neal investigated seventy five animal mutilations at several remote ranches. He jotted in his notebook what he'd witnessed first hand—very careful not to mention UFOs, aliens or a government conspiracy. He coordinated his activities with Sheriff Dan Jeffords and his deputies to ensure their cooperation with the attorney general's office.

On his last day in Twin Falls Neal called his boss, Assistant Attorney General David Randall in Boise to give him a verbal summation of his activities.

Randall sounded frustrated. His first question was, "Were you able to identify the mutilators or come up with anything I can pass along to the attorney general? He's getting hammered by the governor and the media."

"Not on the phone, David."

"Why?"

"I don't want you to have a heart attack."

"Bad as that, huh? Tell me anyway!"

"All right, but don't say I didn't warn you. The mutilators are aliens from a far off galaxy."

The line went dead for a few moments. "Are you still there, David? Neal asked.

"Back up. *Aliens.* Did you say aliens?" Randall sputtered.

"Yes sir! Real grade A aliens."

"Oh, come now! Did you see them?"

"No sir. But I met two reliable eye witnesses who did."

"Were they sober?" Randall chuckled lightly.

"Yes sir. One is the Twin Falls County Sheriff and the other is a medical doctor."

Impressed, Randall asked, "Is there more to the story?"

"Much more," Neal said, "But we shouldn't be discussing it on the phone."

"All right," Randall said. "Get in here to my office as soon as you get back to Boise and tell me the rest of it."

✝

Randall neglected to tell Neal that Allan Moen and Larry Spangler, his other two investigators, had also completed their investigations and were on their way back to Boise. They too had also verbally identified the mutilators as aliens! That left Randall in a quandary! *Should I hear their reports before I notify the attorney general or should I notify him now so he can be in on that first briefing?*

He adjusted his spectacles, shook his head, grabbed the phone and called Attorney General Sam Kennerton.

"It's good to hear from you, David," Kennerton said. "Please tell me you've got some good news! The governor is driving me nuts wanting some answers, and I have none to give him."

"Then I think this may interest you! Our three investigators are on their way back to Boise."

"Did they find out who's been killing and butchering our livestock?"

"I think you'll find their reports extremely informative," Randall answered evasively.

"What kind of answer is that?" Kennerton asked. "Did they or didn't they?"

"It's something we shouldn't discuss on the phone." Randall said. "What they have to tell us is highly confidential and should only be talked about behind closed doors."

"Hot damn! Now we're getting someplace!" Kennerton said enthusiastically. "They must have discovered something really important. Right?"

"Yes sir!'

"How soon can we meet with them?"

"In a couple of days!"

"Good. I'll alert Governor Nordgren. You set up the meeting, David, and call me when the investigators are ready!"

18

AN UNEXPECTED EARLY FALL SNOWSTORM blasted in from the west dumping snow on Idaho's lofty mountains then swirled into Boise. At seven a.m. Governor Nordgren answered his home phone and heard Highway Patrol Sergeant Charlie Schneider's gravely voice. "The roads are slick and icy this morning, sir. Shall I come by and pick you up?"

"No thanks, Charlie, I'll drive it," Nordgren said. "I imagine you've got your hands plenty full this morning without chauffeuring me around."

"We are busy, sir. Cars and trucks are smashing into each other. Visibility is almost zero. The airport's closed and schools are cancelled for the day."

"Any fatalities yet?"

"Not yet, sir. But the day's just getting started! Drive carefully, Governor."

The I-84 freeway was slick and treacherous. Governor Nordgren leaned forward, squinting through the windshield as the wipers swept back and forth keeping slushy snow from blocking his vision. He slowed the big Mercedes to a crawl as he watched several cars up ahead slip slide wildly then spin off into the barrow pit—like watching dodgem cars at an amusement park! *I should have accepted Sergeant Schneider's offer to drive me to work. What a hell of a way to start a day,* he thought as his mind swirled with details of the worst dilemma of his political career—the mutilators! *Who were they? Why couldn't someone come up with some answers? Where did the mutilators come from? Why Idaho? Why were they butchering farm animals?*

The governor was so frustrated it was difficult to concentrate and keep the car on the freeway. Every effort he'd made to try and identify and stop the mutilators had failed big time. Meetings with the state police, the fish and game authorities and sheriffs' reports from Idaho's most populous counties had so far yielded no results. He'd done his best to conceal his depressed bitchy mood from his staff, but evidently not from his wife Gloria, who subtly brought it to his attention this cold snowy morning.

Over morning coffee, Gloria, still in her pajamas, made him aware of his foul disposition as she poured his first cup, when she asked innocently,

"Honey, what's the matter? All week you've been like a big ol' grizzly bear with a sore sunburned ass!"

That brought a light chuckle from the governor and released some of his pent up tension. "Ah, c'mon Honey, am I really that bad?"

"You better believe it!" she grinned.

"I'm sorry," he humbly apologized, feeling ashamed and worn, unaware he'd been inadvertently taking his frustrations out on his wife of thirty five years. He wished things were different. He'd like to ride his horse up into the high country smell the pines and clear his troubled mind. The peace he found in the mountains had always worked in his youth. Unfortunately it was winter now and his problems were now much bigger than they once were. He felt as if the weight of the entire state rested on his broad shoulders.

Nordgren met Gloria's eyes which were brimming with concern, and he wanted to say something, do something, that'd make everything all right. But it wasn't necessary. Gloria knew him all too well! She had a pretty good idea that media pressure was partly to blame his foul temperament. The media never stopped their attacks and seemed to delight in crucifying him with bold-type newspaper headlines like, 'Governor and Police Have no Answers', or TV breaking news stories exhibiting another gory mutilated animal and claiming absolutely nothing was being done by anyone in authority to solve Idaho's mutilator mystery. His howling political opponents kept taking pot shots at him claiming he was incapable of leading the state through this crisis. He must be replaced in the looming election they screamed! To add even more insult to injury, pistol-packing itchy-fingered ranchers and farmers were demanding action to stop whoever or whatever was murdering their valuable livestock, which translated to destroying their livelihoods.

Gloria knew how he thought. She could read him like a book, but there was nothing she could do to help him and to date no one else could either. The feds knew nothing, so they told him; the military knew nothing, or if they did they were keeping it to themselves. His state police didn't have the first damn clue! Gloria knew how he internalized these things. She tried to comfort him by just being there and listening. It usually worked when he got down on himself.

Gloria walked to the stove, checked on the biscuits slowly baking in the oven and grabbed the coffee pot to refill his cup. As she poured steaming fresh brewed coffee she asked, "Are you getting any closer to solving the mutilation problem? Anything new?"

"Possibly," Nordgren said, trying to climb out of his shell of self pity. "Remember those three investigators we sent to different parts of the state to investigate mutilations?"

She nodded. "I remember."

"Well, they've finished their investigations and are back in Boise to report their findings to me today."

"Did they discover any link between UFO sightings and the mutilators?" she asked with subdued excitement.

He shook his head. "I don't know. Even if there is some connection it's too damned weird and complicated to even consider."

"You mean politically?"

He nodded.

"Well, Stan," she retorted in a more serious tone, "You just might have to throw politics out the window. You've got a monumental problem on your hands and you'd better keep an open mind, politics or not."

"I'm trying to," he said quietly, then drew in a long breath. "But there's something else really bugging me."

"What?" she asked.

"A week ago Kyle Howden, director of Boise's FBI field office, barged past my secretary into my office without an appointment. He ordered me to shut the door, and without as much as a by your leave, he lit into me like I was some kind of subversive asshole. He was mad as hell and I had no idea what was going on."

"He was angry with you about something?" she asked

"He certainly was. Evidently it was a damned news release in the Boise paper. He ordered me to put a lid on any further media releases which even hinted that UFOs might be involved in the mutilation problem. I guess what set him off was a statement made last week by the Idaho Fish and Game Department Director who told the press that no wild animals like deer, elk, moose or bears have been killed and mutilated, and he warned ranchers if they spotted UFOs in their area to report them and to be extra vigilant."

Gloria was puzzled. "So he assumed you authorized the Fish and Game director to issue such a statement? Did you?"

"Hell no!" he said emphatically. "I was trying to figure out our next move but Fish and Game jumped the gun on me before we decided on anything. I chewed some ass at Fish and Game about that and warned if anything like that ever happens again they'll all be kicking horse turds down the road!"

"I still don't understand why Mr. Howden was so upset about a simple statement from the fish and game people," Gloria said.

"Damned if I can figure it out either! He didn't say so, in so many words, but I think Howden interpreted it to mean that UFOs and those who operate them are only interested in killing domestic livestock, not wild animals. I think it was the part about UFOs that really ruffled his feathers— and it opened a whole new can of worms. The press is now digging into the statistics of how many domestic animals have been butchered, and they're interviewing biologists at the University of Idaho in Moscow as to why wild animals are totally immune from killing and mutilation. The press indicates that if biologists can solve that problem it would automatically solve the mutilation problem."

Gloria nodded and frowned. "That sounds logical. But what gets me is why is the FBI is so concerned about Idaho's animal mutilations? Isn't it strictly a state problem?"

Nordgren shook his head. "Not exactly. Dozens of cattle mutilations are occurring in surrounding states, over in Wyoming, down in Utah, some in Nevada, well all over the west for that matter.

Gloria nodded. "That's what makes it a federal crime. Right?"

"It does," Nordgren agreed. "But I've suspected for some time there's more to this FBI concern with UFOs than they're spilling to me."

"I'd say so," Gloria said. "Well, dear, the biscuits are ready and the sausage is done. Let's eat. Maybe it'll cheer up that foul mood of yours, and get this snowy day off to a good start!"

Nordgren tried to smile. "Am I forgiven for being a sore-assed grizzly?"

"Well, maybe, Honey," she said slowly, "If you'll let me sit in on your meeting with your investigators. I'd love to hear what they have to report."

"I'll bet you would!" Nordgren said, and leaned back in his chair and stared at her for a brief moment with a broad smile now on his face.

With a mock pout, Gloria said, "Does that mean no?"

"Yep."

Governor Nordgren eased into his reserved parking spot at 700 West Jefferson Street, thankful he'd survived the white-knuckle drive from home. He sat there for a moment thinking, hoping that by day's end he might finally learn the mutilators' identity from his investigators who would recap their investigations with law enforcement officers, veterinarians as well as ranchers and farmers who'd lost hundreds of valuable animals.

Nordgren loved striding up the wide steps leading to the south façade entrance of the state capitol, Idaho's most treasured building. Its renaissance revival style, with beautiful sandstone walls, was close to seventy years old. The grand old building stood majestically, its dome reaching two hundred feet above the street, a solid symbol of law and order in Idaho. The interior was an exciting arena with an atmosphere like no other place he'd ever been. Polished marble columns holding up intricately designed mosaics crafted into the dome were just part of the magnificent architecture not often seen in modern buildings. Legislators, cops, criminals, defense attorneys, prosecutors, court reporters, judges, interpreters, and clerks always kept the building abuzz with the latest scuttlebutt. The main floor, designed to be open and well lighted, seemed to welcome everyone. Its entry way was guarded by an Idaho State Trooper recently appointed to the capitol security detail and ordered to keep an eye out for anything unusual or suspicious. With mutilators marauding throughout the state Nordgren didn't want any unexpected or dangerous intrusions into Idaho's most important building.

The governor brushed snow from his designer topcoat and pulled off his woolen scarf. He doffed his snow-covered Stetson, slapped it against his leg, stomped the snow from his Tony Lama's, and hurried down the long hallway toward the War Room he'd created and staffed shortly after the mutilators began their devastating killing spree five months ago.

Assistant Attorney General, David Randall, met Nordgren in the corridor and greeted him with smile and a firm handshake. "I'm glad you made it here in one piece. Those roads are treacherous this morning."

Governor Nordgren nodded and gave Randall a slight smile. "This would have been a fine day to stay tucked in bed, David, but until we get this mutilator situation cleared up I'm on the firing line. I really need to get to the bottom of this mutilator business—and soon! Are our investigators ready to give me the low down?"

"Yes sir," Randall assured him.

"Have they told you anything about their investigations?"

"Only that they dealt with the situation as best they could. They didn't elaborate or provide any details," Randall answered evasively.

Nordgren nodded. "Being tight-lipped, huh? Well, maybe that's good.

It'll give them a chance to present their results to all of us at the same time. What's the situation today? Are mutilation reports still pouring in from all over the state?"

"No sir," Randall answered with a grin. "The phones have almost gone dead!"

Nordgren's eyes went wide. "What's happened?"

"Damned if I know," Randall said, throwing up his hands. "I've got five dispatchers manning the phones in the War Room. Last time I checked they hadn't taken a call for forty eight hours."

He motioned Nordgren to follow him into the War Room where four male dispatchers sat silently, half asleep, manning the phones. One dispatcher however had a phone in his ear, scribbling notes as fast as he could write. He glanced up from his desk, gave the governor a slight wave and continued talking.

"Give me your name again, Sheriff." Then, "All right. Got it. Owyhee County? Near Duck Lake? Got it. Five cows and two sheep, right? Please Sheriff, talk a little slower. I'm trying to write this down. Yes sir, we'll notify the state police."

As the dispatcher hung up and jotted a few more notes he mumbled under his breath, more to himself than anyone else, "Where the hell is Owyhee County? Do people actually live there?"

"Not many," Governor Nordgren grinned. "It's the most god-forsaken area in the whole state, square in Idaho's southwest corner bordering on Nevada and Oregon—miles and miles of desert and mountains, sprinkled here and there with a few remote cattle and sheep ranches. What was that call all about anyway?"

The dispatcher looked somewhat unnerved as the tall intimidating governor stood there asking him a question.

He answered nervously, "Some rancher down in the Duck Lake area discovered five of his cows butchered and his neighbor, on a nearby ranch, found two of his prize sheep killed."

"Mutilated?"

"Yes sir, all of them totally gutted and their body parts taken."

"Were all those animals still on their summer range?" Nordgren asked.

"Yes sir. Duck Lake didn't get this snowstorm so cattle and sheep in that area are still on summer range."

Nordgren's right eyebrow rose in thought and he stood there for thirty seconds; but it seemed longer to the young dispatcher and David Randall.

"Something wrong, Governor?" Randall asked.

Nordgren shook his head. "What this young man just told me offers some possibilities."

"Like what?" Randall asked.

"Well, for one, most of the animal mutilations occurred in the mountains, on the remote summer ranges, during good weather. Now they've stopped. Maybe whoever is doing the killing has been stopped by the heavy snow."

Randall's face brightened. "Do you really think so?"

"Well, there's really no proof of that," Nordgren said. "Like I say, it's a possibility." He turned and walked out of the War Room and motioned Randall to follow.

"C'mon, David. I'm anxious to get to the conference room and meet with our investigators. Maybe they've come up with something solid as to who or what those sonsabitches are who are killing our livestock!"

19

GOVERNOR NORDGREN AND DAVID Randall passed employees walking in purposeful fashion along the capitol hallways.

"David, which investigator should I interview first? Which one has the most critical data?"

"Neal Harmon," came Randall's immediate response.

Nordgren nodded. "Any particular reason?"

"Some strange things are happening down in the Magic Valley. I think Neal has some valuable information."

"All right," Nordgren said. "He'll be first up."

When Randall opened the conference room door, Nordgren saw Attorney General Sam Kennerton slumped in his chair dozing. He'd not had a full night's sleep for the past month because of the excessive flurry of mutilation reports flooding into his war room.

The three investigators were huddled in animated conversation at the far end of the long polished mahogany table, their papers scattered in disarray. Something was going on! Neal Harmon's arms were extended in the air slowly coming down as if he was describing something descending from the sky. Allan Moen nodded vigorously while Larry Spangler stared at them both with a 'me-too' smile on his face, circling his hands as if holding a large round object of some kind.

"Good morning, gentlemen," Nordgren greeted them.

His greeting jerked Sam Kennerton wide awake, and he started to get up out of his chair, his fatigue suddenly gone.

"Stay put, Sam." Nordgren put a hand on his shoulder. "Is the coffee ready? I'm still half frozen from my icy drive on the freeway this morning."

Kennerton stretched his neck and twisted his head. "Yeah, it is, Stan! I need some too!" He motioned Randall to pour coffee.

Randall walked over to a small table against the wall which held a large stainless steel pot of steaming hot coffee and half a dozen white china coffee mugs. Randall looked over his shoulder. "How many want coffee?" Five hands shot into the air.

Randall poured strong black coffee for each of them. That was the way most Idaho folks drank coffee; no cream, no sugar, just black and strong. He walked around the table and handed each man a mug of hot coffee.

"Thank you, David," Nordgren said and took a sip of coffee, then sat down comfortably and relaxed. He motioned to the investigators, "C'mon up here, closer, I won't bite. Then we won't have to shout."

Neal, Allan and Larry gathered their papers, brief cases and coffee and moved up closer, directly across from Governor Nordgren.

"Welcome home. I'm glad to see you back safe and sound. I've been extremely worried about all of you." He raised his coffee cup in a salute.

The investigators saluted in like manner.

"Friends, I don't mind telling you I've wondered if this day would ever come. Now that it's here I hope you've brought us some answers. Sam and David have kept me partially in the loop about your adventures, though I still don't know a hell of a lot more about the mutilators now than I did when you left. No offense intended, Sam."

"None taken," Kennerton replied.

Nordgren took a sip of coffee. "I'm more than a little curious to learn what you gentlemen may have discovered about the mutilators. Lots of folks, like the news media for example, are even more curious than I am. So I warn all of you, before you leave this room, that nothing discussed here today is to be released, leaked, talked about, or anything else, unless you have my approval. Is that clear?"

Everyone nodded understanding.

"Good," Nordgren said. "Let me take a minute and tell you why the warning. A couple of weeks ago somebody with a big mouth over at Fish and Game released some information that got me in hot water with the FBI. I had to come up with a bogus explanation to save face. I don't want to go through anything like that ever again! So let's get down to business. I'm anxious to hear your reports."

"Who do want first?" Kennerton asked.

"Neal, first. Allan next, and Larry bringing up the rear."

Thirty-year-old Larry Spangler gave a mock pout. "Why do I always have to ride drag?" The solidly built undercover lieutenant with the Idaho State Police was known for his sense of humor as well as his top notch investigative skills.

Nordgren stared thoughtfully at him for a moment. "Well, Larry my man, keep up the good work, and maybe one day you'll move up to trail boss! By the way, how did your investigation turn out?"

"Well Governor, aside from having my ass run ragged over a third of the state of Idaho, and my hair turning gray from chasing the elusive mutilators, it went just fine."

"Sounds fun," Nordgren grinned. "How about you, Allan?"

"Oh I muddled through," Allan deadpanned. "I talked to dozens of pissed off farmers and ranchers, looked at enough butchered cows to last two lifetimes and literally had the mutilators scare the living shit out of me. Other than that it was pretty routine."

The governor chuckled. "Why do you guys always beat around the bush like that? Why don't you just tell it like it is?" He paused for a moment. "Are all of you ready to tell me what happened in your assigned areas?"

They all nodded.

"All right, Neal, we'll begin with you. Your assigned area was the Magic

Valley. As I recall. You started your investigation at a ranch where two race horses were butchered late last summer. Right?"

"Yes sir," Neal answered. "On Randy Johnson's ranch, northeast of Twin Falls. He owned the horses in question." Neal described the layout of Randy's ranch, and how events began escalating slowly when mysterious pulsating blue lights appeared in the night sky above Randy's pasture. Randy and his wife Tessie observed the strange lights several nights in a row before their two race horses mysteriously came up missing from a professionally constructed corral. Their mutilated bodies were discovered a few days later miles from that seemingly escape-proof corral.

Neal then explained young Joe Johnson's eerie experience with those same pulsating blue lights over their pasture one dark cloudy night while driving home from his part time restaurant job in Twin Falls.

From there, Neal provided a very graphic description of the gruesome mutilations he'd carefully studied on each butchered horse. He spoke with the precision of a professional investigator, holding his audience spellbound when he transitioned from the butchered horses to dozens of mutilated cattle. He explained the tranquil, laid-back lifestyle of farmers and ranchers in the Magic Valley before the livestock butchery began and how that lifestyle was suddenly transformed into one of menacing fear when the mutilators suddenly struck ranches all over the area killing and mutilating cattle.

"How many cattle were we talking about?' Governor Nordgren asked.

"I personally studied seventy-five mutilated animal carcasses."

"I had no idea it was that extensive," Nordgren said. "Were you alone when you did that?"

"Sometimes. Usually the ranch owner accompanied me. Once in a while the sheriff or one of his deputies went with me. At that time the sheriff's office was swamped with callers reporting mutilated animals so it wasn't possible for the sheriff or his deputies to accompany me all the time."

Nordgren nodded. "So what did your investigations reveal?"

Neal asked, "I don't think you've ever seen a mutilated animal, have you, Governor?"

"Not a real animal, just a picture or two I saw in the paper," Nordgren answered.

"Then you may want to look at some photos I took." Neal pulled a folder from his brief case, and handed it to Nordgren. "These are some pictures I took of Randy Johnson's slaughtered horses. They will show you the extent of the mutilations close up, which are almost identical to the mutilations we found on cattle and sheep."

Nordgren pulled several 8 x 10 black and white glossies from the folder. He stared at the first photograph for a long moment and then laid it down and stared at the second and then laid that down and stared at the third, which he held up for the others to see. It was a photo of Little Girl with her lips missing, displaying her teeth in a hideous grin.

"My God!" Nordgren gasped. "I can't believe this! Have you ever in your life seen anything so..." Nordgren searched for words. "Gruesome? Damn, Neal, what crazy sick sonofabitch would do something like that? It almost makes the hair on the back of my neck stand up just looking at these photos."

Neal nodded. "I took them, Governor! And the hair on the back of my neck did stand up! It was the eeriest feeling I've ever had. And to top it off, though this may sound kind of weird, I had the strangest sensation that some unseen force was watching my every move. Randy Johnson was there with me—we're both military combat veterans—but standing together alongside those butchered horses, studying their mutilations, was totally outside of anything either of us had ever experienced."

"I can't even imagine something like that!" Nordgren said. "Did Randy have any idea or express any opinion as to who or what he believed killed his horses?"

"I asked him that very question," Neal answered, "and he told me that he and his cousin Bill Martin were first on the scene where the dead horses were found. Based on evidence they discovered at the two different sites Randy and Bill are totally convinced that aliens in a UFO kidnapped, killed and mutilated the horses."

Nordgren reared back in his chair and held up a hand in a whoa Betsy motion—"Let's slow this engine down. I mean slow it way down and back up! You mean aliens like from outer space, from another planet?"

"Yes sir. Alien beings from some far off galaxy."

Nordgren's face remained impassive, quizzical. "That being the case, has Randy or his cousin Bill actually seen any of these so called aliens?"

"No sir. But pod marks they found in the dust near the dead animals could have been made by a UFO setting down on tripod legs or struts. Randy also told me that a reliable Twin Falls veterinarian explained to him that the surgery used to remove the horses' organs was some kind of medical procedure currently unknown to our veterinary science."

Nordgren drew a deep breath. "Did Randy notify the police as soon as he found his dead horses?"

Neal nodded and frowned. "Of course he did. He immediately called Sheriff Dan Jeffords who dispatched two seasoned deputies to investigate."

"What were the deputies' conclusions?"

"I have a copy of their investigative report. Unfortunately they attributed the butchery to predatory animals."

"Unfortunately?" Nordgren questioned. "You seem to disagree. Why? Do you go along with Randy Johnson's theory that the mutilators are aliens?"

"I certainly do!" Neal answered without hesitation.

Nordgren shook his head. "Really? Possible pod marks in the dust? Unusual surgery? That's not much to go on, Neal. Please tell me you've got something more."

"I certainly have," Neal quickly responded. For starters, let me add another bizarre circumstance which occurred on Ben Summers' ranch."

"Who is Ben Summers?" Nordgren asked.

"An old sheep rancher, running sheep on a ranch next to Randy Johnson's spread."

"What about him?" Nordgren asked, eyes wide, now exhibiting keen interest.

"Randy and I found Ben stretched out dead in his pasture, just a short distance from his house. In his cold dead hands, clutched across his chest, was his old 30-30 rifle. We figured he may have been trying to protect himself from rustlers or someone trying to steal his property."

"Was he?" Nordgren asked.

"At first glance we thought maybe so," Neal continued. "We left the body where it lay so as not to destroy any evidence or clues. Then we phoned Sheriff Jeffords who picked up Medical Examiner Dr. James Austin and they rushed out to investigate. Together, the sheriff, Dr. Austin, Randy and I searched every square inch of the pasture and also used a geiger counter to see if we could detect any radiation. We even geigered old Ben's body. We scanned the body from feet to head and were startled when the geiger counter's needle beeped off the chart!"

"What made you suspect radiation?" Nordgren asked.

"Well, sir, dozens of Magic Valley's mutilated animals have exuded high levels of radiation," Neal replied. "So we felt it worth it worth a try to determine if there was any radiation in, on or around old Ben's body."

Nordgren rubbed his chin and shifted uncomfortably in his chair. "Did Sheriff Jeffords authorize an autopsy to determine the exact cause of the old man's death?"

"No sir."

"Why not?" Nordgren questioned. "Under those unusual circumstances any knowledgeable lawman would have immediately ordered an autopsy."

"The sheriff didn't have the opportunity. Dr. Austin told him to wait while he called Dr. Jordan at the Atomic Energy Commission in Arco to report the high radiation levels found on and around Ben's body. Dr. Austin asked Dr. Jordan for instructions on how to proceed. Dr. Austin had never run into anything like the high radiation level he found on the old man's body. Dr. Jordan told Dr. Austin that within the hour he'd have a team of highly trained radiation experts on their way to pick up Ben's body. All of us, Dr. Austin, Sheriff Jeffords and I assumed Ben's body would be autopsied at the AEC lab. However, Dr. Austin thought it strange that Dr. Jordan warned him, in no uncertain terms, to keep his mouth shut about the entire incident.

Assuming the AEC would pick up Ben's body and handle the autopsy, Dr. Austin and Sheriff Jeffords left me alone to turn the body over to the AEC radiation specialists."

"Did those specialists show up to Ben's ranch?" Nordgren asked.

"Yes sir. Very quickly. Weird fellows, very secretive. I turned Ben's body over to them."

"Are you sure they were they from the Atomic Energy Commission in Arco?"

"They said they were."

"Didn't you ask to see their credentials?"

"I did, and the head honcho, kind of a smart ass, told me he was a federal agent and flashed his badge so fast I really couldn't tell what agency he was from. They stuffed old Ben in a special rubberized body bag of some kind, loaded him their van, and smart ass signed for the body. Then they took off and high tailed it back to Arco. When I looked at the signature on the receipt I noticed it was completely illegible."

"Well, why didn't you stop him and find out a little more about what was going on? You're a law enforcement officer," Nordgren challenged.

Neal shook his head. "I should have I guess, but I felt we had enough trouble at that point in time without antagonizing the feds. They do have authority over state law enforcement people you know—and they're not afraid to use it."

Nordgren stared at Neal, apparently puzzled and apprehensive. This startling news that a dead man was now mixed up in the mutilator mystery shook him and sent his mind whirling in several different directions. He gave Neal a piercing glance. "Okay, so 'smart ass' and his people took old Ben Summers' body back to Arco. What were the results of the AEC's autopsy on the old man? Did they let you know the exact cause of his death?"

"No sir, not so far. I phoned the AEC a few days later to obtain autopsy information on old Ben. The young lady who answered the phone explained to me—like I was some elementary school kid—that the AEC is a nuclear research facility and they most certainly have nothing to do with dead bodies."

"Did you believe her?" Nordgren asked.

"Not for a New York minute!"

Nordgren appeared puzzled. "I don't get it. Why the hell would the AEC lie about something like that? I know Dr. Jordan personally and I've always found him to be up front with me, very professional, a good man."

Neal shrugged. "Well sir, for what it's worth I believe it was to keep us from discovering the actual cause of old Ben's death."

"Which was?" Nordgren asked.

"Radiation poisoning. There were no physical injuries of any kind on the body, at least none that Dr. Austin could find after his cursory examination. The Doc felt sure it was radiation poisoning that dropped the old man in his tracks."

"Whoa, hold up!" Nordgren said with a touch of confusion. "This is all very interesting, I guess, but you just lost me! Radiation poisoning? On a remote ranch in Idaho? That's a rather preposterous assumption by Dr. Austin don't you think?" How could something like that be administered?" Nordgren tried to bounce the absurd idea around his brain.

Neal was silent, sitting upright in his chair, feeling uneasy. Nordgren's skepticism was beginning to annoy him, but he remained patient for a moment or two, before dropping a bomb shell on the governor. "Probably by a death ray shot down by alien beings in a UFO," he said forcefully.

Nordgren visibly flinched, like somebody about to be attacked. He studied Neal warily, feeling trapped, now sensing the inevitability that UFOs and aliens would be identified as the mutilators in his investigator's reports. There was no way he could prevent it. "A death ray? That's your opinion?"

"Am I missing something here, Governor?" Neal asked with a touch of frustration in his voice. "You asked me to report what I discovered about mutilators in the Magic Valley, and that's exactly what I'm trying to tell you." Neal's voice rose with irritation. "If I'm going to risk sending my valuable career down the toilet by telling the truth, let's just forget my report and chalk the mutilations up to predatory animals. That's what we've been doing for the last five months and you can see where that's got us!"

Attorney General Sam Kennerton threw up a hand. "Easy Neal. Easy boy! Don't get your balls in an uproar! I assure you the governor has reasons for his caution. So please, don't make this any more difficult for him than it already is."

Neal looked at the Attorney General for a long moment, then asked, "Would it be presumptuous to ask what those reasons are?"

"I'll answer that, Sam," Nordgren interrupted. "Not at all, Neal" the governor broke in. "Do any of you know Kyle Howden?"

Everyone but Sam Kennerton shook their heads.

Sounding strained, Nordgren continued. "He's Director of the FBI's field office here in Boise. A few days ago he called me and said if there's even the slightest chance of something as incredible as UFOs and aliens somehow slipping out to the news media it would cause mass panic throughout the country. People are already living in daily fear of Russian nuclear intercontinental ballistic weapons. They don't need us springing UFOs on them—then Howden issued me a very stern warning to keep a lid on this mutilator business or there will be some very serious repercussions."

"What did he mean by that?" Neal asked curiously.

"From the tone of Howden's voice, and what he said to me, I think he euphemistically meant anyone leaking information to the media might end up in cement overshoes at the bottom of Lake Pend Oreille." Nordgren paused and smiled at Neal. "However, I doubt he'd go that far. But we've got to be very careful from now on."

"Did Agent Howden follow up his warning with anything in writing?" Neal asked.

"Are you kidding?" Nordgren shook his head. "He's smarter than that. What really puzzles me is why Howden and the FBI are even involved. The answer eludes me. Something is going on and I'm not sure what it is."

"I believe I do, sir," Neal said, more calmly now, "and it's more diabolical than you can possibly imagine."

Surprised, Nordgren raised an eyebrow. "You know what it is?"

Neal nodded. "Yes sir. It's all right here in my report."

Nordgren threw up his hands in a sign of frustration. "You've known all along that the FBI is somehow involved in our mutilation investigations? Why haven't you brought it to my attention before now?"

"I didn't know for sure they were involved, sir, until after I had completed my investigation in the Magic Valley. Before you get too upset, I respectfully ask you to hear the rest of my report. There are details in it about the FBI which may clarify their involvement in this mutilator mystery."

Nordgren locked eyes with him for a moment, then finally shrugged. "I sure as hell hope so!" Then Nordgren slowly came up with a faint apologetic smile. "I'm sorry, Neal. It's just that this FBI business is driving me totally nuts—and it's not your problem."

Nordgren looked at his watch.

It was five minutes after ten and he thought about the coalition of ranchers and farmers who would assemble together in his office at one o'clock, to demand answers and action. He wondered what he could—or should tell them, if anything at all.

"Okay, Neal. Let's get on with it. Explain how the FBI was involved in your investigations in the Magic Valley. Did you meet with them down there?"

"No sir! Absolutely not!" Neal growled. "I'd never go outside the chain of command without getting your approval."

"I'm sorry, Neal," Nordgren quickly apologized. "That was a stupid question. May I assume then that the FBI had some involvement with the UFOs and aliens you encountered?"

Neal nodded. "Yes sir."

"Tell me about it!"

20

DAVID RANDALL WALKED QUIETLY AROUND the conference table and refilled everyone's cup then slipped back into his chair next to Attorney General Sam Kennerton.

"Where would you like me to begin, Governor?" Neal asked.

"Let's just cut to the chase. I'm pressed time. Go back to that Ben Summers episode with the Atomic Energy Commission for a moment. I'm confused about those unidentified men from the AEC who took the old man's body. I just don't get it. The receptionist at the AEC told you they don't deal in dead bodies, if that's the case, why would Dr. Jordan at the AEC tell Dr. Austin he would send some of his people to pick up a dead body?"

Neal shook his head. "Damned if I know, Governor. "I got the feeling the receptionist was receiving instructions from someone in the background who was coaching her. She said three or four times, 'hold on a moment, Mr. Harmon,' then she'd come back on line and answer my question according to what someone was advising her to say."

"So you're saying she lied to you?"

"Yes sir. Big time! But let me add some clarification. I assumed the AEC didn't deal in bodies before I called them. So they must be secretly working with some other government agency."

"And we don't know which agency that is, do we?"

"No sir."

Nordgren gave Neal an inquisitive stare. "Do you have any idea what those radiation specialists did with the old man's body?"

"No sir, but I'd lay odds it ended up in some top secret biological laboratory back in Washington, DC—and I've got a gut feeling we'll never hear any more about it."

Nordgren reared back. "Oh, c'mon, Neal, get real! Why in the world would some clandestine lab in DC want an old sheep rancher's body?"

"Very simple, sir," Neal said. "To prevent the media or anyone else from ever finding out that Ben was killed by aliens from another world!"

Nordgren's eyes went wide. He slid to the edge of his chair, hoping to hell the room wasn't wired so no one else in the building could listen to this insane conversation.

He gave Neal a blistering stare and growled, "You're telling me you actually believe Ben was killed by a radiation death ray shot down from a UFO?" Nordgren paused. "That's a pretty wild assumption, Neal, considering that all you have to back it up is a high radiation reading. There's no body, no autopsy, no official police investigation! Did you actually see any of these so called aliens out there on Ben Summers' ranch?"

It was a moment before Neal responded, his voice tinged with a bit of frustration.

"No sir, I didn't actually see them, but I did see their spaceship and I have no doubts that the aliens are the mutilators."

Investigator Allan Moen jumped in. "I've seen the aliens, Governor, even talked to them!"

"Me too!" Larry Spangler said.

Attorney General Sam Kennerton threw up a hand and quickly cut in. "Hang on you two. You'll get your turn. Let's just take it one report at a time. Neal has the floor."

Nordgren was deep in thought, silent now. He absently shuffled through the photos of Randy Johnson's butchered horses, still trying to wrap his head around the concept of UFOs and aliens. He shut his eyes for a second. *What if Neal is telling the truth? Okay, you try to be rational. You try to accept what your top investigator is revealing. Aliens are killing livestock and you've learned an old man has been murdered. You try to work it so it all comes together and is acceptable. You can't ignore it and you can't shove it aside.* He found his staff staring at him.

Sam Kennerton started to say something, but the governor held up a hand. "Hold it Sam!" He turned to Neal again.

"I'm thinking of the consequences that'll engulf us if your alien theory about Ben's death and body removal somehow finds its way to the media. It'll make us look like a bunch of damned fools before the entire country!" He waved a hand toward his staff. "All of you think for a moment how a cockamamie story like this would play with the public. They'd more than likely run me out of town on a rail—maybe the rest of you too!" The governor sensed the first rumblings of an incident which could innocently explode into the local media, then go viral on national and international fronts, like the first tremors of an impending earthquake.

"Screw the public, Stan!" Kennerton growled. "What the hell are we supposed to do, bury our heads in the sand? Those sonofabitchin' aliens are killing our livestock and now our people! We're confronted by a mystery no one on this planet has ever faced before. So let's forget about politics and explore all the possibilities. You wanted answers! My investigators are here to provide them. How about cutting them a little slack and at least let them tell you what they found out?"

Nordgren gave Kennerton a frosty look. "How about you cutting me a little slack, Sam? Damn it man, I'm just trying to sort things out."

"Okay, okay, I'm sorry," Kennerton apologized; but he'd grabbed the governor's full attention for at least a few minutes so they could plow through the details and unravel the mystery. "All I'm saying is let's keep open minds and remain calm so we can analyze and dissect this mess and make some decisions. Do you understand what I'm saying?"

Nordgren raised a hand in a helpless, defeated gesture. "Yeah, Sam, I do!" He then turned to Neal, and for the first time Nordgren's voice softened. He exhaled slowly, and said, "All right, Neal, tell me about UFOs and aliens."

Breathing a sigh of relief, Neal again reached into his brief case and retrieved a brown manila envelope and offered it to Nordgren. "Here are eyewitness accounts written by Sheriff Dan Jeffords and Dr. James Austin describing in detail their face to face encounter with the aliens. You'll find them extremely interesting!"

Nordgren waved the envelope away. "I don't have time to read all of that. Just summarize it for me."

Start at the beginning. Neal thought *Take it slow. Explain carefully what happened to Jeffords and Austin. Win him over!*

"Sheriff Dan Jeffords and his deputies investigated almost every mutilation reported to them in Twin Falls County. They did the best they could under some very trying and unusual circumstances—remember, they'd never dealt with anything like this before."

"Neither have I!" Nordgren said, shaking his head. "And to top it off I've never received one credible bit of information from any law enforcement agency identifying the mutilators. Most of what I've learned about the mutilations comes from the local newspapers. As a matter of fact, the Twin Falls sheriff's office still hasn't notified me of Ben Summers' death. Surely they investigated that, didn't they?"

Neal shook his head. "No sir. They didn't have the opportunity. Those unidentified men from the AEC took Ben's body before they had a chance to complete an investigation."

Nordgren raised his voice. "This goddamn mess gets weirder by the minute! While we're talking weird, tell me what took place when the sheriff and Dr. Austin meet the aliens."

Neal smiled. "You'd better grab hold of something, sir. This is where the story not only is weird but it requires a willing suspension of disbelief on your part."

Nordgren grunted noncommittally. "Get on with it."

"Well, sir, as Sheriff Jeffords and Doc Austin were investigating Ben Summers' butchered ram an alien spaceship suddenly materialized directly overhead and its commanding officer, who called himself Captain John, beamed down to speak to them. He explained that he commanded two ships, his and one other. Both had traveled to our planet together on a crucial mission to secure animal parts to be used for a very advanced type of cloning to replenish domestic animals they'd lost when a huge meteor slammed into their planet."

Nordgren's face was grim, but he restrained himself from scoffing. "That's actually written in those reports?" He pointed to the manila envelope.

"It is."

Nordgren didn't reply for a moment. "Damn, Neal, it's hard for me to wrap my mind around UFOs and aliens. Don't mind me if I seem skeptical. I have to play the devil's advocate so I can better understand what's been happening."

"No problem," Neal said. "I think things will become clearer as I fill in more of the details. Please remember, Sheriff Dan Jeffords and Dr. James Austin are professionals in every sense of the word and I believe their story. Each man conducted himself with consummate skill during the encounter with the aliens, especially Dr. Austin. Had they not, they would have ended up just like Ben Summers."

Nordgren knew he had no alternative but to accept Neal's assessment for the time being. "So the alien told Jeffords and Austin a meteor hit his planet and he was here to collect animal parts? Is that all he told them?"

"No sir, not all," Neal said. "Captain John allegedly told them something so unbelievable I'm still not sure I can believe it. He told them he and his crew were legally justified in killing and mutilating animals in Idaho—that justification came directly from the U.S. government which granted them free rein to take what they wanted."

Nordgren's head jerked back and he shot Neal a suspicious glance. "The alien told them *what*? Good god, Neal, that can't be! Our government conspiring with aliens? No! That's impossible!"

The way the governor said it Neal knew that he was about to get his ass chewed for even mentioning it. But he was wrong.

The governor quickly shifted his gaze to Allan Moen and Larry Spangler. "You just heard what Neal said. You told me you met the mutilators. Did the alien tell you anything about receiving U.S. government permission to butcher our cattle?"

Allan Moen shook his head. "No sir. He didn't say anything to us about that. But you must remember, Dr. Austin and Sheriff Jeffords evidently caught the alien in the act of butchering Ben Summers' ram."

"*Jesus!*" Nordgren mumbled under his breath, shaking his head in disbelief. "Neal, a moment ago, in the interests of time, I asked you not to pawn off those written eyewitness reports on me—but this is down right damn scary. Let me take a look at Dr. Austin's report."

Neal slid the manila envelope across the table to Nordgren. He quickly opened it and took out two separate, stapled five-page statements. He opened Dr. Austin's report and began speed reading word for word Dr. Austin's actual conversation with Captain John. "This is way too much! I just can't conceive…"

Neal held up a hand, clamped his jaw shut and tried to suppress his frustration bubbling up inside. "For hell sake, Governor, I've thoroughly investigated and studied dozens of animal mutilations in Twin Falls County! I saw Ben Summers' body stretched out dead in his pasture. And whether or not you'll believe me, I had an out of body experience with the mutilators myself, along with my friend Randy Johnson…."

Nordgren made a dismissive gesture, waving a hand. "Hold your taters, Neal. I'm not calling you or Dr. Austin liars. Far from it. Maybe I can swallow some of this alien crap, but aliens operating right here in Idaho with our own 'big brother's' approval? Damn it, Neal, that's way over the top! If we even hint to anyone anything like this is happening, our careers, maybe even are lives are in jeopardy."

"Maybe so, Governor," Neal bristled. "But the truth is the truth. If you prefer to discount what I'm telling you, let's just forget the whole thing. All I have to do is shred the photos and my report and the coyote theory wins out. But I warn you sir, there's a danger in using that bogus analogy to solve a crime of this magnitude."

Nordgren glared at Neal for a moment, his thoughts jumbled. Logically what Neal was revealing made sense. Opposing theories such as rustlers, cultists, predators, and weather just didn't stack up as viable solutions to the brutal animal killings and mutilations. However, Governor Nordgren planned to remain cautious. It was the political thing to do!

His reply was very slow and evasive. "You do have a point, Neal. "But remember this, the coyote theory has covered our asses up to now and kept the media off our backs."

Not wanting to appear impertinent, Neal asked, "Sir, you were born and raised in Idaho. Do you actually believe a scrawny coyote or a pack of them could pull down a wild range steer or a bucking bronco?"

Nordgren shook his head. "I seriously doubt it."

"Well then, with mutilations occurring in every corner of the state, are you willing at least to rule out predators as the mutilators?"

Again Governor Nordgren evaded a direct answer, as his political training had automatically taught him to do. "Perhaps. But first I want meet Sheriff Jeffords and Dr. Austin personally and hear their stories first hand. What are the chances of bringing them here to Boise? We're dealing with a touchy situation with implications that could have national or international consequences."

"Is that really necessary?" Neal asked. 'There's nothing they could tell you that isn't fully covered in their reports. And think about this, sir. If you bring them here for questioning, it's the same as telling them you don't believe their story."

Nordgren gave that thought for a moment. "I suppose you're right. I'll dig into their statements first, then decide where we go from there."

Attorney General Kennerton cut in. "You got anything in mind?"

"No, Sam! I don't have the first damn clue. But you can bet your ass if what Neal is telling us is true, we'll have the feds poking around, if they're not already." Nordgren scratched his head and mumbled, "Why the hell did the mutilators select Idaho anyway?"

Kennerton grinned. "Well Stan, we do have the healthiest cattle in the intermountain west."

Nordgren didn't think that was funny!

"Excuse me, Governor," Neal said, "This last part of my report may brighten your day. The two alien ships have nearly completed their mission and secured the animal parts they came for. Captain John's ship was preparing to leave Idaho when he met with Jeffords and Austin. For some unnamed reason his other vessel is little slower, and may remain a bit longer. When its mission is completed it will rendezvous with Captain John at a predetermined destination somewhere beyond the stars and the two ships will fly home together."

"How soon?" Nordgren asked with subdued excitement. "Are we talking days, weeks, months, what?"

"I'd say days," Neal said.

"You really think so?" Nordgren asked eagerly.

Neal nodded. "I'm just going on what Dr. Austin told me. That's how he interpreted Captain John's plans. There must be some truth to it. The aliens have been raiding our cattle herds for the last five months. Why it's taken them so long is a complete mystery. In any case it will be good to see them gone!"

"It certainly will!" Nordgren agreed. Turning to Sam Kennerton he asked, "What do you think, Sam?"

"At the moment, I don't know what to think," Kennerton admitted. "It all sounds so damned bizarre—aliens, secret dealings with our government, butchering animals—but I'm thinking that if those alien sonsabitches fly away, our problems will be solved."

Nordgren smiled, his eyes suddenly drawn toward all five of his closest associates. "That's a mighty big if to hang our hats on, Sam. But it's all we've got right now. I'm thinking that we should just hang tough and wait for a few more days and see what happens. We know for a fact the mutilations have slowed down. That's a mighty good sign as far as I'm concerned. Do you all agree?"

Five hands shot into the air.

Nordgren's mind was running amok with the possibilities that would open up to him if the aliens suddenly left Idaho as quickly as they appeared. It filled him with a sense of anticipation and optimism he hadn't felt in months.

"Anything else, Neal?"

"Well sir, not to burst the bubble, but I'm curious about the warning

FBI Agent Kyle Howden issued you. I've been thinking that it must have come about because the FBI and the aliens have been working together. We must assume the FBI knows that Captain John let the cat out of the bag when he told Jeffords and Austin he had had U.S. government approval for their depredations. So I'm wondering if the FBI plans to take action against any of us."

Nordgren shook his head. "I don't think so. "I imagine the head honchos at the FBI feel Agent Howden's warning to me will be sufficient to keep all of us silent. What worries me now is that they may go after Sheriff Jeffords, Dr. Austin and Randy Johnson. They may want to silence them, so they don't ever tell their story to anyone." Nordgren paused. "Neal, have any of those men mentioned to you any harassment by the FBI?"

"Not yet," Neal replied. "Do you want me to alert them that the FBI may be contacting them?"

Nordgren gave that thought for a minute. "No. Let's not worry them unnecessarily. They've been through enough already."

Sam Kennerton cleared his throat. "Are you sure about that, Stan? If the FBI cuts in on this deal and decides to go after those men down in Magic Valley you can bet they'll by-pass us altogether. You know how sneaky the feds can be. I fight them every day, the BLM, Bureau of Reclamation, Forest Service— it never ends."

Nordgren looked at him for a long moment. "This is a great deal more critical than dealing in land, water and forests, Sam. Let's give the FBI the benefit of the doubt, okay? If we get on the wrong side of them they'll...well hell, Sam, you know them better than I do."

Kennerton threw up his hands in a helpless gesture. "All right, Stan. It's your funeral!"

Nordgren smiled. "It goes with the job, Sam. You know that." He turned again to Neal and asked, "By the way, Neal, before I forget, have you received any updates about Joe Johnson, that young man who had a run in with the mutilators last summer which left him shaken and muddled?"

Neal nodded. "I talked to his father Randy on the phone a couple of days ago and asked him that very question. He told me he took Joe to some counseling sessions with a very good psychiatrist down in Salt Lake City who diagnosed Joe's condition as being similar to PTSD found in some military combat veterans. That psychiatrist told Randy he's never had a case quite as unique as Joe's."

Nordgren smiled. "I'll bet he hasn't!"

Neal returned the smile. "After those counseling sessions the boy has resumed his normal activities."

"Good! And what about Randy? Has he lost any more livestock to the mutilators?"

"No sir. It's been pretty quiet at his ranch. He did tell me a couple of nosey reporters from the Times-News here in Boise showed up at his ranch asking questions. They told him they just wanted to verify some information they had received from an unnamed source about his mutilated horses. Randy graciously escorted them to the remote hillside to observe the dead animals, and answered all their questions, assuming that whatever he told them was off the record. It wasn't!"

"The carcasses are still there?" Nordgren asked with surprise. "After all this time?"

"They are. And those damned reporters, much to Randy's dismay, wrote a story titled '*Slain horses Radioactive.*' Randy is still really pissed about that!"

"Damn! I must have missed that article!" Nordgren snorted, "Did it say anything about aliens?"

"No sir."

"Whew!" Nordgren breathed a sigh of relief. "Thank God for that!" He stood and stretched. "Excellent report Neal. Let's take a short break. Be back here in twenty minutes so we can listen to Allan and Larry's reports, then we can wrap this up and devise a foolproof strategy to inform the public the results of our mutilation investigation—without mentioning aliens or UFOs."

Neal and the others let that sink in.

"What about the FBI?" Sam Kennerton asked.

"Let's worry about that when the time comes," Nordgren said and walked out of the room

27

REFRESHED, EVERYONE RETURNED TO THE conference room, talking, gesturing and shuffling paperwork. The governor rapped his coffee cup with a pen to gain their attention.

He glanced at his wrist watch, then over to Allan Moen. "Your turn, Allan. Give me a quick run down on your investigation in northern Idaho."

Allan began. "I drove up to Council and met with Adams County Sheriff Abe Grover. Council is just a few miles south of McCall."

"I know where Council is, Allan. Move it along, please!"

"Phone calls reporting mutilated animals were pouring into Abe's dispatcher faster than he could answer them. Abe was frustrated, but coping as best he could. He has only five deputies to patrol the county's thirteen hundred square miles, some of it in Hells Canyon. That's a huge chunk of real estate. The western part of Hells Canyon is patrolled by Oregon's Baker County deputies, who were having mutilator problems of their own.

Sheriff Grover was providing adequate law enforcement services to all the unincorporated areas of Adams County—until the mutilators moved in.

We have to give the mutilators credit—they couldn't have picked a more remote isolated spot in the entire country for killing and butchering range cattle. And that kind of panicked Abe because there wasn't a damn thing he could do about it, except try and prioritize incoming phone calls, giving attention to the biggest ranches first, and then working down to the mom and pop operations.

The day before I arrived in Adams County, Abe had received a call from Ned Pearson, owner of the huge Double Tree Ranch, stating that one of his ranch hands had discovered a prime Angus breeding bull dead and mutilated and most of its body parts were missing. It was a fresh kill, probably done the previous night.

Abe asked me to conduct the investigation at Ned's ranch so he could handle a couple of other top priority mutilation cases over near the Oregon border.

Next day I followed Abe's police cruiser to the Double Tree ranch. But we arrived too late to catch Ned before he raced off to the north end of his ranch to look at another newly discovered butchered steer.

Abe introduced me to Nora Pearson, Ned's wife, then he sped off with lights flashing and siren wailing. Nora told me about their mutilated bull—but said she'd be damned if she'd escort me out there. She was scared. Too many weird goings on during the week, she told me, like blue flashing lights in the sky, throbbing engine sounds like a hovering helicopter, her ranch animals were nervous and skittish. She pointed to a loaded 44 revolver on the kitchen table and I had no doubt she knew how to use it! She was nervous as hell—sort of a basket case. She hollered to an elderly Basque ranch hand, who was helping some cowboys prod some wild range steers into the corral and ordered him to take me to the dead bull. The cowboys stopped what they were doing. They were all watching, wondering what the play was. Nora Pearson was hell on wheels! Carlos didn't seem to be the kind of macho man to be pushed around by a mere woman. He said, 'Ah Senora Pearson, let Bill take him. Bill found the dead bull.' Evidently it wasn't a good day to trifle with Nora! She shouted and pointed, 'get your ass in that pickup, Carlos, and take Mr. Moen out there!'

A couple of the cowboys chuckled. Nora was the ranch ramrod when Ned was away! Old Carlos shook his head, gritted his teeth and motioned me to follow him, as he angrily climbed into a rusty battered old Ford pickup. I trailed along behind, eating his dust and smoky exhaust fumes for about three miles over a deeply rutted, rock strewn dirt road., damn lucky I didn't high center my car. Suddenly Carlos threw on his brakes, skidded to a stop, stuck his hand out the window and pointed. He shouted something I couldn't understand, then he spun his pickup around and hightailed it back to the ranch."

"Was there anyone else in that area when you arrived?" Nordgren asked.

"Not a soul. It was deathly quiet—eerie. No birds singing, no chattering squirrels, no cows bawling. Nothing. I spotted the huge black bull sprawled on its back, feet in the air, twenty yards off the road, near a grove of pine trees. I grabbed my camera and walked over to snap some pictures and get a closer look."

Allan paused and stared around at the group. "Gentlemen, I've seen lots of dead animals, well, people too, but I'm here to tell you, that mutilated carcass was butchered beyond human understanding—by far the most grisly cattle mutilation I've ever seen. After a quick examination I was unable to determine its cause of death. There was a huge cut at the back of the jaws, completely across the throat and through the jugular vein. Its ears had been neatly sliced off, its eyeballs were gone, and all the skin and flesh was missing on the lower jaw."

"Did you notice anything unusual about the surgery?" Nordgren asked with intense interest.

Allan nodded. "It was very professional as near as I could tell. The incisions were extremely clean and smooth. Nothing jagged, I have some photos..."

Nordgren threw up a hand. "Never mind that. Move along."

"Well sir, the bull's internal organs were gone, as well as its scrotum and other sexual organs. There wasn't a drop of blood on, in or around the carcass. It..."

"No blood? How could that be? Nordgren interrupted. "You said its jugular vein was sliced open. If it was a fresh kill there had to be blood somewhere."

"I thought the same thing, Governor. I was totally baffled. I've worked as a ranch hand and had to bleed out animals before butchering them. It was always a bloody mess."

"Could the bull's blood have drained into the ground?"

"No sir. I carefully checked every square inch of the area."

"Maybe the bull was killed someplace else and dumped where you found it? That might account for the missing blood."

"That's certainly a possibility," Allan agreed. "There were no tracks of any kind in dust near the carcass, not even of the bull itself. It hadn't been dead very long."

"Did you suspect that maybe the mutilators hadn't completed their work on the bull and might come back?" Nordgren asked

"I did!" Allan exclaimed. "That's why I was so damn scared. From the moment I stepped out of the car I experienced the strangest premonition that whoever or whatever killed the animal was somewhere close by. I was really creeped out. I wasn't armed—though I doubt that would have made much difference at all. There was nothing to shoot at, as far as I could tell."

"So what did you do?" Nordgren asked, tipping his head forward so as not to miss a word.

"My immediate thought was to get the hell out of there, and I should have, but I knew I had to get some pictures, in case the mutilators decided to return and take the carcass. I walked quickly around the animal snapping shots from different angles. While I was adjusting my camera lens for the last close up shot, a dark shadow suddenly slid slowly over me, like a floating cloud blotting out the sun. I glanced up. Two hundred feet directly overhead a long cylindrical-shaped spacecraft hovered silently."

"Just like that? Poof, right out of nowhere?" Nordgren asked doubtfully. "Where did it come from?"

Allan shook his head. "I didn't have a clue. One minute the sky above me was clear, the next moment the space ship materialized. I assumed it had the ability to make itself visible or invisible.

Before I could make a break and run to the car, Captain John unexpectedly appeared, in some kind of movie projection form, and stood facing me, from the other side of the bull's carcass."

"Did he speak to you?" Nordgren asked.

"Yes sir. And his first words, in perfect English, stunned me. He said, 'good morning Allan.'"

"How did he know your name?" Nordgren asked skeptically.

"Someone is providing him with any information he wants about us." Neal answered.

Nordgren stared dubiously. "You mean like the FBI?"

"Yes sir. Just like Neal told us."

Nordgren let it pass. "So what did Captain John want?"

"Nothing. He warned me to leave and not return."

"Did he threaten you in any way?"

"No sir. When I finally got my brain in gear I asked him why he killed the bull."

"Did he tell you?"

"Yes sir. And what he told me was almost word for word what he told Sheriff Jeffords and Dr. Austin—he was here to obtain necessary animal parts for some kind of cloning—but his explanation went way beyond my scientific understanding."

Nordgren nodded. "His honest answer seems to corroborate Jeffords' and Austin's accounts about Captain John and his mission, just as Neal described it to us."

The hint of a faint satisfied smile played across Neal's face. He uttered a silent *Yes!*

Nordgren stared at Allan thoughtfully for ten seconds and then said, "Evidently that Double Tree ranch episode was by far the most important one you handled, given the fact you met an alien."

"It certainly was," Allan nodded. "I investigated three dozen other mutilation cases, but they were basically routine. They're thoroughly detailed in my report." He pushed a brown manila envelope across the desk to Nordgren.

"Thank you. Good job, Allan," Nordgren said. "I'd like to spend more time with you and also with you Larry and hear your report, but in the interests of time we've got to wrap this up now." He looked at Larry thoughtfully for a moment. "Sorry about that Larry. But I promise to read your report in detail and we'll get together soon. You okay with that?"

"Sure," Governor," Larry said. "Just let me know when you're ready."

Nordgren glanced at his watch. "Allan do you have anything else you'd like to share with us?"

Allan nodded. "Well, Governor, like most Americans, I've been led to believe that aliens or extraterrestrials are earth's enemies bent on our total annihilation. It wasn't like that at all with Captain John." Allan laced his fingers together. "It's difficult to put my feelings in words—but Captain John almost seemed like a friend, though he was only a projection of some other type of being. I'm sure he didn't mean me any harm, or I wouldn't be here today. It was as if I'd caught him with his hand in a cookie jar—and he was sorry for killing and mutilating animals. I felt he might even apologize—but I didn't wait to find out. I jumped in the car and raced back to Council! A few hours later I met with Sheriff Grover and described Pearson's mutilated bull, of course leaving out my encounter with Captain John.

Abe was tired and totally frustrated with the cattle butchery devastating his county and asked if I had any ideas or information to help him survive the crisis. I urged him to hang in there, complete the necessary investigations and keep the results strictly confidential. He did perk up a bit when I told him I was sure the mutilation epidemic would soon end."

"Wise counsel" Nordgren said. "Anything else?"

"Not at the moment."

"Then let me see if I've got this straight. From what I've heard here today. there's light at the end of the tunnel as far as animal mutilations are concerned. They will cease as soon as Captain John's remaining space ship has completed its mission—possibly in a few days. Can we count on that?"

Everyone nodded.

Nordgren smiled. "Please accept my personal thanks for your excellent work in reconnoitering and investigating the animal mutilations throughout the state. Your efforts have paid off and gives us a very good chance of saving our careers! It goes without saying, but I'll say it again anyway, everything discussed here today is confidential. Understood?"

Again everyone nodded.

"All right, gentlemen, we're through here."

Everyone stood and Nordgren shook hands with each man as he walked out, Sam Kennerton being last. As Nordgren clasped his hand he said, "Hold up a moment, Sam. Close the door, please."

Kennerton walked over and closed the door and returned to the conference table. Both men sat down.

Nordgren glanced at his watch again. It was eleven forty five. In an hour and a quarter he'd be facing several of Idaho's most prominent and powerful ranchers.

"You look troubled, Stan," Kennerton said. "What are you thinking?"

"It's a cold winter day. It would be a good time to be skiing in Sun Valley."

"It would be, but that's not what you're thinking," Kennerton said.

"No," he admitted. "I was wondering what I can tell those angry ranchers who are probably waiting in my office right now to tar and feather me. They want some answers."

"And you have no answers to give them, right?"

Nordgren shook his head, and raised an eyebrow, "Do you have any ideas or suggestions?"

Kennerton stared at Nordgren for a moment, and managed a slight grin. "I could make a suggestion but you may not like it. You may think it's a little naïve, but it could give us a little time to..." He paused, obviously searching for the right words.

"Go on, Sam."

"Give us time to figure out how we're going to get out of this mess and keep everyone off our backs."

Nordgren smiled warmly at his lifelong friend, Sam Kennerton. "I've seen that devious look on your face before so I assume what you're going to tell me has to be something illegal, unethical or immoral! What do you have in mind?"

"Remember back when we were in law school together?

"That was a long time ago. What about it?"

"Remember that old curmudgeon of a professor, Dr. O'Donnell I believe his name was, teaching a lesson on the duties of defense attorneys?"

Nordgren grinned and nodded. He remembered! *Old Blood and Guts O'Donnell himself! Pounding his fist on the podium, shouting, terrifying half his students while the other half didn't know what the hell was going on!*

"Do you recall his brilliant philosophical diatribe of what to do when you're defending a client and you don't have one shred of evidence to move your case forward?"

Nordgren thought for a moment then shook his head. "I'm afraid not."

Kennerton chuckled. "I've always remembered the old boy, his long jowls flapping, his white hair flying off in every direction, that big fist smashing down on the podium. 'Young ladies and gentlemen,' Kennerton imitated O'Donnell's deep growl, 'when backed into a corner, with no way out, glare at prosecutor, then slowly stroll over and face the jury, carefully study their inquisitive faces, then razzle dazzle 'em with bullshit. It impresses the jurors, throws a monkey wrench into the prosecution's case and buys the defense a little time!'"

Nordgren laughed out loud. "Yeah, Sam, now I remember—and to think we paid good tuition money for that outstanding legal advice! So what's your point?"

"Well, Stan, in your meeting with the ranchers step into your office with confidence, take command and razzle dazzle 'em." Again Kennerton imitated Professor O'Donnell's growl. 'We've been working very closely with some of the nation's top scientists who advised us only last week they are on the brink of a stunning breakthrough in this mutilation mystery gripping Idaho. They haven't yet provided any specific details. The good news is that those scientists are predicting an end to the mutilations within a few days, a month at the most. Until then, they warn all ranchers to be extra vigilant in guarding their herds. Rest assured gentlemen, we'll use the media to keep you advised of further exciting developments.'"

Nordgren stared dubiously at Kennerton. "*Jesus*, Sam, that's not true!"

"You and I know that, Stan—but no one else needs to know. Besides, when did we ever let a little falsehood stand in the way of a good story? It may eventually be true; and the *stunning* information won't hurt anyone."

Nordgren remained skeptical. "What happens if I give that explanation to the ranchers and the media picks up on it?"

"So what? Don't worry about it. A little hyperbole, combined with a touch of mystery coming out in the media, might boost your political career! You know how to manipulate the press, right?"

Nordgren gave that for a moment, and then smiled. "You're one devious son of a bitch, Sam, ya know that? But you do make an excellent point—no one gets hurt. I like that! Old Professor O'Donnell may have just unknowingly saved our asses!"

22

Washington, DC
December, 1975

SEATED AT HIS CLUTTERED DESK, FBI SPECIAL Agent Gary Sheffield, in his late forties, and feeling it at the moment, noticed through his office window the elevator door opening at the south end of the hallway, and Deputy FBI Director Bill Donovan step out and walk rapidly toward his office. In Donovan's hand was a file folder, which probably meant another assignment! Gary got up and opened the office door for his boss.

Donovan didn't waste any time as he motioned Gary back to his chair.

"Idaho's senior Senator, Cyrus Millburn, stormed into my office early this morning, mad as hell, wanting to know what we're doing to solve the animal mutilation problem in Idaho. Why he's involved God only knows."

"What did you tell him?" Gary asked.

"I explained that it's a state problem, and unless he has some proof that it's a federal crime, our hands are legally tied."

"How did he respond to that?"

Donovan shook his head in disgust. "About like you'd expect—angry that we *wouldn't investigate the greatest Idaho crisis since the Great Depression.* His words, not mine!" Donovan paused and exhaled. "Hell, even the boss is leaning on me." The boss he was referring to was FBI Director Charles Halladay. "I'm meeting with him in half an hour, and I'm trying to figure out a way to keep him from going ballistic when I tell him we have nothing new."

"I'm not surprised," Gary said. "Seems like all we've done since the mutilations began is field or dodge complaints coming in from state and federal agencies."

"Yeah," Donovan said with frustration, "And it's all because the aliens don't play by the rules! They don't have to. They hold all the cards. We can't trust a word they say. We don't know from one day to the next what those deviant mavericks will do. First they told us they'd select only cattle, then turned to horses, then it was sheep."

Gary nodded in agreement. "And they told us they'd complete their mission in thirty days or less and it's been five long months."

"It's damn near enough to drive a man to drink," Donovan growled. "Has anything new come in from Kyle Howden out in our Boise office?"

"Not much," Gary admitted. "Just bits and pieces he picks up from scant sources in Governor Nordgren's office. They run a pretty tight ship out there. No one likes to tell the feds what's up!"

Donovan scowled. "Yeah, and those bits and pieces are too fragmentary to do us any good. We simply have to get more detailed information."

Gary looked puzzled. "Do you have something in mind?"

Donovan nodded. "I do. But we've got to be very careful. If we try to take over any part of Idaho's mutilator investigation, it would immediately alert the media and the public that there's something more sinister happening than a pack of coyotes rampaging through Idaho killing cattle."

"And that gives Governor Nordgren a free hand to conduct his investigation however he sees fit," Gary said. "It was a damn smart move on his part to send his investigators to various parts of the state to find out what's causing the mutilations—and that's really got Kyle and me worried. What if those investigators somehow stumble onto the fact that the mutilators are aliens?"

"What makes you think they haven't? They already have!" came Donovan's terse reply, "And now they're back in Boise reporting that to Governor Nordgren."

Gary's expression was incredulous. "How in sam hell do you know that?"

"Captain John told us! I was in Director Halladay's office when the Captain's call came in on the ultra high frequency channel set up from their space ship."

Gary appeared shaken and on edge. "What did he tell you?"

"That Governor Nordgren's investigators and several others had discovered his identity..."

"How did the Captain let that happen?" Gary interrupted angrily.

Donovan held up a hand. "Just hear me out, please. Here's how it all began, at least according to Captain John. His ship was accidentally discovered by an elderly Idaho sheep rancher with an itchy trigger finger—and the old man fired at the space ship with a 30-30 rifle. Captain John had to eliminate him."

Gary's eyes went wide. "You mean he killed him?"

Donovan nodded. "I believe that's what eliminated means!"

"My God!" Gary gasped and slowly sank back in his chair, genuinely caught off guard by Donovan's startling information. "Then what happened?"

"We secretly retrieved the old man's body and brought it here to our forensics lab to run some tests. So we needn't worry about anyone ever finding out how or why he was killed."

"How was he killed? Or do I want to know?" Gary asked curiously.

"The lab report indicates he died instantly from some unknown type of acute radiation poisoning, something like ionizing radiation. Our lab technicians have never experienced anything like it. It's evidently administered by some kind of weapon firing a light beam or ray powerful enough to instantly kill any living creature it touches."

Gary threw Donovan a questioning look. "Okay, so we scratch the old rancher. What happened next?"

"The old man's mysterious death brought Twin Falls County Sheriff Dan Jeffords and Medical Examiner Dr. James Austin into the picture, when they were called to investigate the circumstances surrounding the killing."

"That's when they came in contact with Captain John?" Gary asked.

Donovan nodded. "Captain John admitted he made personal contact with Sheriff Jeffords and also Dr. James Austin, but he didn't provide any specific details. And that's not all, Gary. The good Captain also made direct contact with Governor Nordgren's three investigators!"

There was a mutual silence that lasted for quite some time before Gary, now clearly frustrated, growled, "Then half the state of Idaho knows the mutilators are aliens. This is crazy. Absolutely crazy. How the hell are you going to keep that information from leaking out to the media?"

Donovan smiled. "I'm not. You are—you and Kyle Howden, out in Idaho!"

Gary frowned. "Me? You want me to go to Idaho?"

Donovan nodded. "Yes. You! You're the only man we've got who can get the job done. We want this entire mess to go away—to disappear as though it had never happened. No loose ends!"

Donovan had not the slightest doubt Gary was by far the bureau's best agent to solve Idaho's mutilation problem, quickly and quietly.

"Exactly what am I supposed to do when I get there?" Gary asked.

"Silence anyone who came in contact with the aliens. They must keep their mouths shut or we'll have a nationwide panic on our hands. That must not happen. Do you understand?"

"Silence them? How do I do that? How much authority do I have?" Gary asked.

"As much as you need. Use your imagination," Donovan answered. "But whatever you do, keep the FBI out of it. They were not involved. Understand?"

Gary rolled his eyes and gave a weak smile. "Have you ever been to Idaho in the winter?"

Donovan let it pass. Had an outsider been present they might have questioned whether or not Gary Sheffield was taking this mutilator crisis as seriously as he should. But Donovan knew that Gary's ten years of directing FBI field offices, quickly moving up the ranks into FBI headquarters, coordinating Air Force Blue Book UFO sightings with FBI investigations, made him the bureau's most competent agent in UFO matters. Gary's fascinating assignment with the Air Force ended five years ago in 1970 when the Air Force unexpectedly cancelled Project Blue Book.

Numerous UFO sightings at the end of the Second World War up to 1952 forced the government to look into the UFO craze to quell public concern. The Air Force was assigned to determine if UFOs posed a threat to national security. It was a monumental task! During Project Blue Book, from 1952 to 1970, the Air Force collected 12,618 UFO reports. A small percentage of those were classified, "unexplained." These Gary Sheffield investigated. He quickly discovered that for some unknown reason the names and other personal information from witnesses reporting the UFOs had been changed—names changed, false addresses given—it was like looking for a needle in a haystack. He was unsuccessful in finding out who they were.

Donovan answered Gary's question with a smile. "Yes, Gary, I've been to Idaho in the winter. I remember it was quite cold! Take some warm clothes!"

Then Donovan turned serious. "Kyle has kept a very low profile, very careful to stay in the background and not overstep his authority. He somehow managed to get his hands on a copy of a confidential memo written by Idaho Attorney General Sam Kennerton addressed to Idaho's Governor Stan Nordgren." Donovan slid the file folder across the desk to Gary. "I want you to study it. It might provide some clues or perspective on Idaho's mutilation investigations."

There was a barely perceptible hesitation before Gary asked, "Right now?"

"Yes. Right now! And please pay particular attention to the parts I've underlined. I found them very informative." Donovan glanced at his watch and got up from his chair. "I've got to go see the boss man. When he's through with me I'll be back. Then let's talk."

Gary waved a hand, already engrossed in studying Sam Kennerton's memo. "All right," he mumbled. He didn't even look up when Donovan headed for the door.

The memo's title grabbed Gary's attention: *Summary Report—Cattle Mutilation Problem*

The document consisted of three typed, single-spaced pages. Gary's mind was suddenly sharp and clear. His eyes narrowed as he started reading the confidential memo. It began: Since much publicity has been given to the deaths of cattle throughout the country, particularly in the northwest, and in Idaho specifically, it was decided this office should monitor the reports of Idaho cattle mutilations to determine whether or not there was some common design that could lead investigators to a solution of the problem.

Gary leaned his head down closer to the memo, cursing its single spacing. He hated wearing glasses, but he reluctantly reached into the top desk drawer and retrieved his reading glasses, slid them to the end of his nose and kept reading:

On June 1, 1975, this office began a program of obtaining reports of all known deaths of cattle wherein some type of mutilation was suspected. This program actually involved the coordination of a number of different agencies and the funneling the reports of these agencies into one master file.

Though Bill Donovan had highlighted the memo's most significant information, Gary couldn't help reading every word of the fascinating document, committing to memory its most important parts. Knowing Donovan like he did, Gary knew he'd want to discuss them in minute detail. The next highlighted part read:

In an attempt to standardize the flow of information into this office a statewide broadcast via law enforcement teletype was made to all law enforcement agencies in Idaho and eastern Oregon. This broadcast indicated the desire of the attorney general's office to coordinate reports of cattle mutilations, as well as this office's cooperation with the state Department of Agriculture, the State Brand Department and the Idaho Cattlemen's Association.

In the third week of June the Fish and Game Department told us they were convinced the mutilations were caused by predators. We ordered Idaho National guard helicopter pilots to observe and report any suspicious activity they might encounter during practice flights— and especially watch for any packs of coyotes, cougars or stray wolves.

At that time (June, 1975) 90 cattle mutilations had been reported from 22 counties. So far we have received only 36 written reports from law enforcement. Fremont County indicates they had had 22 cattle mutilations and are deeply concerned with the possibility of human or alien involvement.

That word *alien* jumped off the page and surprised Gary, but he kept reading:

Concerning the tissue samples of mutilated cattle sent to our state lab they told us there was no way of knowing any of the circumstances involved in collecting the samples, so they were dumped. Tissue samples of mutilated horses were more carefully prepared and sent to the FBI Lab in Washington. To date no response has been received from the FBI.

Gary skimmed much of the bureaucratic verbiage on the third page, but his head jerked up as he read the final sentence which Donovan had underlined with a red pen and added a large exclamation mark:

I think the most significant aspect of these animal mutilations is that there is not enough conclusive evidence to determine exactly what caused the mutilations or who or what the mutilators are!

Gary mulled that sentence over in his mind. Then he leaned back in his chair and removed his reading glasses. An idea began to form:

There is not enough evidence as to who the mutilators are? Could that provide an answer? Gary wondered. The memo was written last summer, when no one in Idaho had a clue as to who or the mutilators were. Even so, why couldn't that final sentence work to the FBI's advantage? If Captain John and his people leave and if the FBI plays its cards right they might be able to influence Governor Nordgren to call a news conference and also issue a press release to that effect. Two big ifs to be sure, but the idea had some very definite possibilities!

✝

There came a light tapping on Gary's door, and Bill Donovan walked in holding his trademark cup of coffee. He took a chair in front of Gary's desk.

"Have you read the memo?" he asked.

Gary nodded.

"So? What do you think?"

"Well, for openers, the last sentence you redlined gave me an idea."

"Like what?" Donovan asked.

Gary held the three-page memo in his hand. "This last sentence, *there is not enough conclusive evidence to determine exactly what caused the mutilations or who or what the mutilators are,* may offer the solution we're looking for. The aliens are leaving, so the mutilations will cease. As I see it, all we'd have to do is make sure anyone who knows the mutilators' identity remains silent, then no one would ever be the wiser. I think Kyle and I can handle that. Here's how I see it." Gary explained how he planned to proceed.

Donovan stared at him but said nothing.

"Well? What do you think?" Gary asked.

Donovan's eyebrows rose in surprise, and it was a moment before he said firmly, "It's a great idea, Gary! I believe it could work!" Donovan's voice carried an undercurrent of excitement. "And it may be more important than you know. So let me make sure I have this straight. You will contact Sheriff Dan Jeffords, Dr. James Austin and rancher Randy Johnson and request their silence on anything relating to UFOs or aliens. While you do that, Kyle will contact Idaho's three investigators and request their silence. Then the two of you will arrange a secret meeting with Governor Nordgren and urge, no, demand that he issue a press release that the mutilators have ended their killing spree—and have him state clearly there was not enough conclusive evidence to identify the perpetrators. Right?"

"You got it!" Gary said. "I believe it'll work, if..."

Donovan held up a hand and sipped his coffee as a puzzled look crossed his face. A minute of amicable silence went by before Donovan said, "The whole damn deal hinges on Governor Nordgren, and that worries me. He's a politician, and I've never met one yet who can be trusted. They all have their own agendas."

Gary shook his head. "I wouldn't worry too much about him or his underlings," He'd be committing political suicide if he even mentioned UFOs or aliens, plus ..."

Gary stopped abruptly in mid sentence.

"What?" Donovan asked.

"That's it! That's where I should start—with Governor Nordgren, you just mentioned. I think he'd be cooperative—he'd have no choice—and that would be the diplomatic thing to do—start at the top and work down. I'll meet with the governor as soon as I get to Boise and secure his permission for me to meet with Sheriff Jeffords, Dr. Austin and Randy Johnson—and for Kyle to meet with Nordgren's three investigators and swear them to secrecy. What do you think?"

"I think you'd make a hell of a diplomat, Gary! It'll work!" Donovan said enthusiastically as a huge smile played across his face. "Then we can wrap up this messy mutilation episode in a nice neat package and start the New Year with a clean slate. No more animal mutilations, no more aliens. Ranch life in Idaho could settle back to normal."

Gary nodded, stroking his chin with one hand while he drummed the fingers of the other hand on his desk as if recalling another thought.

"Something else on your mind?" Donovan asked and drank down the last of his coffee.

"Have you heard the latest scuttlebutt about Sheriff Dan Jeffords?" Gary asked.

"No. What about him?"

"Kyle told me the sheriff has kind of gone off the deep end, ever since his meeting with Captain John. Unhinged is the word Kyle used."

"Why haven't I heard about that?" Donovan asked.

"Kyle just told me yesterday," Gary answered.

"Unhinged?" Donovan said. "Elaborate if you will."

"Kyle said the sheriff has arrested some people without cause and he's been accused by the Idaho State Police of brutalizing jail inmates. The county attorney is looking into his conduct."

Donovan chuckled. "Other than that, what kind of man is he—really?"

"The way Kyle tells it he's an ex-marine, one mean rough, tough western sonofabitch and doesn't take kindly to any outsiders poking around in his jurisdiction?"

"People like you?" Donovan grinned

"Yeah, like me."

"He sounds like a hell of a nice guy," Donovan said sarcastically. "You'll have to figure out the best way to deal with him—just be damn careful this thing doesn't blow up in your face—I emphasize again, we don't want the FBI involved in any way, media wise. Do you understand?"

Gary nodded.

"You and Kyle watch your backs," Donovan said. "That sheriff sounds like loose cannon. He could be dangerous."

Gary set the memo down and gave Donovan a slight grin. "What an assignment! UFOs, aliens, politicians, crazy sheriffs! Damn, boss you're all heart, you know that?"

"So I've been told a time or two! Hop on the next plane and get out there to Idaho, and let's wrap this up. Be careful and keep me posted!"

23

Salt Lake City, Utah

ON THE THIRD FLOOR OF THE GRACE Medical Building in Salt Lake City, a private meeting was in progress. Dr. James Austin listened to his psychiatrist friend and colleague, Dr. Wally Davidson, explain details of his examination of Sheriff Dan Jeffords.

Dr. Davidson, a stocky man in his late fifties, with unruly white hair, loosened his tie. "Jim, when you scheduled an appointment for Sheriff Dan Jeffords to meet with me, I had no idea what I was in for! From what you told me on the phone I assumed he was probably overworked and underpaid, which leads to a great deal of stress and other complications. At that time I thought your fears about Jeffords' strange behavior were exaggerated. But after treating him I now understand your concern for the man's well being."

"What have you come up with so far?" Dr. Austin asked.

"Well, he's obviously very depressed and somewhat agitated. He fluctuates between elation and delusional in a very disturbing way. Frankly, I don't know if there is any treatment for his peculiar kind of problem."

"What do you mean?"

Well, so far, I haven't been able to come up with a definitive diagnosis between a bipolar affective disorder…"

"Bipolar affective disorder? That's manic depression," Dr. Austin said with alarm.

"That's true, but hold on, Jim. I said I haven't been able to come up with a definitive diagnosis. I've been looking at every possibility and I'm thinking maybe he's a victim of PTSD, post traumatic stress disorder. Are you familiar with that?"

Dr. Austin nodded. "I've heard the term. Isn't that the new name our medical colleagues came up with for what we front line army doctors called shell shock back in World War Two?"

Davidson chuckled. "Back then we called it a lot of things. But yes, it covers shell shock and several other mental disorders. That damned Vietnam War created an epidemic of PTSD cases, which automatically triggered intense new research to develop the best treatment method for military personnel suffering with PTSD. Those researchers are making some interesting and scientific breakthroughs now that it's considered a real mental illness and not just an excuse for military personnel to fake craziness."

"Such as?" Dr. Austin asked.

"Well," Davidson said, "They're starting to learn what PTSD really is, which comes in many different forms. It's considered a severe anxiety disorder that can develop after exposure to any event that could result in psychological trauma. The event may involve the threat of death to oneself or to someone else, or to one's own or someone else's physical, sexual or psychological integrity."

"In plain English, Wally, what makes you think Sheriff Jeffords may suffer from PTSD?" Dr. Austin asked.

"Well, when he's lucid, he's an intelligent, super law enforcement officer, a man who would go out of his way to help others, very courageous. But when he's in the manic stage he's prone to do and say some very dangerous and strange things."

"Like what?" Dr. Austin asked.

"That's the frightening part," Davidson said. "The sheriff might do something dangerous to himself or to others. He might even consider or commit suicide. I'm not quite sure if Jeffords has reached that state—yet."

"Anything else?" Dr. Austin asked.

Davidson didn't answer for a few moments. "To be honest with you, Jim, I'm not sure about anything when it comes to Jeffords case. I had a hunch that perhaps his physical condition might somehow play into the mental thing—so I gave him a cursory physical examination. He had a couple of old bullet wounds, one from his marine combat experience in the Pacific and the other from getting shot by a felon."

"Other than that, he was in good physical condition?" Dr. Austin asked.

Davidson nodded. "He was." Suddenly Davidson remembered a small detail. "He did have a strange looking triangular scar on his back just below his right shoulder blade, almost like a small brand we see on western range cattle. It wasn't completely healed so I assumed Jeffords must have backed into something which tore open his skin."

"Did he complain of any pain?" Dr. Austin asked.

"His strange answer really puzzled me. He said when he gets angry and depressed the scar burns like someone touched him a hot iron. Right then I began to wonder if his whole problem doesn't stem directly from a wild delusion, a figment of his imagination."

"Wild delusion? You lost me. Can you explain that?" Dr. Austin slid forward in his chair.

"The sheriff told me the wildest tale about seeing spaceships and aliens—actually talking to them. They told him they came to earth to kill and gather Idaho livestock! Is that crazy, or what? Did he ever mention anything like that to you about that?"

"He did mention it, yes," Dr. Austin said, wondering if he should tell Davidson that he himself had been with the sheriff when they encountered the aliens, but he decided to just let it go.

"What did you think when he told you that?" Davidson probed. "Did you believe him?"

Dr. Austin was purposely evasive. "It seemed pretty far fetched, well, right down weird. Nothing like I've ever encountered in any patient before. That's why I sent him to you."

Donaldson nodded. "Well, it took only one counseling session for me to discover that the sheriff actually believes he met an alien, out there in the hinterlands of Idaho. There's no question whatsoever about that in his mind. On subsequent visits I tried a couple of times to eradicate that wild delusion and bring him back to reality using hypnosis."

"I don't think it worked, Wally," Dr. Austin said, "Not the way he's been acting lately!"

"You got that right, Jim! He's too damned stubborn and bull headed for anyone to be able to put him under hypnosis."

"Too bad it didn't work," Dr. Austin said. "Do you think the sheriff's delusions might fall under the PTSD definition?"

"I'm not sure," Davidson admitted. "This PTSD thing is still in its infancy. But it is an intriguing new science and I'm trying to learn more about it. I'm spending a couple of afternoons a week up on the hill, at the Veterans Administration Hospital, working with three top notch PTSD specialists. They're working their hind ends off treating dozens of ex-military veterans coming back from the rice paddies of Vietnam—whole in body, well some of them. But their minds are shot to hell. They've all lost touch with reality, just like Sheriff Jeffords."

Davidson smiled. "As a matter of fact, I'm heading up to the VA Hospital later this afternoon. Would you like to tag along, maybe learn something new?"

Dr. Austin shook his head. "Hell, Wally, I'm way too old for psychiatry. I have a hard enough time being a GP. Besides, my wife rode down with me to do a little pre-Christmas shopping. We're heading back to Twin Falls in the morning."

"Well, don't say I didn't offer," Davidson said. "Are we still on for some Idaho fly fly fishing this spring?"

"Just let me know when you can get away!"

"Do you have any other questions before you leave?" Davidson asked.

Dr. Austin nodded. "A couple."

"Is there any hope that Sheriff Jeffords will ever function normally again?"

"Not unless somebody comes up with some new ideas or methods for treating mental patients. The medication I prescribed should help some, especially during his bouts with depression—if he takes it."

"Then there's nothing else you can do for him?" Dr. Austin asked, hoping for a more positive outlook for his friend Sheriff Dan Jeffords.

"Well, Jim, I believe his condition is treatable, yes, curable—probably not, unless we get him committed to a psychiatric facility—and you can guess what his answer would be if we even hinted such a thing."

Dr. Austin hesitated to ask his other question, but it had to be asked. "Is Sheriff Jeffords dangerous to himself and others in his present frame of mind?"

"Yes, Jim. Yes he is. Very dangerous!"

Twin Falls, Idaho

Dr. James Austin arrived at his office very early and was eyeball deep in paper work, reviewing patient's files, along with a memo from the county attorney suggesting he declare the county sheriff mentally incompetent—and hoping to find time to write up an autopsy report on the two decaying dead bodies discovered by the Highway Patrol a week ago in the barrow pit, just off the freeway.

He glanced at the clock on his bookcase, with an old fashioned dial face, ticking off time faster than he wanted. There was never enough time to get everything done. Today was his wife's birthday. He promised her he'd really try to get his work done early so they could go finish up their last minute Christmas shopping, go to dinner at Antonio's Restaurant and catch a movie.

His nurse stepped in. "Dr. Austin, there's a call from Boise for you on line two."

He nodded, smiled slightly at the nurse, picked up the phone and pushed the second of four buttons.

"Good morning, Dr. Austin. My name is Gary Sheffield. I'm a special agent with the FBI out of Washington, DC, here in Idaho on business. Do you have a moment we can talk?"

Gary's call took Dr. Austin by surprise! *FBI? Damn, Sheriff Jeffords' continual prediction was coming true—'you can bet your ass that one of these days we'll be hearing from the FBI.'*

"What can I do for you Mr. Sheffield? Do you have a medical problem?"

"No sir, no medical problem, just a very urgent matter of business."

"Urgent business?" Dr. Austin asked. "What kind of business? I assume it must have something to do with animal mutilations."

"You assume correctly, Doctor."

"Obviously, you don't want to talk about it on the phone. Right?"

"That's right, Doctor. So I need to meet with you, Sheriff Jeffords and Randy Johnson as soon as possible."

Austin was thinking *I'd rather not.* But how do you say no to the FBI? There was silence on the line for a few moments before Dr. Austin said, "Is it really important? I've made plans..."

"I'm glad I caught you then!" Gary interrupted. "Yes, it's important, a matter of national security. It won't take long to wrap up the details. When and where can we meet? I want this meeting held someplace away from probing eyes, top secret. No one is to know it ever happened. Do you understand?"

"What's up, Mr. Sheffield? Are we in some kind of trouble?"

Gary ignored Dr. Austin's questions.

"What about our meeting?" Gary's voice took on a sharper tone.

"Before we set up a meeting, Mr. Sheffield, I have one concern I'd like to run by you."

"Yes? What is it?"

"I think you should meet with me, Deputy Sheriff Jake Henline and Randy Johnson before you involve Sheriff Jeffords. We need to provide you with some details concerning the sheriff's condition before you make any contact with him."

"What kind of details?" Gary asked.

"I don't want to get into too many specifics over the phone. Suffice it to say Sheriff Jeffords is experiencing some very serious medical problems, and Deputy Henline is unofficially running the Sheriff's office."

"How long has this been going on?" Gary asked, though he was somewhat aware of the sheriff's erratic behavior from info he'd received from Agent Kyle Bowden.

"For several months," Dr. Austin replied.

"Has the sheriff received any professional help for his problems?"

"Yes sir, he has. I referred him to Dr. Wally Davidson, a noted psychiatrist down in Salt Lake City and the sheriff has been receiving treatment."

"A psychiatrist?" Gary asked. "I thought you said it was a medical problem."

"The term medical covers many areas, Mr. Sheffield, and allows folks to maintain their dignity, if you get my meaning."

"I understand," Gary said. "Has the sheriff's treatments by Dr. Davidson helped?"

"No sir, not one bit, I'm sorry to say."

"I'm truly sorry to hear that, Dr. Austin," Gary said. "Then it's your considered medical opinion that there's no way the sheriff could sit in with us?"

"No way at all, Mr. Sheffield, absolutely not!" Dr. Austin answered, wanting to avoid the slightest possibility of arousing Sheriff Jeffords' further suspicions that some plot was afoot to force him out of office.

"Too bad," Gary said. "Based on your recommendation I'll exclude Sheriff Jeffords for the time being and deal with him later. So what about the meeting?"

"How about at my home?" He gave Gary the directions to his small ranch, on the outskirts of Twin Falls. "Tomorrow evening around seven?"

"That would be fine, Dr. Austin. I've got some unfinished business here in Boise, and then I'll drive down and meet you and the others tomorrow evening."

Disgruntled, with incoming phone calls and everything piling up, Dr. Austin scratched his chin, shoved his paperwork aside, grabbed the phone and told his wife he was leaving the office, but he had one quick stop to make before driving home. That quick stop was to determine Sheriff Jeffords' current condition before the FBI agent arrived in town to stir things up. Things could get ugly if the Sheriff was in one of his 'moods' and somehow found out the FBI was cutting in on his territory!

He slipped on his top coat, put on his hat, pulled on his gloves and told his nurse to take his calls. Then stepped out of the office and leaned into the wind and snow and slowly made his way to Sheriff Jeffords' office, just two blocks down the street.

24

ATTORNEY GENERAL SAM KENNERTON'S secretary buzzed his phone. "Mr. Kyle Howden of the FBI is on line one."

"Put him through," Kennerton said. He knew Kyle quite well from working with him on different legal issues involving state and federal jurisdictions in Idaho over the years.

"Sam," Kyle said, "I know you're busy my friend, so I won't keep you. I just need a quick favor."

"If it has anything to do with money, forget it," Sam chuckled.

"Nope, not money," Kyle said. "I wonder if you could arrange for a well connected businessman to meet with the governor for a few minutes early Friday morning? His name is Robert Morely and he represents a large Canadian mining corporation. He's passing through and wanted to feel the governor out about the possibility of developing certain abandoned Idaho mining claims. He wants the meeting to be confidential until further details are worked out."

Kennerton immediately sensed an opportunity for the governor. "How about eight-thirty in the morning? Would that work?"

"Perfect!" Kyle said. "Mr. Morely will be there—and thanks, Sam. I owe you one."

The bitter cold wind that ripped across the Boise airfield was biting, piercing through Gary Sheffield. He bent his head and hurried toward the terminal, holding his hat in place with one hand and his suitcase in the other.

The terminal was crowded with skiers and Christmas visitors either coming to Boise for the holiday or transferring to other flights.

Gary heard someone call his name through the crowd and he paused and stared in the direction of the voice. He saw Kyle Howden wave and make his way through the milling crowd.

The tall, broad-shouldered ex football player and former Air Force officer looked about the same as Gary remembered him from three years ago at a meeting in DC. He still sported a bulldog military haircut. He was ten years younger than Gary and moved with the grace of a trained athlete.

They met in the middle of the terminal and shook hands vigorously. "Welcome to beautiful downtown Boise," Kyle grinned. "I ordered sunshine but it didn't materialize."

"Too bad," Gary said. "But the skiers coming in look happy."

They walked across the terminal out into the drifting snow and got into Kyle's car.

As Kyle drove along the slushy freeway, taking Gary to a motel, he glanced over and said, "I lined up an appointment for you with the governor at eight-thirty in the morning. For that meeting you'll be Robert Morely, a Canadian mining official. That keeps your identity confidential while you're in Boise."

Gary nodded. "Do you know the governor?"

"Not personally. But I know the Attorney General. That gives me a good contact at the state capitol."

"Is the governor someone we can deal with?" Gary asked.

"I think so," Kyle said. "Just take it slow and easy. Ask him gracefully instead of telling him and you'll do all right. These people out here can be lead to water but making them drink can be tricky."

Gary grinned. "I believe I've heard that a time or two!"

Kyle said, "I think your plan to meet with the governor is well thought out. I hope he'll give you his blessing for us to talk to those people who came in contact with the mutilators."

"Well, if he doesn't, we'll have to by-pass him," Gary said. "Do you know the governor's three investigators?"

Kyle kept his eyes straight ahead as traffic slowed to a crawl on the icy freeway. "I do. The last time I worked with them we were trying to apprehend cattle rustlers from Montana who stole cattle and brought them to Idaho to be auctioned off. It was quite the scheme—like the old wild west, all within the bounds of our little area—and lots of money too!"

"They sound like good guys," Gary said, "do you anticipate any problems when you meet with them and warn them to keep quiet about their investigations?"

"None at all. I suspect they are looking for a way to do just that—as soon as you get the governor's permission."

Gary nodded. "This Sheriff Dan Jeffords you mentioned, do you also know him?"

"No, but I've heard about him?"

"Bad?"

Kyle nodded. "Bad! If I were you I'd talk to Dr. James Austin first before you talk to Jeffords. He can give you some tips on the safest way to approach the sheriff."

"I've already done that," Gary said. "What about Randy Johnson?" Gary asked.

"Don't worry about him," Kyle said, "He lost some race horses to the mutilators, so he'll be happy to talk to you."

"I wish you could go with me to Twin Falls," Gary said. "But in the interests of time we have to move fast. The longer we wait the greater the danger of something leaking out to the media. The brass in Washington want this mutilation business put to bed quietly and quickly. And above all, they want us to make sure nothing slips out about the FBI's involvement with the aliens or the word alien even mentioned! If we can't get the job done, you and I will be looking for new employment!"

✝

Gary unpacked, then took a shower. He opened the blinds in his motel room and watched snow blowing and drifting across the Boise River and hoped that someday he might have enough seniority to get a permanent assignment in sunny Hawaii!

Alone in his motel room, Gary sat up late into the night, unable to let his mind wind down and get some rest. *How the hell can we cover all the bases? Too many people involved. Who is the most dangerous—the one who might expose the FBI's conspiracy with the aliens?*

He finally drifted off to sleep about midnight. He awoke at six, dressed, brushed his teeth and shaved then went to the lobby. He took his time and had coffee and a Danish in the lobby lounge and read the morning paper. Then he buttoned his top coat, walked out to the parking lot, got in the rental car Kyle had secured and drove on the icy freeway to the state capitol building.

Attorney General Sam Kennerton met him in the foyer. "Mr. Morely, I'm Sam Kennerton. I'll take you to Governor Nordgren." Kennerton smiled. "Is the weather as bad as this in Canada?"

"Oh yes sir! Every day," Gary replied.

Nordgren's secretary smiled as Kennerton said, "This is Mr. Morely, here to see the governor." Then he turned to Gary. "The governor is expecting you. Through that door." He pointed.

"Thank you, Mr. Kennerton," Gary said and walked into Nordgren's office.

The governor got out of his chair behind the large cluttered desk, walked around and extended his hand to Gary. "Welcome to Idaho, Mr. Morely. I'm pleased to meet you." Morely had a grip like steel. Nordgren liked that—a man you could trust.

"We have a fresh pot of coffee, Mr. Morely. Would you like a cup?"

"Yes sir! You folks run a pretty chilly winter in these parts," Gary said, trying to establish some charisma and rapport with the governor before getting down to business.

As Nordgren poured two cups of coffee he turned his head. "Have a seat." He brought the coffee, one for Gary and one for himself, and sat down comfortably next to Gary. Nordgren sipped his coffee. "Damn, that's good on a bitter cold winter morning! Now, sir, what may I do for you?"

Gary smiled. "First off, Governor," Gary said, wanting to get off on the right track, and show he was a man of integrity, "Let me tell you I'm flying under false colors. My name is actually Gary Sheffield and I'm a special agent out of FBI Headquarters in Washington, DC." He showed Nordgren his badge.

"Washington, DC?" Nordgren was completely surprised. "Out here in Idaho in the dead of winter? To what do I owe such an honor, Mr. Sheffield? Have you come to arrest me?"

"Oh no sir! Not today," Gary said, cracking a grin.

"Damn, that's a relief! Federal people always give me goose bumps! I assume you're visit has something to do with the animal mutilation epidemic we've been wrestling with for the last five months."

Gary nodded. "Your assumption is correct."

"So what does the FBI want with me, Mr. Sheffield."

"Before I answer that, let's have an understanding. Anything we discuss is strictly confidential. All right?"

Nordgren nodded and said, "Okay, Mr. Sheffield, I'll agree to that or tell you when we've crossed a line where I wouldn't be comfortable. Go ahead. Ask away."

"Fair enough, Sir. Does the name Captain John mean anything to you?"

Nordgren's face showed incredulity at the question. The governor stared at him for a long moment. "I've heard the name."

"Then you can probably guess what brings me to Idaho."

Nordgren shook his head. "I'm not sure I follow you, Mr. Sheffield. There seems to be a large leap of faith in there somewhere."

"Well for starters, you and I both know who and what the mutilators are, right?" Gary saw a strange look cross Nordgren's face.

Nordgren shrugged his shoulders. "So?"

"Well sir, if there's even the slightest chance that any information gets out about the mutilator's true identity the consequences could be catastrophic."

"To whom? The FBI?" Nordgren asked, with a stone cold face. "You wouldn't be here if you weren't trying to cover your backside. May I assume that?"

Nordgren's caustic remark troubled Gary, and brought his quick response. "And we're covering your backside too, Governor! You're probably thinking you have a good chance to climb out of this crisis with a feather in your cap by laying the blame for the animal mutilations on an FBI conspiracy, right?"

Nordgren nodded. "I won't lie to you, Mr. Sheffield, the thought has played on my mind since my staff and I deduced what must be happening." He decided to cut it off here and see if Mr. Sheffield would tighten the noose any further.

Gary stared at Nordgren. "I think you know you would come out on the short end of that, so you don't even want to go down that road. Dismiss that thought entirely," Gary warned, trying to get the upper hand, but finding this western governor and politician a bit more practiced in this sort of thing than the FBI kingpins would have suspected.

"And if I don't?" Nordgren asked, still not showing a bluff in his hand.

"Let's just say that wouldn't be wise."

"Is that a damn threat?" Nordgren asked, with a touch of anger.

"No sir. Certainly not." Gary forced a smile "We'd like to take a positive approach by asking you to cooperate and work with us so you remain in office as Idaho's popular governor and boost your chances for re-election next fall."

Nordgren looked apprehensive. "I'm not sure I follow. Can you please explain that a bit more in detail how you are suddenly going to save my ass when you've screwed this thing up as bad as you have?" There was a touch of anger in Nordgren's voice.

"Yes sir. To begin with, the aliens have left Idaho, so the mutilator problem is over. There will be no more animal mutilations—at least for the foreseeable future…"

Nordgren interrupted and stared at Gary. "My investigators have already told me that. C'mon, Mr. Sheffield, you're sidestepping! There's more to your visit than to tell me that everyone lives happily ever after—or you wouldn't be here. Right?"

"You're very perceptive, Governor, and quite correct. It's the aftermath of the mutilator's destruction the FBI is concerned about—the mysterious mess they left behind—and the people they came in contact with—which I assure you wasn't supposed to happen. We need to make everything about the mutilator's visit disappear as though it had never happened."

"Just how do you propose to do that?" Nordgren asked.

"Well, for starters," Gary said, "by contacting the six people who came in contact with the aliens and warning them against divulging any information about their alien encounters."

"Which six people are we talking about?" Nordgren asked, thinking to himself, *damn, this boy is sharper than I thought.*

"Three of them are your investigators. I need your permission for the FBI to contact them."

"Is that really necessary?" Nordgren cut him off and protested, "I've already warned them, as well as my personal staff, to keep quiet."

"I appreciate that, sir. Your warning to them makes the FBI's contact just a routine follow up, but emphasizes the federal government's concern for tight security.

"Who are the other three?" Nordgren asked, knowing he couldn't refuse to give up his guys.

"Dr. James Austin, Sheriff Dan Jeffords and rancher Randy Johnson."

"You don't need my permission to speak to them," Nordgren said.

"I know," Gary said, "but we need you in the loop because you're going to be the key player when we bring this case to a close."

Governor Nordgren leaned forward in his seat, his eyes wide with interest. "Me? What the hell do you mean?"

"Well sir, to be perfectly blunt, you are going to lie to the public..."

"I'm going to do what?" Nordgren voice rose.

"Lie!" Gary repeated. "Isn't that what shrewd politicians sometime do at crisis time? You are going to set up a TV and radio news conference and tell the public how pleased you are that your dedicated law enforcement people have driven the mutilators from Idaho. Then you publicly thank God the mutilations have ended. You are, however, disappointed that the police were unable to uncover enough conclusive evidence to positively identify the mutilators."

Gary watched Nordgren seriously thinking it through. "Do you think the public will buy it?" Nordgren asked, frowning slightly.

Gary nodded. "They'd be absolutely overjoyed!"

"I don't know..." Nordgren stroked his chin, not fully convinced. "What if some astute reporter asks if we've received help from any federal law enforcement agencies—like the FBI for example."

"That's simple, Governor," Gary said. "Yes you did! You tell the public you contacted the FBI for help and they told you condescendingly that they had more important matters to attend to than riding around Idaho in jeeps looking at dozens of dead range cattle."

Nordgren shook his head gravely. "You don't leave me much choice, do you?"

"Not really, sir," Gary said firmly. Then lowered his voice persuasively. "Please look at it through our eyes as well. You come out of this situation totally exonerated. You dealt with a very serious state problem by coordinating law enforcement activities. Remember your "war room" and sending investigators out to get the bottom of the problem? The voters will remember and respond to that in the upcoming election. It's a win-win situation for you and the FBI."

Impressed, but still a bit ill tempered, Governor Nordgren took a few moments to mull that over, realizing now there was some pretty sound logic in Agent Sheffield's overall assessment. "You've thought this out very carefully, haven't you?" Nordgren said evenly, measuring each word.

"Yes sir, we have," Gary answered.

"And the FBI brass in Washington are okay with this plan?"

"Yes sir. That's why I'm here."

"How soon would you want me to call such a news conference?" Nordgren asked, acquiescing that he'd probably now accept the FBI's plan for closing the mutilator investigation.

"I'll let you know," Gary said. "Probably sometime around mid-January, if I can get all the details worked out by then."

Gary stood and extended his hand in gentlemanly fashion to Nordgren, assuming that the good governor had met his match and would accept the fact that the FBI's plan for bringing the mutilation episode to a close would work.

"You've been very helpful sir, and the bureau and I do appreciate it."

Nordgren shook Gary's hand, trying at the same time to suppress the sense of excitement he felt. *The mutilations were over. The mutilators were gone. The problem was almost solved!* These words went around and around in his brain.

For a second Governor Nordgren was about to say something happily flippant, something about that crazy Captain John and little green men from Mars. But he saw from the expression on Gary Sheffield's face the man was all business!

"I don't want anything to happen to you down in Twin Falls. Please be careful and keep me informed."

"I'm always careful, sir," Gary said as Nordgren walked him to the door.

25

SHERIFF DAN JEFFORDS' MORNING HAD gone from bad to worse, and it didn't look like things were going to improve any time soon. He stood behind the desk in his office and stared out the window at the whirling snowstorm. Winter still had its grip on the land. Twin Falls seemed to get bleaker every day—dark in the morning, dark at five in the evening.

Jeffords' head was splitting with another migraine headache, the second one today. He was wound up tighter than a drum, jumpy, ready to explode and he couldn't figure out why. Dizzy, he settled into his squeaky old leather chair. He opened the desk drawer, found a bottle of Tylenol, opened the plastic lid with one hand and popped two pills into his mouth then washed them down with water mixed with whiskey in his coffee cup. He closed his eyes and waited for the Tylenol to take effect.

Ever since his confrontation with Captain John last fall he'd been unable to get a full night's sleep. Weird dreams of aliens and spaceships filled his mind and he'd wake up in a terrified sweat.

Jeffords' deputies, with exception of Chief Deputy Jake Henline, were on Christmas leave, happy to get away from the sheriff and his erratic behavior—continually shouting and screaming orders at them, cursing them as if they were green military recruits rather than professional law enforcement officers with years of experience. Every one of them was nervous, wondering what the new year would bring and whether they'd be able to hold onto their jobs.

In Jeffords' mind they were all conspiring against him, sneaking around, giving him looks, talking about him behind his back, and probably devising ways to push him out of office. The truth of the matter was that everyone but Dan Jeffords was aware that he'd been acting very strangely of late. Take early this morning for example.

When Jeffords walked down the long corridor, checking the jail cells, Jimmy Camacho spat out, "You gringo bastard!" Or at least Jeffords thought he did.

Ticked off, the sheriff unlocked and threw the cell door open, shoved Camacho against the wall and smashed an iron-hard fist into his stomach. He would have slugged the weaselly-faced mouthy little son of a bitch square in the face if Jake Henline hadn't stepped in at that moment for his day shift, grabbed Jeffords' arm and pulled him off.

"Goddamn you, Jake!" Jeffords hissed. "Don't you ever grab me like that again or I'll..."

"Or you'll what?" Jake interrupted angrily. "What the hell's the matter with you? Get hold of yourself!" Jake was a big burly man, towering over the sheriff.

Jeffords stared hatefully at Jake. "Mind your own business. You don't come into my jail and start shoving me around. Understand? You and the others—I know what you're up to! Sneaking around, talking behind my back." The knot in Jeffords' stomach tightened. His pistol was back on his desk. *Jake was trying to take over. Damn him to hell.* If he could just get back to his desk...

"I'm not shoving you around, Dan," Jake said calmly. "Loosen up, man! I'm just trying to save your ass. You can't arrest people without cause or beat on them. The county attorney has warned you..."

"Piss on him, Jake. Who the hell does he think he is, God Almighty? This is my county. He can't tell me what to do!"

"Oh yes he can," Jake countered. "And if he can't the attorney general up in Boise sure as hell can."

Sheriff Jeffords just stood there with a 'where am I' confused look on his face.

Jimmy Camacho was lying on the floor, doubled up, groaning, gasping for breath. Jake reached down and helped him to his feet, and asked softly, "Are you okay, Jimmy?"

Jimmy stared hatefully at the sheriff who was standing there in a daze.

"Muy loco," the young man whispered to Jake, circling his finger around his left temple. Jake leaned over and shook his head. "Shh." He whispered. And pointed Jimmy to the other side of the cell. He took Jeffords' arm and led him out into the hall and locked the cell door.

"C'mon, Dan," Jake said softly and escorted Jeffords back to his desk and gently pushed him down into his chair. "Just relax. Take it easy. You'll be all right."

Startled, Jeffords drew back and looked up. "Jake?"

Jake smiled. "Yeah, it's me, Dan. Feel Better now?"

Jeffords nodded.

"Good. Why was Jimmy locked up?" Jake asked.

Jeffords' brow wrinkled in concentration trying to remember. "He was staggering drunk last night, singing, pissing on the sidewalk, raising hell. I received several calls to get him off the street. He was out of control."

"You've seen him that way before, Dan. He doesn't drive and he doesn't hurt anyone. We always let him sleep it off when we bring him in. He was probably staggering home to his wife and kids."

Jeffords looked blank, like he couldn't fully comprehend what Jake was talking about.

"Why did you hit him?" Jake asked.

Jeffords jerked back to reality. "The little son of a bitch called me a gringo. Nobody calls me names...'

"Nothing's wrong with that," Jake grinned. "You are a gringo, and a mighty damn mean one at that! You can't hold Jimmy for calling you a name. I'm going to release him to his wife—and let's hope to God he doesn't file a complaint against you for brutality."

Jeffords scowled! "You do whatever you think is best. You and the other deputies never back me up anyway. You want my job so bad you can taste it, don't you Jake? Always scheming behind my back, countermanding my orders—all of you conspiring against me. Well, you just try taking my job away from me and see what happens."

Jesus! Jake gritted his teeth angrily, shook his head and threw his hand in the air. He was so pissed off he couldn't see straight. It was futile and frustrating to argue with Jeffords. He'd gone completely over the edge. His suspicions of everyone grew worse with each passing day. In the back of Jake's mind lingered the frightening thought that he didn't know what Jeffords was capable of in his present condition. *Something had to be done. But what? One of these days Dan was going to beat one inmate too many and that one would eventually fight back and probably kill the sheriff. It would serve the crazy bastard right!*

Jake quickly walked back to Jimmy's cell, opened it and motioned him to follow him out the back door to his patrol car. When they were seated, Jake was still so pissed off he couldn't even talk. He hadn't said a word to Jimmy.

"Senor Jake," Jimmy said, "how can you work with that crazy gringo every day?"

"It ain't easy, Jimmy!"

Jake hit the steering wheel with his fist and swore a blue streak. "That crazy son of a bitch—I've told him over and over again. Oh never mind."

Jake knew he shouldn't say things like that in front of a prisoner, but damn it, he'd almost reached his breaking point, which always brought the same thought. *He could easily switch jobs and join the Highway Patrol.*

"Are you mad at me, Jake?" Jimmy asked mildly.

Jake shook his head and kept his eyes on the snow-covered road leading to Jimmy's tiny rental home.

"No, Jimmy, I'm not mad at you. Did Sheriff Jeffords mirandize you when he arrested you last night?"

"Mirandize?" Jimmy asked.

"You know. Tell you you have the right to remain silent..."

"No, Senor Jake." Jimmy said. "He jes knock me down and put on me—how you say, cuffs, and shove me into his patrol car. He say to me, "you little Mexican prick, you say one word I will shoot you.""

Jake pulled the patrol car into Jimmy's driveway. He looked over at Jimmy and smiled. "I'm sorry this happened, Jimmy. You okay?"

Jimmy grinned. "Damn right, man! No more bad ass sheriff to beat on me!"

Jake grabbed Jimmy's hand and shook it. "Tell Maria and the kids hello and that I wish them a Merry Christmas. And Jimmy, for hell sake stay sober!"

Jimmy grinned. "That's asking quite a lot, Senor Jake, but I will try. Thank you, my friend, for letting me out of jail."

For a moment Dan Jeffords sat at his desk, perfectly still, stunned. *What the hell have I done?* He tried to remember. He felt sweat seep out of his forehead and his cheeks grow damp. His shirt was suddenly too tight. He pulled it open so violently that he ripped off a button.

I hit Jimmy Camacho? Did I kill him? He couldn't assemble his thoughts. They were a tangle.

At that moment Dr. Austin stepped into the sheriff's office unannounced and slapped his snow-covered Stetson against his leg. Jeffords, still in a daze looked up. His office was messy and cluttered as usual, smelling of stale tobacco smoke.

The first words out of Dr. Austin's mouth were, "What's wrong, Dan? You look like hell! Are you all right?"

"No, Jim," Jeffords growled.

"What's the problem?"

"Jim, sit down, please," Jeffords said.

"But what..."

"Jim, please. Sit down."

Dr. Austin slid into the closest chair in front of Jeffords' desk. He had never seen Jeffords like this—even his big hands were trembling involuntarily. He and Jeffords had always been direct with each other, so maybe today the sheriff would finally come clean, level with Dr. Austin and tell him what was troubling him.

Facing Dr. Austin, Jeffords confessed." I think I just beat a prisoner."

Surprised, Dr. Austin said, "You did? Why?"

"I don't know. He irritated the hell out of me. That's all."

One of Dr. Austin's thick eyebrows cocked as if what the sheriff was telling him was completely off the wall. "You can't beat prisoners, Dan! Good God, man, you could lose your job, your pension, your family..."

Jeffords face was instantly tense, his jaw became rock hard. He shook his head as if it was full of cobwebs, and stared at Dr. Austin for a few moments without saying anything. "Damn you, Jim. Don't you lecture me! I run this jail..."

"Whoa, Dan. Take it easy! I'm not lecturing you. I'm trying to help you."

Dr. Austin knew he'd hit a raw nerve with Jeffords and he'd have to proceed with caution.

Jeffords apologized. But his expression was as hard as ever. "I'm sorry, Jim. I know you're trying to help me. In fact, you're the only one in this whole county I can trust. Can I talk to you in confidence?"

Dr. Austin nodded. "Certainly."

"Jake's trying force me out of my job!"

"What makes you think that?"

"He threatened me this morning. He said I'd be up on charges for treating prisoners like I do. He told me I couldn't arrest anyone without mirandizing them. Hell, Jim, I know that, but I've never much believed in that Miranda bullshit, wasting time. A crook is a crook. I don't baby 'em..."

Dr. Austin shook his head, his face coldly business like. "Jake's right, Dan. You should listen to him. He's not only your chief deputy, he's your friend too."

Jeffords' head snapped up and his face was again instantly tense. *Jim's siding with all the others! Why is my best friend betraying me?* His mind filled with sudden dread.

"You're plotting against me too, Jim?" Jeffords asked almost pleadingly. "How can you do that to me?"

"I'm not plotting against you, Dan," Dr. Austin responded softly. "You've had some bad days, and they're starting to tell on you. You've gone through a rough time and I'm really worried about you."

"What's wrong with me, Jim?" Jeffords said, almost with a sob.

"I truly believe it stems from that horrifying alien experience when you met Captain John last fall. Remember? You came away pretty rattled."

"More than rattled," Jeffords admitted. "I've had dozens of nightmares about what happened that night on old Ben Summers' ranch. Those nightmares play over and over in my mind and never stop. Why is that, Jim?"

"I don't really know. Maybe it's because you're a law enforcement officer and you were suspicious of Captain John from the first moment he appeared. He was the enemy. He mutilated our animals. You not only wanted to arrest him, you were even going to shoot him!"

Jeffords nodded. "So?"

"You posed a threat to Captain John's authority. He doesn't tolerate threats. Remember? He killed Ben Summers. It may sound diabolical, but maybe Captain John deliberately planted something in your brain or psyche that caused you to become like you are."

That sounded logical to Jeffords, but it also raised a question in his mind.

"What about you, Jim? Why weren't you affected?"

"This is just a wild guess," Dr. Austin said, "but maybe it's because I wasn't a threat or an enemy to Captain John. In fact I rather liked him and I would have really enjoyed spending more time with him, learning more about his civilization, his travels through the universe and how far their medical science has advanced."

Here Dr. Austin stopped. "I think we got sidetracked. We were talking about your problem."

"Do we have to?" Jeffords asked without much enthusiasm. "I have a headache."

"Yeah, and that headache's only to get worse unless we figure out what's causing it!" Dr. Austin said without waiting for any response. Then he asked a question to which he already knew the answer. "Did you talk about your alien experience with Dr. Davidson, the psychiatrist I sent you to down in Salt Lake?"

Jeffords nodded. "Yeah. But it didn't do a damn bit of good. He always uses big fifty-cent words like schizophrenia and manic depression. I get so damned confused! I don't know what the hell he's talking about half the time! One thing I do know though, he didn't believe a word I said about meeting Captain John."

Dr. Austin smiled. "That's understandable. I'm not sure I would either if I hadn't been there with you. Are you taking the medications Dr. Davidson prescribed?"

Jeffords shook his head. "No. they didn't help at all. They made me feel all mixed up inside like I wasn't in control. I was like a walking zombie. I can't sleep. My nerves are shot to hell. Sometimes I think I'm going crazy."

"No, Dan. You're not going crazy…you…"

"Oh no?" Jeffords argued. "Then why is everyone after me?"

"Everyone?" Dr. Austin said. "Like who?"

"My deputies. That smart-ass smirking county attorney who wants me to step down. The Twin Falls Chief of Police who called me a low-life, overbearing son of a bitch because I roughed up one of his officers who told me I was out of my jurisdiction. All of 'em, Jim. They're all out to get me…"

Dr. Austin threw up a hand to stop Jeffords' rant. "Whoa, Dan, you've got to calm down. Take a little time away from the office. Let Jake handle the office for a couple of weeks. Take the wife on a vacation—go someplace where the sun is shining."

"Do you think that would help?" Jeffords brightened, thinking through the possibilities.

"It sure wouldn't hurt," Dr. Austin said. "And I want to you to start taking your medications again."

Jeffords leaned forward in his chair and started to object.

Dr. Austin again held up a hand. "I know, I know, Dan. You don't want to. But if you take your medications faithfully every day your mind will clear up. How about it? Will you do that for me?"

Jeffords' mind was still a shambles but he knew Dr. Austin was right—and the gentle way Dr. Austin asked, touched Jeffords. A slight smile crossed his face for the first time. "If it was anyone else asking me I'd tell 'em to kiss my ass. But for you Jim, I'll give it a try. I really will!"

"That's all I can ask for right now, Dan. It'll work and you'll feel better. Trust me."

For a second, Jeffords just sat there thinking—*vacation? Damn that sounds good. Get away from these crazy people conspiring against me.* He took several deep breaths, waiting for the oozing perspiration to abate, he mopped his face dry and pulled up his tie. His fingers felt thick and unmanageable. He knew he could not trust himself to drive home on the icy roads in his present condition.

He leaned forward in his chair and said, "Jim, will you do me a favor?"

"Sure, Dan. Just name it!"

"Would you tell Jake I'm taking a few days off? I don't want to run into him the way I feel right now. Then will you drive me home?"

"I'll be happy to. Give me an hour. I'll close my office and come by and pick you up."

26

KYLE HOWDEN WAS ON THE FREEWAY approaching downtown Boise. Despite eighteen inches of new snow and blizzard conditions, Kyle's mind was focused on solving Idaho's animal mutilation problem, and his boss, Gary Sheffield being in town. Suddenly he took his foot off the gas pedal and allowed his Chevy to slow down to avoid a six-car pile up littered across two freeway lanes. The driver of the car behind him honked angrily in protest, then passed him, his horn blaring and his middle finger extended.

What a Crazy bastard! Kyle thought and ignored him and drove on, but wider awake now and more cautious. He pulled off onto the Fifth Avenue off ramp and breathed a sigh of relief as he drove across the icy parking lot into his parking spot behind the FBI field office.

The sun wasn't up yet when he walked into the office and breathed in the pleasant aroma of fresh brewing coffee.

Helen Rissom, his confidential secretary, greeted him with a smile and said, "Good morning, Mr. Howden. Ready for a new day?"

Kyle wasn't a morning person and he'd never figured out how Helen, at 7:30 in the morning, could look so neat and be so pleasant, not a hair of her gray-streaked black hair out of place, and her attractive figure dashing about the office keeping everything in perfect order.

Kyle smiled back. "Hi yourself," he replied, taking off his coat and hat. "After that icy drive on the freeway I wasn't sure I'd have a new day."

"This might help." She handed him a mug of hot coffee.

"Thanks," he said, taking the mug in both hands. "Anything new happening?"

"Attorney General Kennerton called last night just after you left. He wanted to verify your meeting with him and his investigators tomorrow afternoon at one-thirty. I told him you'd be there."

"Good," Kyle nodded. "Can you check and see if we've received a report from Sheriff Buck Tobin over in Bear Lake County. He promised me on the phone last week he'd mail it to me. I'd like to review it before my meeting tomorrow."

"It came in the mail late yesterday afternoon," Helen said, as she reached over and took it from her in basket and handed it to him.

Kyle gave it a quick glance. "This is all? Only one page?"

"That's it," Helen said. "Isn't Sheriff Tobin the one who investigated the deaths of sheep and goats over near Bear Lake?"

"Yeah," Kyle said, "and as far as I know they're the last animals killed by the mutilators in Idaho. That's why I figured his report might be important."

Helen stared at him. "Even with Sheriff Tobin's report, you don't have much detailed information to work with, do you?"

Kyle shook his head. "Very little. Sam Kennerton keeps a pretty tight lid on most of the specific information he and his investigators have gathered. I get the idea they don't want the FBI messing in Idaho's business. Sam's succeeded damn well in that endeavor."

"Maybe you can pry some information out of him tomorrow," Helen offered.

"I'm not holding my breath," Kyle said. "Do you have those confidential agreement forms ready for the meeting—you know, the ones swearing Kennerton and his people to secrecy,"

"Yes sir. They're typed and on your desk—one for each man, ready for their signatures. I also typed three agreements for Mr. Sheffield to take with him to Twin Falls—but I was kind of puzzled by one of them."

"Which one?" Kyle asked.

"The one I typed for Deputy Sheriff Jake Henline. I thought Dan Jeffords was the Twin Falls County Sheriff."

"He is," Kyle replied.

"Well, how come you didn't have me type an agreement for him?"

Kyle smiled. "Remember our need to know rule?"

"That means you're not going to tell me, are you?"

"That's a negative, Helen." Kyle said.

"Okay. If that's all you're going to tell me, I'll go back to my typewriter," she said with a mock pout on her face. She started to walk out of his office, then turned and asked, "Is Mr. Sheffield coming in today?"

"A little later this morning."

"Good. Maybe he'll tell me why he's meeting with the deputy instead of the sheriff."

"Don't even think about it!" Kyle said. Then he smiled and said playfully, "Will you please get out of here and go back to work. And please hold my phone calls. I've got some catching up to do. No interruptions. Okay?"

"Yes sir." She walked out and closed his office door.

Sipping hot coffee, Kyle settled in his chair at his desk and studied Sheriff Tobin's report along with bits of information he'd been able to gather from the news media and from Idaho's tight-fisted officials—and a few other odds and ends picked up from a few cooperative law enforcement officers. However, the critically important data he needed in this investigation was under lock and key in Attorney General Kennerton's safe, unavailable to the FBI. And that circumstance worried and disturbed Kyle who wanted to know exactly what Idaho investigators knew and when they knew it.

Kyle was slightly frustrated. He'd been pulled into this mutilation crisis far too late and he didn't have all the facts! Washington was often very slow in notifying its field offices, especially when national security was involved—too many political decisions had to be made before appropriate action could be taken. He sat back and placed the tips of his fingers together trying to come up with some ideas on how to diplomatically obtain full disclosure from the attorney general then get the confidential security agreements signed by him and his investigators. He'd need to be extremely careful to avoid any antagonism that often interferes with developing a compatible working relationship between state and federal officials, both of whom normally want to protect their own turf—*almost like playing a game of chess where there is only one winner.*

He looked up with annoyance when he heard a quick knock on his office door.

"I said nobody, Helen!" Kyle called out.

"Does that include me?" Gary Sheffield asked as he slipped around Helen, who was holding the door open.

Kyle knew something was wrong as soon as he saw Gary's face, which wasn't particularly happy.

"Of course not. C'mon in," Kyle motioned him. "You're always welcome. I just hadn't expected you this early. Anything wrong?"

"There certainly is!" Gary said with disgust. "As if we didn't have enough trouble already. Take a look at this newspaper I found in the news rack at my motel!" He unrolled the latest copy of a San Francisco Chronicle and held it up so Kyle could read its bold, glaring headline: Eerie Cattle Mutilations Spread Westward: Is California Next?

Kyle looked very uncomfortable, almost alarmed. "Damn!" he said with a frown. "And just when I thought we were getting on top of things. Do you think the mutilators are going to start killing and mutilating California livestock?"

"It sure as hell looks like it," Gary said. "Go ahead and read the article, then let's talk. I'll grab a cup of coffee from Helen." He handed the paper to Kyle and he started reading:

RENO—Nevada has joined the list of western states perplexed by the eerie mutilation killing of livestock. Hundreds of such incidents have been reported in twelve other states this year, including Oregon. But there is as yet no confirmed mutilations in California. The carcass of a young male calf, drained of blood and minus its sex organs was recently found in a pasture five miles west of Denio in northeastern Nevada. The animal was taken to the state lab facilities in Reno where an autopsy was performed. Veterinary diagnostician Charles VanDamen said, as have examiners in other states, that he had never seen anything like it. "The penis, rectum and tail had been removed almost surgically with a very sharp knife or scalpel," VanDamen added. There was no evidence of an attack by a predator. Bulls, cows, calves and horses have been killed mysteriously in a number of western states, with various organs— including eyes, tongues, ears, udders and genitals—removed.

Gary again walked into Kyle's office, a cup of coffee in his hand, and sat down in front of his desk.

"Damn, Gary," Kyle said, shaking his head, "I just can't believe this! All their body parts missing…just like here in Idaho." He stared at Gary for a few seconds. "What the hell is going on?"

"There's more," Gary pointed to the paper. "Read the rest of it."

Kyle took a deep breath, and plunged back into the article:

In nearly every case no cause of death has been determined. Human or vehicle prints have not been found around most of the bodies, which frequently have been drained of blood. This has led some to conclude that the mutilators arrive by helicopter. One dead animal reportedly was found in fresh snow. Its tracks were visible, but there were no other prints around. Theories are widespread and frequently blood-chilling. Among the most popular attempted explanations: vampires, crazed morticians or veterinarians, devil worshipers, visitors from outer space, or predators with razor-like teeth. Last fall a rancher in Idaho's Magic Valley, Randy Johnson, said two of his horses were killed and mutilated and he saw nothing. He said, "They needed sophisticated equipment to do this work." VanDamen concluded, "One of the problems associated with these cases is that by the time the animals are discovered, decomposition has usually set in and it is too late for real evaluations.

"Randy Johnson?" Kyle said. "Why the hell did they mention him?"

"Damned if I know," Gary said. "Maybe to warn California people to watch their horses?"

"I hope they do," Kyle said. "Are we expected to do something if the mutilators strike in California?"

Both had assumed the mutilation epidemic was over. Captain John and his two ships had flown out of Idaho weeks ago. So who were these new mutilators now raiding ranches and farms in Nevada and might soon do the same in California? Against the remote—but nevertheless—real possibility that Captain John had secretly returned, they didn't have the first damn clue!

"So far as I know right now our current assignments are all we need to be concerned with," Gary said. "Unless Washington notifies us otherwise, let's just concentrate on the job at hand—ensuring that all these Idaho witnesses, in any way connected to the alien animal mutilations, remain silent. We'll have to let Washington try and sort out what may happen in California."

Kyle grinned. "I'll go along with that!"

Gary chuckled. "Getting back to the matter at hand, after we've gotten the confidential agreements signed by all parties involved I'll meet with Governor Nordgren and have him issue a press release that animal mutilations in Idaho have ceased."

"Good luck with that," Kyle said. "You met him, so you know he can be pretty testy if things don't go his way."

"That's why I'm not going to ask him, I'm going to tell him."

Kyle frowned slightly. "A man like Stan Nordgren is not easily intimidated."

"Did I mention intimidation?"

"You didn't have to," Kyle said. "But I certainly understand the need for it if we're ever going to mark this case closed."

Gary nodded. "Don't worry about it. I'm not expecting any trouble from the governor, though I'm sure he'll want me to identify exactly what steps we've taken to prevent any further mutilations here in Idaho."

"How do you plan to do that?" Kyle asked.

"Well he knows Captain John is gone so I'll tell him there's nothing for him to worry about."

Kyle stared at him for a moment. "I'm not sure that'll solve the problem. You and I and the governor know that Captain John is gone. But Idaho farmers and ranchers are still scared half to death wondering when the mutilators may zoom into this area again and start butchering their animals. The local news media spews out daily reports about domestic livestock being slaughtered by the dozens in Wyoming, Montana and Utah—and today we learn that California may be next. That'll probably be splattered all over on TV in a day or two. That'll just add fuel to the fire and keep these pistol-packing Idaho farmers and ranchers on edge twenty four hours a day."

"Well, there's not a hell of a lot we can do about the media," Gary said. "If, and that's a mighty big if, our government is doing something covert, besides working with Captain John, they're not letting us in on it. For all I know they may have made secret agreements to let other alien groups come into this country."

Kyle nodded. "Frankly, that wouldn't surprise me a bit. If they've made any such agreements it would certainly answer a lot of our questions. I find it difficult to believe that aliens can be flying around the western United States, almost like commercial airliners, and no one back in Washington seems to know diddly squat about what is going on."

Gary agreed. "Well, whatever Washington may or may not be doing to help solve the mutilation problem, we seem to be out of their loop for some reason. When you meet with Sam Kennerton tomorrow be careful what you say. I'll do the same when I'm down in Twin Falls."

Gary took a sip of coffee. "Anything else?"

Kyle shook his head.

"Then we've got our bases covered," Gary said. "If you're free this evening how about having dinner together?"

Kyle nodded. "Sounds good. I'll pick you up at your motel around six-thirty."

Kyle stared at Gary for a long moment.

"Something else on your mind?" Gary asked.

Kyle nodded. "I don't know why, Gary, but I have a bad feeling about you going down to Twin Falls alone. Please be very careful."

Gary saw the concerned look on Kyle's face. "Are you worried about Sheriff Dan Jeffords?"

"Your damn rights I am. That crazy sonofabitch, if you'll pardon the French, is someone to worry about. Do you have your gun? You're going to..."

Gary stopped him with an uplifted hand. "Right here!" He patted his small snub nose 357 Smith and Wesson revolver, in its well worn leather holster, on his left hip, from which he could crass draw with lightning speed.

"I hope you don't have to use it," Kyle said.

"Me too," Gary said. "Anything else?" Gary said as he stood to leave.

Kyle motioned him back to his chair. "Do you have a few minutes?"

"There's nothing on my agenda until tomorrow."

"You want a refill on the coffee?" Kyle asked.

Gary handed him his empty cup.

Kyle spun his chair to a table behind his desk, which held a small Pyrex pitcher of hot coffee. Kyle poured coffee and carefully handed Gary a refilled cup then sat one on his desk.

"What's on your mind?" Gary asked.

27

KYLE SIPPED HIS COFFEE AND LOOKED AT Gary thoughtfully for a moment. "Could you postpone your trip to Twin Falls for a day or two and go with me to meet Sam Kennerton and his investigators tomorrow? Then I could go with you down to Twin Falls." Kyle paused. "I don't know why Gary, but something just keeps nagging at me about you going down there alone. There's safety in numbers."

There was a moment of silence. Gary was pleased but not really surprised by Kyle's suggestion. He'd thought about it himself. "I appreciate the offer. Not that I wouldn't enjoy your company and your back up, but I want you here in Boise to take care of business. You're special agent in charge here in this region. The last thing you need is me, a Washington outsider, poking around in Idaho's business, except for the governor of course. I'll handle him when the time comes."

Kyle mulled that over. "I didn't think about that. But maybe you're right. I do have to work with these local law enforcement people—and they can be a little obstinate at times. All the same, I'm glad you're here."

"Anything else?" Gary asked.

Kyle nodded and hesitated for a moment. "It's kind of personal, and if it's none of my business just say so."

"Let's hear it."

"I know you worked undercover as an FBI liaison officer with the Air Force during Project Blue Book. Could you share with me a few details of your experiences during that assignment? It might help me better understand UFOs and aliens and how this bizarre situation came about. Would that be out of line?"

In the FBI there it was standard operating procedure that highly confidential cases were not to be discussed unless an agent had a definite need to know, so Gary took a moment to consider the request; then said, "I suppose not, if it's just for your information and it goes no further."

"You have my word," Kyle said.

"All right, since we're off the record, what you do you actually know about Project Blue Book?"

"Not a hell of a lot," Kyle answered. "I know there were a lot of UFO sightings back in the days shortly after World War Two. The world press called those sightings mass hysteria. The Air Force downplayed the whole deal, labeling anyone who claimed to have seen a UFO a nut case!"

Gary sighed audibly with a smile. "That's the perception most folks seem to have of the Blue Book era. Let me give you some facts so you'll have a clearer understanding of what actually took place. To begin with, Project Blue Book was one of a series of systematic studies of unidentified flying objects (UFOs) conducted by the Air Force."

"Why the Air Force?" Kyle asked. "Why not some policing agency, like the CIA, federal marshals, you know, people like that?"

"Good question," Gary answered. "According to the information I got directly from Air Force General Tom Carradine, Air Force and commercial pilots reported several run ins with UFOs. The government decided UFO phenomena should be investigated by the Air Force which controls American air space. The question then became how does the Air Force do that?" Gary sipped his coffee. "Are you still with me?"

Kyle nodded but didn't reply.

Gary continued. "The Air Force's prime objective was to determine if UFOs posed a threat to America's national security by analyzing whatever data they could get their hands on."

Kyle raised an eyebrow. "And they did that for eighteen years as I recall. Did they ever come up with any specific evidence that UFOs were extraterrestrial?"

"They labeled UFOs as actual misidentifications of natural phenomena such as clouds, stars, commercial or Air Force aircraft."

"All twelve thousand UFO sightings?" Kyle asked.

Gary said, "Twelve thousand eight hundred and sixteen to be exact."

Kyle frowned. "And they all turned out to be natural phenomena?"

"Oh no, not all of them!" Gary said. "Seven hundred and one of those reported UFO sightings remain unidentified to the very day!"

"Interesting," Kyle said. "Do you think any of those seven hundred and one UFOs carried alien visitors?"

"I was extremely curious about that," Gary said. "So I asked General Carradine and he told me, 'there's no evidence whatsoever to indicate that any of those seven hundred and one unidentified flying objects were extraterrestrial vehicles.'"

Kyle gave Gary a penetrating stare. "Evidently that's what General Carradine believes. I'm interested in what you believe. You investigated twelve thousand UFO sightings…"

"Whoa," Gary interrupted and held up a hand. "No, no. I wasn't involved in anything that had to do with specific UFO sightings. That wasn't my job. The Air Force handled those. I was involved mainly with the unusual cases which the Air Force marked 'inconclusive' after their investigations."

"Meaning?" Kyle asked.

"Incidents where aliens in UFOs may have come in direct contact with American citizens."

Kyle stared at him for a moment. "I don't recall that being mentioned in Project Blue Book. You mean the Air Force actually interviewed some of those victims?"

"I don't really know," Gary said. "If they did, they never told me. As a courtesy they provided me names of a few of people who claimed to be victims of aliens or had made alien contact; but as I sadly learned, when I tried to contact some of those people their names turned out to be fictitious."

"Then why did the Air Force give them to you?" Kyle asked with mounting interest.

Gary stared at him for a long moment, almost visibly deciding whether he could trust him with what he was about to say. "Perhaps the Air Force wanted to show the FBI it was being cooperative. However, my personal feeling is the Air Force didn't want the FBI or the news media to ever find out or identify those people who had come in direct contact with aliens."

"You're probably right," Kyle said. "Were you ever able to discover their identities?"

Gary nodded. "A few of them—after one hell of a lot of digging and calling in a few favors from a couple of friends in the Air Force hierarchy."

"And you interviewed those folks you identified?" Kyle asked.

"Yes."

"After you interviewed them did you write reports of what they told you?" Kyle asked with subdued excitement.

"What interviews?" Gary smiled deviously. "Yes. I wrote a very detailed analysis of each interview and turned them in to my boss. He reviewed them for a few days, then handed them back and told me to destroy them."

"But why?" Kyle asked. "That doesn't make any sense since you'd put so much time and effort into the interviews."

"I'm guessing, but I think the Air Force may have found out that we knew too much about those alien encounters, so they ordered the FBI to destroy any written information or any other physical evidence concerning UFOs and aliens."

"Did you destroy your report?" Kyle asked.

Gary nodded. "I did. An order is an order—but it really pissed me off! I was so damn mad I was nearly ready to resign. I guess my boss sensed my anger and frustration so he explained that if we inadvertently embarrassed the Air Force our future careers wouldn't be worth a plug nickel. His explanation sure as hell didn't improve my attitude or morale!"

Kyle waited for Gary to continue. But he remained silent.

"You mentioned physical evidence—like what?" Kyle prodded.

"The most interesting item was an implanted metal-type device about the size of a cigarette pack taken from the body of a female victim. Our lab technicians drew a total blank when it came to figuring out what it was or how it worked. They couldn't even figure out what kind of metal it was. It wasn't any type of metal found on our planet. The aliens also accidentally left behind what appeared to be some kind of medical apparatus made of the same type of unidentified metal. There were a couple of other things—but it's all water under the bridge now, if you pardon the cliché, which I really shouldn't be talking about."

"Maybe not," Kyle agreed, "but you can't just leave me hanging. Do you remember any of those people you interviewed?"

"I certainly do! They're hard people to forget," Gary said quietly.

"Can you tell me a little bit about them? Do you believe they actually had alien encounters?"

Gary looked at Kyle for fifteen seconds, then finally said, "Yes, Kyle, I believe they did." As those words came out, he detected a slight look of skepticism on Kyle's face.

"What convinced you?" Kyle asked.

"It was a combination of several things."

"For instance?" Kyle slid to the edge of his chair.

Gary stood and stretched his six-foot-two inch frame, twisted his head sideways a time or two then sat down again. "Well, Kyle, looking back on that moment in time, the most convincing evidence of those folks' encounter with aliens came about when they were placed under hypnosis."

"Hypnosis?" Kyle asked with surprise.

Gary nodded. "Yes. Hypnosis conducted by a highly qualified FBI psychiatrist on the five subjects, which included three men and two women, who lived in different states back east. They didn't know each other. Within a controlled environment, at different times and in different locales, the psychiatrist hypnotized them. At that point I took over and asked them specific questions about their face to face encounter with aliens. Each subject responded in identical fashion. In a nutshell, here's what it boiled down to. They were snatched from their natural earthly environment and beamed aboard an alien space craft, then physically examined by strange unearthly beings who were evidently trying to learn more about the human body and how it functions."

"How did those subjects react when they recalled those events?" Kyle asked.

"Use your imagination. Several of them screamed in terror, they fought me and tried to run away. I had to physically restrain them. When the psychiatrist finally got them calmed down they freely admitted to me that once they were inside the alien craft their captors, whom they feared, treated them well, though they did spend hours physically examining their bodies. The two women, with some embarrassment, told me the aliens seemed extremely interested in their reproductive systems."

Kyle leaned forward. "Did the aliens speak to them or ask any questions?"

"Not vocally, no. Not like you and I are communicating," Gary replied.

Kyle looked puzzled. "Are you saying the aliens and the subjects communicated with each other without speaking? That would be mental telepathy, right?"

Gary nodded. "That's what I assumed."

"What happened to those five people after you and the psychiatrist finished with them?" Kyle asked.

"To put it bluntly the Air Force ordered them to keep their mouths shut about their abductions, and threatened them with severe penalties if they failed to do so."

"Excuse me, Gary, but I find it hard to believe that our own government…"

Gary interrupted. "Not the entire government, Kyle. I'm not sure how high up the chain of command this alien cover up went but I felt deeply and still do to this day that either the Air Force or the FBI or both had some obligation to help these folks through their trauma, and get them back to some sense of normalcy. I argued the point with my boss as much as I dared, but it was a waste of time. The Air Force and my boss slapped my hands and ordered me to destroy my files and forget the entire matter."

"Damn, Gary, this is so far out…it boggles the mind…"

"Well, my friend, I was there and those are the facts, not pleasant facts, but facts, and we have to deal in facts, not with things as we wish they were. Those five people I interviewed sure as hell didn't want to come in contact with aliens—just like you and I sure as hell don't want aliens slaughtering western livestock like they've been doing."

"I understand," Kyle said. "But it all seems so damned sinister! Why are all of these things happening?" Kyle seemed to be speaking more to himself than to Gary. "Oh well." Kyle's voice trailed off. "What ultimately happened to those five subjects? Are they still alive?"

Gary shook his head. "Two of them have passed away, and the last I heard the other three are terminally ill with severe physical and mental health problems."

"Do you think their abductions had anything to do with their deaths and illnesses?" Kyle asked.

"It's quite possible," Gary said.

Kyle sat there, silent, several questions running through his mind.

"What are you thinking, my friend? Gary asked.

Kyle rubbed his chin, pondering. "Maybe there's a time line? Perhaps those aliens of the Blue Book era discovered the earth and its inhabitants, flew home, then returned later and zeroed in on our livestock. Could there be a connection?"

"I'm not sure I follow you." Gary said.

"Well, when Project Blue Book was discontinued you were interviewing humans who claimed they had been abducted by aliens. Today we are both investigating weird animal mutilations inflicted by aliens. I'm just wondering if there's any connection between the two events."

"Maybe. Maybe not. Who knows?" Gary said.

"I think maybe there is," Kyle countered. "Maybe the aliens of the Blue Book era were exploratory expeditions from other worlds trying to find out if different life forms existed in the universe. They succeeded in finding both human and animal life, here on earth, and now they've returned to kill and mutilate our animals. What do you think?"

"It's all conjecture at this point in time," Gary said. "We may never know the answer."

Before Kyle could respond a quick knock came on the office door and Helen opened the door. "Excuse me, Mr. Sheffield, Assistant Director Bill Donovan is on the phone from Washington. You can take it at my desk." She pointed to her desk with a chair and the secure phone.

"Are you alone, Gary?" Donovan asked.

"Yes sir."

"Good. Have you seen the article in the San Francisco Chronicle telling the whole damn world the mutilators may move soon move into California?"

"Yes sir."

"So have we and we're in panic mode back here. We don't have the faintest idea who these new mutilators may be. Have you heard any talk or chatter out your way? Anything I can pass along to the director?"

"Not at the moment, sir."

"Have there been any more mutilations in Idaho?" Donovan asked.

"None that I'm aware of."

"Thank God for that! How soon can you finish your current assignment?"

"I need at least a week."

"Is that the best you can do? No way to finish up sooner?" Donovan said a little sharply.

"No sir. There are several loose ends to tie up."

"Okay then. As soon as you're finished I want you on the first plane to San Francisco."

"What do I do when I get there?"

"If the mutilators hit California I want you to be there to coordinate law enforcement activities. Work with our other agents and do whatever you can to muzzle the news media from spreading stories about UFOs and aliens— and keep this in mind, these unidentified aliens may be dangerous, so keep me posted. Understood?"

"Yes sir."

Gary walked back to Kyle's office and poured himself a fresh cup of coffee.

"What did the boss want?" Kyle asked.

Gary pointed to the Chronicle on Kyle's desk. "He read that article and it got his balls in a big uproar. He wants me to finish up here as quickly as possible, then hop a plane to San Francisco."

"What the hell for—why is having you in California so important?"

Gary shrugged. "I honestly don't have the first damn clue! But if we don't do something soon the whole situation could blow up in our faces—aliens in California, butchering livestock—*Jesus H. Christ!* That's all we need!"

Kyle and Gary exchanged doubtful glances, then Kyle said, "Did Bill provide any suggestions to help out?"

"No."

"Well then let me throw one at you," Kyle said. "What if Washington could make contact with these *new* aliens? Maybe they could work out some kind of deal or arrangement like they did with Captain John."

"That's an interesting thought," Gary smiled. "There's only one little problem with that. We have no way to communicate with these aliens unless they contact us first."

Kyle nodded. "So where does that leave us?"

"Up the creek without a paddle!" Gary said.

There was a long moment of silence, which Gary finally broke, with a slight jerk of his head: "Do you have a Nevada map?"

Kyle opened a desk drawer and took out a map. He unfolded it and laid it out on his desk.

Gary stood and examined the map for a moment. "That San Francisco Chronicle article highlights animal butchery in Denio, Nevada. Where the hell is Denio?" Gary checked the map coordinates, A-2, and slid his finger north along Highway 95 to the junction where it intersected with Highway one-forty, running west to Denio. Gary tapped his finger on that spot. "Here it is, about one hundred miles north and west of Winnemucca."

"What's your concern about Denio? Why is it so important?" Kyle looked puzzled.

"Because Bill Donovan thinks it is—and because it's mighty damn close to northern California."

Kyle stared at the map and nodded agreement.

Gary continued. "Denio is the latest reported mutilator strike zone. That makes me believe those alien sonsabitches are moving west! See? Look here! From Denio west it's about a hundred miles to one of the most remote isolated spots in California, Modoc County—cattle ranches everywhere! A prime area for the mutilators to do their dirty work!"

"So?" Kyle asked, still puzzled, as he examined the Nevada map with interest. "How does that help us?"

"Well, this is just a hunch on my part," Gary said, "But I'm going to pass it along to Bill Donovan. If he wants to pursue it, he can ask the Modoc County Sheriff to report any unusual UFO sightings or slaughtered animals directly to the FBI."

"What good will that do?" Kyle asked.

Gary grinned. "It'll get Bill Donovan off my ass long enough for me to go down to Twin Falls for a face to face meeting with a couple of people who met Captain John, as well as a rancher who lost two race horses to the good Captain. I have no idea what I may run into down there. Both of us are involved in a dilemma which no FBI agent has ever faced before!"

"I'd say so," Kyle agreed. "Do you think these new mutilators know what we are doing?"

"I doubt if we'll ever find out, unless of course, Washington gives them free rein to rampage through the countryside like they did with Captain John!"

"Do you think Washington will do that?"

Gary shook his head. "Nope." Then he offered Kyle his hand and put the other hand on his shoulder. "Let's just take care of our current assignments, all right?" There was a tone in Gary's voice that Kyle knew meant further discussion was closed.

"We're on for dinner this evening?" Gary asked.

Kyle nodded. "Yes sir. "I'll pick you up at six-thirty."

Kyle watched him go, watched the door close behind him. He didn't move for a time. He just sat there, and stroked his chin a few times. He wished he could have convinced Gary to let him accompany him to Twin Falls.

Though Kyle had never met Twin Falls Sheriff Dan Jeffords he couldn't get him out of his mind. The few discreet inquiries he'd made about the man didn't inspire any trust! The county attorney told Kyle the sheriff had lost his mind! *The same kind of answers came in from other shakers and movers in Twin Falls— the guy is crazy, paranoid, needs psychiatric help and several more cryptic comments even worse…Ah, what the hell? Gary Sheffield is a tough as nails cop who didn't grow old in his line of work by being stupid! He could take care of himself—couldn't he?*

28

GARY EASED THE FORD LTD ONTO Interstate 84, and headed toward Twin Falls, 130 miles south, usually a two and a half hour drive, allowing for a relaxing coffee break. But a sudden unpredicted blizzard slammed into central Idaho and slowed freeway traffic to a crawl. Gary found himself in bumper to bumper traffic and wondered how the hell Idaho folks live through one storm after another in what must seem like endless winter. He couldn't see more than thirty feet in front of him and wished he'd heeded Kyle Howden's advice to cancel the Twin Falls meeting and wait for better weather.

But it was too late now! Here and there, where snow completely blocked parts of the freeway, Gary edged the car through very slowly. Twice he pulled off into the emergency lane to clear snow from the windshield and rear window.

Thank God for truckers Gary thought as he eased back into traffic and slipped in behind a slow-moving18-wheeler, its tail lights leading the way through the whirling snow like a beacon; but why was the truck now pulling off the freeway onto the Mountain Home exit? Then Gary saw the red and blue flashing lights on two Idaho State Police cruisers blocking the freeway ahead, and the officers diverting traffic into Mountain Home until the howling blizzard abated and settled into gently falling snow.

Gary smiled. *Murphy's Law in action.* If anything can go wrong, it will! Well no matter, the drive so far had Gary yawning, wishing for a cup of coffee to keep him going. Three hours and four cups of coffee later, Gary was finally on the freeway again, now cleared of ice and snow. At the north Twin Falls off ramp he exited the freeway and drove onto Main Street.

According to the directions Gary received from Dr. Austin he was to travel west, about halfway to Buhl, then turn north and drive five miles to where the pavement ended and a rural dirt road began. There he would see a sign with large block letters reading: END STATE ROAD MAINTENANCE. Dr. Austin's small ranch was located just west of the sign.

Leaving Twin Falls, Gary again found himself behind a truck, this time a large well-lit state snowplow heading in the direction of Buhl. The snowplow's huge, V-shaped blade cleared a drivable path, while the spreader at the truck's rear flipped ice melter on the asphalt—and on any autos which got to close.

Sixty-year-old snow plow driver Ed Hurley noted headlights a ways behind his truck, and wondered why a few damn fools ventured out during snowstorms—but what the hell, those fools provided job security. The pavement widened out and ended in a turnaround at the maintenance sign. In his rear view mirror Ed watched the headlights of the car following him turn into Dr. Austin's driveway. The snow had let up somewhat so Ed turned the truck around and stopped for a short break. He turned off the headlights, turned on the overhead lights, poured a cup of hot coffee from his thermos into a cup and sipped it slowly, enjoying its refreshing warmth against the bitter cold seeping through the old truck's drafty windows. He lit a cigarette, and relaxed. He noticed a sheriff's patrol car parked in Doc Austin's driveway. Behind it was Randy Johnson's pickup and behind it the car that had followed him from Twin Falls. The driver stepped out of the LTD, leaned into the wind, and made his way to Austin's well-lit front door. *Maybe Doc is having his monthly card game with the sheriff and other friends.* To Ed it seemed a hell of a cold snowy evening to have folks over for a card game. He sipped his coffee and smoked his cigarette, and thought no more about it. All he wanted to do was get home in Twin Falls and fall into bed. He started the truck, drove to the junction and turned east.

Off to his right, four miles from Austin's ranch, Ed could see Sheriff Dan Jeffords white, well lit two-story New England style house, unusual in this rural landscape.

Ed had known Jeffords more years than he liked to think about and over the years they'd become good friends. During good weather when Ed was out that way filling in chuck holes with hot asphalt he always stopped to visit with the sheriff if he happened to be working out in his yard.

Ed slowed his truck, as its headlights outlined a man standing in the middle of the road, waving his arms, hailing him down. Ed leaned forward, and peered through the windshield, surprised to see that it was Sheriff Dan Jeffords, who he'd assumed was playing cards at Doc Austin's place.

Ed slowed to a stop and rolled down the window as Jeffords jumped up on the running board.

"You headed home, Ed?" Jeffords asked.

"Yeah, Dan. I'm on overtime and worn to a frazzle. It's been one long hellacious day!"

Jeffords smiled. "I can imagine. That's why I almost hate to ask you for a small favor. Would you mind running your snowplow down my driveway?"

Ed didn't answer. His eyes studied Jeffords' face curiously.

"Have I got something on my face?" Jeffords asked. "Why are you looking at me like that?"

"Oh, it's nothing, Dan. I'm just surprised to see you. I thought you were playing cards over at Doc Austin's place."

"Why?"

"Well, I saw your patrol car parked in Doc's driveway. Randy Johnson's pickup was parked behind it and a stranger, who followed me from Twin Falls, parked behind Randy's truck. I just figured you guys were having a card game."

Ed's statement brought an immediate angry scowl to Jefford's face, which surprised Ed, who said, "Did I say something wrong?"

Jeffords eyes smoldered through the puffy skin surrounding them, and he gritted his teeth angrily. "That wasn't my patrol car you saw, Ed." It's Jake Henline's!" Jeffords mind was awhirl. *Randy? A stranger? Jake Henline? He's supposed to be on patrol east of Twin Falls.*

"Those goddamned sonsabitches!" Jeffords growled and smashed his fist down on the on the truck's window sill. "They're plotting against me!"

Startled, Ed jerked back and asked, "Who?"

"All of them! Especially that bastard Jake. He's been trying to take my job away from me for months. Well, by God, we'll see about that! I've taken all I'm going to take!"

Ed didn't have a clue what Jeffords was rambling on about, but one thing he did know for sure—Jeffords had one God-awful mean temper when he got mad! "Calm down, Dan," Ed said soothingly. "You sound madder than hell. Why not wait until tomorrow then you can have a sit down with Jake and iron out your differences, whatever they are."

"Don't you start telling me what to do!" Jeffords snarled.

"Okay. Okay. Don't bite my head off. I'm sorry," Ed apologized. "Shall I plow your driveway now?"

"No! Go on home," Jeffords snapped, "I've got more important things to attend to right now." Jeffords paused, then hissed a warning. "And Ed, you keep your mouth shut about this, understand?"

Ed threw up both hands in a helpless gesture of confusion and anger. "If you say so."

Jeffords stepped down. Ed rolled up the window, put the big truck in gear and drove off, still puzzled and concerned by his friend's irrational behavior—he'd never seen him so angry.

Mumbling under his breath Jeffords walked quickly through the deep snow back to his house. When he stomped through the front door his wife, Claire, stared at him, "What's wrong, Honey?"

"That goddamn Jake Henline is over at Doc Austin's place plotting to take my job. He's probably telling Jim to commit me to the nut house!"

Poor Dan looked like death warmed over. There were dark shadows under his eyes. His hair hung limp, wet from the snow.

Claire tried to calm him—a little too quickly! "You don't know that for sure."

"You too?" Jeffords growled. "Isn't there one person in this entire world on my side?"

There was a moment of awkward silence before she apologized. "I'm sorry, Dan." He just glared at her and she wasn't sure what he would do next. So she phrased her next remark carefully when she said, "Why don't you have Jake come over? Talk things out."

The question didn't register with Jeffords. He shook his head. "I trusted Jake completely. I expected loyalty. I hired him, gave him his start in law enforcement. Anytime I needed anything Jake was right there. I made him my chief deputy—and now he's..."

"I know, dear," she interrupted. "He's been like a son to us since the day you swore him in and pinned on his deputy badge."

"Like a son?" Jeffords snorted derisively. "A son doesn't stab a man in the back! He's trying to get my job and he's used every dirty trick in the book!"

"I think you're wrong, Dan!" Claire countered. "He can't take you're job. You're an elected official—he'd have to run against you and he wouldn't do that." She paused for a moment. "He's over at Jim's place right now. Why don't you call him? He could be here in a few minutes and the two of you sit down and talk things out."

"That's enough! Back off, Claire! I mean it!"

Claire felt her self-control begin to unravel. "Don't you threaten me, Dan Jeffords. And please don't speak to me in that tone of voice. I know Jake Henline and he's a damned good man, no matter what you think. You'll play hell finding his equal!"

"You don't know anything! You don't have to work with him every day!"

Maybe not, she thought. *But I have to be around you every day!* Dan had changed so much over the last few months she hardly recognized him any more. Their loving relationship had deteriorated and forced her to move her things into the small guest bedroom—and there she stayed, despite Dan's daily assurances that he would not act irrational, flying off the handle at every little detail life threw at him. What had happened to him? Claire really didn't know. Ever since that day he went to Ben Summers' ranch to investigate the old man's death he'd become a stranger to her. She was convinced that something happened that day which caused Dan's personality change. When she pressed him for details he just stared at her. Then something inside him snapped, something that lay hard in the center of him he couldn't control.

"My work is none of your business! Don't you ever ask me that again!"

Claire didn't move for a time, then in a trembling voice asked, the question that was now upper most in her mind. "What are you going to do?"

He didn't respond, trying to control his temper. Then he brushed past her to the coat closet and grabbed his gun belt hanging on a peg and buckled it around his waist.

"You're going to work on a night like this?" she asked with concern. "Have you been called out?"

Still Jeffords didn't answer. He pulled the .38 revolver from its holster, opened the six-shot cylinder, whirled it, then stuck it back in the holster. He grabbed his coat, zipped it up, and put on his Stetson. He stared for a quick moment at his Sheriff's star lying on the coffee table. *Pick it up! You carry that badge to remind you who you are—what you stand for.* He shook his head lightly. *No! Not this time! This isn't police business—this is a matter of my personal survival!*

Jeffords met his wife's eyes for a long moment then answered her question. "Yes, Honey, I've been called out." He walked over to her, pulled her close and gently kissed her on the forehead. "I'm sorry, Claire. I don't mean to be…"

"Shh." She put her arms around him until he pulled away and quickly walked out the front door.

Clair stood there for a few moments in a frightened daze. She'd involuntarily panicked inside the moment he buckled on his gun belt—and she knew she'd used a poor choice of words almost as soon as she said them when she questioned Dan about being called out! She'd meant to ask are you going out on a call to help someone in trouble.

Not many folks knew, though she certainly did, that in western parlance, *being called out* meant two men facing each other in a gunfight, with the loser being shot dead!

Her mind was racing. *This is crazy!* Dan was going to Jim Austin's place to confront Jake Henline; and there was nothing she could to prevent it. She stared at the phone. *Well maybe she could call Jake and warn him that Dan was on his way to Doc Austin's house.* She could. But she didn't—and she would live to regret it!

Jeffords leaned into the icy wind and fought his way through the deep snow to the garage. As frigid as it was, the triangular scar on his back was burning like a hot branding iron was being applied to his shoulder blades. He was mentally out of control. *They are talking about me, conspiring, telling lies.*

One by one their faces flashed through his mind—faces of people who had once been his closest friends. Faces he had once trusted. *Jake Henline…Jim Austin…Randy Johnson.* Now it dawned on him they had been placed in his life to test him. His gloved right hand reached down and wrapped around the butt of his pistol. It was still there, ready for action!

Then all at once he remembered what had eluded him all these months. The night he and Jim Austin met Captain John on a lonely stretch of rocky ground on old Ben Summers' ranch the Captain had ridiculed him and put him down like he was not worthy to even speak to such an important being as the captain. Jeffords hated the alien then and he hated him now. From that time forward Jeffords world had been shot to hell—his mind didn't function properly, he had weird dreams, some kind of scar on his back burned every time he had to make a lawman's decision. Jeffords believed Captain John had devised some diabolical scheme to force him out of office, destroy him subtly, just to teach him some respect for a superior being.

Jeffords' normal thought processes had evaporated. His mind was locked into one thought. *Destroy those traitors who were conspiring against him!*

He opened the garage door, slid into his patrol car, hit the starter and the big V-8 engine roared to life. Angrily he backed out onto the sloping driveway, gunning the engine, spinning the back tires to a squealing pitch as they turned snow to ice. The car was stalled and wouldn't move! *Son of a bitch!* He turned off the engine and walked back into the garage, got his snow shovel and began shoveling the deep snow off his driveway.

29

IT WAS A LITTLE PAST SEVEN AND DARK when Gary pulled into the driveway of Dr. Austin's two story log home. Swirling snow whipped in from the west drifting snow across the barren farmland. Gary climbed out of the LTD, leaned into the wind, made his way to the front door and rang the doorbell. Dr. Austin opened the door.

"Dr. Austin?" I'm Gary Sheffield. I believe you're expecting me?"

"Ah yes, Mr. Sheffield," Dr. Austin said enthusiastically. "Come in, come in!" He grabbed Gary's hand in a firm handshake, pulled him inside out of the snow and closed the door. "I'm James Austin and we've been worried about you driving through the snow. Let me take your things then I'll introduce you to the others."

"Thank you," Gary said as he unbuttoned his topcoat, took off his hat and handed them to Dr. Austin.

The doctor ushered Gary into his comfortable living room where two men were standing in front of the fireplace chatting. "Mr. Sheffield, that big guy in uniform is Deputy Sheriff Jake Henline. The cowboy next to him is Randy Johnson. He has a big spread over on the other side of Twin Falls. The mutilators butchered two of his best horses."

Then Dr. Austin smiled, pointed to their guest and said, "Gentlemen, this is FBI Special Agent Gary Sheffield from Washington, DC."

They shook hands all around, then took seats on the couch and surrounding chairs. Gary's right knee popped when he sat down—in cold weather it gave him trouble caused years ago by a fall he took while chasing a bank robber. He adjusted his Smith and Wesson five-shot revolver in its hip holster, and slid it further toward his back. The small snub nose 357 magnum with its two-inch barrel, loaded with magnum cartridges, could kill a bear close up. Its man-stopping power had saved his life more than once!

When they were comfortably seated, Dr. Austin's wife, Barbara, brought coffee, poured them each a cup, then walked back to the kitchen.

There was the usual western getting-acquainted small talk. Gary Sheffield wasn't anything like the FBI agents portrayed in movies thought Randy Johnson. He seemed like a personable ordinary guy. His brownish gray hair was trimmed neatly, yes, but far from a military cut. He had an easy country boy charm about him, friendly, talking with a slight southern accent. He called himself a Texican. But beneath the affable, easy going guy exterior Randy sensed that this man was a very sharp dedicated federal agent.

Gary quickly learned that the three men were military combat veterans which added to the comfortable camaraderie. The smell of wood smoke from the rock fireplace scented the air, while firelight played against the walls.

Then it came time to get down to business. Gary took some papers from his brief case, stood, with his back to the fireplace, and said "Thank you for meeting with me on such short notice."

Dr. Austin smiled. "I didn't know we had a choice."

"Nonetheless I appreciate your cooperation, gentlemen," Gary said.

"What brings you all the way out here from Washington, DC in the middle of an Idaho winter?" Dr. Austin asked cordially.

Ordinarily Gary would not be doing this himself. He would have assigned it to Kyle Howden or one of the other FBI agents in the western region. But given the sensitive nature of animal mutiltions related to UFOs and aliens the brass in Washington specifically assigned Gary to handle the case. He never left anything to chance which might come back later and embarrass the powers that be at FBI headquarters.

"My main reason for being here is to swear you to secrecy concerning your involvement with UFOs, aliens and animal mutilations. So anything discussed here is top secret, never to be referred to again privately or publicly, or in writing. To put it very bluntly you are to keep your mouths shut. Divulging any information about aliens or UFOs in conjunction with Idaho's animal mutilations will bring severe penalties down on you, and I do mean severe." Gary held out some papers as if he were offering them to the three men. "I have three government confidential agreement forms which I need you to sign. Do any of you have any problem with that?"

"Are we in some sort of trouble?" Dr. Austin asked.

"No. Quite the opposite," Gary replied. "In the interests of national security the FBI has been assigned to make certain anyone involved with the animal mutilations here in Idaho keeps it to themselves."

Dr. Austin cut in. "There are several others here in Idaho besides us who have sensitive information about animal mutilations. What about them?"

Gary quickly answered, "Kyle Howden, the director of our Boise field office is meeting with them as we speak and will have them sign confidential agreement forms. So let me ask again, "Do any of you have a problem with signing these forms?"

"No problem," Dr. Austin said.

""You, Deputy?" Gary asked.

"No sir."

"You Mr. Johnson?"

"No sir.'

"Good," Gary said. He handed a form to each man. "Please sign your name at the bottom."

Each man quickly glanced over the form, then signed and handed it back to Gary.

"Any questions so far?" Gary asked.

Deputy Jake Henline moved uncomfortably, shifting in his chair.

"Something on your mind, Deputy?" Gary asked.

Jake nodded. "Sheriff Jeffords has been involved clear up to his eyeballs with these animal mutilations. Why isn't he here? If he ever finds out about this secret meeting my life won't be worth a plug nickel. He's dealing with some very serious emotional problems and none of us know what he's capable of."

"I've heard about that, Deputy, and I'm sorry that the sheriff is having problems. From reports I've heard he's been an outstanding law officer. Because of his situation, I plan to meet with him privately before I leave Twin Falls and see if I can find out what's troubling him and do whatever I can to help him. Maybe you can fill me in and tell me a something about him. You work with him every day."

Jake looked somberly at Gary. "Well, sir, for the last four months he's been going downhill, acting really strange. He's been, I don't know, moody. Everything gets on his nerves, and that's not like him."

Gary listened, then nodded. "Go on."

"Well, on top of everything else he's been having terrible headaches. Sometimes I think he's suicidal. He keeps complaining about some kind of weird scar on his back that troubles him. He doesn't know when or where he got it. He says it burns like hell when he gets stressed."

Gary nodded. "Sort of like a ticking time bomb ready to go off?"

"Exactly. He was especially worked up last week—I mean ranting and raving, full of hate." Jake shook his head, "And that hate is directed at me. Like how I want to take his job, I'm always plotting against him, I'm insubordinate. I don't mind telling you, sir, it scares hell out of me just to be around him."

"That's certainly understandable," Gary said. "That's why none of you must mention this meeting to him. Understand?"

The three men nodded.

"Okay. Let's get on with it then," Gary said, "I believe you are all ahead of me as far as animal mutilations here in Idaho are concerned. Do any of you have any questions for me concerning any part of that episode?"

"I do," Dr. Austin said. "I'd like you to verify something Captain John told me and Sheriff Jeffords. It's really been bothering me. He said he was he operating in Idaho with U.S. government approval. Was that true?"

"It was," Gary said without hesitation. "He was supposed to keep his mouth shut about that. But Captain John held all the cards. He said he'd take what he wanted whether we gave him approval or not—and if we got in his way he had enough weapons to destroy life as we know it here on planet earth."

"Do you think he will come back?" Dr. Austin asked.

Gary made a dismissive gesture with his hand. "Forget about him. He's gone back where he came from, thank God. Let's close that chapter and never mention it again."

"That's fine with me," Dr. Austin sighed. "No more animal mutilations!"

Gary shook his head. "I wish that were true, Doctor. But these Idaho mutilations are just the tip of a gigantic iceberg. Animal mutilations are still occurring all over the west—and what's most frustrating is—it seems to be a strictly an American phenomenon."

"Excuse me, Mr. Sheffield," Randy Johnson broke in. "I'm all mixed up. You say Captain John is gone. He's the one who killed my horses. There seems to be a real contradiction here. Are you telling us there are more mutilators out there? I could end up losing more of my animals?"

"It's a distinct possibility," Gary answered honestly. "I'm beginning to believe America has been selected by some kind of inner galactic conference or council as a prime location for securing farm animals or parts thereof which may be unavailable on their planets." He stared momentarily at their shocked, somber faces. "However, gentlemen, that is sheer speculation on my part."

Jake Henline wasn't buying it! "Do you have any evidence to support such a theory? If there are alien mutilators out there why would they concentrate only on America?"

"Good question," Gary said. "The short answer is, I don't know. The FBI isn't the only agency that has no answers. None of the other federal agencies do either."

"What other federal agencies?" Jake asked with surprise.

"The Federal Aviation Administration, the North American Air Defense Command and the National Aeronautics Administration, to name just a few," Gary answered.

Dr. Austin jumped in. "Let me get this straight. None of those agencies have any specific information on the aliens?"

"If they have," Gary said, "They haven't shared it with the FBI."

Jake spoke up. "You mean to tell us all you government guys working together don't know who these aliens are?"

Gary shook his head. "No."

Dr. Austin made a gesture with his hands indicating he was confused. "I'm still thinking about what you said about an inner-galactic council. I'm not sure I follow you. Can you explain your theory in a little more detail?"

Gary nodded. "Well, Doctor, to me these on-going mutilation attacks appear to be coordinated and controlled by some type of intelligent beings who dispatch various groups to U.S locations. Hundreds of animals have been slaughtered all over the United States. However the mutilators for some unknown reason recently shifted their depredations entirely to the western states to obtain the animal parts they need."

"But why?" Dr. Austin asked.

"Damned if I know," Gary answered.

Randy Johnson raised a hand. "Well, if Captain John has gone back to his planet, are you saying these unidentified mutilators have replaced him?"

"It's a possibility," Gary admitted. "But gentlemen, to make sure we're on the same page, let me digress for a moment to clarify why I look at this situation the way I do. At the moment we're in a cold war with the Soviet Union, right?"

The men nodded, wondering what Gary was getting at.

Gary continued. "Because of cold war secrecy it's impossible to obtain information concerning livestock mutilations from any communist country. However, I've spent many hours researching what scant few records are available from non-communist countries in Europe, Latin America, Asia and the South Pacific and to date I haven't uncovered one documented case of animal mutilations in any of those areas."

"You left out Canada and Mexico," Dr. Austin said. "What about them?"

Gary chuckled. "Well gentlemen, that's where things start to get a little bit weird! As far as I know there have been no animal mutilations in either country, at least none that were publicly announced in the news media. To date, over seventy mutilations have occurred in northern Montana, almost on the Canadian border. At exactly the same time, numerous animal mutilations were taking place in Texas, just this side of the Mexican border."

"That just doesn't make any sense," Dr. Austin said, as he leaned forward in his chair, now totally consumed with interest.

Again Gary chuckled. "Tell me about it, Dr. Austin! My colleagues and I have met behind closed doors several times, scratched our heads and kicked around a few ideas. But all we come up with are more questions which have no answers."

"Well, since we are speculating," Dr. Austin said, "Why do you think alien mutilators are so interested in planet earth?"

"Well," said Gary, "I can only venture a guess, based on the results of my investigations along with bits and pieces I've overheard heard in government offices. The earth must have something the aliens want. Exactly what that is, no one knows. We know for a certainty they want animal parts. But other than that..." Gary threw up his hands, "Who knows? What would we want if we traveled to another planet?"

Dr. Austin was quick to respond. "First we'd want to know if the planet was inhabited, and if so by whom or what—and whether they were friendly or hostile; and being Americans we'd probably make it a top priority to figure out a strategy to claim it."

Gary chuckled at that. "Really? When have we ever taken land from anyone?" Then he turned to Randy, who looked like he wanted to say something. "You have a question?"

"What happens if these new mutilators hit my ranch again and kill more of my animals?

"Oh, I don't think that will happen," Mr. Johnson.

Randy persisted, with a touch of frustration. "But you just told us it's happening right now, especially here in the western United States. You FBI guys are in charge—you have to do something to make sure the aliens don't hit us again!"

Gary looked at Randy thoughtfully for a moment before asking, "What would you like us to do, Mr. Johnson?"

"Hell, I don't know," Randy said, throwing up his hands in frustration. "How about alerting the military? How about warning the people what's going on…"

"It's not that simple, Mr. Johnson," Gary interrupted. "As far as the FBI or any other federal agency is concerned there are no such things as UFOs or aliens. That makes it one big paradox—like we're fighting a war against an invisible enemy, and if there's no enemy there's no war. That makes people in high places damn scared."

"Scared of what?" Randy asked.

"To put it bluntly they're scared of the aliens and they don't know what to do stop them. Of course their major fear is how their actions—or inaction, might affect their government positions. Influential bureaucrats in Washington are catching hell from western governors, senators and congressmen…"

"Hold up there, Mr. Sheffield," Dr. Austin interrupted. "Are you saying this whole mutilation business is being swept under the rug, just like it never happened? You're kidding, right?"

"I wish I were, Doctor. But that's about it in a nutshell. It never happened! That's why I had you sign the confidential agreement forms. You are prohibited from mentioning anything about the mutilations. Anything else?"

Randy said, "Talking about those forms, I have a question. Newspaper and television reporters came to my ranch and inspected my butchered horses and took pictures. Then they asked if I had any ideas about who killed them. Maybe I should have said no. They kept after me until I told them I thought UFOs spotted in the area that night may have had something to do with the butchery. Was that a breach of security?"

"Certainly not," Gary answered. "At that time you were under no written obligation to maintain your silence. You had every right to express your opinion. However, if the mutilators should come again and attack your animals you must not express any opinions that mention UFOs or aliens. If you feel inclined to say anything, stick to the predator theory—predatory animals killed your livestock—and only if it becomes absolutely necessary."

Randy nodded and took a deep breath. "Let's hope it doesn't!"

Gary glanced at his watch. "It's getting late gentlemen, so let's call it a night. Any more questions?" The men shook their heads.

The meeting at an end, Dr. Austin started to rise, but sat down again when Gary said, "Hold on a moment Doctor."

"Yes?"

"Would you be kind enough to accompany me tomorrow morning when I call on Sheriff Jeffords? I should have Deputy Henline go with me, but the situation being what it is, I think you and I might be better able to communicate with the sheriff and find out what we can do to help him."

"Of course I'll go with you," Dr. Austin said. "He's my friend."

"All right with you, Deputy?" Gary asked.

Jake nodded. "Fine. But if you need me just let me know."

Barbara Austin sat at the kitchen table sipping coffee. The door knob of the back door slowly turned and she watched Sheriff Dan Jeffords quietly open the door and step inside the kitchen. His face was so masked with hate she hardly recognized him.

Startled, Barbara set her coffee cup down and jumped to her feet. "Dan, what are…"

Jeffords put an index finger to his lips. "Shh! Quiet!" he whispered, as he moved slowly and stealthily toward her, a .38 revolver clutched in his right hand.

Oh my God! He's going to kill me! She could hear the sound of her heartbeat.

Terrified, she just stared at him, too paralyzed to move, wishing she could just close her eyes and he would be gone.

With a jerking motion of the pistol he moved her out of the way and growled, "Stay put and don't move! It's killing time!"

Barbara let out a blood-curdling scream, "Look out Jim! It's Dan Jeffords and he's got a gun!"

30

JEFFORDS SLIPPED BY HER AND MATERIALized from the kitchen hallway and barged into the living room, his pistol covering the four startled men standing there chatting.

"Jake Henline, you low-down scheming bastard!" Jeffords shouted. "I caught in the act! If you think you can to take my job away from me—you've got another think coming!"

Totally stunned Jake shook his head in amazed disbelief at his boss's sudden unexpected appearance, screaming wild accusations.

"Sheriff," Jake stuttered and held up a hand, "Please, put the gun away and let's talk…"

"Bullshit!" Jeffords growled. "I'm through talking!" Shaking his head he growled, "You don't have the first damn clue how humiliating this is for me to walk in and see you plotting against me, do you?"

"You've got it all wrong, Dan," Jake protested. "We're working on a case."

Jeffords looked at Jake a long moment and kept his pistol pointed directly at the deputy badge on his chest. "You son of a bitch Jake, you're unbelievable, you know that? I didn't assign you to any new case. That's a bald faced lie!"

"Whoa, Sheriff, hold up there," Gary Sheffield took a step toward him and held out both hands, palms toward the sheriff, and said calmly, "What's this all about? Please put the gun away and I'll explain what's going on."

Jeffords turned his head slightly and glanced at Gary for a moment. "And just who the hell are you?"

"I'm Special Agent Gary Sheffield with the FBI. Would you like to see my ID?"

Jake Henline knew there was no time to ruminate on Sheriff Jeffords' state of mind now. What happened next, all too quickly, was a series of events that occurred in a blur. Jake's adrenaline ignited in an explosive fury. He heard the low, rageful howl of his own voice as if it were separate from him. In a smooth swift draw Jake's pistol was in his hand.

"Drop your gun, Dan!" Jake shouted. "Do it now!"

"What? You'd shoot me down like a dog—after all I've done for you? Go to hell!" He started to squeeze the pistol's trigger, but he was just one tenth of a second too slow.

Jake's weapon fired and the bullet tore into Jeffords chest with a force that slammed him back against the wall. He looked at Jake, his eyes wide with stunned surprise that suggested bewilderment, like, how could this happen? He weakly and slowly raised his pistol again.

Gary Sheffield's pistol was now in his hand and when he fired, the snub-nose 357 recoiled upward in his hand. The slug tore into Jeffords. He dropped his pistol and fell face forward, dead before he hit the floor.

Staring at Sheriff Jeffords' lifeless body Jake felt sick. Dr. Austin knelt down and felt Jeffords' neck for a pulse. "He's dead, Jake."

"What did you say?" Jake asked.

"Dan is dead."

Jake sounded panicked. "You all saw it, didn't you?" he asked, still holding his pistol in his hand.

When no one said anything Jake nervously asked again, "You all saw what happened! Dan gave me no choice!"

Jake didn't know what to do. He breathed a soft sigh of relief when Gary Sheffield weighed in and took over, now every bit the man in charge; but the first thing Gary said and who he said it to surprised Jake.

"Dr. Austin," Gary said, pointing down at the Sheriff's lifeless body, "It's most unfortunate that Sheriff Jeffords has suffered a massive heart attack here this evening. I assume that with the stress of these animal mutilations he was overworked to the point it caused heart failure. Right?"

"Oh, no, Mr. Sheffield!" Dr. Austin protested, "You can't get away with that! I'm a doctor and I can't do what you are suggesting."

"Oh yes you can, and you will!" Gary said forcefully.

Surprised, Jake interrupted. "What are you saying, Mr. Sheffield, that I didn't kill him?"

"Oh you killed him all right, Deputy. But don't you or anyone else here try to second guess me on this one. The Sheriff died of a massive heart attack in the line of duty. Are we clear on that?" The three men nodded. Gary raised his voice and repeated, "Are we clear?" Dr. Austin and Jake Henline nodded. Randy Johnson stared at Gary.

"I can't be party to something like that, Mr. Sheffield. I won't do it."

Gary didn't reply immediately, as if considering what he would do to Randy for refusing to cooperate. Gary looked Randy right in the eyes. "You're telling me you are going to buck the FBI and the United States government? That wouldn't be a wise choice. By tomorrow I could have agents going over your ranch with a fine tooth comb and I'm sure they could find something that we could use to detain you for a long long time..."

"Jesus!" Randy sighed disgustedly, "You win. But you always do, don't you?"

"Most of the time, Mr. Johnson, most of the time."

"Okay," Randy looked somewhat nervously at Gary. "The sheriff died of a heart attack. Am I off the hook?"

Gary nodded. "Wise choice, Mr. Johnson."

Gary walked over and grasped Jake's elbow and wrist and guided the deputy's .38 into its holster. "He was going to kill you Deputy—and maybe the rest of us too."

Gary caught a glimpse of a visibly shaken Barbara Austin walking slowly from the kitchen toward the living room. The two blasting gunshots echoing through the house had caused something almost like panic inside her. What was happening? Her uneasiness grew when she saw only Gary, Jake and Randy standing by the fireplace. *Where was Jim?*

Gary blocked her way and held up both hands, palms forward meaning come no further. He pointed to Dr. Austin, down on one knee, examining Sheriff Jefford's body stretched out on the living room floor.

"Please Mrs. Austin," Gary said softly, "there's been an accident and this is no place for you right now." He nodded to Randy Johnson, and Randy walked over and took Barbara's arm and escorted her back to the kitchen. "It's okay, Barbara," he assured her quietly as he sat her down in a kitchen chair and patted her shoulder. "Just stay calm. Mr. Sheffield and Jake have things under control. They're both police officers and know what they're doing. It was just a very unfortunate accident."

When Randy returned to the living room Gary said in a very menacing voice, "Gentlemen, this is now a matter of national security!—and that got their attention!

"Dr. Austin, do you know someone who can come get the sheriff's body, ask no questions and keep his mouth shut?"

Dr. Austin nodded. "I have a married son over in Twin Falls. He has a station wagon and can be here within a few minutes and I'll have him take the body to the morgue. There's no one there this time of night. Will that work?"

Gary nodded. "Get him over here!"

Dr. Austin went to the phone, called Steve and spoke to him briefly. When he hung up the phone, he nodded to Gary. "He's on his way."

Jake Henline appeared damned uncomfortable with the whole deal and didn't look like he was buying into it. "So we ex out the sheriff just like that, cover it up and everyone walks away scott free?"

Gary didn't appear the least bit phased or ashamed to admit it. "That's right, Deputy—unless you want to explain to the public why you shot the sheriff to death."

Randy Johnson jumped in. "Damn it, Mr. Sheffield, we've let you complete your investigation and we haven't hindered you in any way. We signed your confidential agreements. We sure as hell didn't expect it would get our sheriff killed or put us in a very adversarial position with our own government. What guarantee do I have you won't arrange some other diabolical plot against me or the rest of us?"

Gary knew they were not stupid men. He'd learned that very quickly. Unruffled, he said, "That's a good question, Mr. Johnson. "You were a military officer in Vietnam so you probably found out you had to make decisions that went against your grain upholding American values and traditions. Sometimes you had to decide which American value to sacrifice in your decision making. Right?"

"So?" Randy asked.

"So, my friend, that's what we're doing now. We're going against our American value of fair play, honesty and belief in the law. We're covering up the death of a good man and keeping our national security in tact. You have only my word that there will be no repercussions against any of you in this entire matter. I want to make it disappear, like it never happened, and so will the people in Washington."

"Like the war in Vietnam?" Randy asked sarcastically.

"No, Mr. Johnson. That war will never go away. Fifty thousand casualties proved that."

"So what happens next?" Randy asked.

"Sheriff Dan Jeffords, who died of a sudden heart attack, will receive a hero's funeral and be buried with full military honors. Police officers from across the state as well as a marine honor guard will head the funeral procession. Do any of you see a problem with that?"

"Aren't you biting off more than you can chew, Mr. Sheffield?" Dr. Austin asked.

Gary shook his head. "No, I don't think so."

"Do you actually believe you can get away with it?" Dr. Austin asked skeptically.

"If we don't, and the facts come out, you can lay the blame on me and the FBI. But don't misunderstand me, gentlemen! I'm just trying to save time. I've got to be on my way. Those goddamned mutilators are rampaging all over the west. If any of you open your mouths about what happened here tonight, I'll have your asses and you'll rue the day you were ever born. I hope I've made myself perfectly clear."

Dr. Austin chuckled. "I think you have!"

"Good," Gary said. "Do you have a blanket we can use to wrap the sheriff's body in?"

Dr. Austin nodded.

"Get it. Let's have the body ready to go when your son gets here. Do you think he can he be trusted to keep this situation to himself?"

"Of course! He's an attorney..."

"Oh, Jesus!" Gary deadpanned.

Again Dr. Austin chuckled. "Don't dismiss him so quickly, my friend. With what you've done here tonight you might need him to save your ass someday when the locals find out what you did here tonight!"

"That'll never happen," Gary said.

"You'd better hope not!" Dr. Austin said.

Gary looked at Dr. Austin and feigned a mock grin, then turned to Jake Henline. "Deputy, get some towels and a bucket of water and let's get this mess cleaned up."

✝

Within the hour Dr. Austin's thirty-year-old son Steve arrived and walked into the living room. He knew everyone but Gary Sheffield. He stared at his father then glanced at the blanket covered body on the floor. He leaned down and pulled back the blanket.

"Jesus, Dad! What happened here?" Steve asked. "You said something about a body. I didn't know it was Sheriff Jeffords. "Did…"

Dr. Austin looked at Steve. "Don't even *think* of asking what you're thinking."

Steve shrugged. "If you say so."

"It was a simple case of self defense," Dr. Austin offered. "That's all there was to it."

Steve remained silent. Dr. Austin could see Steve's eyes were moving quickly, as if he were considering asking more questions, wanting answers, saying what was on the tip of his tongue.

Dr. Austin shook his head. "You don't even want to know, son! That man," he pointed to Garry Sheffield, "is with the FBI—and this is a very special case."

"Am I allowed to ask anything about this special case?" Steve asked.

"No!" came Gary's immediate response. "Deputy Henline and Mr. Johnson will help you move the sheriff's body to your station wagon so you can take it to your Dad's morgue in town."

"Then what?" Steve asked.

"Go on home and forget what you saw and did here."

✝

It was ten p.m. when Gary got back to his motel room in Twin Falls. He picked up the phone and called Kyle Howden at his home in Boise.

"What's up?" Kyle asked sleepily,

"Did you get your confidential agreements signed?" Gary asked.

"Yes sir."

"Any problems?"

"No sir," Kyle said. "How about you?"

"We've had a little trouble down here," Gary said, "and I'll be here three more days to wrap up some loose ends. I'll meet you in your office Thursday morning at eight a.m. sharp. Okay?"

"All right," Kyle said. Then asked, "What kind of trouble?"

There was a perceptible pause before Gary replied, "I can't discuss it on the phone. We'll talk about it Thursday morning."

Gary replaced the telephone in its cradle and turned on the television to *Breaking News*. A pretty blonde newscaster was reading a script, "Just in from California—rancher Tim Holloway found five of his horses dead and horribly mutilated. Tim's ranch is located about ten miles west of Alturas in the Modoc National Forest, thirty miles west of the Nevada border. We tried to get an interview with Mr. Holloway but he was unavailable. No further information has been received. Now on to the international news...the Soviet Union is rattling its sabers again over American intrusion into its air space... Gary turned off the TV. *Those mutilating son of bitches are on the move again!*

He turned out the light and pulled up the covers. It was cold. He listened to the howling wind blowing sleet against the motel windows and drifted off to sleep.

✝

Thursday morning in Boise the temperature hovered at 22 degrees. In the FBI field office Kyle Howden was seated behind his desk. Gary Sheffield had a chair to the side of the desk, and was explaining what happened at Dr. Austin's home in Twin Falls.

Kyle listened intently then said, "My God, Gary! You and Deputy Henline shot and killed Sheriff Jeffords?"

Gary nodded. "We did, but it was self defense. He left us no choice. The man had lost his mind and might have shot us all." Gary explained that after the shooting he'd deceitfully declared Sheriff Jeffords' sudden death as being caused by a heart attack.

"I can understand the shooting," Kyle said, "But why the hell did you make up the heart attack story?"

"Mainly to prevent an investigation by non-FBI law enforcement officials who would subpoena Dr. Austin, Deputy Henline and rancher Randy Johnson and force them to testify under oath in open court—and what they would have to say would cause extreme embarrassment to the FBI and several other federal officials in Washington."

They heard a light tap on the office door and Kyle's secretary Helen Rissom stepped in. "Would you two enjoy a cup of hot coffee?"

"Damn, that sounds good, Helen," Gary smiled. "I'm still not thawed out! Idaho is the coldest damned place I've ever been assigned to!"

After Helen brought coffee and closed the door, Gary asked, "May I use your phone?"

"Who are you calling?" Kyle asked.

"Governor Stan Nordgren. It's time for him to issue a press release that animal mutilations in Idaho are over—and all the evidence and information he received from state officials indicated that the mutilations were committed by predatory animals."

Kyle frowned. "Do you think you can sell that to the governor? He can be pretty obstinate—and we can't afford to antagonize him. He's already pissed off at me because I made his investigators sign those confidential agreement forms." Why not just let the situation play itself out? Let it fade away?"

"Mainly because it's an order directly from headquarters in DC."

Kyle considered that for a moment, then nodded and grinned. "I guess that answers my question. Do you want me to go with you?"

Gary shook his head. "No, you have to live and work here until your next assignment. It'd be best for you to stay uninvolved and above this mess."

"Okay, my friend, if that's the way you want it. It's your funeral," Kyle said as he reached into the credenza behind his desk for his private phone directory of key Boise people. He opened the directory and pointed to Governor Nordgren's private phone number."

Gary dialed the number and got Nordgren's secretary, and in less than thirty seconds heard the governor's very businesslike voice. "What's on your mind, Mr. Sheffield?"

"I think you already know—and it's not something we should discuss on the phone. I'll be leaving Boise tomorrow, so let's meet in your office at two this afternoon."

"It's about a press conference, right?" Nordgren asked.

"We'll talk this afternoon," Gary said.

"I don't have time this afternoon! I'm booked solid," Nordgren snapped.

"Make time, Governor! I'll be there at two!" Gary hung up the phone.

Goddamn feds! Nordgren fumed. *I'm the governor, not someone to be ordered about like some menial servant. Oh well, Sheffield is just doing his job. But does he have to be such an arrogant bastard? Never so much as a sir, or a thank you. Well tomorrow I'll be rid of him!*

Governor Nordgren buzzed his secretary. "Cancel all my afternoon appointments, something urgent came up. Reschedule the important ones for tomorrow morning."

37

GARY SHEFFIELD'S PHONE CALL UNNERVED Governor Nordgren and left him in a dark mood of frustration, edgy and nervous. He sat at his desk drumming his fingers on the desk top cluttered with mutilation investigative reports forwarded by Attorney General Sam Kennerton.

Neatly typed, those reports provided the actual facts uncovered by Sam Kennerton's three investigators, blaming the animal mutilations on aliens. Kennerton wanted the reports out of his hands, out of his office, and the sole responsibility of the governor!

Whatever the governor decided to do with them, Kennerton knew they'd never get into the media. That damned federal cop, Gary Sheffield, would see to that!

Though Governor Nordgren was elated the mutilations had ceased he now faced the dilemma presented by Gary Sheffield—to call a local news conference in which he'd need to fabricate a story that wasn't true—and present it to the citizens of Idaho! *How the hell can I get out of this?* He thought about it for a few moments and couldn't come up with any plausible ideas. He needed help, someone to talk to. Only one name came to mind, long time friend, Cyrus Millburn, Idaho's Senior United States Senator!

Nordgren called in his secretary. "Get me Senator Cyrus Millburn on the phone. It's urgent!"

In a few moments the secretary buzzed Nordgren's phone. "Senator Millburn is on the line."

"What's going on, Stan?" Millburn said. "Your secretary said it's urgent."

"Thanks for taking my call, Cyrus. I'm meeting with a special agent from the FBI in Washington this morning, and he's going to order me to put together a news conference for the local media about cessation of animal killings."

"How do you know that?"

"He's already told me that's the plan."

"So what's the problem?" Millburn asked.

There was an awkward pause.

"Well, he…wants me to say some things that are not correct."

"You mean he wants you to lie?"

"Exactly."

"Did he tell you why?"

Nordgren said, "Yeah. He said it's a matter of national security."

"That sounds pretty serious, Stan. What do you expect me to do about it?"

"You carry a lot of weight back there in Washington. Can't you get the FBI to recall this hot shot special agent and let us work out this mutilation business on a local level?"

"No, Stan, I can't do that!" Millburn said forcefully, but to soften the blow, added, "I wish I could. I've already been over to the FBI's main office, raised some hell, but it was a waste of time. They ordered to get my ass back to the senate where I belong and keep my long nose out of their business."

"So there's nothing you can do?" Nordgren asked weakly. The prospect of meeting with Gary Sheffield appalled and frightened him.

"No, Stan, I'm sorry. You'll have to deal with the FBI yourself. Good luck!"

✝

Promptly at two p.m., Governor Nordgren's secretary pushed open his office door. Nordgren looked up and saw Gary Sheffield. Nordgren didn't stand or offer his hand. He merely waved Sheffield to a chair in front of his desk.

"You're very punctual, Mr. Sheffield," Nordgren said without a smile.

"I always try to be."

Sheffield's presence in the governor's office, even in the state of Idaho, annoyed Nordgren and made him feel uneasy. *Damn it, I'm the governor;* but the smug FBI agent was pushing him aside and calling all the shots.

Nordgren swallowed his pride, and tried to be pleasant. "I hope your trip to Twin Falls was successful."

"It was," Gary said.

"Would it be presumptuous of me to ask what happened down there? Did you get signatures on your confidential agreement forms from the people you went to see?"

Gary rubbed his chin and hesitated for a moment. "I did. But there was a slight complication I need to tell you about. Before I do, however, I want it understood that this meeting is off the record. What is said here stays here. All right?"

Nordgren made a face of frustration as his smile vanished. "I've assumed that's always the case when I'm talking to you! Everything you guys do is secret! Damn it, Mr. Sheffield, we're in this situation together. I think you should trust me enough to know I'd never betray a government confidence."

"Okay, okay!" Gary held up a hand. "Unfortunately Twin Falls County Sheriff Dan Jeffords died while I was in Twin Falls and that created some problems."

Nordgren's head jerked up, he took a deep breath and swallowed hard. "Sheriff Jeffords is dead?" The news shook him. For a moment his mind raced off in several different directions trying to comprehend the implications of this startling information. "I hope to God the mutilators had nothing to do with his death—did they?"

Gary shook his head, and wanting to avoid specific details, said, "Well sir, the sheriff's death was just as much of a shock for me as it is for you. While I was meeting with Dr. James Austin, the Twin Falls County Medical Examiner, Deputy Sheriff Jake Henline and rancher Randy Johnson, getting their signatures on the confidential agreement forms, Sheriff Dan Jeffords came rampaging into Dr. Austin's living room unexpectedly, waving his pistol in our faces—mad as hell, shouting and cursing, babbling on about some perceived threat to his job. Before any of us could calm him down and figure out what the hell was going on he suddenly gasped for breath, stiffened then dropped dead right there in front of us."

"You mean he keeled over and died—just like that?" He stared at Gary disbelievingly. "How could that happen? The man was an ex-marine, strong as an ox, so I've heard."

"I'm sure he was," Gary agreed. "Dr. Austin jumped in immediately and used every emergency procedure he knew to revive the sheriff, but it was no use. The Doc told us the sheriff had died of a massive heart attack."

Nordgren was silent, sitting upright in his chair, absently thumping his fingers on his desk.

"What are you thinking, Governor?" Gary asked.

"You said the sheriff came rampaging into Dr. Austin's living room. I don't understand. Wasn't he participating in your meeting? I thought he was one of the key people you went to see."

Gary tried to squirm out of the hole he'd dug for himself. "No. I didn't invite the sheriff to the meeting."

"Why not?" the governor asked.

Gary wasn't prepared for the governor's probing question, though he'd thought seriously about the fall out which might occur because of Sheriff Jeffords' death—so he answered carefully. "The sheriff had been suffering with some mental issues for several weeks so I planned to meet with him separately." Gary went on to explain Sheriff Jeffords' shaky erratic mental condition, as he had learned it from people most closely associated with him, and how that condition finally lead to a complete mental breakdown and ultimately to the sheriff's death.

Governor Nordgren listened impassively as Gary related in short fragments the stressful events which occurred that cold winter night in Dr. Austin's living room, concluding, "The sheriff was overwrought, mentally disturbed and died of a heart attack."

Still not satisfied, Nordgren cocked his head and looked quizzically at Gary. "You said he was waving a gun in your face. Did he use it?"

"No. He died before he had a chance to pull the trigger."

Nordgren didn't buy it. "Tell me, Mr. Sheffield, do you actually expect me to believe a cock and bull story like that? There's got to be more to it than what you're telling me. I plan to make some inquiries…"

Gary shook his head and waved a finger. "You can forget that right now!"

"And if I don't?"

"The matter is not up for debate, Governor! I warn you—accept what I've told you and let it go at that!"

Nordgren backed off and was silent for a time, thinking it through. "It's a hell of a mess, Mr. Sheffield."

"What do you mean?" Gary asked.

"Well for starters, losing a good sheriff like Jeffords will be a terrible blow to the folks in Twin Falls County. Though I didn't know the man personally I've heard good things about him. He was a three-term Idaho lawman." The governor pulled on his earlobe for a moment, then said softly, almost as if thinking out loud, "I'll need to send condolences to his family then get in touch with my attorney general to find out what we need to do to find a replacement for Jeffords."

Gary shook his head. "You needn't bother, sir. I arranged for Chief Deputy Jake Henline to take over as acting sheriff until the county attorney and others decide what they want to do. I assumed you'd want the matter settled quickly. I hope I didn't overstep my authority."

"No, I guess not," Nordgren said, sounding somewhat relieved that the delicate matter had been taken care of. "I assume you checked Deputy Henline's credentials to ensure he has the experience to handle law enforcement matters for Twin Falls County?"

"Of course. I made a few phone calls and got some good references. I also interviewed him privately. He's personable, has a good reputation, and is well thought of in the county, an exceptional lawman with several years of experience. I have no doubts he's fully capable of filling in as interim sheriff until other arrangements are made."

"I appreciate that," Nordgren said. "What about funeral arrangements? Do I need to be involved?"

"No. Dr. James Austin, a very close friend of Jeffords, has taken care of it. He's also arranged for a marine reserve unit to provide an honor guard. You should alert your attorney general to notify all Idaho law enforcement agencies. They'll want to provide a motorcade to the cemetery."

"An excellent suggestion. I'll see to it," Nordgren exhaled with relief.

Gary glanced at his wristwatch. "As you know Governor, I didn't come here to talk about events in Twin Falls."

Nordgren looked at him with a sour face. "Yeah, I know. You want me to hold a press conference. Right?"

Gary tried to lighten the mood. "All in the line of duty, sir, so let's not make this any more difficult than it has to be."

Nordgren wanted to tell Gary Sheffield to go straight to hell—but he bit his tongue! *You never win a battle against the feds!* He'd learned that early on when he first became governor and found out how tough federal bureaucrats in Washington can be in controlling the forests—well hell, the whole damned environment for that matter, logging, mining, water and dams, treatment of Native Americans, transportation and on and on.

"What do you want me to do?" the governor asked weakly.

Gary reached inside his coat pocket and pulled out an envelope which contained the press release he'd drafted before he left his DC office—and had it approved by the FBI director. It contained no department letterhead or signatures—just in case it might fall into the wrong hands.

Holding the envelope in his hand for a moment, and lowering his voice to indicate the gravity of the decision he'd been ordered to relay to Nordgren, Gary said, "I want you to call a news conference and read this short public statement."

Nordgren reluctantly took the envelope from Gary, slowly opened it, and removed the memo which contained two short typed paragraphs. He studied it for a moment.

"You've got to be kidding!" Nordgren said sarcastically, his temper simmering just below the surface. "You expect me to tell our citizens that predatory animals were the mutilators? I can't believe this!"

Gary managed an icy laugh. "I assure you I'm not kidding, Governor!"

"Why the hell do I have to say anything at all to the press?"

"Mainly because it's an order from the Federal Bureau of Investigation," Gary growled. "Let's just leave it at that! Okay? Why are you being so damned obstinate anyway? What we're asking you to do will only take ten or fifteen minutes of your time and the mutilation crisis in Idaho will be over and done with."

Nordgren disagreed, raising his voice. "For you maybe, but not for me! You want to know why I'm being so obstinate? Well let me be perfectly frank. I don't want to go public and spew out these lies to the people of Idaho." He held up Gary's typewritten statement. "Our people are smart enough to know there is more to the mutilators' identity than predatory animals."

"Perhaps," Gary agreed. "Just remember there are a number of possible scenarios if you are hard pressed by the reporters to come up with some answers. For example, your law enforcement people have looked into the possibility of rustlers, ranchers killing cattle for insurance money, cultists, etc. That gives you some leeway. Your hands are not tied—but you must remember, and let me make this perfectly clear—if a question comes up about any UFO connection to animal mutilations, you must vehemently deny there is any such connection, and move on. Understood?"

Nordgren rubbed his chin letting his anger cool for a moment. Suddenly an idea popped into his mind. "What if I could arrange a TV and radio interview with Idaho's most popular news anchor, Mara Esplin? I've worked with her several times and with a little prompting from me before hand she could ask the 'right' questions and scoop the other stations." Nordgren paused. "Would that work?"

Gary remained silent and stared at the governor, contemplating the pros and cons of Nordgren's suggestion. It made perfect sense. Gary smiled and in a more conciliatory tone said, "Good idea! That might work even better than a public press conference."

Nordgren grinned and stuffed the memo back into the envelope and handed it to Gary. He'd finally gained a concession from the FBI!

"If I can set up this interview with Miss Esplin will this horrible nightmare finally be over? I mean will the FBI will get off my back and go away?"

"What FBI?" Gary grinned. "You know the FBI has never been involved in any way in animal investigations in Idaho or any other state, right?" Gary put out his hand. Without thinking, Governor Nordgren took it. "Do we have a deal?" Gary asked. "

Nordgren exhaled softly and grinned. "Deal! But I have to tell you, you feds are the most devious bastards I've ever had the pleasure of working with! I hope I never see you—ever again!"

"I can live with that, my friend!" Gary heartily agreed.

Gary strolled out of the state capitol building feeling good about the results of the meeting and stood relaxing on the steps for a few moments. The winter sun was shining, and there was no wind. He gazed out across the snow covered mountains, not really seeing them, noticing them only in an absent way. He was thinking of Governor Nordgren and his upcoming interview with Mara Esplin. Gary did not like deceiving the people of Idaho anymore than Nordgren did, but he'd carried out his orders and it was time to move on to another assignment. He had no doubts Bill Donovan back in DC would have something lined up. Reluctantly he walked to the parking lot, got in his car and drove back to the Boise field office.

Kyle's Howden's door was open, and he was sitting at his desk talking on the telephone. He waved.

"Hang on, Chief," Kyle said, "Gary just walked in." He handed the phone to Gary who pushed the speaker button so Kyle could listen in.

"How did it go with Governor Nordgren?" Donovan asked.

"About like you figured it would," Gary answered. "He wasn't a happy camper."

"Angry, was he?"

"Pissed might be a better word. When he cooled down and we got down to the specifics of calling a news conference, he came up with an excellent suggestion."

"Like what?"

"A one on one TV/radio interview with Mara Esplin, a well known media personality in this area. He knows her quite well. It would keep publicity to a minimum and accomplish our purpose."

"How soon?" Donovan asked, as if he'd already accepted the change in plans. He trusted Gary's judgment in making crucial decisions.

"Tomorrow," Gary said, "Then we can mark the Idaho mutilation case closed."

"Good. That means you can get out of Dodge in the morning and head on down the road."

"How far down the road? I'm not sure I like the sound of that!" Gary said.

"How about Northern California? I assume you've heard the mutilators did move into that area?"

"Yes sir. I saw something about it on Boise TV and Kyle found a small write up in an Oregon newspaper about a rancher somewhere in northern California, just south of the Oregon border, who found some of his cattle dead and mutilated similar to those here in Idaho."

"Exactly like those in Idaho!" Donovan said. "That rancher has a big spread in the Modoc National Forest, near the town of Alturas; and since that story broke, three more ranches in that area have been hit and at least a dozen cattle have been killed and mutilated. I want you to get over to Alturas as soon as possible."

"Where the hell is Alturas?" Gary asked.

"In the northeast corner of California, near the Oregon border on the north and the Nevada border on the east. Get Kyle to show you on a map."

"Sounds pretty remote," Gary said.

"It's damned remote," Donovan said, "a perfect spot for the mutilators to continue their dirty work."

"What's the law enforcement situation in that area? Can't they handle the situation?"

"If they could, I wouldn't be sending you! Alturas is the county seat of Modoc County. There's a sheriff and a few deputies. The Bureau of Land Management has some people there, as well as the National Forest Service, which has a few rangers. The California Highway Patrol has an office there."

"Damn. Locals and feds—that's a problem right there," Gary said.

"Not if you get over there and coordinate the investigations—and make damn sure none of the killings and mutilations reach the headlines of any California newspapers, and for hell sake, whatever you do, don't let any breaking news stories air on television. Got it?"

"Do they have television in Alturas?"

"Don't be a smart ass!"

"Okay, boss, I got it. By the way, are these mutilators..." Gary hesitated for a moment, wondering if he dared ask the question on his mind, "any intergalactic folks we may know?"

"Is there anyone in the office besides you and Kyle?" Donovan asked.

"No sir."

"Then to answer your question, Gary, no we don't have the first damn clue who these "*people*" are. We know it's not Captain John or his group. It's like we've been discovered and have become a way station or a stop over for intergalactic travelers—but we have no hard proof of that. But why here, in the western states? It's driving us nuts."

"And you expect me to stop them?" Gary asked. "Just how the hell am I supposed to do that?"

"You can't stop them, Gary. None of us can. Just try to keep those law enforcement people under control. You know what happened to Sheriff Dan Jeffords when he tried to pull a gun on Captain John. No guns! Let them mutilatin' sonsabitches take what they want—a few cows and they'll be on their way again. You were here when we talked to Captain John. They have weapons that could wipe us out in an hour."

Gary chuckled. "You're all heart, Bill, you know that?

"I've been told that a time or two," Donovan responded.

"Okay, Bill, how the hell do I get to Alturas?"

"Rent a four-wheel drive vehicle there in Boise and drive over to Alturas…"

"Drive?" Gary interrupted. "Wouldn't it be faster to fly?"

"No. You'd have to fly to Sacramento, rent a car there and drive almost three hundred miles north. Alturas is only three hundred and fifty road miles west of Boise. You can take I-Eighty-four to Ontario, Oregon, there turn south to Burns, then hit three ninety-five for a straight shot into Alturas. Any questions?"

"Not at the moment."

"Good luck, then. Call me when you get to Alturas," Donovan said, and hung up.

Gary put the phone back in the cradle. "Well, Kyle, you heard the man,"

Kyle nodded and smiled. "Sounds like a nice assignment!" he said sarcastically.

Gary shook his head. "Yeah, lucky me! You want to go in my place?

"Not unless they raise my pay grade at least three levels!"

"You chicken shit!" Gary grinned. "Okay, get your maps out and show me where the hell Alturas is, then let's go rent me a jeep Cherokee. That ought to work all right in that California outback. I want to get moving on this while it's still fresh."

"You're not staying to watch the governor's television interview?" Kyle asked.

"No time. You watch it. I'll keep my car radio on. If Nordgren keeps his word and does the interview tomorrow, maybe I can pick it up."

"All right, if that's the way you want it," Kyle responded. "I am kind of curious though. You're going up against unidentified aliens this time. Doesn't that worry you?"

Gary nodded. "Yeah, it worries the hell out of me; but what aggravates and bugs me most is how totally helpless we are in trying to stop them. All we can do is follow them around, clean up their messes and try to keep their true identities from the public—and that's becoming more difficult with each passing day!"

32

MARA ESPLIN—TOP IDAHO TV PERSONALITY and a stunning thirty-five-year-old blonde, lived alone with her twelve-year-old son, Johnny, who never seemed to have his nose out of adventure books. Mara's troubled marriage had lasted only one year and she told friends the only good thing that ever came from it was Johnny. She should have known better than to marry William, a loser with no life goals and little respect for work—and she soon discovered he was an alcoholic. She also found out the hard way what a macho bastard he actually was after he brutally assaulted her during one of his drunken rages.

Back then she was a very bright, energetic college student at the University of Vermont, majoring in journalism—at a time when good jobs were hare to come by. Her professor told her of a position in broadcast journalism in Idaho and urged her to check it out. She still smiled as she remembered her famous reply, "Where the hell is Idaho?"

But she followed through and made the phone call to KBOI's general manager. Her sexy, melodious voice, strong personality and ability to answer questions secured the job, sight unseen.

Relocating to Idaho had given her a new start in life and with hard work and her relaxed, glamorous movements in front of the TV camera quickly moved her into prime time—and into the arms of the handsome, athletic sportscaster, who had taken an interest in her and Johnny. He'd taken Johnny fishing, boating, camping and became the father figure Johnny had never had.

Mara quickly learned that Idaho politics, like politics in most western states, was basically a good-ol'-boys club, and if you could wiggle through the club's front door your career could move along and upward very smoothly, and provide many fascinating informational tidbits to pass along to the public. Soon she was talking to Stan Nordgren, Idaho's governor. However, she still hadn't quite figured him out. Their personalities clashed at times, so she was careful and cautious in her approach to him and his closest associates.

It was seven p.m. when Mara Esplin stepped out of the shower, slipped into her robe and was drying her hair with a towel when the phone rang. She was very surprised to hear Stan Nordgren's voice. "Sorry to bother you at home, Mara, but I need a quick favor."

"Name it, Governor," Mara said. She'd known Nordgren for several years and if he called her at home, she knew whatever he wanted was mighty damned important!

"I need you to set up a radio/TV interview—just you and me, one on one."

"How soon?"

"Tomorrow morning."

Mara hesitated. "That's pretty tight, Stan. Can you give me a little more time?"

"No, I'm sorry. But this may interest you. I have some new information about the animal mutilations I'm sure your viewers will be interested in. The attorney general has finally submitted to me the full report provided by his investigators."

"Really?" Mara asked with subdued excitement. "Tell me more!"

The mutilator crisis was the most intriguing story she'd ever covered, and her viewers latched onto every tantalizing detail with intense interest, especially ranchers and farmers who'd fought challenges of predators, drought, forest fires, insect infestation, animal diseases and fluctuating beef and mutton prices—but none of them had ever confronted the mysterious, unidentified mutilators who ravaged their herds.

"Well, Mara," Nordgren said, sounding upbeat and positive, "the mutilations are over, finished, done away with!"

There was a just-perceptible hesitation before Mara said, "Finished? How do you know that?"

"It was in the attorney general's report."

Another pause. Then Mara said, "I'm kind of sorry to hear that."

"Why?" Nordgren said. "I thought you'd welcome the good news."

Mara chuckled. "A reporter's dream come true, a once in a lifetime story? And you tell me it's finished?"

Nordgren quickly responded. "Maybe it's bad news for you, but not for me!"

"Oh well," Mara replied casually, "that's the way it goes sometimes—

win a few, lose a few. Did the attorney general's report happen to identify the mutilators?"

Nordgren was slow to answer. "He did. But I want to keep it under wraps until we go on the air."

"That's understandable," Mara said. "But I've just got to ask, were UFOs and aliens involved?"

Nordgren hem hawed and cleared his throat. "I'd certainly appreciate it if you wouldn't bring that up during the interview—not even the slightest mention. Okay?"

"Why not? So far all we in the public have heard is that the predatory animals killed the cattle. But damn it, Stan, that just won't work any longer. All of the ranchers I've interviewed know they are not being told the truth."

"Okay, let's talk about that—and the serious consequences we face if we go public against the predator theory."

"What do you mean, serious consequences?" Mara asked with surprise. "Is the federal government involved in this? It's got to be someone higher up the food chain than you. Right?"

"Look, Mara, you're a friend so please take my warning seriously— during the interview do not mention UFOs or aliens. I mean leave that topic strictly alone."

"Why?"

"Mentioning it on the air would be very dangerous for me—and for you."

Mara thought about that for a moment before she said, "I'll keep it in mind, but you're sidestepping as usual. What's your own personal feeling about the mutilator's identity—out of school, of course?"

"Not even out of school, Mara! So what about it? Will you set up the interview?"

"You goddamn politicians are all alike, you know that! The scoop of the year and you've tied my hands."

"I'm sorry, but that's the way it has to be. We've got a situation that's much more complicated than it appears."

"Says who?" Mara asked angrily.

"I do, and I'm not going to argue with you. Do I get the interview or do I get one of the other stations to handle it?" Nordgren said forcefully.

"I'll set it up for tomorrow morning."

"And you'll follow my guidelines? No UFOs or aliens?"

"I'm not making any promises, Stan, but I'll try. Remember, I've got thousands of loyal listeners out there who depend on me for the truth."

"Well, give 'em truth," Nordgren said, "the political truth, just as I've given it to you."

"Meaning razzle dazzle 'em with bullshit! Right?" Mara snapped, expressing her chagrin at the parameters Nordgren had set for the interview.

Nordgren chuckled. "Damn, Mara, I couldn't have said it better myself. See you in the morning!"

West of Boise, Gary Sheffield was speeding along in a Jeep Cherokee on Interstate 84, almost to the Oregon border. He was tuned in to radio station KBOI, when station manager Bill Chadwick broke in, "We're sorry to interrupt the program in progress, but we have some breaking news concerning the cattle killings and mutilations. Governor Stan Nordgren is here in studio with Mara Esplin to provide the latest information. Go ahead, Mara."

"Thank you, Bill," Mara began. "Welcome as always, Governor Nordgren," Mara said pleasantly. "We appreciate you joining us this morning. I understand you've received a detailed report from the attorney general and his investigators concerning the recent cattle killings and mutilations. Our farmers and ranchers have waited anxiously for several months to find out what those investigators discovered." She held out a hand. "Go ahead, Governor."

Nordgren nodded and smiled. "Thank you, Mara, and good morning ladies and gentlemen. Today I'm very pleased to announce that the cattle mutilations which have plagued Idaho for the past seven months are finally over. Our investigators concluded that in most of the animal deaths and mutilations it was determined they were caused by predatory animals. The actual number of animals killed and mutilated here in Idaho, under unusual circumstances, is unclear, though it numbers in the hundreds. We're still trying to tally the exact number as more reports come in from outlying areas. It's been a very unusual phenomenon on which the attorney general as well as his investigators and local law enforcement agencies have spent hundreds of man hours searching for answers."

Mara broke in with a broad smile. "So you now have conclusive proof that predatory animals were the culprits?"

Nordgren nodded. "That's what I've been told by the investigators."

"Really? Mara feigned surprise. "You mentioned most of the killings were committed by predators. What about the others? Has any person or persons of interest ever been apprehended, questioned, or arrested in those killings?"

"Not that I'm aware of," Nordgren answered truthfully.

"That's rather strange, don't you think? I assume it will be very difficult for ranchers and farmers to accept your investigators' conclusions."

Nordgren was visibly upset by her question and comment. "I find nothing strange about it at all."

"I'm not sure our listeners will agree with you, Governor!" Mara said. It came out more sarcastically than she intended and she saw frost for a moment in Nordgren's eyes.

But Mara plunged ahead. "To help clarify and explore this predator theory for our audience would you mind answering a few questions?"

"I'll do my best," Nordgren responded, as perspiration oozed out on his forehead. He wiped it off with a handkerchief and had a warning thought! *The FBI is watching and listening. Be careful!*

Mara said, "Dozens of ranchers, whose cattle were killed, reported seeing UFOs in the immediate vicinity just prior to the killings. Did your investigators come across anything like that?"

Goddamn her to hell! She's stabbing me in the back. Nordgren knew he had to head her off.

Gary Sheffield, hitting 75 miles per hour on I-84, turned up the radio's volume. His pulse was racing. He spotted an off ramp coming up. He turned off the freeway and sped into a Chevron gas station parking lot, threw on the brakes and skidded to a stop. *This I gotta' hear! You'd better make it good, Governor!*

"Well, Mara," Nordgren said casually, "opinions are divided as to the nature and cause of this phenomena of cattle killings. Some of the wildest theories have surfaced—UFOs of course being absolutely the wildest! Some conspiracy theorists have suggested that secretive governmental or military agencies may be involved. But let's think this through for a moment. Cows are found dead in various places—and suddenly we're deluged with the craziest ideas as to what happened to them, which by the way, makes for exciting breaking news flashes here on KBOI—UFOs, Satan worshippers, the government's black helicopters, and on and on. Our investigators wasted hundreds of precious man hours reviewing and discarding all those weird theories pouring in to the attorney general's office via mail and by phone."

Mara wasn't buying it, and Nordgren felt betrayed by her persistence. He'd have to be damn careful if he didn't want to end up as the object of an FBI investigation!

And FBI Agent Gary Sheffield was just as apprehensive as Nordgren as he sat there in the Cherokee, hanging on every word. *Don't screw this up Governor.*

Mara was like a hound chasing a fox to ground and threw caution to the wind. "Did your investigators observe close up any of the meticulous surgery allegedly found on the butchered animals?"

"Of course they did!" he said impatiently, shifting nervously in his chair.

"What did they think about that strange type of surgery? Several prominent Idaho veterinary surgeons described those cuts as a type of laser-precision surgery they'd never encountered before."

"Unusual type of surgery?" Nordgren scoffed. "There was nothing unusual about it, though the media tried to exaggerate it to add to the excitement! Do you or any of your listeners actually believe Idaho's highly trained veterinary surgeons were out in the field performing weird surgeries on wild range cattle?"

"I didn't imply that 'our' veterinary surgeons were involved in the mutilations, Governor!" Mara said with a touch of anger.

"Who are you talking about, then?" Nordgren asked.

"Perhaps alien surgeons?"

Nordgren chuckled. "Oh, come now, Mara! That's completely absurd. Alien surgeons mutilating cattle? What the hell for, if you'll excuse the French. If such things as aliens were flying around, wouldn't they be more interested in humans or our culture or civilization?"

"What about the missing body parts of the mutilated animals?" Mara persisted.

"Ranchers reported eyes, ears, tongues and other body parts missing. What did your investigators have to say about that?"

"Just what you'd expect! Their report indicates predatory animals and scavengers enjoy eating those particular body parts. I don't find that hard to believe—do you?"

Damn him! Mara Esplin's voice crackled with irritation and frustration as she tried again, "Then so as far as you and your investigators are concerned what you're telling us is that there were no UFOs, no laser surgery to remove vital organs and no cattle were taken from their habitats and mutilated elsewhere? It was just an unusual predator infestation?"

"Yes, Mara," Nordgren nodded with a broad smile, "That is absolutely correct."

Mara realized she'd created a stalemate. "Is there anything else you would like to tell our viewers and radio listeners about the animal mutilations?"

"Yes, I certainly would, thank you," Nordgren said pleasantly. "The people of Idaho can rest assured that the animal mutilations have ended, and if ranchers or farmers or anyone else has any additional information they would like to share with us they should pass it along to the attorney general's office and their reports will be added to our on going files." (To this day, those meticulously stacked files lay forgotten, gathering dust in the top drawer of a file cabinet in the A. G's office in the state capitol building. Perhaps one day a file clerk may accidentally open that drawer and glance at the top sheet—*Cattle Mutilations, 1975–76 Confidential*, and wonder—what's that all about?)

Station Manager Bill Chadwick stepped in quietly and handed Mara an incoming news bulletin. "Excuse me for a moment, Governor," Mara said. "We've just received word from a wire service in San Francisco that will be of special interest to our listeners. Dead and mutilated cattle have just been discovered on a couple of remote ranches in northeast California. Would you care to comment on that, Governor?"

"I'm truly sorry to hear that our good friends in California are having that problem," Nordgren said sincerely. "With drought, low prices, predatory animals ravaging the herds, bureaucrats and environmentalists, it's a wonder ranchers anywhere in the west can still make a living."

"I don't think you'll arguments from anyone about that," Mara said as she and Nordgren stood. "Thank you for coming in this morning, Governor Nordgren." She extended her hand.

Nordgren forced himself to extend his hand to her, but Mara could see from the distrustful look in his eyes it was very doubtful she'd ever get another *head's up scoop* from Governor Stan Nordgren!

✝

Gary Sheffield sat there in the Cherokee for a moment, disappointed with the tone of the interview, but he breathed a sigh of relief that no real harm had been done, and the governor walked out the interview with his credibility still in tact. Gary opened the driver's side door, stepped out and stretched in the Oregon sunshine. He walked into the Chevron station where soft western music from KBOI radio echoed softly through the station. He put a coin the Coke machine and a can of Coca Cola bounced noisily down the slot. He popped the top, nodded to the bored attendant, and took a long drink of Coke.

"Have you been listening to you car radio, Mister?" The young man asked.

Gary nodded. "Station KBOI. The Idaho governor was speaking."

The attendant smiled. "Boy, that was a real crock of bullshit."

"Why do you say that?" Gary asked, friendly like. "I'm not from around here."

"My Dad's a rancher and has a small ranch twenty miles north of Payette just over the border there in Idaho and two of his best cows were gutted out about three months ago. I seen them butchered animals with my own eyes and I hope I never see nothing like that ever again! I can tell you, no goddamn predatory animals done that!"

"What did your dad think?" Gary asked.

"The same as me."

"So neither you nor your dad believe wild animals killed them?"

"Hell no! The night before dad found the dead cows he seen flashing blue lights over the ranch and a big UFO hovering right over our pasture. It scared the living hell out of him. He's still shaking!"

"What did he do about it?" Gary asked.

"Nothing much he could do. He called the cops and they come out to the ranch, took a quick look at the butchered cows, then told dad predatory animals had killed them. He argued with 'em, but it was no use. They told him to report it to the Idaho Fish and Game guys and they could do some tracking, maybe kill the predator." The young man shook his head disgustedly. "Hell, my dad ain't seen a wolf, a bear or a cougar for twenty years and coyotes don't kill cows."

"That's really weird, huh?" Gary said. "I guess animal killings and mutilations have hit Idaho ranchers pretty hard. I'm sorry your dad lost those two cows."

"Me too. He's just barely making ends meet as it is."

"Well, son, I've got to hit the road. You take care now." He waved as he walked back to the Cherokee. The Coke washed away Gary's consuming feeling of apprehension, knowing now that Governor Nordgren had cleverly held up his end of the agreement. He'd quashed the UFO alien questions; however, Gary suspected nearly everyone in Idaho still believed the mutilators were aliens.

Gary climbed into the Cherokee and headed back to the freeway, deeply troubled, wondering what strategy he could devise to use against the mutilators now raiding cattle herds around Alturas, California. He also curiously wondered about the relationship between Captain John and these new mutilators now plaguing the west, or if there was any relationship at all—but Captain John was long gone, back to where he came from, and Gary knew he'd never find out.

Twenty miles down the freeway it finally dawned on him there was nothing, not one damn thing, he or anyone else could do to stop the mutilators! They'd come from some far off galaxy and when they finished their grisly work they would leave. It was as simple as that!

33

LONG TIME TWIN FALLS MORTICIAN, SILVER haired, sixty-year-old Will Fowers, studied Sheriff Dan Jeffords' body stretched out on the embalming table. The neatly stitched incisions resulting from Dr. Jim Austin's autopsy were typical of Austin's expert work—but Will stood there staring, puzzled and concerned by the two cleverly concealed bullet holes near Dan's heart.

Something wasn't right! Will had worked on too many corpses to be fooled by anyone trying to cover up a crime. Something was going on which Will wanted no part of.

It all started yesterday when Dr. James Austin called Will and informed him he'd finished his autopsy on Jeffords' body and his son Steve would deliver the body to Fowers' Funeral Home to be prepared for funeral services.

Why, Will wondered, was an autopsy necessary if Dan had died of a massive heart attack as Dr. Austin claimed—and why was Steve Austin transporting the body? Usually Will sent his hearse to pick up bodies of those who had died of natural causes.

Steve Austin pulled up at the funeral home within half an hour of Dr. Austin's call and backed his inconspicuous red Suburban up to the receiving door where he and Will and an employee carefully loaded Jeffords' body onto a gurney. Then Steve jumped in the Suburban and gunned back to the highway.

As Will positioned Dan's body on the embalming table he wondered how and why the sheriff got shot. He'd not heard read or heard of any shootings lately in the Magic Valley. He knew he needed to start asking some questions to find out if something illegal was being pawned off on him.

He grabbed the telephone and called Dr. Austin. "I'm Sorry to bother you, Jim. But I need to talk to you right away."

"About what?" Austin asked just a bit too sharply as though he expected to hear from Will as soon as he examined Dan's body.

"I'd rather not discuss it on the phone."

There was a perceptible pause before Austin reluctantly replied, "C'mon over."

✝

Twenty minutes later Shawna Knudsen, Dr. Austin's receptionist, stuck her head around the door into his office. "Mr. Fowers is here."

"Send him in."

Austin stood, greeted Will and shook his hand then waved him to an upholstered chair. "Now what can I do for you?"

"I'm sure you already know," Will said, looking tolerantly at him. "You told me Dan Jeffords died of a heart attack. I don't think so, not with two large caliber bullet wounds in his chest. What's going on?"

Austin drew a deep nervous breath. "You're right, Will. There's no fooling an old pro like you."

"But why all the secrecy?" Will asked. What the hell happened to Dan?"

Austin dodged answering the question. "How long have we been friends, Will?"

"Over thirty years."

"Do you know me to be an honest man?"

"Why hell yes, Jim. You know that."

"Well, my friend, you've caught me red handed on ethically thin ice with your question. What happened to Dan is a one time occurrence and I guarantee nothing like it will ever happen again."

"I sure as hell hope not," Will said. "It could cause me to lose my license, my business…"

Austin interrupted with a warning of his own. "You could lose a lot more than that if you start poking your nose into matters that are none of your business!"

"What are you talking about?" Will asked, surprised by Austin's sharp retort.

"Just let it lie, Will! Lots of crazy things have happened in the last few days."

"Obviously," Will said, thickly sarcastic. "Look, Jim, I didn't come here to cause any trouble or pry into matters that don't concern me. What I really want and need to know—was Dan Jeffords murdered?"

"Good hell no!" Austin replied forcefully.

Will didn't buy it. "Well, he sure as hell didn't shoot himself twice in the chest!"

"That's right, Will!" Austin agreed. "So just forget it."

Will shook his head. "You've pulled me into this mess," he said with a touch of anger. "If you want me to take care of Dan I want to know what's going on or you can find someone else to do the job."

"God, Will, don't get your balls in an uproar!" Austin said. "Can I trust you to keep your mouth shut if I explain what happened?"

Will nodded.

"I need more than a nod, Will. Swear to me you'll keep what I tell you confidential. It's not to go outside this room."

Will's face was grim. "All right, Jim, you've got my word. Now quit pussy footing around and give me some answers!"

"All right, but I can't go into all the details. What it boils down to, Dan and an FBI agent ended up in a gunfight and Dan lost. Evidently they were in a secret meeting comparing notes on several of these vicious animal mutilations here in Twin Falls County. The FBI agent evidently said something that pissed Dan off. He's been meaner than a stepped on rattlesnake for a couple of months. Anyway one thing led to another and Dan drew on the FBI agent—but he was just a hair too slow. The FBI man outdrew drew him and shot him in self defense. It's as simple as that."

It was a moment before Will could say anything. He felt a sense of fear, fear of being dragged into a situation he really wanted no part of. He'd have to be cautious.

"I'm truly sorry to hear that about Dan. He was a damn good man."

Austin nodded. "So now you know how Dan died. That's about all I can tell you."

"I appreciate that, Jim. But why all the secrecy?"

"The FBI doesn't want any information slipping out that they've been working behind the scenes on these animal killings. They want it to remain strictly a state matter. Can you imagine the publicity if the newspapers ran a headline like: FBI agent kills popular Idaho sheriff in old west style shootout? That would create all kinds of problems for the FBI—so we've got to be mighty damn careful what we do and say until we get Dan buried. Understand?"

Will nodded. "I think I've got the picture."

"Good," Austin smiled. "Let's go ahead and get Dan buried and that'll be the end of it. In the meantime no one, absolutely no one, is to see Dan's body until it's in the casket ready for viewing—and I mean it, Will!"

Will shook his head. "Even his wife?"

"Especially his wife."

Will was silent for a moment, still chewing on Austin's wild tale of a shootout between the FBI and the sheriff. "All right," Will said.

"Any questions?" Austin asked.

"Just one." Will raised an eyebrow. "Why was The FBI involved in the animal mutilations here in Idaho?"

"God damn it, Will!" Austin swore, "Don't mess into this any further! Leave it alone! You asked why Dan was shot and why it has to be kept quiet and I've told you. That's all you need to know. Keep this to yourself. Are we clear?"

"And if I don't?"

"Then I won't be responsible for what happens to you or your family."

"What are you talking about? Is that a threat?"

"No, Will. Just some friendly advice if you want to stay healthy. You don't want to end up like Dan, do you?"

Will gave that serious thought for a moment. "No, Jim, I sure as hell don't."

"Good! Then keep your mouth shut and just do your job and make certain Dan's body is properly prepared for the funeral. Be sure he's in his dress uniform. Law enforcement officers will be coming from all over the state. After the viewing and the funeral seal the casket. Got it?"

Will nodded. "Yeah, Jim I got it. But I sure hope you know what the hell you're doing!" His tone was on the edge of sarcasm.

"I do, Will. Trust me!" Austin said, as he stood up behind his desk and slipped on his leather jacket.

"Are we still friends?" Will asked hesitantly.

"Why hell yes, just like always," Dr. Austin replied. "C'mon. I'll buy a cup of coffee!" He grabbed Will's hand and pulled him up from his chair. Then, still holding Will's hand, he said, "There are some people I intuitively know I can trust. You're one of them."

Will nodded. "Thank you, Jim. I appreciate that."

✝

That evening Deputy Sheriff Jake Henline sat quietly at Sheriff Jeffords' desk, deep in thought, and felt as if his mind was ready to snap. The tension and guilt of shooting Sheriff Jeffords had finally culminated in a fevered pitch, unlike any guilt feeling he'd ever experienced before—and he feared that somehow details of the shooting might slip out to the public—and that would finish his career

Jake looked up, startled out of his reverie as the door to the sheriff's office opened slowly.

Claire Jeffords appeared, an expression of sadness on her face that was also part anger. "Jake," she said and her voice was soft, "I need to talk to you. Do you have a minute?"

Jake quickly rose to his feet. "Come in, Claire, come in." He motioned her to a chair in front of the desk. He had known her for several years and normally she was neat, well dressed and her gray-streaked black hair made an attractive frame for her strong featured face—but this evening she looked completely frazzled, causing Jake to think she may have had a drink or two or maybe been in a fight.

Foregoing the normal pleasantries, Claire came right to the point. "Jake, you've got to help me! I've been to the Fowers' funeral home twice and both times Will refused to let me see Dan's body. All I wanted to do was make sure everything was being taken care of—maybe spend a few moments alone with him."

"Did Will tell you why he refused your request?" Jake asked courteously.

Claire nodded. "He gave me a bunch of gobbledegook about instructions he received from the medical examiner, Dr. Jim Austin. No one was to see the body until the viewing. Will told me Jim Austin performed an autopsy on Dan and the body wasn't in the best of shape. He said he had to obey the law and follow Dr. Austin's orders."

"Then what?" Jake asked. *God, this isn't happening! If Claire gets a look at Dan's body and sees the bullet holes in his chest the game is up!*

"He told me the only legal way I could see Dan's body would be for me to produce a court order."

"That might be difficult, Claire," Jake said. "It takes quite a bit of time and Dan's funeral is already scheduled."

"Couldn't you step in and speed up the process?"

Jake shook his head. "I'm afraid not."

"Well, could you at least go with me to the funeral home and make Will let me see Dan's body?"

"No, I'm sorry," Jake said hesitantly "I can't force a businessman to break the law. Like you, I'd have to obtain a court order." Jake thumped his fingers on the desk and appeared to be thinking of a way to comply with Claire's request. "Tell you what I will do though, I'll talk to Will privately and see what I can work out. Would that work?"

Claire nodded. "I'd appreciate that very much." She drew a deep breath. "You know, Jake, I wouldn't be a bit surprised to learn that Dan was murdered—and someone is trying to cover it up. I've been thinking of going to the state police and asking them to help me find out what's going on. I think I'll call them in the morning."

Startled, Jake's head jerked back. "Murdered? State police? I think you're blowing this way out of proportion."

Claire shook her head. "I don't think so, besides, I know some key people with the state police. I'm sure they could figure out what's going on."

As much as Jake hated lying there was no way he could tell Claire the truth about the shootout at Jim Austin's place—but her accusation was beginning to make him very nervous. "Are you sure you want to do that? I think we should try to keep this matter confined to the local level until we figure things out."

"What are you saying, Jake?"

"I know you need some answers, but I'm not the one who can give them to you. Would you be willing to talk to Randy Johnson before taking any further action?"

"Randy?" Claire stared at him, puzzled. "What's he got to do with it?"

"More than you might think."

"I'm listening," Clair said.

"I think he can answer your questions and explain what happened better than I can.

"Why don't you explain to me what happened?"

"I can't, Claire, but Randy can. Will you talk to him?"

Claire gave him a dirty look. "Why are you beating around the bush, Jake? You can be so frustrating at times! Just tell me what happened!"

"I can't. I have my reasons and after you talk to Randy I think you'll understand." He stared at her. "Will you talk to him?"

Claire shook her head in frustration. "It looks like that's the only way I'm going to find anything out. When do you want me to talk to him?"

"Tomorrow."

"All right, but I'm tired of playing around—Randy better be able to provide more information than I've received from you!"

Claire moved toward the door. Jake walked over to her and held out his hand, which she took. "Are we still friends?" he asked as he opened the door.

With a half smile she said, "We always have been."

34

MAYBE IT WAS A MISTAKE TO BRING RANDY INTO
this mess, Jake thought. But what else could he do? There was no way he could
tell Claire he'd shot her husband without opening up the entire episode to
local scrutiny. Yet if he wanted to keep her from going to the state police the
truth had to come out. But how much of the truth?

Jake also needed to consider the U.S. government's confidential forms
he and Randy had signed stating they would never reveal anything about the
FBI's involvement in animal mutilations or with UFOs and aliens! Disclosing
a single detail *and getting caught* could land them in federal prison.

Reluctantly, Jake grabbed the phone and dialed Randy Johnson's
number.

Tessie answered. "Tess, this is Jake. Is Randy available?"

"I'll get him, Jake. Just a moment."

Jake thought about hanging up, worried about involving Randy, and
maybe trying to find another way to rein in Claire's concern that her husband
had been murdered. But when Jake heard Randy's reassuring voice on the
line, he took a deep breath and told Randy why he was calling.

Aghast, Randy said, "You volunteered me to explain Dan's death to
Claire?"

"I did," Jake said.

"Why me?" Randy sounded upset.

"Because you were there the night Dan died and know how that
came about. Telling her what happened would be better coming from you.
Remember I shot her husband—and it would mighty damned awkward for
me to explain that to her."

"You have a point," Randy said. "Just how much of what happened
should I tell her?"

"Explain we were having a brainstorming session with an FBI agent
about animal mutilations in the area and Dan tore into the living room,
unannounced, pistol in hand, angry and out of his mind, threatening to shoot
me. I had no choice but to defend myself. The FBI agent had no choice but to
back me up—and be sure to tell her the FBI doesn't want this information to
go public."

The line was silent for a moment. Then Randy said, "I don't know, Jake. Maybe we shouldn't tell her the truth. Maybe there's such a thing as being too honest. Maybe..." His maybes trailed off into unspoken fears and doubts.

"Well, I'll leave it up to you Randy." Jake said. "Do whatever you think will work out best. We've painted ourselves into a corner by lying, and covering up the details of Dan's death,—and that's created more lies. It's got to end. Claire is an intelligent woman. She'll understand—won't she?"

"We shouldn't build our hopes too high," Randy said truthfully. "Telling her the truth would be the logical step. But doing so will present some very serious repercussions for you which you'll have to live with the rest of your life."

"I've carefully considered that," Jake said, his voice sounding relieved. "Will you meet with Claire?"

Randy chuckled. "You knew damn well I would before you called, didn't you?"

"I suspected you might! So I wish you luck, my friend—and don't worry about me." After Jake hung up he knew Randy's meeting with Claire would cause him more pain than he could think about, more than he could bear.

She had always been like a mother to him—kind and generous—that would change to loathing as soon as she learned he'd shot her husband!

✝

A light dusting of snow covered the ground the next morning when Randy drove to Claire Jeffords' home. She met him at the door, staring at him through wet, blurred eyes. She'd been crying.

"Is this a bad time?" Randy asked. "I could come back..."

"Oh no, Randy, come in! Thank God you're here." She ushered him to the front room and he sank gratefully onto Claire's living room couch. He hadn't been in this room since he and Tessie's last visit two or three months ago.

"Would you like a cup of coffee?" Claire offered.

"No. I'm good." Randy said nervously. "I guess you know why I'm here?"

Claire nodded. "Jake told me you could provide some details concerning Dan's death." Claire paused. "I thought it strange that a deputy like Jake wouldn't know everything that happened to Dan—apparently he doesn't, so it's up to you to tell me."

Randy nodded. "Jake was very concerned about your suspicions that maybe Dan may have been murdered?"

"There is nothing else I can think! Dan is dead. I was told he died of a heart attack. Evidently that's a lie! Since then I've been treated like I have the plague. I'm not permitted to see Dan's body; and if I ask any questions everyone clams up. It doesn't make any sense." Claire's eyes narrowed. "Isn't there anyone in this town who can help me? Dan was a damned good man and I think someone owes me an explanation as to what happened to him!"

Randy stared at her for a moment before responding, "There's me. Hopefully I can provide the answers you're looking for. First off let me tell you Dan was not murdered!"

Claire was quick to ask, "Then what happened to him?"

"Let's start with Dan's investigation of animal mutilations, and move on from there. He got so damn grouchy I hated to be around him. I suppose you noticed that also"

Clair nodded. "Did I ever! Those investigations totally engulfed him day and night. His mind never seemed to rest."

"Did he ever tell you anything about his investigations?"

"No. He seldom ever said anything about his work."

Randy nodded. "A while back Dan seems to have suffered from some kind of mental breakdown. What happened? Do you recall when that started?"

"I certainly do! The day after he and Jim Austin traveled out to Ben Summers' ranch! He found old Ben dead and his prize ram butchered."

Randy nodded. "I know! I was there!"

Claire stared at him. "Then you must know that something happened to him at the ranch. Do you know if UFOs and aliens were involved?"

Startled, Randy said, "What makes you ask a question like that?"

"Because several times Dan mumbled in his sleep something about aliens and a Captain John. Do you know any Captain John?"

Randy shook his head. "No. Never heard of the man."

"Well, whoever he is I think he had something to do with Dan's personality change,"

"Why do you think that?"Randy asked. "

"Because that's when Dan started to change from a loving husband to a bullying brute!" She paused for a moment. "What happened out there at Ben's ranch that could change him like that?"

"I don't know," Randy answered evasively, "But shortly after Ben was found dead, along with his ram, the state invited the FBI to help them solve the mystery of who was killing Idaho's cattle herds. A special FBI Agent, Gary Sheffield, invited Doc Austin, Jake Henline and me to a brain storming session to compare notes on the status of the local investigations."

Claire's head snapped up and her eyes went wide. "Why wasn't Dan invited to that meeting?"

"Sheffield told us he'd made inquires about Dan's strange-paranoid behavior. He told us he planned to meet privately with Dan the next day, so we didn't think much about it."

Claire raised an eyebrow and nodded. "Paranoid behavior, huh? I won't argue with that, Randy. That accurately describes how far gone Dan was."

"How did you deal with it?" Randy asked with concern.

"I thought seriously about leaving him and getting a divorce. I put up with his abuse, hoping he'd get better. I really tried—until he hit me a couple of times. Then our relationship turned into a living nightmare—and Dan wouldn't talk to me about what was troubling him. Then he went completely bonkers, I mean delusional, about Jake Henline, claiming Jake was trying to take his job. Once I heard Dan say it would be a cold day in hell before a deputy like Jake could steal his job. He'd kill him first!"

Randy stared at her and took a deep breath. "Then it will come as no surprise to you that he was acting like a raving madman that night he unexpectedly busted into Jim Austin's living room, madder than hell!"

Clair shook her head and gasped, "My God! What did he do?" she slid to the edge of her chair.

"Well, Claire, what I'm about to tell you will come as a shock, but to make a long story here's how it went down. Agent Sheffield was peacefully explaining to us what the FBI was doing to solve the mutilation problems. Dan snuck through Jim Austin's kitchen door and stomped into the living room, waving his pistol—almost frothing at the mouth he was so angry, shouting he was going to kill Jake. You can imagine Jake's stunned surprise. He just stood there unsure what to do. Sheffield asked Dan to put his gun away and tried to reason with him, but there was no reasoning with the man. He was completely out of his head. He threw down on Jake, starting to pull the trigger, when Sheffield made a fast draw and shot Dan before he could kill Jake."

"Good God, Randy!" Claire said. "You're telling me that my husband, a three term sheriff, was gunned down by an FBI agent?"

Randy nodded

Completely stunned, Claire shouted angrily, "Why didn't you or Jake or Doc Austin do something? Are you telling me all three of you just stood there and watched Dan get shot down?"

Her question clearly rattled Randy and made him angry. "Whoa! You just rein in there for a damn minute! What the hell could we do? Doc Austin and I were unarmed..."

"I'm sorry, Randy," Claire quickly interrupted and apologized. "That was uncalled for."

It took Randy a moment to get his temper and voice under control. "It's all right. We need to get things out in the open," he replied.

All along Claire had assumed Dan was murdered—and Randy's story confused her; but deep down she knew there must be some truth to it. She vividly remembered that cold snowy night when Dan angrily buckled on his gun belt and growled: *That goddamn Jake Henline is over at Doc Austin's place plotting to take my job!* He stormed out of the house in a killing mood!

Suddenly, she understood. It was like watching the fractured pieces of a puzzle knit themselves together into a unified picture. She gave a half smile. "It's becoming clear to me now, Randy. But why did all of you try to cover up Dan's killing? I don't understand that at all."

Randy wished he could ease her torment, and tell her the complete truth and put her mind at rest. But he assumed doing so would do more harm than good. He had to tell the rest of it the best he could and try to keep Jake's actions in the drama confidential.

"The FBI wanted Dan's death covered up to protect their agency from adverse publicity and to protect Dan's reputation. If the media got hold of the story it would destroy Dan's credibility as a lawman. Think of headlines like this: *Delusional sheriff shot by FBI agent:* or *Local lawman and FBI shoot it out, old west style.* The FBI sure as hell didn't want the spotlight of negative publicity such a story would bring, and I know our local sheriff's department wouldn't want that either. Don't you agree?"

Claire appeared more thoughtful and less antagonistic. She was silent for a moment before saying, "You're right. Thank you for telling me. I hope you can understand what a traumatic and heartbreaking ordeal Dan's death this has been for me." She paused for a moment. "And for you too. We've both watched Dan's personality change and neither of us could do anything about it."

Randy nodded and issued a warning. "Because of the nature of this entire situation I'm sure you realize that you must never discuss with anyone the details of what happened to Dan at Doc Austin's home."

Claire nodded. "I understand."

"Any questions?" Randy asked.

"Only one," Claire said with a slight smile. "Now that you've told me what actually happened to Dan, I'd like to go to the funeral home and spend a few minutes alone with him? Do you think that would be possible?"

Randy noticed Claire was different. Her anger was gone. Their conversation had changed her. Softened her.

Randy straightened his shoulders and over his face came a slow smile, warm and friendly, the smile of a man who had succeeded in saving a friend's honor and reputation and providing peace of mind to Dan Jeffords' wife.

"Yes Ma'am! I can arrange that, "Randy agreed enthusiastically. "May I drop by and pick you up this afternoon?"

Claire felt a sense of exaltation. Things were beginning to work out!. "You bet! I'll be waiting."

Randy stared at her. "Would it be all right with you if I stop by the sheriff's office and pick up Jake to go with us?"

A broad smile lighted Claire's face. "Oh, I'd like that! I'd like that a lot. Jake's always been just like a son to me. Hopefully I can make it up to him for the way Dan's treated him these last few months."

There was an awkward silence for a few moments then Randy started for the door. He stopped and turned. "I'll see you this afternoon."

Claire walked over to him and gave him a hug. "Thank you for always being such a great friend, Randy."

35

NOW THAT DAN JEFFORDS WAS DEAD county officials quickly appointed Chief Deputy Jake Henline as acting sheriff. He was qualified on several counts, the most important was having served as Sheriff Jeffords' chief deputy, working closely with him on every major case—gaining the hands on investigative skills necessary to handle any future crimes committed in Twin Falls County. But he quickly learned that sheriff's duties didn't seem too much different from the duties he'd been performing as a deputy! In fact he'd already apprehended and arrested a burglary suspect this morning before he'd had his morning coffee. When he walked into the Sheriff's station his chief deputy, Jim Munford, stood at the doorway.

"Good morning, Sheriff,"

"Morning, Jim," Jake said almost absently waving him into his office. He took off his hat, and sat down. "Got any hot coffee?"

"I'll get you a cup," Jim said and walked to the coffee maker near the front door, poured Jake a cup, returned and handed it to him.

"What's on the docket for today?" Jake asked.

"The FBI wants to talk to you. An agent by the name of Kyle Howden called about twenty minutes ago. When I told him you weren't in he said he'd call back about nine."

God! Jake jerked upright in his chair. "What did he want?" The mere mention of the FBI scared hell out of him. In the back of his mind lurked the nagging thought that they might try to indict him for killing Sheriff Jeffords. He'd wrestled with that thought ten ways to Sunday analyzing all the angles— no one knew about that night at Dr. Austin's house, except the ones who were there and they were all sworn to secrecy. So what the hell did the FBI want?

"He didn't say, Jake. Just said he'd call you back at nine." Jim glanced at his watch. It was nine a.m.

The dispatcher called over to Jake, "FBI Agent Howden from Boise is on line two." Jake exhaled deeply, sat his coffee down and reluctantly grabbed the phone.

Howden's voice was friendy and it surprised Jake. "Congratulations, Sheriff Henline! I just got word you've been sworn in as Twin Falls County's interim sheriff. From Gary Sheffield's glowing reports of you they couldn't have picked a better man."

"Well that was mighty kind of him," Jake said, breathing a long sigh of relief. "By the way, how is Gary?"

"That's what I'm calling you about, Sheriff," Howden said. "Before Gary left Boise for his new assignment he instructed me to notify you that a rumor is circulating in your area that there may have been some foul play associated with Sheriff Jeffords' death."

"Excuse me?" Jake gasped with surprise. "How the hell did a rumor like that get started?"

"We figured you might know something about that," Howden replied.

Jake was silent for a moment. "I have a pretty good idea."

"You do?" Howden asked with surprise. "Tell me."

"It has to be Steve Austin," Jake said angrily, "Dr. Jim Austin's son. He transported Jeffords' body from Austin's house to the mortuary. I'm sure it was him. Gary Sheffield swore the rest of us to secrecy! Do you want me to bring him in for questioning?"

"Don't even think about it, Sheriff," Howden warned. "That would just add to the speculation. Let's let it lie and get Sheriff Jeffords buried as quickly as possible and put this entire nightmare to bed. Okay?"

"Yes sir! Sheriff Jefford's funeral is scheduled for tomorrow at eleven a.m."

"Excellent!" Howden exclaimed, his voice back in friendly mode. "You asked how Gary is doing. He's on his way to Alturas, California."

"To investigate some mutilated cattle?" Jake asked. "I heard on the news that a couple of ranchers over that way discovered some of their cattle dead and mutilated—very similar to the mutilations we experienced here in this area."

"That's right. Gary's on his way to check things out," Howden said. "By the way, have you had any more mutilations in your area?"

"Not lately," Jake replied. "But I did get a report of some suspicious activity near Rogerson..."

"Where the hell is that?" Howden interrupted.

"About twenty-two miles south of Twin Falls."

"What's going on down there?" Howden asked with a touch of concern in his voice.

"Flashing blue lights, strange noises, skittish animals running amuck, UFOs…"

Again Howden interrupted again, with a gasp. "UFOs?"

"Yes Sir!"

"I assume that means we may be in for more trouble, right?"

"It could. It's just a matter of time. "Wherever ranchers in this area spot a UFO it's not long before our phones start ringing off the hook with reports of dead butchered animals," Jake hesitated for a moment. "If we do get any reports of butchered animals coming in from Rogerson do you want me to notify you?"

"Hell yes!" Howden said forcefully, "And just as quickly as possible! Be sure to keep me posted on anything suspicious—and remember sheriff—try to keep the media from getting involved, and above all remember this, the FBI is not involved!"

"Yes sir. I understand," Jake said as he hung up.

He neglected to inform Agent Howden that one of those Rogerson ranchers had already called in and reported that two of his horses were missing and he thought they might have been stolen. Jake didn't want the FBI poking around in his territory until he'd had a chance to check things out.

✝

From all corners of the county farmers, ranchers, businessmen and others reverently poured into the high school gymnasium for Dan Jeffords' funeral. The gym was filled with metal folding chairs, from front to back, with an isle separating the room into two parts, one for civilians the other for law enforcement officers from every Idaho jurisdiction, in dress uniform—state police, sheriffs and city police. Behind them sat the marine honor guard, resplendent in dress blues.

Reverend Trebow, Jeffords' pastor, and a very popular clergyman, felt a sea of eyes on him as he walked to the microphone on the portable pulpit.

"Please stand," Trebow said as Will Fowers and his assistants slowly wheeled Dan Jeffords' flag-draped casket to the front of the gym. Following the casket Jake Henline escorted Claire Jeffords and behind them came Jeffords' relatives, who took seats in the section reserved for them in front. Will Fowers carefully positioned the casket ten feet in front of the family.

"Please be seated, ladies and gentlemen," Trebow said, and waited a moment. Then he held out a hand toward the casket. "We've all been saddened by the untimely death of Dan Jeffords and we've gathered here to pay our last respects to him and to his family. "I've known Dan for many years and I won't fib and tell you he was a devout go-to-church-every-Sunday sort of man. But that's never mattered much to me. I don't judge men or women by how many times they warm a church bench." That brought chuckles from the congregation as he continued. "Dan was raised right in the valley and loved his family, served his country and his community with honor."

Trebow cited some of Dan's military exploits in the jungles of Vietnam, then alluded to a couple of vicious crimes Dan solved, putting his life on the line both times in shootouts with the criminals. "He made the county safer for everyone," and that brought nods of approval from the audience. "Why he had to be taken from us at the prime of his life only the Lord knows." He paused for a moment. "Some things happen for no known reason. It's useless for us to try and draw a moral from them. When something shocking, like sudden death occurs, we must put aside needing to understand or to fit it into a system that makes no sense to us. What happens happens and we have no control over such events. Perhaps, after life is over, it will all be explained. Let's hope so. Dan never forgot his God, his country or his duty as a police officer—and he adored and deeply loved his wife Claire. Please keep her in your thoughts and prayers. These next few months will be difficult for her."

Despite her efforts to control her emotions Claire Jeffords began to weep silently, making no attempt to wipe away the tears as they traced down her face. She leaned over and whispered to Jake, "Oh, Jake…" but that's all she could say. He softly patted her arm and whispered back, "Hang in there."

Reverend Trebow said, "I assume many of you folks, friends of Dan, can easily recall some act of kindness he provided to you or your family. I've asked Dan's lifelong friend, Randy Johnson, to provide a few details about that friendship, after which the pall bearers, consisting of sheriffs who have come here from other counties, will carry Dan to the hearse. We will follow a police motorcade to the cemetery. There the marine honor guard will fire a final farewell salute to Sheriff Jeffords. Thank you for being here today. Please take your time and drive carefully." He motioned Randy to come to the pulpit.

Tall, and rugged, in a western cut suit, white shirt and bolo tie and polished cowboy boots, Randy, a former army officer exuded a commanding air, ready, yet relaxed as he walked to the microphone.

"Good morning, ladies and gentlemen. I was thinking about Dan as Tessie and I were driving to the funeral today, trying to sort out or remember vividly some special event he and I shared. I don't know why, but suddenly an afternoon some years ago came drifting in—the afternoon Tessie and I got married! Dan was only a deputy then, but he secretly organized an affair Tessie and I have never forgotten." Randy smiled nostalgically." As soon as we'd said our I do's we ran to the car, threw it in gear and tried to speed out of town to avoid being shivered!" The audience chuckled as Randy continued. "We almost made it—but Dan and the other deputies ran us to ground at the edge of town with lights flashing and sirens blaring."

Randy shook his head with a humorous grin. "What a miserable affair that turned out to be! Now for you younger folks who don't know what shiveree means, I'm here to tell you that for Tess and me it meant me wheeling her to the jail in a wheelbarrow where we spent most of our wedding night in separate cells. It was all in good fun of course—but a night Tess and I have never forgotten." He saw an embarrassed smile light Tessie's face.

"Friends, there are so many memories we've shared with Dan and Claire, but time is short so forgive me for getting serious. Randy's demeanor noticeably changed, and he struggled for words to express the depths of his feelings about his friend with whom he'd grown up. He choked with emotion for a moment and the audience noticed tears wetting his cheeks.

"I still don't know what happened," Randy said quietly. "A few months ago our lives were shattered by unusual circumstances none of us could comprehend. Some of our precious animals were mysteriously killed and we had nowhere to turn for help except to Dan Jeffords and his deputies. In fact, Dan's last law enforcement duty was trying to apprehend whoever was responsible. Like always, he was there when we needed him."

Randy paused for a moment to control his emotions. "The two of us enjoyed hunting in the nearby mountains, dating girls, then marrying our sweethearts and settling here in the valley. We went off to war together and through the grace of God we both came home. Many times Dan and I talked about why we got to come home and many of our buddies didn't. Of course we never came up with any answers. Perhaps there is some unknown purpose as to why we are here. Whatever it is Dan served his time here on earth and has now crossed over the great divide to other adventures. Though I'm not an overly religious man, I like to believe what the good book tells us, *for as in*

Adam all die, even so in Christ shall all be made alive. May our friend Dan rest in peace."

Randy turned his face to the casket and snapped his right hand to his forehead in a final military salute then walked over and sat down next to Tessie.

Two deputy sheriffs stepped to Dan's flag draped casket and carefully lifted the flag, then slowly and methodically folded it. One of them took it over to Clair Jeffords and presented it to her. She lovingly took it in both hands and pressed it to her chest.

Reverend Trewboy said, "Will the audience please rise."

Will Fowers and his assistants wheeled the casket to the hearse. The audience dispersed to their cars to follow the hearse to the cemetery.

36

SIX UNIFORMED IDAHO COUNTY SHERIFFS carried the casket to the burial plot. A brief grave dedication by Reverend Trebow, capped by a bugler playing taps and the marine honor guard firing a farewell salute, ended the funeral service.

Tessie Johnson and other friends and relatives gathered round Claire and visited and offered her help in the coming weeks. Jake unobtrusively took Randy Johnson's arm and steered him off to the side.

"I want to thank you, Randy, for straightening things out with Claire and protecting me from…well you know, having her find out I shot her husband."

Randy shrugged. "All in a days work, Jake. Uh oh, looks like trouble coming." He pointed to Deputy Sheriff Jim Munford's mud-splattered patrol car pulling in to the cemetery.

"Damn it!" Jake growled. "I told Jim to take care of things until I got back!"

Jim stepped out of the patrol car and walked over to them. "I hate to bother you Jake," he apologized, "but we've got an emergency."

"*Jesus!*" Jake said softly, a tone of exasperation in his voice. "What now?"

Jim reached in jacket pocket and came out with a couple of sheets of yellow lined paper filled with scribbled notes. He handed them to Jake, who threw up a hand. "Never mind that! Just spit it out Jim and tell me what the hell is going on!"

"Cory Langdon, owner of the Big Bend Ranch east of Rogerson called me on the phone about an hour ago. You know them two horses he reported missing? Well he found 'em," Jim said, glancing at his notes. "They been killed and mutilated."

"Anything else?" Jake asked.

"Hell! Ain't that enough?" Jim grinned. "Cory told me to tell you to get your lazy ass on down there quick as possible and take a look at his dead horses. He said he's tired of them goddamn mutilators killing his stock and you've got to do something to stop them!"

Jake shook his head. "That sounds like Cory!"

"Didn't you go down there a while back and investigate five of his steers that got killed?" Jim asked.

Jake nodded. "Yeah. That's when I first met him. He's a real sweetheart— an A number one asshole! His brother is a big honcho in the state legislature so Cory acts likes he owns the whole state."

Randy, standing quietly nearby, grinned. "That's an apt description, Jake. I know old Cory. I've done some horse trading with him over the years and he's got a disposition only a mother could love!"

Jake nodded then turned to Jim. "Did Cory tell you anything more about those dead horses?"

Jim took a quick glance at his notes. "He said he last saw the two horses alive on Tuesday afternoon about a mile from his ranch house. When he checked on them the next day he found them dead. Both of them had been gutted out,"

"You mean dead and mutilated?" Jake asked.

"Ain't that what I just said? Anyway, Cory said he did a quick walk around looking for evidence, but there was nothing to indicate who killed his horses—not a track or ground mark of any kind."

"Is that all he said?" Jake asked.

Jim shook his head. "He told me it scared the shit out of him when he found his dead horses. He said he could live with the sonsabitches killing his cows, but he'd be goddamned if he could figure out why any human would kill his horses and he was real puzzled trying to figure out how they could do it without leaving any footprints in the snow. There was no sign of a struggle—like the horses just laid down and died?"

"Anything else?" Jake asked.

"He told me he seen some weird shit in the sky the night before he found his horses."

"Define weird shit, Jim. Was it a UFO?"

"Yeah. Cory said it was a dark triangular craft as big as an aircraft carrier. I ain't sure about that. I just figured old Cory must have been drinking. There ain't anything as big as aircraft carriers flying around Idaho."

Jake let it go. Sightings of UFOs usually coincided with most animal mutilation cases and Jake didn't want to delve into further details with Jim.

Jake scratched his head for a moment. "I guess I'd better head down that way in the morning," he said, "before old Cory throws a hissy fit and calls his brother."

Jim smiled. "How about me going down there with you?"

"No!" came Jake's immediate response. "I need you here to handle things until I get back," Then he turned to Randy, "Would you be willing to ride down there with me?"

Randy hesitated a few moments. "How long would it take?"

"Not long if we leave first thing in the morning. You could take a look at Cory's butchered horses and determine if there are any similarities to the mutilations you found on your mutilated horses."

Randy thought for a moment. "Okay. Joe and Tessie can probably take care of things until I get back."

"You coming back to the office before you go down there?" Jim asked.

"No," Jake answered. "Right now I'm going to take Claire home. If anything else comes up, call me at home—and Jim, you don't say one word to anyone about this, understand?"

Jim looked at him doubtfully. "Okay, if you say so." He turned and walked back to his patrol car.

Jake turned to Randy. "You still got that old Army forty-five of yours?"

Randy nodded.

"Good. Make sure it's loaded and bring it along. I'll pick you up at seven in the morning."

Randy looked curiously at Jake. "You expecting trouble?"

Jake grinned. "Now why the hell would I expect trouble?" He glanced around to make sure no one was within earshot, and then lowered his voice. "Just for your information, this mutilation at Cory's place is the third one reported this week. I've been keeping them on the QT so the media doesn't start poking around before we come up with some answers."

Randy acted as if he could not believe his ears. "Do you think Captain John and his crew have returned?"

"I don't have the first damn clue," Jake said. "But I doubt it. The UFOs being reported are nothing like Captain John's."

"How do you know that?" Randy asked.

"I had a call from Deleon Gifford owner of Magic Mountain Ski Resort just east of Rogerson…"

"I know the place," Randy interrupted. "Joe and I have been skiing down there several times."

"Well, Deleon told me that for the past week at sundown every evening he's observed two huge UFOs zooming in low from east of his place in the Sawtooth National Forest, then disappearing from sight At daybreak they come zooming by, heading back to the forest. They're huge triangular-shaped outfits…"

"Do you believe him?" Randy asked.

Jake shook his head. "I don't know what to believe any more. I'm kind of thinking that maybe whoever or whatever is flying those UFOs may have stopped by Cory's ranch and gutted his horses."

It crossed Randy's mind that Jake's theory was right on the money. "Did Deleon report those huge UFOs to anyone else?" Randy asked.

"I asked him that very questions," Jake said, "and he said hell no. I don't want people thinking I'm a nut case. He only told me about the UFOs because he knows he can trust me."

They looked at each other for a long moment. Randy broke the silence. "So you think I can help? "

"I do."

Randy was silent for a time and felt uneasy, thinking back on his own experience with the mutilators and then what happened to his old friend Ben Summers when he came in direct contact with the mutilators.

"What are you thinking?" Jake asked.

"I was just remembering what happened to old Ben Summers when he tangled with the mutilators. I hope to hell Cory doesn't end up like that."

Jake shook his head, looking very worried. "I've got a bad feeling about our trip tomorrow, like those sonsabitchin' mutilators are somewhere around Rogerson just waiting for us."

"So what are we going to do?" Randy asked.

"What can we do?" Jake sounded helpless. What can anyone do against them? They're untouchable. We'll just have to play it by ear." Jake paused. "I'm not sugar coating what we may run into down there tomorrow, Randy. It could be mighty damn dangerous—and you don't have to go. You can still back out now and no one will say a word about it."

Randy shook his head and smiled. "Oh no! I'm not letting you go down there alone, my friend! Quit your worrying and consider yourself damned lucky you've got me backing you up."

Jake shook his head and chuckled. "Geez, I wish you hadn't said that! Now I'm really worried!"

Randy nodded, took a deep breath and exhaled and waved at Tessie visiting with Claire Jeffords. She waved back and started walking toward him. "Well, I guess I'd better tell Tess I'm going with you tomorrow to look at some mutilated horses."

Jake shook his head vigorously. "No! You tell her only that you're going to ride along and keep me company on a routine patrol south of here. There's no need to alarm her now. Maybe later you can tell her why we went to Rogerson—after we learn more about what's going on down there. Okay?"

"If you say so," Randy reluctantly agreed, though he didn't like the idea of leaving Tessie in the dark wondering what was going on.

✝

That evening after Randy finished his chores he was completely exhausted. When he and Tessie finally crawled into bed she snuggled next to him but he didn't move. "What's wrong, Honey?" she asked. "You've hardly said a word to me since we left the cemetery except to tell me you're going with Jake in the morning."

"It's nothing," Randy said casually. "Just tired. That's all."

"Are you worried about going with Jake tomorrow?"

"A little," he admitted.

"Why does he want you to go?" Tessie asked softly. "He's got deputies."

Randy was silent for a moment. "We're good friends."

"Well, if you're worried, you don't have to go," she said.

307

"That's the rub, Honey. I do have to go."

"Why?"

"I really don't know how to explain it. Maybe it's just to be with Jake in case he needs me."

Tessie knew there was more to it than what he was telling her. He was holding something back—and it frightened her. But she knew enough not to pry—but she just had to ask, "Going with Jake is more than just a pleasure trip, isn't it?

"What makes you think that?" Randy said, trying to formulate an answer.

"Because I can tell when you're keeping things from me…oh, never mind," she said. "When you're ready to tell me what's going on I'll be ready to listen." She snuggled up tight against him and soon fell asleep.

Randy lay awake, listening to Tessie's steady breathing, feeling the warmth of her body beside him. Though they were both reaching middle age they were still like lovers. There had never been anyone else for either of them. He loved her more than words could convey.

Off in the distance a lone coyote howled. The real world was still out there, cold, dark and dangerous. The wind murmured hypnotically around the corners of the house. He turned on his side with a sigh of surrender and drifted off to sleep.

That's when the dream came! He was standing on a rocky hillside with his cousin Bill Martin, staring down at the butchered remains of his sturdy little mare, Miss BJ. He was angry. Her killers had come and gone like smoke, drifting in, killing and mutilating, and then wafting away with the wind. He was helpless against them. How do you fight smoke? Suddenly he was whisked from the hillside to Old Ben Summer' pasture and he stood there alone staring down at the old man's stiffened body, studying the once kind old face, now twisted beyond recognition with terror.

Randy wandered from the pasture along a waist-high sagebrush-lined trail and stopped dead in his tracks when he bumped into old Billy's huge curved horns protruding above the sage. He ran his hand slowly and lovingly down the old ram's face and touched his nose. It was still warm. Steam was wafting up from the ram's empty stomach cavity. He'd been gutted! The mutilators were close by! He couldn't see them, only sense them, like a dark evil blanket had been cast over him. Terrified, Randy gazed out across the endless sea of sagebrush, where a cold breeze now created patterns along the tops, bending them toward him, followed by a dense rolling white mist.

From the mist a shadow rose up and materialized in the form of a man. The man called his name. *Randy!* The hair on the back of his neck prickled. The words were so quiet they might have been a thought!

"What do you want?" Randy asked, his voice trembling.

"You!"

"Why?"

The man started to say something but the rest of his words faded as the figure turned and slowly floated skyward without another look back.

"Stop!" Randy shouted, waving his arms. "Stop!" He ran, trying to catch the disappearing shadowy figure...

Randy jerked awake, sat up and cleared his throat and rubbed his eyes as he fought to clear the nightmare from his brain.

"What's wrong, Honey?" Tessie mumbled sleepily.

"Nothing. Just a bad dream. Go back to sleep."

Randy took a few deep breaths, lay back down. When he woke it was daylight. He looked at the clock on the nightstand. 5:30. Jake would be here at seven. A chill ran down Randy's spine and he didn't want to get out of bed! He stared at the .45 lying on the nightstand. He closed his eyes. *What the hell good would that do against the mutilators?*

37

SHERIFF JAKE HENLINE PULLED THE POLICE car off the interstate into the local McDonalds drive through and picked up two cups of coffee—then jumped back on the freeway to the turnoff to Randy Johnson's ranch. He was glued to the police radio and caught several updates on the robbery at the truck stop south of town just two hours ago. Two of his deputies and two state police officers now had the robber cornered near the Union Pacific storage building.

Between crooks robbing truck stops, mutilators killing horses and his recent shooting of Sheriff Jeffords, Jake was teeming with frustration. Nothing made sense any more—and he was less than enthusiastic about the drive down to that god-forsaken area east of Rogerson to look at some dead horses when he could be doing something useful like apprehending lawbreakers!

Jake drove into Randy's driveway promptly at seven and Randy stepped out of the house, with Tessie at his side. She waved to Jake, gave Randy a quick kiss and he walked to the police car and got in. Jake handed him a cup of coffee.

"Ready to roll?"

Randy nodded. "Let'er rip!" Randy held his coffee and pushed back deeper into the seat. He felt the .45 in his belt dig into his leg as he pressed against the seat.

"Take your jacket off and enjoy the ride," Jake said as he backed out of the driveway and headed for Highway 93, the road to Rogerson.

"So how are..." Randy started to ask.

"Shhh!" Jake help up a hand. "I want to hear this!"

The police radio crackled with staticky calls between police officers. It was close to seven thirty when an updated report brought a wide smile to Jake's face. *The suspect, holed up at the Union Pacific storage area, wounded in a shootout, surrendered and is now in custody...*

"They nailed the sonuvabitch!" Jake threw a fist in the air, as if he were cheering a football touchdown.

"What did he do?"

"He robbed the truck stop east of town. Luckily two of my deputies got there within five minutes of the call and tracked him down. A couple of highway patrol boys got in on the act and helped out."

"That's great, Jake," Randy said. "Too damn bad we can't catch the mutilators that quick, huh?"

"Yeah," Jake agreed, "only it doesn't work that way with them. I've wracked my brain trying to figure out a strategy to find out who they are—then what to do to stop them."

"Have you come up with any logical answers?" Randy asked.

"No, and it's driving me nuts."

"Tell me about it."

"Well, I wouldn't mind identifying these mutilators are who are killing animals down by Rogerson. I know it's not Captain John and his crew. They're long gone. Hell, Randy, we don't even know for sure that it was Captain John who killed your horses. Maybe they're the same ones who killed Cory Langdon's animals."

"Well, I guess it really doesn't matter any more, does it?"

"Probably not," Randy agreed. "I figure my biggest problem is that tracking down the mutilators is not in my job description. I'm not trained to unravel the mysteries of UFOs and aliens—but here I am driving toward the boondocks to ferret them out and get rid of them."

Randy grinned. "Maybe you should have been smart and majored in Ufology in college."

"Yeah, maybe I should have," Jake grinned back, "except there are no schools, academies, associations or licensing exams available for teaching a person how to track down aliens in UFOs flying around Idaho—or any other place!"

"Well you'll just have to fly by the seat of your pants and figure out this mutilator phenomenon as you go along?"

"You got it, Randy! It's way beyond a simple county sheriff's ability to solve the mutilator mystery. All I can do is observe, think, jot notes and maybe turn them over to the FBI. But that causes them a problem—what the hell will they do with that kind of information? They're as much in the dark about the mutilators as I am."

"You got a point," Randy agreed. "The FBI knew about Captain John— they even had an agreement with him! But like you said, he's long gone. So who the hell are these other mutilators? Where do they come from, why are they here and most importantly what do they want, animal parts?"

Jake shook his head. "There's got to be more to it than that, Randy."

"Like what?"

"God damned if I know!" Jake answered honestly. "It's like they get some perverse pleasure out of toying with us, like we're puppets on a string."

"What do you mean?"

"From what little I know about them, I believe they could easily destroy us in the blink of an eye. But they don't." Jake paused for a moment. "Take your boy Joe for example. That night I picked him up after his meeting with the mutilators he was terrified, but perfectly all right physically. They could easily have killed him so he couldn't tell anyone about them."

Randy gave that thought. "Yeah, they could have. Thank God they didn't!"

Jake slowed just north of Rogerson and turned east toward Magic Mountain Ski Area where he'd turn off onto the dirt road leading to Cory Langdon's remote ranch nestled next to the Sawtooth National Forest. He'd called ahead and alerted Cory he'd be at his ranch at nine thirty so take a look at his dead horses.

This time of year the ski season was over and there was not much traffic on the road. They saw only one car heading west toward Rogersson. Randy leaned over and said, "Hey, Jake at the next wide spot in the road pull off. I need to take a leak. That coffee went right through me."

Jake nodded. "Okay. Hang on." Ahead he saw a level pull off, suddenly conscious of another vehicle following about half a mile behind. He pulled off the pavement onto the dirt and turned off the engine. Randy opened the car door and started to get out.

"Hold up a minute, someone is coming," Jake said

Randy got back in the car and shut the door.

The Idaho Fish and Game pickup slowed as it came closer. The driver honked and waved as he passed by.

"You know him?" Randy asked.

"Yeah. That's Mike Steadman. He's the game warden in these parts. Probably trying to find that damn deer poacher who kills big bucks for their antlers and leaves the meat to rot. Knowing Mike, he'll catch him…" Suddenly Jake stopped in mid-sentence as the bright morning sun was blocked out almost as if a blanket had been thrown over the car, and a dense dark shadow covered the entire parking area, extending at least a block on all sides. Jake and Randy heard a low throbbing rumble of some kind of engine which vibrated and jostled the car.

Jake turned the key to start the engine, but nothing happened. He rolled down the window and stared up at the huge UFO hovering directly over them. "Oh my God!" he said as he tried to open the car door but he was locked in. He smashed his shoulder against door but it refused to budge.

"What's happening, Jake?" Randy asked nervously.

Jake's mouth was hanging open, and he was breathing hard, eyes wide. He'd grown pale and appeared to be in shock.

"Jesus, Jake! Are you okay? You look like you're having a heart attack or something."

Jake waved his hand and pointed up. "Roll down your window and look up! Tell me what you see!"

Randy rolled down his window and stared up.

"Well?" Jake said.

"It's a UFO. A big sucker!" Randy said and turned as pale as Jake. What do we do now?"

"I'd like to shoot the sonsabitches!" Jake growled angrily, "but they got us cold, Randy. We're sitting ducks! Just sit tight. It's their move. Let's hope to hell they don't kill us!" Jake reached for his pistol and was frozen to instant immobility. Randy tried desperately to open his locked car door, and he too was instantly immobilized.

Two hours later, Mike Steadman, driving west toward Rogerson, noticed Jake Henline's police car still parked in the same spot he'd last seen it.

He slowed and pulled his pickup off the road close to the car and stopped. Something wasn't right! The two occupants were slumped forward, either dead or asleep. Mike apprehensively unstrapped his pistol. He slowly walked to the driver's side of the car and looked through the window at the driver. It was Sheriff Jake Henline. Mike didn't know the other man slumped in the passenger seat.

Mike knuckle tapped on the driver's window but Jake didn't move. Mike apprehensively glanced in every direction. Everything appeared normal, except for the deathly silence—no raucous blue jays, no cawing crows or magpies and no chattering squirrels.

Carefully Mike opened the now unlocked driver's door and studied Jake's limp form slumped forward against the steering wheel. There was no blood or bullet holes in the body that he could see." Jake?" Mike shouted. No response. The sheriff appeared to be sleeping. Mike grabbed Jake's left shoulder and shook him gently. "Hey, Jake, c'mon man, wake up!"

In an instant Jake jerked back. The mutilators had him! He grabbed his pistol. "Back off you sonuvabitch!" Jake growled, now in kill mode.

Stunned by Jake's sudden move, Mike backed up a step, silent and still. "What the hell's going on, Jake? Have you guys been drinking? Put the gun away before somebody gets hurt!"

Jake felt his heart hammer faster. He was confused but he slowly pushed the pistol back in its holster.

"What's the matter, Jake? Don't you recognize me? I'm Mike Steadman."

"Mike? Mike Steadman? Do we know each other?"

Mike stared at him, incredulous. "Why hell yes! We've been working this territory for years, you catching the bad guys and me the poachers. Are you after some bad guys?"

"I don't think so," Jake said. His forehead wrinkled as he tried hard to remember.

"Then what the hell are you doing way out here in the middle of nowhere?"

Jake was frustrated. "My God, Mike, I don't know what the hell's going on. Where are we?"

"You're just a ways east of Magic Mountain Ski Resort."

It didn't seem to register with Jake. "You got a cigarette?" he asked.

"Yeah, but you don't smoke, remember!"

"I do now!"

Mike took a pack from his shirt pocket, pulled a cigarette out and passed it through the open window. He waited until Jake's trembling hands got the cigarette to his mouth, then Mike lit it. Jake inhaled greedily, then coughed.

"Who's your buddy over there?" Mike pointed to Randy still slumped against the dashboard.

"Randy," Jake said. "Randy Johnson." He turned and shouted, "Hey Randy, wake up, we've got company!" Jake reached over and shook Randy, who slowly came to, shaking his head back and forth like a dazed prize fighter.

"You gonna' tell me what happened?" Mike asked.

"There's no way to explain it, Mike. It's just too crazy. You've just got to trust me—until I figure out it out."

Mike stroked his chin and nodded. "Well, maybe I can help you with that. I assume you were headed out to Cory Langdon's ranch, right? It's the only place out this way. I was just out that way and stopped by to see how old Cory was getting on. I learned the old boy suffered a heart attack last night. He's in pretty bad shape. The Doc's out there now and he told me he doesn't expect him to pull through. He said Cory told him a cop was on his way to take a look at some mutilated horses, but he never showed up."

"Who are you talking about? Jake asked, looking very confused. "Cory who?"

"You okay?" Mike asked. "Cory Langdon. His ranch is just down this road."

Jake searched his memory. He'd never heard that name before. He looked over at Randy. "Do you know a Cory Langdon?"

Still dazed, Randy shook his head. "Never heard of him."

Jake turned back to Mike. "You said something about mutilated horses. What did you mean?"

"Well, hell Jake, livestock's been getting killed and mutilated in these parts for months. You telling me you don't know about it?"

"No, Mike, I don't!" Jake replied with a touch of anger.

"Well, excuse my French," Mike said with slight exasperation, "then what the hell are you two doing out here?"

Jake turned to Randy with a questioning look. "Do you know why we're here?"

Okay, Think, Randy…swallowing hard, he shrugged. "Honest to God, Jake, I don't know—I can't remember."

Mike shook his head with frustration and frowned. "Boy, you guys are really screwed up! You want me to radio in to your dispatcher and have him send a deputy out here to take you home?"

Jake and Randy glanced at one another in confusion. Then Jake said, "That won't be necessary, Mike. I can drive."

"Are you sure?" Mike looked doubtful. "I'm really worried about you. "Would you like me to follow you back to Twin Falls?"

Jake shook his head. "Thanks, but no. That won't be necessary either." Jake was silent a long moment then stared at Mike. "I would like you to promise me you'll not say anything to anyone about this, uh, situation. You can imagine how embarrassing that would be for me if you…"

Mike threw up a hand and interrupted. "Hell, Jake, don't worry about that at all. Whatever happened here is none of my business. You got your job, I got mine…" Mike chuckled. "But your job is a little weird—and I do mean weird!"

Jake smiled at that. "You got that right! Thanks, Mike, I appreciate it."

Mike nodded. "Well, if there's nothing more I can do for you, I'll head back to Rogerson. If you need me give me a call on the radio."

Jake watched Mike walk back to his pickup. He turned and waved, then climbed into the truck and drove away.

Jake chuckled nervously.

"What?" Randy said.

"I'll bet that guy will be wondering from now till doom's day what the hell happened here! Maybe we ought to try and figure it ourselves!" That set Jake to thinking about something—something Mike had said—something that shifted loosely in his mind. What was it he'd said? Mutilations? Mutilated horses? Mutilators! That was it. That was it! *The mutilators? Something to do with animals. What? What? Who? The mutilators.* Try to remember. *What am I trying to remember?*

"Jake! Hey, Jake!" Randy shouted. "Where are you? You're a million miles away!"

"Sorry, Randy, I was just thinking, trying to remember. Something Mike said about mutilations. Does that ring a bell with you?"

Randy scratched the back of his head. "Horses. I remember he said something about mutilated horses." Randy shook his head. "Aw, hell, I just can't remember."

"That makes two of us," Jake said. "So where do we go from here?"

Randy chuckled and threw a hand in the air with a dismissive gesture. "I don't know, my friend. You're driving!"

Epilogue

IDAHO'S FBI FIELD DIRECTOR, KYLE HOWDEN, stepped into his Boise office, took off his coat and settled himself comfortably in his high-backed brown leather chair, exhaled deeply, finally ready for an unstressful day. No new animal mutilations had been reported. Gary Sheffield should now be in Alturas, California taking care of business and Dr. James Austin and Sheriff Jake Henline had carefully and cautiously smoothed over Sheriff Jeffords' death, closing the file on a very troubling case.

Kyle glanced through the daily newspaper his secretary Helen Rissom placed on his desk every morning.

She poked her head around his door. "Would you like a freshly brewed cup of coffee?"

"Yes Ma'am!" Kyle said enthusiastically, with a broad smile. "Any phone calls?"

"Not so far," Helen replied, just as her phone rang. She hurried over to her desk and grabbed the phone. "FBI. Mr. Howden's office."

"Is he in, Helen?" She instantly recognized Bill Donovan's deep, gruff voice.

"Yes sir. One moment please." She covered the mouthpiece with her hand. "It's Mr. Donovan in Washington!"

"*Oh God! Now what?*" Howden muttered under his breath and his smile disappeared. He picked up the phone.

"Where the hell is Gary Sheffield?" Donovan growled.

"He should be in Alturas, California."

"Well he's not!" Donovan said.

"Are you telling me you lost him? You're the one at headquarters. I thought you guys back there had all the answers."

"Don't be a smart ass!" Donovan said, sounding strained.

"To answer your question, Bill, if Gary's not in Alturas, I don't know where he is. He drove away from here a couple of days ago It's only a five or six hour drive."

"We know that, Kyle that's why we're worried about him. We haven't had one damn word from him. Did he plan any stops along the way?

"No sir. He told me he was driving straight through."

"Then he hasn't made any contact with you since he left Boise?"

"No sir, not a word. But I didn't expect him to. He'd finished his business here in Idaho."

"Damn!" Donovan sounded frustrated. "You know the route he was following, so I want you to track him down. Get the Idaho State Police to fly you along Gary's proposed route in their chopper, and follow his trail. He had to travel through part of Oregon so contact the Oregon State Police and see if they can provide any help or .information. Do whatever it takes to find him!"

"Yes sir. But why the urgency?" Kyle asked.

"Cattle around Alturas are being killed and mutilated by the dozens . We've got to get someone in there ASAP to keep those killings from getting blown out of proportion in the media. They're already sniffing around looking for a story. We've somehow got to keep a lid on these animal killings before the press sends in reporters."

"Do you want me to drive over to Alturas?" Kyle asked.

"No. I want you to find Gary Sheffield, understand?"

"Yes sir.'

"And Kyle, call me the minute you have something!"

✝

A young Oregon state trooper, Jimmy Rivera, wearing a Smokey Bear hat, was taking a break, sitting in his patrol car at a pull off on Highway 20, near Juntura, Oregon, midway between Ontario and Burns. It's a boring, desolate stretch of highway and the wind was swirling dust and tumble weeds across the highway. The only reason anyone lived in the area was because the Malheur River, alongside the highway, brought water to the parched region. Native American Paiutes used to winter along the river's middle fork until the mountain men and settlers pushed them out.

Though Trooper Rivera would rather be patrolling Oregon's super highways closer to Portland, he knew he'd have to patrol on the state's remote highways to earn enough seniority to move up. But no problem! He felt damn lucky to have landed a job with the Oregon State Police when he returned home from Vietnam, and got his discharge from the Marine Corps. He filled out applications for highway patrol jobs in Washington, Nevada and Oregon.

He would always cherish that lucky call he got from the Oregon State Police. *Mr. Rivera, we would like to talk to you about a possible opening with the OSP if you are still interested...*

A staticky radio call from the Ontario dispatcher jerked Trooper Rivera wide awake.

"Jimmy, we need to locate a red nineteen seventy-four Jeep Cherokee with Idaho plates. Have you by any chance seen a vehicle matching that description along Highway Twenty?"

"Not today," Rivera replied. "Do you have any additional information on the vehicle?"

"Single occupant, no passengers. Last seen at a truck stop in Ontario yesterday and believed to be traveling south on Highway Twenty."

"Is the driver wanted?" Rivera asked.

"No. He's an FBI agent out of Washington, DC, name of Gary Sheffield and he's disappeared."

"An FBI agent? Sounds important," Rivera said. "You got a description?"

"Yeah. He's in his mid-fifties, about six two, two ten, grayish brown hair."

"What the hell is he doing out in this God-forsaken part of the world?"

"We don't know, but right now finding him is top priority for the FBI— so that means it's top priority for the Oregon State Police. Our people in Salem are calling us every hour—so keep your eyes open and radio me the minute you come up with anything."

✝

Shortly after ten a.m. Trooper Rivera started his police cruiser and headed south on Highway 20 toward 4200-foot Drinkwater Pass. The plain wrinkled up toward the mountain's jugged upheaval. Suddenly Rivera caught a glimpse of sun shining off glass or chrome about a mile or more west of the highway. He slowed and pulled off to the side of the road, trying to get a glimpse of whatever was causing the bright mirror-like flash. He couldn't see anything. Slowly he backed the car looking for a way to get to the shining object. He spotted the faint outline of an old sheep trail which seemed fairly level. He drove the cruiser off the highway into the desert. Rocks hit the undercarriage until he had reached the first of several hills and gullies and parked on the rim of a gully.

Where the ground dropped away into a deep gully below, Rivera spotted the red Jeep Cherokee with the sun glinting off its windshield. He parked, grabbed the mike and called Ontario. "I found the Jeep Cherokee you're looking for. It's in a gully about a mile or more west of the highway, just north of Drinkwater Pass."

"Anyone in it?"

"I can't tell from here."

"Haven't you inspected it yet?"

"I'm going to. I just wanted to let you know I found it."

"If there's no road out there, how did the Cherokee get into a gully?" the dispatcher asked.

"It's a four-wheel drive, but I haven't found any tire tracks."

"Well go take a look around!" said the dispatcher with a touch of frustration his voice, "then call us back as quickly as you can. I'll let headquarters know you've found the car."

Rivera stepped out of his cruiser, slipped on his jacket, and walked and slid down to the Cherokee. Its exterior was in perfect condition, not a dent or scratch any place. Rivera scratched his head and walked around the vehicle trying to figure out how the Cherokee ended up in a gully. His first impression was that it must have been dropped here by something in the sky, but how could that be?

The passenger side door was locked. The driver's door was slightly ajar, a key chain hanging from the ignition. And the interior light was on, but very dimly. But how could it still be burning, when the dashboard was burned black, its wiring fused and burned almost as if it had been scorched with a blow torch? There was no one in the car.

Rivera nervously slid into the driver's seat and looked around. He pried open the glove compartment. It was empty. Then he felt under the seats. Nothing.

As he climbed out of the Cherokee he had a gut feeling he'd stumbled into a situation almost beyond his ability to understand. Where the hell was Gary Sheffield? With his hand on the butt of his .38, he bent low examining the ground as he walked along searching for footprints. A hundred yards from the Cherokee he spotted a faint set of footprints heading west, deeper into the desert.

As Rivera climbed up the far side of the gully and topped a small hill he saw a man maybe a hundred yards off, walking slowly.

"Hey, hold up, there!" he shouted. But the man kept walking, staggering slightly.

Rivera quickened his pace and caught up. Out of breath he moved in close to the man. "Are you Gary Sheffield?"

The man turned and stared at Rivera. Sheffield's brow wrinkled, like he was trying to remember. "Yeah, I'm Sheffield," he said slowly.

"What are you doing out here, Mr. Sheffield?

Without warning Sheffield threw a sucker punch at Rivera who was knocked backward and hit the ground stunned. His head thundered with pain. He opened his eyes to slits.

Sheffield stood there, zombie like, expressionless.

Rivera rose up on one elbow and shook his head. "What the hell did you do that for?" he asked as he wiped his sleeve across his eyes and got to his feet. "Don't ever do it again!" he warned.

But Rivera's warning had no effect. Sheffield shuffled toward him, his right hand made into a fist.

Rivera stepped back and held up a hand. "Stop, Mr. Sheffield! I don't want to hurt you!"

Sheffield stopped. He shook his head and blinked his eyes rapidly like he was waking from a deep trance.

"Are you all right?" Rivera asked.

Sheffield seemed confused and didn't answer. When his eyes finally came into focus he studied Rivera for a moment then said slowly. "Are you one of them?"

"One of who?"

"Them!" Sheffield pointed toward the sky.

"No sir. I'm a trooper with the Oregon State Police, name of Jimmy Rivera." He pulled open his jacket and pointed to his badge on his shirt.

"You sneaky bastard! I don't believe you!" Sheffield glared at him. "You're one of them!" And he opened his jacket and his right hand streaked back to his hip holster and came out with his snub nose .357 revolver. Rivera judo chopped his arm and he dropped the gun. Suddenly a terrible muted cry came from Sheffield's throat that made Rivera's hair stand on end, and

Sheffield began twisting and squirming wildly, screaming and tearing at his back with both hands.

"Oh God, Trooper, help me! My back is on fire!"

Rivera grabbed Sheffield and hurled him to the ground on his stomach then jerked up his shirt. There, pulsating on Sheffield's back was the strangest mark Rivera had ever seen—long, deep red, in the shape of a crescent moon. Rivera put his hand over the scar and pressed down as hard as he could and instantly gasped and sucked in his breath as a strong surge of some kind of electricity coursed through every part of his body. Then the scar suddenly turned cold under Rivera's hand and he jerked it away, away, shaking it violently back and forth several times.

Sheffield lay motionless on the ground. Rivera assumed he was dead and he wasn't sure what to do. Maybe go back to the police cruiser and call Ontario—*and tell them what?* Cautiously he leaned over, took Sheffield's hand, turned it over and felt his wrist for a pulse. Nothing! Rivera shook his head, totally baffled.

He turned and tried to judge the distance to his cruiser on the other side of the gully. He knew he couldn't carry or drag Sheffield's body that far. He'd have to leave it here…he heard a stick break behind him and whirled around to find Sheffield on his feet, holding his 357 Rivera had carelessly left lying on the ground. Sheffield raised and aimed the pistol and started to pull the trigger.

Rivera had no time to issue a 'drop the gun' warning. He fast drew his pistol and squeezed the trigger three times, in rapid succession hitting Sheffield in the chest. He sprawled forward, dead before he hit the hard ground.

✝

Rivera was breathing rapidly when he jammed his pistol back in its holster. He just stood there trying to come to grips with the fact that he'd just killed an FBI agent. He wasn't sure what to do. That's when he heard a muffled sound, much like a jet aircraft makes. Coming in low from the east was a huge triangular shaped UFO, its speed relatively slow. It kept coming until it was about five hundred feet above Rivera, then the engines stopped. The craft had no lights and it hovered silently,

Rivera looked up, now a player in a scenario he'd only read about— and wasn't sure if what he was seeing was real. Squinting against the bright morning sun he carefully studied the object above and realized it was not a helicopter or any other common flying vehicle. Right now what he really wanted to see more than anything was a friendly helicopter bringing help in his hour of need.

He didn't want to accept the fact that what he was seeing did not fit into this world. But why in God's name was it hovering over him—just to watch him or do him harm? Suddenly it dawned on him that he was not alone, Gary Sheffield was stretched out dead on the frozen desert floor. Could someone or something in the UFO be monitoring the body? If so why? Was Gary Sheffield in some way connected to the UFO? Rivera reasoned that Sheffield must have had some connection else it wouldn't be here.

Finally the huge triangular shaped UFO began to move south, very slowly, but building up speed as it went, still perfectly visible. It floated like it weighed nothing. When it was about a quarter of a mile away, its needle sharp nose turned a point or two west, and the back end tipped from side to side as if the pilot was waving his wings in a farewell salute.

✝

Rivera knew he had to call in a report to the Ontario dispatcher. He left Sheffield where he lay and made his way back to the police cruiser. He sat there for a few moments trying to gather his thoughts. Then he took the mike in his hand and turned on the radio. Still he waited apprehensively before he trusted his voice to say what had to be said—knowing his words might cost him his career.

"Ontario, this is Unit four nineteen, Trooper Jimmy Rivera."

"Go ahead, Jimmy," the dispatcher responded immediately.

"I've located Agent Sheffield."

"That's good news! I have FBI Agent Kyle Howden from their Boise office here with me. The Idaho police flew him here in their helicopter. He's anxious to speak to you. Here he is."

"Hello, Trooper Rivera," Kyle said. "I'm relieved to hear you've located Agent Sheffield. Is he all right?"

There was a short pause before Rivera answered.

"Sir, I don't think we should discuss this over the radio. Can your pilot fly you down here "

"Is that really necessary?" Kyle asked.

"Yes sir. I'll park my car along the highway so you can see it. Okay?"

"Okay. We can be there in a few minutes," Kyle said, wondering why

Trooper Rivera was reluctant to provide more information. He handed the mike back to the Ontario dispatcher and turned to Lieutenant Boyce Jacobson, chopper pilot for the Idaho State Police. "Did you hear that, Boyce?" Kyle asked.

Jacobson nodded. "The chopper's gassed and ready to go."

There was a round of handshakes as the Kyle thanked the dispatcher and several Oregon State Police officers who'd gathered to listen in on Rivera's unusual call.

✝

Lieutenant Jacobson was navigating by reference to Highway 20. He looked over at Kyle sitting next to him in the co-pilot's seat. Kyle was staring straight ahead. He hadn't said a word since they took off from Ontario.

"Something bothering you, Mr. Howden?" Jacobson asked.

"Yeah. I'm wondering what happened to Gary Sheffield and why Trooper Rivera wouldn't tell us."

Suddenly Jacobson's eyes went wide as he stared past Kyle through the chopper's right window—then he threw up his arm and pointed. "Look!"

When Kyle turned his head he saw a huge shiny triangular craft of some kind flying alongside at the same altitude in the same direction, just two hundred yards to the right of the helicopter.

Jesus! Kyle muttered, and shook his head in wonderment as he studied the gigantic UFO.

"My God, Mr. Howden," Jacobson said, "is that real? In all my years of flying I've never seen anything like that!" He stared unbelievingly at the UFO which had slowed to match the helicopter's speed. "Do you think they mean us harm?" he asked nervously.

Kyle shook his head. "No. if they wanted us dead, we'd be dead!"

"Do you think that craft had anything to do with Agent Sheffield's disappearance?" Jacobson asked.

Kyle stared at the UFO with unabashed curiosity and nodded affirmatively. "You can bet your ass on that, Lieutenant!"

For Further Reading

IF YOU ARE FURTHER INTERESTED IN ANIMAL mutilations you can search the internet. Look up "Animal Mutilations." There you will find a great deal of information. Of particular interest are images of mutilated animals. You may also wish to look up FBI—Animal Mutilation. In addition to the information furnished by the FBI there is a "Disclaimer," which is very interesting.

Quoting from that disclaimer you may find this of interest. "…some of these records are no longer in the physical possession of the FBI eliminating the FBI's capability to re-review and/or re-process this material. Please note that the information found in these files may no longer reflect the current beliefs, positions, opinions, or policies currently held by the FBI. …some information in this site may contain actions, words or images of a graphic nature that may be offensive and/or emotionally disturbing. The material may not be suitable for all ages. Please review it with discretion."

www.ingramcontent.com/pod-product-compliance
Lightning Source LLC
Chambersburg PA
CBHW020428030726
47495CB00006B/1709